A YEAR
OF THE
MONKEYS

SHORT FICTION BY THE
INFINITE MONKEYS CHAPTER
OF THE LEAGUE OF UTAH WRITERS

I0587359

Edited by
Lyn Worthen

CONTENTS

Introduction:

AN INFINITE NUMBER OF MONKEYS

Lyn Worthen

There is a theory that says if you give typewriters to one hundred monkeys, and let them type for one hundred years, they will eventually reproduce the works of Shakespeare. We decided to put that theory to the test—with a few minor modifications.

We didn't have one hundred monkeys—but we did have the membership of a League of Utah Writers chapter that calls itself "The Infinite Monkeys." Most of them didn't have typewriters, but worked on laptop or desktop computers, smartphones, and tablets. And instead of one hundred years to perfect their prose, we gave them one year to get from blank page to published anthology. So while you won't find any reproductions of Shakespeare here, what you will find are thirty-five short stories that will make you laugh, make you cry, make you think, and sometimes make you glad you don't live in the unsettling worlds of the imagination.

The authors in this collection are as varied as their stories, a mixture of brand-new writers seeing their first publications, to long-term professionals, many of whom acted in mentoring roles at different stages of the project. But the overarching vision of *A Year of the Monkeys* came from the collective minds of Terra Luft, Johnny Worthen, Paul Genesse, and Talysa Sainz, who, as the leadership of the Infinite Monkeys, had the goal of creating this anthology from the earliest days of the chapter. It was their idea to create a teaching anthology—one that would give our members the experience of writing, revising, editing, submitting, and finally seeing their work in print—that formed the foundation for this anthology, and remains at its core.

Ambitious dreams like these don't come true without a lot of effort. As the initial Managing Editor, it was Paul Genesse who oversaw much of the behind-the-scenes planning and organized the authors into small groups to work on refining the stories from their initial rough drafts to publishable quality, before handing the project off to me to see it to its completion. I cannot thank him enough for his time, dedication, effort, and friendship. Working with small groups of writers, Jenn Adams, Jennie Stevens, Johnny Worthen, Karla Jay, Laurie Jones, Masha Shukovich, Paul Genesse, and I each had the opportunity to see these amazing writers develop their skills, and I am incredibly impressed with the level of dedication and effort toward improving their craft I saw across the board.

Also deserving of acknowledgement are our amazing copy-editors, Jennie Stevens, Laurie Jones, and Talysa Sainz, who read through every word of every story in this collection looking for the missed punctuation, copy-and-paste errors, and typos that are often so hard for an author to spot in their own work. Rachael Moody painted our amazing cover, and Caryn Larrinaga waved her magic wand to convert the raw document into the beautifully formatted book you hold in your hands.

Stepping into the role of Managing Editor partway through the process gave me the opportunity to read every story, encourage all of the authors beyond my small group, arbitrate editing questions, and generally coordinate production of the anthology around the lives and schedules of the many participants. But the biggest challenge that fell to me was determining the order in which the stories would be presented. After much consultation with my fellow editors and shuffling of lines on spreadsheets, I believe I have organized the stories so that, when reading the book from front to back, the reader will ease into the worlds the Infinite Monkeys have created, get to know the characters, and find the time they spend with them—through their highs and lows, laughter and tears, chills and thrills—to be an experience they look back on fondly at the journey's end.

This, then, *is* my circus, and these *are* my Monkeys. Working with them on *A Year of the Monkeys* has been a barrel of fun, and I am very proud to present them to you.

Fly, my Monkeys, fly!

– Lyn Worthen
Sandy, Utah
June 21, 2018

When not writing speculative fiction for a living (her day job is writing computer software manuals), Leigh Saunders enjoys writing "social science fiction"—stories that focus on people (or "things" that are also people) in distant places, and how futuristic events or advances in technology impact their lives. A 1995 Writers of the Future finalist, her recent short fiction can be found in multiple Fiction River anthologies and BundleRabbit collections, and her first novel, "Memoirs of a Synth: Gold Record" is available through all the major ebook retailers. To learn more about Leigh, visit www.leighsaunders.com.

About this story, Leigh says: "There were many times, as my children were growing up, when I wished for even the simplest of magics that might make our lives easier—particularly during those difficult times between jobs, when the pantry routinely resembled Mother Hubbard's cupboard. And while all magic comes with a price, I don't know of many mothers who wouldn't gladly pay it if it meant their children were better off."

This gentle story of real-world needs and quiet magic was the first place winner in the 2017 League of Utah Writers short story competition, and provides an introduction to many of the themes in this collection.

STONE SOUP
Leigh Saunders

Trishla stared at the handful of rolled oats in the bottom of the cardboard container and the few saltines in their crumpled, wax-paper wrapping. She could use the oats and the last can of evaporated milk for the children's breakfast in the morning, but the otherwise empty pantry left her with nothing for dinner and mouths to feed.

Again.

Trishla closed the door, leaning her head against it with a sigh. Jake was doing his best, but even with three part-time jobs, he barely earned enough to cover the rent and keep the lights on. Of course, their three young children didn't understand things like layoffs and recessions and food stamps. They just knew that they were hungry all the time.

Trishla pushed herself away from the pantry and turned to watch three-year-old Andy playing in the living room. The toddler scooped up a handful of brightly colored plastic blocks and dropped them into a large yellow dump truck with a clatter, then drove the truck across the room, energetic *vroom-vrooms* bubbling from his lips.

Trishla smiled weakly, pushing a strand of dark hair out of her face with a thin, trembling hand. Crossing the kitchen, she pulled a slim picture book from the high shelf where she kept her cookbooks. Keeping her voice light, she called out to Andy.

"Would you like Mommy to read the baking story, sweetie?"

Long ago, when Trishla was just a little girl, her mama often read bedtime stories to her and her little brother, Amir, the sing-song, accented English of her native New Delhi lulling the children sweetly to sleep.

Sometimes, she would read the lively Panchatantra tales of talking jungle animals and their foibles, mimicking the characters with silly voices and grand gestures that cast shadows on the wall. Other nights, they would clamor for tales of the Arabian Nights, shrieking and giggling as they engaged in mock battles until they were so worn out that they slipped away into an adventure-filled dreamland.

But there were also the times when Trishla's mama would read simple tales of quiet, everyday things—like the adventures of the hungry little boy named Viku and his friend, Haatee the elephant, who took him to a banana grove where they picked and ate their fill of the sweet fruit. Trishla was sure it was just her imagination that filled her dreams with Viku's laughing and Haatee's happy trumpeting, but the next day so often brought a breakfast of fresh, hot bread spread thickly with mashed bananas and honey, or a tray of her grandmother's fried *pazham pori* banana fritters cooling on the kitchen counter, that Trishla and Amir looked forward to story time, licking their lips in anticipation of the yummy foods the stories described.

Trishla settled Andy onto her lap, his trusty tan teddy bear cuddled on his own lap, and opened the picture book.

"There once was a little red hen…," she began.

As she read, she found herself slipping into the rhythm of her mama's sing-song accent, the syllables of the story falling off her tongue like musical notes. Around them, the air began to move, brushing gently across her skin.

Andy shivered, looking up at Trishla with happy anticipation lighting his wide brown eyes. Trishla pulled him closer and kept reading.

In the kitchen, a chicken clucked.

"…The hen planted the grains of wheat," Trishla read.

A current of air brought with it the fragrance of rich, loamy soil, freshly turned, and the soft hint of warm spring rain. Trishla could taste the droplets on her tongue, feel the sunshine on the side of her face nearest the kitchen.

Ignoring the gnawing emptiness in her own stomach, Trishla read on.

Their parents had gone out for the evening, leaving seven-year-old Trishla and six-year-old Amir with a babysitter. Amir had been restless and fretful, and the sitter impatient, and she had sent the two children to bed early, shouting up at Amir as he lay on his bed and kicked his feet against the wall.

Trishla knew that shouting at Amir would do nothing to settle him, so she crept down the hall to his room and slipped inside.

"Shall I read you a story, Amir?" she asked, switching on the light.

"Mm-hmm," he replied, giving the wall a last one-two kick before rolling over onto his belly.

"What would you like to hear?"

"The ps-ketti story."

Trishla retrieved the tattered copy of *Strega Nona* from the bin of children's books and began to read about the old, grand-motherly witch, Strega Nona, and the overflowing cauldron of spaghetti, sending Amir into fits of giggles as she embellished the tale with silly voices and grand gestures like she thought their mama would.

In the kitchen below, a large pot full of steaming water grad-ually shimmered into existence.

———

Andy giggled as the pig squealed, the dog barked, and the little chicks cheeped from the next room, and Trishla continued to read. Soon, she heard the whispery swish of the scythe as the mature wheat was harvested.

"Who will help me grind the wheat?" Trishla read, her voice clucking at the end of the sentence just as her mama's had. This far into the story, the voices were seldom her own.

"Not I," growled the dog.

"Not I," squealed the pig.

"Hen will do it," said Andy with a smile.

Trishla clucked in agreement and laughed as Andy clapped his hands to his ears to muffle the crushing whine of stone on stone as the grain was milled into flour.

———

"Help! Oh, help!"

Trishla and Amir barely heard the babysitter's shouts over their own laughter at the silly tale of magic gone awry. Together, they threw open the door and ran out of the room, peering through the railing at the top of the stairs in amazement.

"A mountain of spaghetti...," whispered Trishla as ribbons of pasta flowed beneath them.

"A river of hot, slurpy sauce...," breathed Amir as waves of marinara, fragrant with onions and garlic splashed on the walls.

"And meatballs the size of softballs!" they cried out together as large, dark meatballs rose to the surface of the river like giant fish. Some rolled across the top of the pasta while others sank under the waves of sauce.

Screaming in terror, and oblivious to the children watching her from above, the babysitter waded toward the front door through the deepening stream of spaghetti and meatballs that seemed to be pursuing her from the kitchen. It had already risen above her knees and was still rising.

The sitter reached the door, but there was too much spaghetti pressing against it and she couldn't force it open. As the children watched her stand there, pounding on the door, a new wave of spaghetti washed from the dining room and into the entry, raising the level to the sitter's thighs.

"Amir, quick! Get the book," Trishla whispered.

Amir was back in a flash, and Trishla skipped forward several pages, reading and rereading the passages where the townspeople ate away at the mountains of spaghetti that had been cooked up in the story.

"It's working," Amir whispered.

Trishla didn't dare look, couldn't stop reading. She read the pages over and over until Amir finally put his hand on top of the pictures. "Stop."

The spaghetti was gone, not a noodle or meatball in sight.

The sitter was curled up by the front door, crying, her head against her knees.

And Trishla suddenly realized that she was ravenously hungry—for anything *except* spaghetti.

———————

Little Andy clapped his hands in delight, his teddy bear forgotten, as Trishla rose from the living room chair where they had been reading and carried him into the kitchen. She set him gently on a chair at the kitchen table, tucked the picture book into its place with the rest of her cookbooks, then turned toward the oven.

A lovely loaf of bread sat on the cutting board, the luscious aroma filling the home with its warm, wonderful fragrance. Beside the loaf sat a small crock of freshly churned butter and a jar of clear, golden honey.

Trishla cut a slice of the bread, spread it with butter and honey, and gave it to Andy, who quickly began to gobble it up.

As she turned away from the toddler, she saw Jake standing in the kitchen doorway. "You're home early," she said.

"Just in time, it seems," he said with a smile. He crossed to her and kissed her, then nodded toward the loaf of bread now cooling on the counter. "Shall I cut you a slice?"

Trishla turned away, hoping Jake hadn't noticed her involuntary shudder. "It's for the children," she said. "Sara and Lilly will be home soon."

"You hardly eat anything anymore."

"I'm not hungry." She went over to the counter and cut a second slice, buttered it, then placed it on a napkin and handed it to Jake.

"You're getting so thin. I'm worried about you," Jake said.

He looked at the warm slice of bread in his hand. "I know it's been hard to make the money stretch so far—I don't know how you manage to put food on the table every day. Please, promise me you'll at least eat something for dinner."

"Of course," Trishla said with a tired smile that she hoped was more convincing than it felt. She'd never told Jake that she was conjuring up the food—or that the smallest bite would turn to sawdust on her tongue and nauseating slurry in her stomach. The magic fed her children and gave her husband the strength to juggle three minimum-wage part-time jobs while he looked for something better. If feeding them well every day meant she had to survive on water and a daily protein bar—bought with the precious food stamp money and hidden away where neither Jake nor the children would find them—that was a price she was willing to pay.

He'd find a new job soon, and things would go back to normal.

As Jake left the room to go change for his evening shift at the warehouse, Trishla looked from the closed pantry door and back to her cookbook shelf. With a tired sigh, she pulled out a slim picture book. She ran her fingers over the title embossed on the cover—*Stone Soup*—as she went over to sit next to Andy.

"Would you like Mommy to read the soup story, sweetie?"

Julie Frost writes every shade of speculative fiction and lives in Utah with her family—six guinea pigs, three humans, a tripod calico cat, and a "kitten" who thinks she's a warrior princess—and a collection of anteaters and Oaxacan carvings, some of which intersect. A 2016 Writers of the Future prize winner, Julie's short fiction has appeared in The District of Wonders, Cosmos, Unlikely Story, Plasma Frequency, Stupefying Stories, and many other venues. Her second novel, "Pack Dynamics: A Price to Pay," will appear in mid-2018, published by WordFire Press. She whines about writing, a lot, at www.agilebrit.livejournal.com.

About this story, Julie says: "The inspiration for this story was a contest prompt about artwork with an unusual property. I'd been noodling an idea where someone is trapped in a painting anyway, and I thought 'What if someone did it on purpose, and why?' Me being me, of course the answer was 'Because werewolves.' Add the 'what could possibly go wrong?' element, along with True Love, and that was the story, right there. The end bit with the professor let me put an exclamation mark on the sacrifice they'd made for each other."

You'll have to decide for yourself if this story ends in tragedy or with a happily ever after. Then again, perhaps the answer depends entirely on the phase of the moon.

PORTRAIT OF THE ARTIST AS A YOUNG WEREWOLF
Julie Frost

"You're not a monster."

The four rows of butterfly bandages decorating Liana's face from cheek to temple belied her statement.

"You're lucky I didn't hurt your hands, honey," Jasper said, his voice strained and unhappy. Standing in front of his easel, he drafted a nighttime landscape onto a stretched canvas with a few rough pencil strokes. The shadowy outline of a grotesque wolf dominated the foreground.

"I just don't think trapping yourself in one of your own paintings over the full moon is the way to go, even if it is temporary." She brushed her fingers through his hair. The fingers she used to carve stunning, lifelike animal sculptures, the fingers he could have utterly crushed if she'd been a bare *second* slower yanking away. Liana was a tactile person, always touching things to feel their texture. More often than not, she'd have a hand resting on him as they sat together reading or doing homework in their cozy studio loft, crowded with art supplies and partly finished projects.

Jasper loved her hands, and the very notion that he could have ruined her forever gave him cold shudders. His own hands were steady and determined while he took stronger precautions, leaning into her caress as he worked. "Well, I'm doing it anyway." He mixed his colors using wolfsbane spirited from the university's magic supplies closet, along with silver nitrate for the full moon he would place, oversized, in the sky. His own blood, along with rowan berry juice, went into the red to tip the wolf's claws, and a frame of mountain ashwood stood by to receive the completed work. Specific ingredients for his specific condition. He had less than a month before the next full moon.

———

Liana caught her breath when she saw the finished painting. "It's beautiful." Of course she would think so. She adored him, and thought *he* was beautiful in whatever form he took, which was why she'd gotten close enough for him to hurt her.

He set the framed picture inside the cage and waited for his next changeover with no small amount of trepidation, preparing the incantations beforehand. He didn't tell his professors what he was up to. This was illicit magic he could get in deep, expellable trouble for. If anything bad—or worse—happened, Liana would handle his affairs.

She locked him in the cage just before moonrise. "I love you."

"I love you back," he said, just before a choked groan tore its way from his throat. A ripping sensation down his back, a yank through dimensional fabric—

———

The wolf stares at unfamiliar moonlit trees and a running brook. A human voice makes him turn his head, but he doesn't under-

stand, and snarls. The scents in this place are sharp and alien, but he recognizes inimical odors: wolfsbane, silver, rowan, all of which nearly paralyze him. Maybe the cage was better. He whines on his exhales, flat on the ground.

Something huge materializes out of the darkness and strokes his back. He snaps instinctively, tasting blood and hearing a cry. A female human looms overhead, enormous, with damp eyes. He yelps and retreats into the shadows under the trees.

He's never been afraid before.

The moon set, and Liana waited for Jasper to emerge from the painting like he'd planned. He'd be dizzy and disoriented; he always was after a night like this.

But nothing happened. The wolf glared, frozen, from the gloom of the woodland, eyes glowing malevolent amber. Liana rubbed her bandaged hand. Drawn to its beauty, she'd thought it would be safe to touch the painted wolf, never expecting it could reach out and bite her. She wondered if lycanthropy was contagious in this situation. He'd caught her with his claws the previous month, and that had healed over, leaving a set of pink and white ridges across her cheek. But that hadn't involved contaminating her bodily fluids with his. Did biting her while in his painted form count?

A sick feeling roiled the pit of her stomach when she realized her hand didn't hurt anymore. She stripped off the bandage to find the wound completely healed. A look in the mirror showed the scars on her face were gone as well.

Something had clearly gone wrong with the incantation. Jasper was stuck in the painting. The idea of a life without him was unbearable; the idea of being a werewolf alone was worse.

A pang knifed through her as she thought of her unfinished sculptures, of the family that would never know what happened. But if he couldn't come out, then she'd be a wolf with him. He'd sacrificed for her. She would sacrifice for him, so they could be together, always.

She wasn't as skilled on canvas as Jasper by any means, but she'd taken a few painting classes and knew animal anatomy. With the oils and wolfsbane left over from his efforts, she painted a smaller, more lithe wolf onto the canvas, using her own blood and more rowan juice to tip its claws.

Jasper had jotted down the incantations, and she settled herself in the locked cage. Liana timed the spell just so—

His pain has faded to a dull ache. The wolf steps out of the forest to greet the female, his tail wagging. She shrinks away momentarily before realizing he means her no harm, then licks under his chin. He touches his nose to her no-longer-wounded paw, then cocks his head and bounds a few steps, inviting a romp. She follows.

For the first time in his short life, he understands what "happy" means. Maybe he's not a monster after all.

Doctor Rasmussen, dean of the university's School of Art, let himself in to Jasper and Liana's apartment a few nights later, calling for his young students, who hadn't been to their classes for several days. He stopped short when he caught sight of the painting in the cage. It was a masterpiece, beautifully detailed. The moon glowed with lambent light, and he could almost hear the brook burbling. Even the leaves of the darkened trees appeared to be in motion, waving in a breeze only they could feel. The pair of wolves playing in the foreground were imbued with grace and power, fur nearly rippling.

He stepped back when the wolves *did* move, jerking their heads around to gaze at him. Then they turned away and melted into the trees, a faint howl sounding behind them.

Soon enough, he found the incantation and realized what they'd done with a flash of understanding.

"Oh, you young, foolish lovers," he murmured, shaking his head. Two wrong words in the incantation meant they'd trapped themselves in the painting forever instead of temporarily. He set a match to the spell, so no one else might fall prey to the error. This was a pretty mess. He carefully lifted the painting by the corners of the frame, where the wolves couldn't reach him, and carried it out of the room.

Rasmussen hung it in his den. He discovered that the image froze by day, but he watched the wolves playing at night while he worked, almost envying their reckless passion.

Almost.

Victoria Lisowski lives in Utah where she tries not to disturb her neighbors with the contents of her brain. She's been published in Dark Moon Digest and Peony Magazine, and was the winner of Margaret Young's "Rick Walton Children's Story" contest. She lives with her twin three-year-olds, a cat she rescued, a dog she bought on a whim, and a husband who supports her but wishes she'd stop bringing small animals home. You can find her on Twitter @vic_liso.

About this story, Victoria says: "'The Weak Amazon' came to me when I got a front row seat to the pain and pure love a mother has for a child making horrible decisions. It got me thinking about what a person is worth, even when they're doing everything wrong, and why they are still valuable. I liked the idea of looking at it from a vaguely non-human point of view, and the Amazons just kind of came to me. I wanted to explain to an outsider why someone could love another person, even when on a simple, societal level, they were essentially worthless."

Sometimes the truth we think we know falters in the face of the truth we discover when we get close enough to really see.

THE WEAK AMAZON
Victoria Lisowski

The first time I saw his face, I was planning to kill him.

I can remember it so clearly. He was young, his back broad and arms thick from working in the coffee fields of Brazil. He had a strong jaw and bright eyes, his skin darkened from labor in the sun. Attractive and of suitable age. He displayed all of the base characteristics of the weaker sex: aggression, pompousness, arrogance. He was the perfect choice.

I watched him from the jungle, leaves obscuring my body, melding into the background of green foliage as I followed him home. Nobody ever noticed me. I had been trained and prepared for that moment.

The moment I would follow him home, seduce him, and get rid of him.

But I had failed.

***

"Elena," Kaiala says. She sits above me, her golden dress encircling her shoulders and draping over her long body in waves. The life tree, dripping with fruit, is woven into the bodice. Her throne nestles in the trunk of a great Kapok, its bark grown into a seat rather than being cut into one with a human's rudimentary tools. Vines fall around her, the leaves of our rainforest offering us cover. The other Amazons stay to the edge of the trees, leaning against them while I stand in the center. Unprotected.

I keep my shoulders back, head high. I am unaccustomed to the shame that pricks at the back of my eyes, but I force myself to meet Kaiala's gaze.

The coarse brown garments they put on me chafe against my breasts and hips. The skirt comes to my knees, as is custom, but it does nothing to protect me. I miss my armor, but I am not here to be protected. My hands are empty, my spear torn from my clenched fist.

"Do you understand the charges brought against you?" Kaiala's eyes are fixed on mine. "Do you realize the seriousness of what you've done?"

"I extended mercy," I say.

"You risked us all." Kaiala doesn't sound angry. More disappointed. Our sisters had lived in the secret places of the world for hundreds of years, and now I have placed them at risk of exposure. "You know what we must do."

The urge to please her, to throw myself at her feet and beg for forgiveness, is overwhelming, but I try to contain it. "Please." The word bursts from my mouth as though seeking escape. "Don't kill him. He knows nothing."

Kaiala shakes her head. "It is the law. Do you think we would make an exception for you because you loved him?"

I drop my hand to my round, bare belly. The life that exists there fills me with joy, but that is not the issue here. "I accomplished what needed to be done," I say. "My daughter will be brave and wise."

"You did not answer my question." Kaiala's beautiful brown eyes are not without kindness. They look at me with the same love and belonging that I've felt my entire life. My mother had those eyes, as did many of my sisters who surround us. How could they be full of such love, understanding, and compassion for me and our clan, but not realize that same emotion could be shared and given to others?

And how would I ever be able to explain?

"I beg you to spare him," I say. "It is not for myself that I ask."

Kaiala's eyes narrow. Murmurs spread around us as the other Amazons whisper to each other. I do my best to remain tall and strong, but a little of that shame starts to curl my shoulders inward.

"Explain," Kaiala demands.

Where to begin?

When I'd followed the man from the fields to his home, I hadn't noticed the poverty. The city was dark, which made it easy to sneak unseen through streets littered with trash. Tiny houses of various colors were crammed into the mountainside, begging for space. Children played in the muddy ruts in the road while their mothers stared at them with hollow eyes. The road, wide enough for trucks, narrowed until it would barely fit a laboring mule.

I was callous towards their suffering. The rainforest we had claimed as our own was a perfect protection against such human difficulties. I had been watching the man for weeks, studying his patterns, his weaknesses, and with them my understanding of his kind had increased. I'd heard stories, but seeing their degradation for myself had solidified my opinion of mankind. They were good for one thing, and that thing only.

Yet, upon reaching the man's home, even I couldn't deny its destitution. I watched him push aside mud and wood in order to crawl inside his hovel. I peered through a window with no glass into a dim room lit only by a small oil-burning lantern.

An old woman sat in the corner, her hair wispy and thin as it hung in her lined face. The man walked to her, put his arm around her, and gently kissed her on the cheek.

"Home at last, little man?" the woman said, her eyes sharp and twinkling despite their age. The man sighed and shook his head, rolling his eyes.

"How are you, avó?" he asked. "And I'm not little anymore."

"If I do not call you little, who will?" the grandmother said. "Your head is too big!"

I tensed at this. I had seen him throw beer bottles at his companions for such slight insults. If he attempted to harm the woman, I would have no choice but to intervene. I could not allow such violence against a woman, even if she was only human.

But to my shock, the man chuckled, his eyes shining with a light I had never seen from him before—one I had yet to see from anyone of his sex. He disappeared behind a ragged curtain and returned with a hairbrush. Then, kneeling, he began to gently brush the old woman's hair.

"I do not know why I put up with you," he said, his eyes crinkling in the corners. He brushed her hair back from her face.

"Because you respect your elders," the woman said with a cackle, but love shone from her as she leaned into his touch.

I couldn't understand what I was seeing. Was this the same man I had been following? The man who had knocked someone's tooth out in a fight just the day before? Who screamed and cursed with the fluency of habit, throwing his head back and laughing boisterously as though he hadn't a care in the world?

Yet he cradled the old woman gently, as though she were something precious.

I listened as he sang to her and fed her, his bulging muscles and hard-lined face suddenly soft, melting into expressions and mannerisms I could barely understand. She patted his cheek, love shining from her eyes.

"You're a good boy, Gabriel," she told him, her hand cupping his chin.

"Only you think so, avó," he whispered, then kissed her palm and pulled away.

I was supposed to take him to my bed that night but found I couldn't do it.

———

"There is a woman," I say. "An elderly woman who needs him. How can we abandon our sister and kill her caregiver?"

A few of the younger Amazons look shocked, their eyes widening as they turn to each other. I can hear their disbelief. Many have never been beyond the forest that bears our name, have never seen a man. But we all knew men weren't strong enough to care for other people. I can't blame them for doubting me; the idea of a male caregiver is still strange for me as well. I would not have believed it myself if I hadn't seen it with my own eyes. But the older Amazons just look sorrowful, as though they know how my story will end.

Kaiala's expression changes to one of pity.

"Was he a good caregiver, Elena?" she asks.

I want to defend him. But smoke comes to mind. Little blue pills and a short temper. Tears.

I look away.

"Tell us what happened, child," Kaiala insists.

"I did my duty," I mutter.

I berated myself for becoming so distracted and approached him the next day. Knowing he was caring for the aging woman had spiked my interest rather than depleted it. We were a warrior race, and therefore those with the qualities closest to the war god's were considered desirable. But there was something fascinating about a man who could break someone's skull choosing to comb her hair instead.

I wanted to know more, to understand how this man, who was so full of arrogance and pride, could also be as soft and caring as a mother with her new child. I justified it, thinking that if he was so kind to his aged relative, then perhaps our daughter would be both strong and loving. Perhaps she'd be an Amazon beyond anything we had ever seen.

He was, of course, enthralled with me. I am descended from the gods—my beauty, like that of all of our kind, exceeds that of human women, and it took very little to seduce him. He handed over his heart without objection. My own was untouched by the hyperbolic stories he told or the simple gifts he crafted in his attempt to gain my affection. He resisted bringing me to his home, instead begging to show me off to his friends. I refused. The law dictated that I was to remain unseen by anyone but the man I had chosen as my mate, and I was uninterested in any humans beyond the man and his grandmother.

I followed him home to watch as he carefully made feijão, the simple dish of seasoned black beans he shared with his grandmother. He enchanted me when he brushed her hair, bantered with her, and laughed. He was patient, even kind. The strength his sex so often neglected was on display every second he was with his elder, and I couldn't understand why he refused to let me in, to see her in person.

But he was embarrassed. He didn't want to bring me to his home. The more I insisted, the more brisk he became. When I finally managed to convince him to allow me inside, he apologized uncomfortably whenever his grandmother was in the room. He started hiding her behind an old dirty curtain when I visited, wanting more and more time alone with me.

It was all horribly…dissatisfying.

"I distracted him from his duties," I say. "I should never have chosen him as a mate. I should have left him to take care of his grandmother, but he is a man, and once he knew me…" A small smile can't help but curl my lips, even as I loathe myself for it. I look up at Kaiala and see the same understanding in her face. We are Amazon. Men cannot help being attracted to those superior to themselves.

"I had already become pregnant with my daughter." I touch my belly again, feeling the small kick there. "I thought that if I left, the man's attention would return to his duty. He didn't know who I was. He didn't know where I came from. I didn't think it would be a difficult transition."

"Your duty called upon you to end the father's life, so he

would be unable to tell anyone about us," Kaiala reminds me. She no longer looks sympathetic. I had broken the law. I must be punished. "Your duty was to kill him."

"He needs to care for his grandmother," I say. "He will not come looking for me."

"You underestimate man's desire for the pleasures of a woman," Kaiala says.

I bow my head, no longer able to meet her eyes. "Yes, I did."

Once I left him, I hadn't intended to ever return. I knew the law; I knew I risked banishment, debasing my name and that of my line by letting him live. But how could I slaughter a man who had the capacity for kindness? I didn't love him, no. What Amazon could love a man? But I loved the love he had for the woman under his care. I loved the way she looked at him, as though she knew he would never let her down.

I couldn't stay away. I found myself hiding in the woods, watching his little house. I wanted to be sure that everything had returned to the way it was.

It hadn't.

He no longer brushed her hair or sang to her. Instead he would sit outside, his eyes bloodshot and wet, a bottle of porradinha in his hand. Occasionally he would go somewhere by himself and weep.

Months passed and his grandmother wasted away from his neglect. When she called his name, he would avoid her, his eyes darkening. I did not understand it. I couldn't understand why he was acting this way.

He spiraled into despair. He'd always been prone to drink,

but never at home, never around his grandmother. Now he was drinking, taking other substances—things I didn't recognize, couldn't place. They put him into a state of complacency and bliss, but when they wore off, his eyes were more bloodshot and tear-filled than ever.

His grandmother tried to rise to the challenge, but there was nothing she could do. The fire in her eyes dulled as she tried to help him, and I grieved for the pain I had caused her. My sister. She was not Amazon, but she was female. It was not right that I had abandoned her to this. But it wasn't her own well-being that she mourned. The lack of food, the clean clothes, none of it seemed to bother her.

Instead, she worried for him.

"Gabriel," she said. "You will give your grandmother a heart attack staying out this late. What are you doing?"

"Nothing, avó," he said bluntly. "I will be out with friends."

"Again?" Sadness entered her eyes. "You know they are no good."

"You don't get to decide who I spend time with. I am not a child."

"You are a better man than this, Gabriel," she said, voice sharp.

He turned to look at her with rage in his eyes, but it died and his shoulders slumped. He looked away. "What do you know about it?" he muttered and then left.

Tears shone in the woman's eyes, but she stubbornly held them back. Despite all of this, her love didn't waver, and the look in her eyes when she saw him never changed.

"I made a mistake," I say, raising my head once more. "I took a good man, one who had very little. All he had was his grand-mother. And then I seduced him, deceived him. Made him believe that there was something better in this world than the destitution he lived in. I blinded him. I took him in my arms and made him believe I loved him—and then I vanished without a trace. Perhaps it would have been easier if I *had* killed him. But I didn't, and now he has sunken into despair.

"But there is a woman, a woman who needs him, a woman who refuses to give up on him. She has fire and spirit, a heart to match an Amazon. How can we take him away from her?"

Kaiala sighs, her hand traveling to the sacred tree embroi-dered on her gown, her eyes staring at something far overhead. Then she stands and leaps to the ground, the distance nothing to her strong legs. As she walks toward me, shivers travel up and down my spine.

"Elena," she says, her voice filled with sorrow. "You misjudged. You thought you found a man with the strength to care for another, but you did not. It was not your actions alone that brought him to this fate. A man weak enough to be seduced by the pleasures of the flesh would have fallen to vice eventually."

"No." I shake my head. "I do not believe it."

Kaiala sighs and cups my chin in her hand. "You are not to blame for his decisions," she tells me. "Only your own. You broke our laws and now must suffer the consequences. Don't you think the man's grandmother would rather have her pain ended quickly than have it drawn out as she watches her grandson spiral into nothingness?"

I pull free of her grip, holding her hand in my own. "No," I say again. "She wouldn't."

The grandmother's face is still so vivid in my mind. Her eyes as bright as a flame when she knelt on the dirt floor, clasping her hands together, almost in challenge, holding the cross necklace between her palms. Weak and feeble, yet she looked as powerful as a queen.

"God," she said. "Help me." It didn't sound like a plea, but a request for assistance, as though between equals. "Gabriel is all I have left in this world. And he is a good man, Lord. He forgets himself. He is afraid to show weakness, but he has always been a good man." She drew in a breath, steadying herself. "He is hurting. He no longer believes that good exists in the world. All that is good has been taken from him throughout his life. So he flees into those noxious poisons, and they're killing him. Oh, God. They're killing him!" Her voice broke, barely above a whisper. "Please help him. Please help me help him."

No matter how many nights he left her alone, how often she was forced to drag her aged body away from her soft blankets to cook and clean. She still knelt every day and prayed to her God to watch over her grandson. To take care of him.

To keep him alive.

———

"I think that for as long as she has breath, she will try to save her grandson. There is a reason he was the person he was before I came, Kaiala. There is a reason he loved his grandmother enough to take care of her the way he did. If she can overcome the innate selfishness of man once, who is to say that she cannot do it again? We have to let her try."

Kaiala sighs and removes her hand, walking back toward the great Kapok. My warrior sisters step from the edges of the clearing and grab my arms, pinning me in place. "I see you cannot be reasoned with," Kaiala says, looking back at me over her shoulder.

I keep my head high, my back straight.

"You will not perform your duty," she says, forcing me to admit it once again.

"I cannot betray her," I say.

"As he did." Kaiala's eyes are locked on mine, and I fight with the shame she expects from me. "Can no others care for her?"

"No," I admit. "She won't let them."

It took a long time before I made up my mind to approach the old woman. My daughter had swollen in my belly and it was becoming more difficult to move silently amongst the trees, but I still did it. The man's weakness had become repulsive to me. I found myself more and more angry as I watched him.

He was supposed to be different. I'd *seen* him be different than the other men in this world. I'd seen his strength, and now he was throwing it away because he couldn't have what he wanted. It was pathetic. I never should have spared him. I had risked my people's safety, my status amongst my sisters, for him. And for what? It was becoming painfully clear that he was too selfish to appreciate what he had. Everything I had done, and it was all for nothing.

I should have killed him then. He was walking out of the house, his eyes dazed, his hand clutching a bottle, dragging it to his lips, and draining it. He stumbled away from their tiny hovel, his step already swaying. I knew where he was going. I knew the den where he would pump himself full of poison, dulling his mind and forcing him into a state of stupor.

My spear was heavy in my hands. I could do it. Great with my child or not, it would take little effort to destroy him.

I was halfway out of the trees before a voice reached my ears. "Elena," she said. "You came back."

The grandmother had been watching her grandson leave through the window and had spotted my movement. Her eyes betrayed no hostility, though they were carefully guarded as they flickered down at my spear and then up again. Whatever she thought of my appearance, she kept it to herself. I drew myself up to my considerable height, staring down at her.

She looked at my swollen belly, and a hint of a smile touched her face. "Foolish child," she said softly. "I should have known. I thought I'd raised him better."

Her face was pale and thin, her hands shaking ever so slightly as she looked at me, her hair in vicious snarls around her face. My anger surged in my veins. How dare he? After everything I'd done, all that I'd sacrificed and risked for him, he'd abandoned her. The only good man I'd ever met, and he'd thrown it away in a temper tantrum.

"Why do you put up with him," I growled. "Why don't you leave him to rot in his own putrescence?"

Surprise flashed across her face. She shook her head, as though bemused by my ignorance. Her obvious pity made me bristle. I was Amazon. I came from a line of warriors, descended from an ancient race that had spread across the world over two thousand years ago. We had taught the native women to defend themselves, and the people had named the great forest in our honor. She was nothing but a human woman being taken advantage of by a man—how dare she look at me like I understood nothing.

"Come with me," I said. I reached forward and grabbed her hand. The bones felt as fragile as a bird's. "I can take care of you so much better than he ever could. Even before, when he loved you. I can do even better than that."

"Oh, Elena," the grandmother sighed. "He still loves me."

I scoffed. "Men are incapable of love."

I do not know if she knew what I was, or if she guessed. But she looked at me for a long time, studying me, pinning me with her gaze. It was uncomfortable, as though she were attempting to examine my very soul.

She pulled her hand free and reached into her pocket. After a moment, she pulled out an old photograph. It was wrinkled and stained, as if it had been folded and unfolded many times.

She held it out for me. The photo was of a young boy, no more than three years old. He was grinning, holding a large fish in front of him, eyes shining with pride. Someone in the background helped him hold it up.

"Do you want to know why I put up with it?" the grandmother said softly. "Why I don't kick him out of my home, send him to destroy his life out of my sight? It's because of this little boy, right here." She tapped the photo, her wrinkled finger gently touching the child's face.

"This little boy needed me," she said. "When his parents died of malaria, I brought him here to live with me. He was so tiny, so scared. He knew me, of course. But he missed his parents and would cry out for them in the night. He needed me to be strong. He needed me to love him. And when I see that man"—she pointed down the path, where her grandson had disappeared—"when I see him hiding another drink or downing another pill, I think of this little boy."

I stared at the photo. The child was so young. His eyes were bright and full of the light I'd seen in the man's eyes when I'd first seen him with his grandmother, before I had come into his life and ruined him. Inadvertently my arm encircled my belly, feeling the kicks of my daughter. Looking back into the grand-mother's eyes, I saw her smile.

"This little boy is still somewhere in that big man," she said. "The world took this baby and destroyed him. It stole his parents from him, forced him to grow up in poverty. Convinced him that in order to be strong, to be protected against the cruelty of the world, he needed to be tough, hardened. That emotions were for the weak. It broke him. And I failed him, because I wasn't able to stop it.

"This little boy?" She touched the photo again. "This little boy needs me now just as much as he did that first night he came to me. He needs me, and I'll be here. I'll be here until the day he draws his last breath, because he is my grandson and I love him."

"What if he no longer loves you?" I whispered.

She smiled and put her hand on my cheek. "Dear child," she said. "That was never the point."

Kaiala shakes her head and turns to the warriors lined up against the trees. "Elena, daughter of Amazon," she says, addressing me. "You have shamed our people, broken our law, and must therefore be punished."

I brace myself, my eyes closed.

"You are stripped of your rank as warrior," Kaiala says, each word a blow to my heart. "Your daughter will be known as the child of a traitor and a weakling. You will never hold a spear again."

I try to stay upright, proud, but my shoulders bow and I drop to my knees. The shame I have been fighting wells within me, and I fear I will choke on it. I know I must stand and accept my fate, for my daughter, but I cannot get myself to do it.

Kaiala watches me with pity in her eyes but doesn't waver in her decision. She turns back to the Amazons. "Hunt the man down and kill him. We must clean up this mess."

"No!" Stupid, stupid child that I am, I can't help the word as it bursts from my lips. The Amazons all turn back to me, surprise crossing my sisters' faces. I force myself once more to my feet. Shame hangs on me like a cloak, but I straighten my shoulders.

"Please, Kaiala," I whisper. "You cannot do this. Study him. Watch his grandmother, as I have. Do not take my words alone. See for yourself. But please, please. You must spare him. For our sister."

Kaiala stares into my eyes. "I do not understand," she says eventually. "Why do you care so much?"

"Because she does," I whisper. "I was fascinated when I saw him love and care for his grandmother. I had never seen a man act with such compassion, but to the grandmother, it did not matter. When he was kind to her, when he was cruel to her, she acted the exact same way. She loves him, Kaiala. With the love that a warrior has for her child." At this, I touch my expanded belly, my heart still flush with the shame I've brought upon my child. "If we kill him, we will not be serving some great justice. We will only be taking away the last relative of an old woman who doesn't deserve to be alone."

"Maybe she should be alone," Kaila says bluntly. "Maybe she doesn't know what is best for her."

"Please," I say. "Please, let her try to help him."

Kaiala and I hold each other's gazes for a long time. "No," she says, her voice quiet. "I cannot do that."

Looking into her eyes, I do not blame her. It is impossible for her to understand. My heart beats painfully in my chest, and it is as though I can feel the heartbeat of my child syncing with mine. I take several steps backward, planting myself between my queen and the path to the village. She watches me with hooded eyes, not understanding. I am unarmed. I have been stripped of my spear. As far as my sisters are concerned, I am nothing.

But I am *not* nothing.

"Then you will have to mow me down," I say. "For I will not let you hurt him."

Kaiala's eyes darken. Her brow furrows in frustration. She holds out her hand and the rays of light filtering through the trees condense together, forming a golden spear. My heart races at the sight of it, but I hold my ground.

"You would risk this for him?" she says. "You would risk your child?"

For a brief moment, I hesitate. I can imagine my daughter, how strong she would be, how kind. The thought of her being taken from me is a pain I cannot imagine. But then I think of that little boy in the picture. The hope in his eyes. The smile on his face. My beautiful sisters will take that beloved child and destroy him, taking him from an old woman that has already had the world turn against her.

I cannot let them do it.

"Please," I whisper. It is all I'm able to say. I know I will not live through this. My sisters walk toward me with the grace that we have all been blessed with, their spears sharp and their grips steady. I look into their eyes, hoping to see some glimmer of empathy.

There is none.

When this is over, I pray they will save my daughter, raise

her as one of their own. And that, maybe, their bloodlust will end with me.

"He is not worth this," Kaiala says.

I clench my hands and set my feet. "It isn't about him. It was never about him."

Effie Graves is an author of short stories, novels, flash fiction, and poetry, who lives out her life chasing dreams and recording truths. She mostly writes contemporary YA, but has also published nonfiction articles for various magazines. This is her first attempt at horror. No matter what the genre, all of her work explores the inner workings of friendships, boundaries, family dynamics, siblings, and mental illness. She also likes dogs and fish and cats. You can learn about Effie, read more of her work, and stay connected with her at effiegraves.com.

About this story, Effie says: "Life is messed up. Thanks to dysfunction and insomnia, I have spent countless hours watching murder shows and as a result have allowed madness and suffering to fill my head. I needed to get some of it out, so I wrote 'Angel.' It, like life, is pretty messed up."

Like a photograph pinned to the wall, the chilling imagery of this story will stay with you for a long time.

ANGEL
Effie Graves

The cold comes faster this time. Sapping color. Numbing, freezing them where they huddle, pressed in the darkest corner of the hollowed-out building. Perfect crystals of ice shimmer on exposed pipes and wires.

"It's too cold, Momma." Storm clouds burst from him with each ragged breath. "I can't do it. Can't stop shaking." Angel's soft round features quiver with each word. He struggles to see, his baby blue eyes obscured by the frosty air. "Sorry, Momma."

"Try again," she says. "You have to concentrate. Remember, golden light. Soft carpet. Warmth." She moves her hands up and down his exposed arms to comfort him. "Close your eyes. Try. Again."

His lids sink. Flutter. Reopen.

Momma leans closer, searching his face. He's somewhere else, she can tell. "What do you see, Angel?"

"The windows. Curtains. They're open, but it's okay. There isn't anyone outside." Angel jerks his head. "Candles are everywhere. They're dancing, Momma. Do you see them?"

"Yes, yes, I see them. They're lovely. What else?" Momma asks. She presses her forehead to his and whispers, "What else, Angel?"

"Hey, my fort. It's here. Same as always. Pillows are all messed up. Dumb dog." Angel chuckles at what he sees. He shakes his head almost imperceptibly, once, then twice. "I'll put them right. Charlie? Get in here."

"Go into your fort, Angel." Momma tells him as she places a small harp at his side. "Play the song I taught you. Your pup will come when he hears the music." She pulls him closer to her, heats his hands with her breath. Arranges his little fingers on the strings.

His fingers twitch and jerk, but produce no sound. No melody.

"That was beautiful, Angel." She notices a purple tinge to his lips. The shallowness of his breathing. "Now, how about you snuggle under a blanket? I bet your fort is full of them."

"I'm okay, Momma. I don't need a blankie. I'm not cold anymore." His mouth hardly moves, his jaw almost petrified. He exhales one final time.

She swipes at her eyes, knocking ice-chip tears to the frozen concrete. "Oh, Angel, at last you're finally ready."

Momma. That's what she made him call her. What they all call her.

She runs the back of her hand along his cheek. He truly looks like an angel now. Pure white and glistening. He's perfect.

Momma carries the lifeless boy to his place in the assembly, her holy choir of angels. There are hardly any spots left to fill. With so many children clamoring for a position in the unspoiled choir, her biggest issue is sorting out the rotten ones, those she could do without. She waves her hand, dispelling the thought from her mind, and focuses on her boy. She adjusts Angel's robe and hair. Smiles at his flawless features.

Snaps a Polaroid.

If only they were all like him.

Momma heaves open the freezer door and walks out into golden shafts of sunlight streaming through high windows. Inside the house, her feet sink into deliciously soft carpet. With a pushpin in one hand and the photo in the other, she tacks Angel's perfect image to her wall.

Momma settles on the couch and pats the cushion beside her. Tiny, shaggy Charlie hops up and circles over and over again. He folds his paws beneath his chest, lifting his ears and squinting toward the light as Momma scratches his neck.

"You're quite sweet, Charlie. I see why Angel hoped to get you back. Children love you. You draw them right in," Momma says. "Yes, Charlie, you'll stay a while. It'll be nice working together."

Charlie sighs, rests his head on Momma's thigh as she looks up at her wall of photos.

Her divine collection.

The empty spaces yet to be filled.

She considers the audience of grieving parents, photos clipped from so many newspapers. Momma shakes her head. They'll understand soon enough. When they finally gather to see her flawless host of angels.

Tomorrow she will begin again.

Some say that Patrick M. Tracy is an evolutionary throwback to prehistoric times. While the full scientific truth of this has yet to be proven, he does play the bass guitar, which is generally considered to be evidence enough. His written work spans fantasy, science fiction, and horror, as well as poetry and the occasional literary piece. One of the principal creators of the Crimson Pact universe, he was included in all five volumes of that series. He's also appeared in Kaiju Rising: Age of Monsters and Mech: Age of Steel. When not writing and dragging his knuckles along the ground, he loves playing the guitar, archery, and doing feats of strength. For more information, please check out his website, www.pmtracy.com.

About this story, Patrick says: "A piece of art that showed a disembodied door standing in a benighted forest kicked off a movie reel inside my brain, wherein I hit upon the idea for the first part of the story, 'Door to Dreamland.' I wrote it up and sent it to her, and she asked, as one does, "What happens next?" Rachael kept asking, and I kept writing more flash stories about this world, beset by exterior forces bent upon its destruction. In the end, I knit them together to create a single narrative, but their symbolic links had always been there, in my mind."

In every world, there are those who sacrifice so the rest may live in peace. In these three interconnected shorts, and the family whose lives they follow, the price of that peace is costly, indeed.

WHO STANDS AGAINST THE FALL OF NIGHT
Patrick M. Tracy

ONE: THE DOOR TO DREAMLAND

Elizabetta held the hatchet close to her thigh. The cold iron head held the remnants of the dead. The fragments of banished spirits reached out, bridging the distance to the skin below her dress, sending shivers through the muscle of her leg. The door and casement stood in the gloom of the forest like disembodied parts of bodies. Betta stood before it as the night mist began to rise, feeling smaller even than her ten summers.

She knew what had to be done. Mama Iadra had trained her, shown her how to fight. The ax-head could never come to rest, a furious partner who danced in twirling circles. Betta couldn't make it look so effortless. Her slim arms were not strong enough, her movements still inexpert, but she gritted her teeth and tried her hardest. Mama Iadra said that the family had always stood this vigil alone. Every girl child had borne the sorrow and the honor, from the time of her ancestors. She thought of the look in her mother's eye, how strong she seemed. How sad her face would become when she thought no one could see her.

"When they come from the golden light, you have to hit them. Cut them deep, before they can get used to our world." She felt her body reverberate like the bell that called them to the Conclave. Mama Iadra's words lived inside her, as did those of the angry-eyed Catechist. Their expectation of her, the weight of their need. She couldn't look at the Catechist's face when he spoke. The way his voice would rise higher and higher, rough and angry, sounding like blood boiled in his throat. The terror of his words, when he'd tell them about the end of the world.

"It shall be the fault of the people, the failing of their strength, at the last. This world, grown small and crushed between the nameless forces of the Many Hells. Rejoice, ye who are called to defend us, who can be the needed warriors of our fading kingdom. Rejoice in the honor to give the Angry Gods their due!" His words, and the dark sleeve of his holy garb, swinging wildly, a fleck of spit shining in the gleam of the afternoon sun. His words, the stuff of Betta's night terrors. She brought the hatchet's metal against her belly, pushing the flat metal against the place that made her want to throw up.

"Let me be strong enough," she begged. Her heart filled with a nameless something. Fear and power. Shame—that every time she had to do this, her eyes filled with tears and she wanted to run away. She thought again of the Conclave, where all put their foreheads to the stone and spoke the words that kept the Angry Gods asleep. They would eat the world and everyone upon it. It would be the end of everything, doom in the bloody jaws of madness. Whatever burden fell upon her, she had to carry. She knew the fearsome consequence if she ever faltered.

Betta gripped the smooth maple of the ax handle and swallowed. This door where she stood guard only opened two nights in the month. In the light of day, when the sounds of crickets and frogs down by the marsh kept the silence at bay, these nights seemed unreal. Like a different girl stood before the door to dreamland and killed the beautiful things that came out into the night. The shadow hid deep within her heart, invisible. Only in the darkness, when it billowed out of her and hung above her straw bed, did the truth of the bloodshed return. Like Mama Iadra, would Betta be doomed to cry out in her sleep, tearing at her blankets, soaked in the sweat of fear? Would the sadness be painted as thick upon her soul as the black paint on an iron bell? The Angry Gods cared not.

Betta felt it begin. The door rattled in its frame, that out-of-place portal that stood without a building. It started like a rustling, like the breaking of small sticks, far off in the beyond. The door opened, just a flicker of golden light at first, then more and more. It waxed until the brightness hit her like a bonfire without heat. The feeling. That peaceful feeling fought against what she'd have to do. Betta knew enough to not trust the peace of dreamland, but she felt her fingers relaxing, the hatchet almost falling from her grip. The fragment of a song promised that she'd always sleep easy, that all the pain in the world could be eased, floated out of that golden glow.

"We do what we must, for the sake of the world, for the sake of our souls," she whispered. The words, meant as a tonic, just made her feel a deep well of sadness open behind her ribs. It would be years. She'd have to stand this way until she had her woman's blood and could pass the awful burden to someone else. Only the young could see the dream creatures. This war belonged to her now, as it would belong to some other unfortunate girl when the blindfold of maturity slipped across her eyes.

The door eased open. They came so quiet, so calm, their huge and luminous eyes glowing with the same gold light as their world. This one, ten times her size, puffed and billowed along the ground, weighing nothing, its ten legs rustling along the leaf litter.

It saw her. The eyes, each one as large as her fist, focused on her. It made a sound like a purr and a hunting horn, all together. It billowed toward her, so innocent, so gentle. Its existence made a hundred promises to her heart. Held within its light, she would know a peace that had escaped her at her very birth. She'd never have to kill again. The burdens would slip from her shoulders. She would float like a leaf upon the surface of a still pool on a day without wind. The beauty of dreams always lied. The night songs couldn't survive the light of day.

Betta's hand clenched. The hatchet came up and whipped down. The iron tore through the dream beast. Blood as sweet as tree sap sprayed across her face, blurring the vision of one eye, touching her tongue as her teeth skinned back like an animal's. The eyes flared, then darkened. The beast cried out as it died, a trumpet of surprised pain that caused every bird in the trees to take flight. The sound always hurt her the deepest. It sounded like hope dying.

Betta tried to wipe the gore off her face, out of her eyes. The blood didn't even sting. The beast broke into a thousand bright fragments, carried by the wind, hungrily consumed by the canopy of trees. The door eased shut again. Her eyes blinked against the night as it asserted its dominance upon the forest once more.

"As the Angry Gods require," she said, her head bowed in prayer. She held the hatchet up against the starlit sky. The dream-sweet blood cooked against the iron and wafted as vapor into the sky. Betta heaved it into the forest, heard it scuttle against a sapling tree and fall to earth.

She couldn't do it again.

She wouldn't.

But she said the same thing every time, and bloodied the hatchet once more.

TWO: MIDDAY'S BROKEN LINE

Janosh watched the other boys run away. After swearing, with heads against the stone and before the eyes of the Angry Gods, they had run. He looked down at his own palms, feeling the shameful urge to do the same. Each beat of his heart brought him closer to the moment of his demise. Alone, the only one who hadn't turned coward, he retained no hope at all. He wouldn't live past sixteen. He would never have a family. The children would never gather at his feet next to the winter's fire and listen to his stories of the old times.

Davo, Rurik, and Tev disappeared into the verge of the trees, the soft noise of their footfalls gone just as quickly. "You will carry it a long time. You'll carry the guilt all your lives," Janosh said. Perhaps they would. The blessing of forgetfulness might save them. He wasn't certain which one he hoped for. They had been his friends, close as brothers. Next to the terror of their task, though, those bonds failed. He closed his eyes, thinking of his mother and his little sister, Betta. They'd both had to be brave for so long. He only needed to be brave this one day. He could do it. He had to.

A gray stone lay in the field of grass. He knelt, putting his forehead against the rough granite surface. Did it matter that he did so? Did the hateful Angry Gods who required such bloody service from his family hear his words from any valley or mountaintop? Janosh found that he didn't care. Not on this day. These words were for himself as much as for them.

"They say that we should find gladness in the burdens of the world. Those who pay the dearest price are the highest honored in the places beyond. I say it's a lie, a sin. I give myself, not for you, you awful gods, but for the hope that Betta will have a world in which to live for a while longer. In hopes that my parents and my sister will grasp a moment of joy in the years ahead. I go to my doom, hoping you starve in your sleep and never awaken."

He stood, his throat working with the aftermath of his words. Janosh scanned the field, the anger spent with his sinful final prayer. For just a moment, he waited for guilt to rise, waited to be crippled with the chill touch of every agony a body could feel. Nothing. Nothing happened. No reprisals came, and the time had arrived.

The peak of summer cooked the last of the night's dew from the high grass. The sun could shine no brighter, climb no higher in the sky than this. It didn't take the Conclave Catechist to know that today the creatures of the dark world would come and require appeasement. The feel of it, whatever thrumming the drums of the beyond could produce, Janosh could feel the touch of those vibrations against his skin.

Stripping to the waist, Janosh felt the sun reach down, its heat like a gentle weight upon his shoulders. In the center of the shaggy grass of the field, he faced west, the beginnings of sweat blooming on his neck. All hallmarks of time fell out of the day. No sparrows swept low over the meadow. The murmur of the nearby river, just beyond the trees, hushed to silence. Even the insects of the earth drew down to a hush.

"Come. Come, you who wait in the unseen shade of brightest day. I am here. I await the claws of your touch."

Those words. The Catechist taught them all, taught them until they dreamed the phrases in their beds. Janosh had never imagined that he'd stand alone to say them at the last. He had finally admitted it. The hatred that had burned within his gut like an invisible disease. In speaking it, the molten metal in his stomach cooled, leaving him suddenly chill and barren.

A crack formed in the surface of the air, thin as spider's silk, dividing the sunlit field.

The Chooser in the Gloom came. The broken place in the day didn't seem to widen so much as grow closer, the magnitude of it revealed with proximity. Once confronted with it, all thoughts of escape, all thoughts of anything but the jagged ribbon where the dark realm loomed, everything departed.

Time, always a trickster, told only lies when Janosh tried to understand how long it took for the crease between worlds to form. He only knew that sweat covered his chest and stung his eyes before he could peer deep into its shadow. The folded place where the realm of shade opened was simply there.

"There are always many. I am accorded the honor of a choice." The voice, no more than a beckoning whisper, came from far back. Janosh could only see her eyes. It seemed a female voice to him. It held a sort of allure, a pull that any reasonable mind recoiled from. Like the moment, when peering down a tall steep cliff, a small voice urges you to leap, to pay for the momentary joy of flight with death upon the rocks below.

"There... is just me. I am sorry."

Her eyes, far above his own, came to the bare verge of the rift. They cast light, just enough to hint at horns and fangs and scales. "I would have chosen you regardless." The force of her words reverberated between worlds, shivering in his belly.

"Why?" The question escaped him before he could quell it.

Janosh had the impression that the Chooser smiled.

"Because you would dare ask. Because you have gone beyond devotion and found a reason closer to your own beating heart. Because I can taste the charcoal remnants of anger upon you. Come, now. Enter my realm. Give yourself to me, if you would forestall the coming of the long night."

He met her eyes. Coming to this moment took bravery, but here, he found that he wanted to take that step. He wanted, in that moment between moments, to see the far side of the broken line. Janosh stepped forward. The shadow felt warmer than he'd imagined. The Chooser's talons wrapped across his limbs, solid as the steel of a plow's blade.

As all he'd ever known fell away, he heard the birdsong begin. The mutter of the river. The swaying of the tall grass in the wind. The rift eased shut, quiet as dusk in a vertical horizon.

THREE: THE HUNGER OF THE GREEN

We came together in the last hour of day, clasping hands before the forest verge. Dressed in our best clothes, we found the heart to smile when we stood together for the convocation, the blessing, and the speaking of the task. Like a marriage, like the ritual that had bound us together two decades before. I remembered that long-gone day, when the crone came and wrapped our wrists with a rope made from supple river grass.

"You needn't do this. Your family has given so much." The Catechist's words held a rare mercy, a softness. I watched his face, seeing something outside the hard doctrine his kind had always preached. A human moment.

I looked at Iadra, touching her face as the light filtered through the trees, going from amber to peach in the waning of the day. She smiled at me, wrinkles next to her eyes, the cares of our lives written like the course of rivers across her skin. No less beautiful, no less my love, but marked by the scars that time will impress upon us all. It had been so long since that look of fatigue had been absent from her features. That feel of being worn down thin by the cares of the world. I'd done my best to avoid my own eyes in reflection, as I didn't want to know the bereft chill they held. What the world had asked, we had given. Few families had been so blessed as ours, according to doctrine. So blessed that little remained of us.

She nodded. "I am no less sure than I was yesterday."

I turned to the Catechist. "Our Elizabetta yet lives, and is married now. Janosh has been gone for many seasons. What need does this world have of us? We are cracked cups, Iadra and I. We cannot hold the waters of life as we once did. Better to serve the good and do what the Angry Gods require. Better us than others."

The Catechist's chin touched his chest. He looked at his own clasped hands. "Very well. I will pour the wine. The dark and narrow path awaits." I could see the tremor in his grasp as he upended the jug, the blood-dark draught flowing messily into his ornate chalice. With both hands, he proffered it to me, the tool of this last ritual.

"Let the time of the final dusk be outside the lifetime of any who now live, and beyond the ancient age of their children, and their children's children. Let the Angry Gods slumber for a thousand years. Through bravery, through reverence, through sacrifice, may it be so. I thank you, Iadra and Davlin, and commend you above all others. The road of flesh is short, but the spirit road stretches beyond even the farthest shore."

I hesitated for a moment, the chalice to my lips. As much as I imagined my courage to be strong, my hand didn't want to tilt the cup. My throat refused to open. The animal in which we ride, this vehicle of flesh, can sometimes balk at what the soul demands. Only a moment, though. Only a passing eyeblink that others would likely miss. I drained the cup, the hot, sharp sensation of the draught tracing down the corridors of my chest. Iadra, upon her turn, upended the chalice without a single hesitation. Always braver than I, always quicker to grasp the need and turn herself to that purpose. Only a few knew the cost. Only a few guessed at the bright and keening demons who haunted her sleep, calling out from that realm where slain dreams go. I knew, and that had always been enough.

Within a hundred heartbeats, I could already feel the wine doing its grim work. Colors I had no names for crept up the inside of the twilight trees. The sound of the whispering forest ahead of us took on timbres unknown.

"Your hands," the Catechist said, producing a thin, sharp dagger from his belt.

The feel of the cut across my palm, deep enough that blood welled wild and sudden against my skin, was no more than a faint echo across a wide ravine.

"How long?" I asked. My feet felt further away with every passing moment.

The Catechist met my eye. "Not so long. I think you already feel the poison." He put his hand upon his chest. "Davlin... your family's strength will not be forgotten."

I nodded, words being of no more use. Whether we would linger in memory or be forgotten held no interest for me. The Catechist's earnest face fell away and became unreal. Taking Iadra's hand, our wounds pressed together. The falling fruit of our veins formed a dotted line of blood as we went. We stepped below the forest's boughs together. The darkened path would not take us far. The soft poison of the wine lit the dimness with the dancing of rainbow lights and nearby stars, our feet scuffing in the leaf litter until we fell.

As we lay upon the loamy ground, hearts nearly stopped, I looked up into the canopy of trees, into the illusory fire of the heavens, and knew that Empress of the Green would stay her hand for one more season. I knew she would eat of our flesh and be made quiet in the cathedral halls of the blood forest.

Heidi Voss got her start writing novels in spiral notebooks and drawing comics for her middle school drumline. That interest continued, and she graduated with her degree in English, capping her experience with an honors thesis about retaining reader interest while juggling world building and character development. While her preference is for long formats, she's working to improve her other skills, and her story "Scrollvana" was awarded in the Vera Mayhew short story competition. Besides writing, Heidi works full time and spars at a local MMA gym, and gets a lot of bloody noses no matter how much she tries to stay hydrated. Follow her on Twitter (@rarevoss) and Instagram (@ubervoss) for updates on upcoming writing workshops and recaps of her latest fights.

About this story, Heidi says: "Acacia is a character in a novel I'm working on about witches. I figured Acacia, the witch who has been practicing longest, would have an interesting dating history. The natural first choice would be for Acacia to have dated a demon, but it didn't take long for me to think of other comparable stories with demon or 'bad boy' ex-lovers in the lives of the main characters. What about going the other direction? What if Acacia used to date an angel?"

Surviving a critical illness is difficult enough without also getting an unwelcome glimpse of the 'other side.' Then again, sometimes it helps to be scared straight—and have someone both hot and heavenly to look forward to.

Breaking Up with an Angel
Heidi Voss

I know you won't believe me when I say I kissed an angel, but that's understandable. I don't love telling the story anyway. It'd probably be a good idea to at least write it down. Maybe I'll never see this guy again in this life or the next, but I owe it to myself to remember.

When I told the story to Carmen, she had a billion questions. What did he look like? Did he have wings? Where would you even meet an angel?

I'll start with that last one.

I met him at a hospital.

I was in the cancer wing at a hospital in St. George. It was a long way from my apartment in Salt Lake City, but that's where my mom was, and cancer isn't something you tough out on your own. It wasn't supposed to be a big deal, but I ended up staying a lot longer than I thought I would. There was this super old lady in the bed next to me. I kept thinking, *Damn, if I was that old, I'd just ask them to put me out of my misery.* But I wanted to be put out my misery anyway.

Not because of the cancer. Like I said, it wasn't a big deal— the skin cancer I had came with a high survival rate. I just didn't care whether I lived or died. That's why I was such a nightmare for my family. Any time I called, they thought I was calling from some jail, asking to get bailed out again.

But I hadn't been caught with anything for years. Not since I switched to dealing in prescription meds. All my friends were chasing after the loaded suburban good-kids-gone-bad, but I knew better than that. You should've seen my fake doctor signature. If you wanted Ritalin, I'd get you Ritalin. If you wanted Vicodin, you got a prescription from me, Dr. Acacia.

I was supposed to be in and out, home recovering and making more bad decisions, but one day I woke up and I wasn't in bed. I was on the ceiling above, looking down at my lifeless body below. There was a man next to me, laying out like ceilings are as comfy as couches.

"Are we dead?" I asked him. I hoped he knew more than I did. After all, he'd been there longer. He jumped at the sound of my voice.

"Yes." He stopped to think about it. He had curly brown hair and eyes with his feelings written all over them. I bet he was a poet in a past life. "I mean, no. You are not dead, not yet."

I couldn't place his accent. I never traveled or anything, so I wasn't sure. Maybe Italian?

"I am here to watch over her." He pointed to the bed next to mine. That's where that old woman, Ethel, was sleeping. I don't know how she could sleep through all the noise—a nurse had just found me and was yelling down the hall for help—but there she was, drool dripping down her chin. I checked out the other beds on the ground, looking for the body that matched the ceiling spirit next to me. From here I could see over the curtains that separated the beds. Only ladies on either side.

"Are you"—I tried to work it out—"a protector ghost? Are you haunting this hospital?"

He kind of laughed at that.

"I am a guardian angel."

A guardian angel? In washed-out blue jeans, a white shirt, and a flannel top wrapped around his waist, he didn't look much like an angel. Throw in his accent and I would have guessed he was some Euro tourist who got lost on his way to Moab.

"I am surprised you can see me," he said.

"Yeah, but that's probably not a good thing."

Both of us looked down at my body. The doctor gave me chest compressions, like the kind I learned when I was taking lifeguard lessons at the YMCA.

The angel looked at me, his eyes round and soft.

"That is unfortunate, but the next place is good, too. I am from there." He held out a hand. "My name is Daniele."

I shook it, like it was the most natural thing in the world to meet someone on the ceiling of a hospital room.

"Is it okay if I call you 'Danny'?"

I wasn't sure I could call him 'Daniele' with a straight face. I'd met plenty of women named 'Danielle,' but no men that I could think of.

I knew it was rude, since I'd just met him, but I was kind of angry.

"Where's my guardian angel?" I said. "I'm dying down there, and they can't send someone to watch out for me?" I was all ready to launch into a lecture about how broken religion is, but he just pointed down at the doctor saving me. There were three nurses with her, messing with equipment and trying to get me to breathe.

"That one. There," Danny said. Clearly I didn't see what he was seeing, so he pointed. "The woman with the red hair. She is not a nurse, she is your angel. She cannot interfere much—that is not really what we do—but she stopped the doctor from leaving to eat lunch so she could be here for you."

That shut me up quick. After I thought about it, I turned to him. He already knew what I was going to ask.

"Ethel's disease is fatal. I would help with the nurses, too, but my assignment is to watch over and give her comfort."

"So I'm going to live, but Ethel won't?" I looked from my choking, shaking self to her wrinkled and frail old body. Danny shrugged.

"Things do not look good for you, either. There is fluid in your lungs."

"Fluid?" I stared back at him. "It's skin cancer, not lung cancer."

"Sometimes after an operation like yours, the fluids build and get in your lungs. I am not a surgeon. I cannot explain the process. But that is why Garnet was assigned to you." They were still having a hard time getting me to breathe right, and my body was turning ghostly pale.

I was nervous. I talked big and I acted like an idiot, but I wasn't really ready to die. I grabbed Danny's hand, and he didn't pull away, he just held it. His skin was soft, like feathers on a goose, but his hands were strong, like they could carry the weight of the world.

I don't remember exactly what he said, but he was very soothing. He was a good choice for someone getting ready to move on.

He told me about Heaven. He said there are all kinds of flowers there. Way more than what we have on earth, and you don't have to weed them or anything, they just grow there. He said he has a little cabin by a lake, and when he's off duty, he paints. It was surreal there, lying on the ceiling, watching myself dying while this angel next to me talked about cubism.

I felt a yank and suddenly I was back in my body, gasping for breath. It was like I was drowning. Now that they had me breathing a bit, they were wheeling me back into surgery. I didn't want to be in that aching body, though. I wanted to go back on the ceiling with Danny. I wanted to know if there were any ducks on the lake by his cabin.

That night, I was pretty drugged up, but feeling better. They said I wasn't out of the woods, but I could breathe again. I was flipping through a magazine, but it just seemed so stupid reading about lipstick when the lady next to me was headed for death and I probably wasn't far behind.

Danny came down from the ceiling. I hadn't seen him up there earlier, but I guess that was kind of his home base while watching over Ethel. I looked around to see if anyone else just saw what I saw, but the curtains were drawn between me and the other patients.

"May I join you?" he asked.

Like I'm going to turn down an angel for company.

"Sure, knock yourself out."

He sat in a corner, in a rocking chair that wasn't there before, and started knitting. That's when he told me about the prayers. He had this huge, gold ball of yarn and what looked like a six-foot-long blanket in the works. He said a lot of people had been praying for Ethel, all those kids and grandkids praying for her to get better. Sometimes it heals people, but not always.

"Those calls are above my sanction," he said, pointing up. I wondered if God was up there too, hanging out on the ceiling, making cosmic decisions while all the hospital people ate their pudding and watched TV, unaware God was watching them pick their noses.

"They have made an appointment for Ethel, but they want to

give her time to say farewell to her family. So I make a lot of these to give her comfort."

He showed me the blanket. Each strand of the yarn glittered with the words of Ethel's family. "Please help her get better." "Help the cancer go away so she can come to the family reunion this summer." "Let her feel comfort even though she's very sick." I started to tear up, reading stuff like that. I thought, if anything, my mom probably told her friends at church not to pray for me.

Of course, Danny could tell what I was thinking from the look on my face. He pulled something from his pocket.

"Garnet is helping the doctor sleep so she can take good care of you, but she wanted me to give you this."

It was a glittering, gold scarf. It was a lot smaller than Ethel's blanket, but I didn't care. I was just happy to have anything. He wrapped it around my neck, and I felt the pain in my lungs melt away. I felt my fears calm. I looked at the words in the yarn. "Please bless Acacia to get better. I'm not ready for her to go." "Sometimes she can be kind of a pain, but we love her so much. Please bless the surgery to go smooth."

That dumb prayer scarf, it broke my heart. I knew that last one came straight from my mom. I saw prayers from my cousin Sarah woven in there too. And my dad across the country, he must have taken a break from watching the stock market ticker long enough to send a prayer up for me. I felt like I didn't want to be so awful anymore. Like I ought to find an honest way to make money.

Then I pictured myself sitting in an office, answering phones or something for the next thirty years.

"If I go, would I even get to Heaven?" I asked Danny. "I'm not a very good person."

He paused from his knitting and looked at his hand, like

he'd written it down or something. Maybe an angel's hand is like a phone screen and he could look things up on it. I don't know.

"You are on the list," he said. "If you get to the other side, I would love for you to live in my neighborhood."

"You don't even know me," I said. I was so stupid. Defensive because I thought an angel was hitting on me. A heavenly being asks to live next door to me for eternity, and I'm offended because I think he's trying to get in my pants.

"I have seen your whole life," Danny said. "I think painting would be healing for you. My brother used to sell false medicine, and painting has been wonderful for him."

I scowled. "I don't sell snake oil."

He frowned at me, and I shut up. We were quiet for a minute except for the sound of his knitting needles clicking together. I tried flipping through my magazine some more, but he caught me staring at him over the pages, so I set it aside.

"Is there anything you want to know about Earth? It sounds like you haven't lived here for a while."

Man, you should've seen him light up at that. He asked questions faster than I could answer them. Why does everyone draw their eyebrows on so big? What is "the cloud" and how do you put pictures and books in there? If vaping smells so much better than smoking, why do people get so annoyed with it?

He didn't believe me for most of it, but we ended up talking all night. He took breaks to wrap Ethel up in her prayer blanket and sing her to sleep, but then he was right back in the rocking chair with another giant ball of yarn, starting on a hat and gloves for her. I thought Ethel might sweat to death with so much comfort.

We spent a week like that, him telling me about Heaven and me telling him about earth. My condition wasn't getting any better, and I was getting into the idea of living next to Danny by a lake, sitting on the front porch and painting flowers. Maybe I could help Danny with his knitting, or maybe I'd get my own job. I decided maybe I could be like a "scared straight" angel, and I could visit rotten people like me and say, "You're going to die and get stuck knitting if you don't clean up your life."

Then things got really bad. One night, after Ethel was asleep, Danny was sitting in the chair next to me, holding my hand and asking me about what a Beyoncé was when I saw Garnet run in with the doctor. I thought they must have been mixed up, but it turned out they were just in time for another fluid-in-the-lungs episode. This time, instead of getting thrown out of my body and onto the ceiling where I could hang with Danny, I was in pain the entire time. I couldn't see what was happening, but I could feel every squeak of breath trying to force its way through my wrecked lungs. I could feel my limbs go numb, suffocating along with the rest of me.

All I could think, over and over again, was, *Please, just take me to Heaven where I can live next to Danny. Please, take me to Heaven where I can stay by the lake.*

I didn't see a white light. I didn't hear a chorus of angels. Everything went dark, and the first thing I noticed was a smell.

It wasn't flowers.

It was like the time I tried pulling over to help a raccoon that was stuck by the side of the road. Except it had already been half crushed, and there were maggots eating him while he stared out, stiff and sightless. It was that smell of rotten flesh, baking in the sun.

I saw a gaping mouth in front of me, with rows of teeth like a shark, but instead of a tongue reaching out to grab at my feet, it was hands. There were all these hands reaching for me, pulling at my hospital gown, grabbing for my ankles, my toes. I curled up to get away from them, but I was getting pushed closer and closer to them. They got hold of me, and every touch was sticky. The smell made me want to puke. I called out to Danny, to God, to anyone for help, but the hands kept pulling me farther down, down into the throat.

I woke up in an operating room with a doctor standing over me with a scalpel. I tried to roll away from him, but my hands and feet were tied in place. A motion from his hand had a nurse at my side with a gas mask to put over my face.

I screamed and thrashed.

"Don't send me back!" I begged. "Don't send me back!"

The nurses won, of course.

When I woke up in a hospital room after that, I let out a relieved breath. No mouth, no smell, and Ethel was still in the bed next to me. That meant Danny was still here.

There was a mistake, there had to be. Danny said I was on the list for Heaven, and I'm sure Heaven doesn't smell like rotten meat.

I'd been mad at God before, but it was always with the idea that he might not be real and that the crappy things in my life were all on me. Now I was livid. Miserable, broken, and livid.

My mom came to see me, to fuss over me and to feel tragic about herself for having a daughter with cancer.

"Baby girl, we'll make it through this together." She brushed her hands through my hair, sitting at my side. She'd never been the kind of mom to brush her hands through my hair before, but now that I was one step away from being a Hallmark special, she was suddenly mother of the year.

The minute she was out of the room, Danny swooped down from the ceiling, taking my hand.

"That looked very painful. How do you feel?" He had flecks of gold all over his lap from the prayer yarn rubbing against his clothes. He held out a mitten for me, trying to pull it over my hand. "Garnet has not finished the other one, but I thought you could at least have this."

I slapped the prayer mitten out of his hand. His eyes widened.

"Your list is shit," I told him.

He winced. I didn't care.

"I nearly got dragged to Hell today, and you told me I was going to some nice place with flowers and ducks and water and all that garbage, you bastard."

I wanted to sock him. I thought that maybe angels lied to people to get them to move on without putting up a fight. Maybe that's why I got fed some story about healing at a cabin.

I tried to suck back in my tears, but they ended up dripping down my face.

"I know I'm not exactly Mother Theresa, but that's not"—I gasped, trying to catch my breath—"that's not fair. I don't deserve that." I wanted to go on, to tell him that I could change, that I haven't had enough time here, but I couldn't. My lungs were on fire, and every shock of breath felt like knives in my chest. Wasn't this torture enough? Couldn't cancer be my punishment?

I expected Danny to fight back with me or to tell me off. I wanted him to list all the terrible things I'd done, rub it in my face, so I could shout back at him that if God wanted me to be a good person, he should've given me a better shot at life. Should've given me a real mom, not a walking prescription zombie. Should've given me a dad who knew how to function in a relationship, not shut down at any sign of conflict.

Should've given me a chance for an athletic scholarship, not jacked up my knee during my senior year of high school soccer.

But Danny didn't yell at me, and I couldn't yell at him because my lungs were beat. I couldn't even see him through my tears, just a white glow and two brown blurs where his beautiful eyes were. I felt a tissue touch my hand and I turned away from him, wiping my face, wheezing against the curtain separating my bed from the bed of Danny's real concern. For a moment I wondered if Ethel was going to Heaven or if Danny had lied to her, too. As a matter of fact, there was no reason to assume he was an angel at all.

I turned back to him to use whatever breath I could to tell him he was a phony, but I stopped short when I saw his face was red, swollen with tears.

"When I looked at the list, you were on it, I swear to you!" His hands were shaking, wrapped around my unwanted prayer mitten. His eyes were sincere. I swallowed my nasty words.

"Check it again," I said.

"I cannot." He dabbed at his eyes with the mitten. "They have taken away my access. I was not supposed to tell you anything. I just... I could not bear to see you hurt so much." His hand reached for mine, but he caught himself and curled it up against his side instead.

I wanted to snatch up his hand and command him to stay by my side. I wanted more stories of Heaven, to cocoon myself in prayer yarn, and to forget about a gaping mouth drooling for my wicked spirit.

But I couldn't stand the idea that I was being tricked. I couldn't deny the sights and smells burned into my memory. I wrapped the thin hospital blankets around myself as tight as I could.

"Get out," I said. I didn't dare look up into those cinnamon brown eyes of his. I looked at my lap instead.

There was a pause. I wondered what he was thinking. I wondered if he loved me.

Then he was gone.

If you can believe it, things got worse from there.

My mom got pretty spooked when I asked her to bring me different versions of the Bible and essays on scripture. I think I even had her find a Talmud and Qur'an for me. I didn't read much of the content, just hunted through the index for anything about angels. Specifically, how to tell the good ones from the bad ones.

There's plenty in there about Hell. Weeping and wailing and gnashing of teeth. Lots about Jesus, too. Dining with the sinners and healing the sick. But not a lot of details about angels.

Not that I was a very precise reader at the time. I complained constantly to my doctor about my aches and pains, pressuring them to give out more medication. The minute Danny was gone, I called my roommate to bring me a stash of unsold pills I had from the apartment. At one point I wasn't even looking at the bottle labels anymore. I was just taking whatever my hand landed on first. Anything that would take me away, even for a minute.

At least, that's what I guess was going through my head. I learned about the pill stash secondhand after everything was over. I don't remember much about that time except crying a lot and squeezing my prayer mitten in my hand until it all but unraveled.

There was a break in the haze where I saw my mom yelling

at me, shaking a bottle of pills in my face, but it was like I was watching someone else's life. I couldn't even hear what she was saying. I just thought, *There's no way I'm going to Heaven. There's no way I can fix this.*

Painting classes weren't going to heal me. Wrapping up in prayer blankets could never put me back together.

The next thing I really remember is the wheelchair on the way out of the hospital. My first breath of fresh air after being stifled with chemical smells and the stink of cancer for weeks.

"Acacia, you're going home," my mom told me, bending to look into my eyes. She must not have liked what she saw. "Oh, Lord, are you even in there, baby girl? Acacia, you're cancer free. All that poison you swallowed is out of your system. We're going home."

"I don't have a home." I was being dramatic, of course, but the thought of going back to my cramped Salt Lake apartment after everything that had happened was bleak.

"Don't be like that, Acacia. You always have a home with your family." Mom reached for my hair again, but I pulled away. She sighed and wheeled me out to her newly leased SUV. I half expected her to tell me not to get my hospital stink on the seats.

So that's how I met an angel. I doubt he remembers me as nice as I remember him, but it was a real comfort to have a visit from someone who honestly cared about me at a time when things looked their worst.

The next few years were tough, but everyone's life is tough. I tried to go back to my old network. I was out of stock after my mom raided my apartment and took all my product, but I never lost my touch for forging prescriptions.

I wanted my best friend, Lily, to take care of me. Mom couldn't make me stay with her, and Lily had a whole new flock of customers waiting for me when I came back. But for some reason every time she reached over to hand me my share of fries or a blanket while we watched TV, I'd get this whiff of rotting meat. I tried to ignore it, sure my nose got messed up while I was in the hospital, but after a few months I couldn't take it anymore. That was the beginning of the end of my prescription-dealing days.

I had a dream once, years later, where I saw Danny's lake. The water was so clear you could see all the way to the bottom, and there wasn't gross mud and algae in there. Just these little fish, who almost looked like they were smiling at you. The water wasn't freezing, either, the way it is up in the mountains here. It was just right for swimming, or even for dipping your toes in on a hot day.

There were ducks—or at least, I would call them ducks. They had blue and pink feathers, which seemed to change color in the sun. What a tough color to try to copy. If you were trying to paint one of those ducks, you'd mess up the color a lot before getting it right.

Then I remembered. Painting lessons.

I turned around.

There was a little cabin by the lake. A glowing figure sat in a rocking chair, watching the clouds move across the sky. He was nodding off, his lap full of gold yarn and a half-finished sweater.

When he saw me, he jumped out of his seat, rocks and dry grass crunching under his feet as he ran to me. A mountain breeze tossed his brown curls in a frizzy halo around his head. I walked to meet him, a big smile plastered on my face like nothing had ever been wrong.

He grabbed my hands, explaining everything, words falling out of his mouth faster than he could keep up. It made sense, it was perfect, he was perfect. He wanted to ask me about how the rest of my life was, pulling me to join him on the porch of his cabin, but I stopped him. Before he could say another word, I wrapped my arms around his waist and pressed my lips to his.

It was more warmth than my heart knew how to handle. I thought it might burst, and all my happiness would shoot out my ears and my eyes and into the sky. I thought I'd turn into an angel right there on the spot, like a heavenly chorus was blessing our kiss, blessing the lake, blessing me.

When I opened my eyes, though, it was just my phone screen staring back at me. Three minutes from when my alarm was supposed to wake me up.

I grabbed a paper from my desk to write down what the explanation was, why there had been some kind of mix-up at the hospital. But I couldn't remember, of course.

I was a changed woman after that. Changed in that I knew I wasn't ready to face death. Not then, not ever. Sure, Danny apparently had an explanation about why I was headed for Hell that day, and it was nice to get a preview of what a peaceful afterlife might look like.

But no one knows when they're going to go, and seeing the other side made me more scared, not less. What if by the time I'm hit by a bus or shot in a holdup, the scales are tipped a little bit the wrong way?

I wasn't much of a reader before, but now I've always got a book in hand. I'm still looking for something, anything, to give me another option, no matter how wild it sounds. I mean, I met an angel for crying out loud, so maybe this book isn't so far off saying I could steal a magic staff from the ocean and live forever. That's the one I'm obsessed with right now. Between the devil and the deep blue sea, I don't think I'd mind the waves.

Maybe if my mom can't get a Hallmark special about my cancer, she can get one about me going crazy.

I do catch myself, though, after all these years—when I know I've messed things up and I don't know how to fix it, I pray. I pray to someone else's guardian angel, hoping he'll bring me some gold, knitted comfort. I pray that one day I might grow the guts to do the right thing. Not just once in a while, when I get a vision of Hell, but all the time. I spend the rest of the day imagining what it might be like if I could earn a seat next to an angel.

#1 *Amazon bestselling author Michael Darling has worked as a butcher, a magician, and a librarian. He wrote his first story on a scrap of paper for his mother named Sandra. That previous sentence was constructed with a misplaced modifier on purpose. In part, because Michael sometimes teaches English to terrible middle-grade monsters, but mostly because people reading this will wonder if the scrap of paper was named Sandra instead of his mother. The possibility of such a thing happening is the kind of world Michael likes to imagine. Humorous and unexpected and potentially frightening. Michael's award-winning short stories are frequently anthologized and his first novel, Got Luck, hit #1 on Amazon. He continues to work on that series and other projects. Visit Michael at www.michaelcdarling.com*

About this story, Michael says: "Sailing on the Tides of Burning Sand" began with an image. One of those pictures that surfaces when you're halfway between sleeping and waking; when you're in that pre-dawn consciousness and your imagination is crossing realities. The image was a married couple sitting together in the bow of a boat, moving over rust-colored sand dunes. I wondered how they got there and what they were going through together, and the story came out of asking those questions and listening to the characters for the answers."

There's a Dali-esque quality to this story that warps time and stretches perception, and may leave you wondering about the reality you have sailed into. Just name your constellations and let them guide you.

SAILING ON THE TIDES
OF BURNING SAND
Michael Darling

Falling. The whole room. Falling. The lightness of his own weight. Air rushing outside the walls. He remembered everything. All he had learned. All he had been. His mind strained with the accumulated wealth of experience. Then, like a grain of sand in a midnight sea, everything sank and faded away. His only memory was that of having remembered.

The room thudded, landed, stopped. Blackness. No sense of time.

Lips pressed against his. Soft.

He opened his eyes.

The room moved. Swayed. He felt dizzy. Maybe from the motion of the room. The chamber where he laid no longer falling but going forward.

Maybe it was the kiss.

The woman hovered over him, smiling, holding herself up with her hands beside his shoulders. Long, tousled hair fell, tracing lines on his face. Her eyes locked onto his.

He had no idea who she was.

"It's okay if you don't remember me," she said. "I didn't remember you either. Not at first." She slipped off him. She wore a gray shirt. Gray pants. Gray shoes. He did too. She grasped his hand and pulled him to his feet. "Come on. It's beautiful outside."

He looked at the room.

Four walls. Each wall with a round window. One window set in a door. On the floor, a box with a lid. Various copper fixtures decorated the walls and ceiling. Opposite the bench he'd been lying on, a small bin. A bronze metal plaque bolted to the wall above it. Blank.

Outside, a narrow deck. Blue sky and brown sand, flowing by. Susurrations of particles trickling around the walls. The woman pulled him to a heavy railing. Sand roiled in tumult behind them like a wake.

"A boat. I remember boats." He laughed. "Hey! I remember boats!"

The woman squealed and let go of his hand to jump and clap.

He followed the deck around the cabin to the bow, holding the rail. Touching the solid metal reassured him the boat was real. The view atop the prow supplied a splendid view of hot sand under a pale, blue sky. Beautiful indeed, in its way. The sun burned directly overhead, offering no sense of direction or time. He asked, "Do you know where we are?"

She shook her head, smiling shyly. "I woke up in your arms and came outside. I've been remembering bits and pieces for an hour, at most. I got afraid you weren't going to wake up." Her laugh was soft. "So I…"

"I remember. It was nice."

She hopped and clapped her hands again. The gesture was familiar. As if he'd seen her do it hundreds of times before. Thousands. Not just once.

The vast empty landscape remained a mystery in every

direction. Flat. Endless. Trackless. The starboard view was no different from the port. He returned to the cabin. His inspection of the entire world had taken only a minute.

He opened the box and found two silver packets, two bottles, and a metal tube.

"Where did you get those?" The woman put a hand on his shoulder and took a silver packet. She opened it. Sniffed. Her eyes brightened. "Bacon, lettuce, and tomato sandwich."

They ate. He didn't remember having a sandwich ever before. "Delicious," he said.

"You didn't tell me where you found these." She drank from the bottle with a sigh.

"In that box."

The woman eyed the box. "It was empty."

The man lifted his shoulders. One shoulder rising a moment before the other. A habit returning.

Her lips twisted in a wry half-smile. "I remember hating that shrug."

"Really? Shrug, huh? I didn't know I did that."

She kissed him again. Her hands came to rest on his chest and he found himself holding her in his arms. She whispered, "There's something else you might not know you did."

The metal tube was a spyglass. He remembered what it was called after he'd pulled it open and looked through the lens. Delighted with the view, he surveyed the horizon.

An object.

The sky had faded with the setting of the sun, turning from blue to pink to purple, but there was something. A patch of gray on the brown sand and a plume of dust.

The woman looked. Her nose and mouth scrunched up. "Where? Oh. Hmm. I see it!" She bounced on her toes. "What is it?"

"A vessel. Two of them. One straight ahead and one straight behind. Vessels like ours."

She laughed. "'Vessels?' You love fancy words. I remember."

"Accurate words," he corrected. "And you always tease—" He stopped. "I have a brother. Do you remember that?"

She hesitated. Thinking. Shook her head.

"He pointed it out. How you tease me about using fancy words." He tried to remember other things but came up blank. He shrugged. One shoulder, then the other.

The sun slipped past the horizon. A blanket of stars faded into view like a cloth infused with diamonds unrolling across the sky.

"Vessels," he mused. "Going where?" He looked forward to the horizon. A fuzzy line of orange light flickered in the distance.

The woman reappeared, carrying silver packets and bottles and a copper lantern, already glowing. She said, "The box had stuff in it again."

He tried to remember if boxes normally went from empty to having things in them.

The packet gave off a savory aroma as soon as it was opened. He inhaled the steam before looking inside. "Spaghetti and meatballs?"

"Yay! You knew it!"

She was often upbeat. Supportive. He remembered that about her.

They sat in the bow again, legs dangling. The sand *shush-shush-shushed* below them. There were little sticks with little hooks in the packets. They figured out how to use them to eat spaghetti while they looked at the stars.

"Cheese," he remembered, tasting. "Parmesan."

"What's that bunch of stars called?" She pointed at the sky with her eating stick.

"Constellation," he said.

"They're called Constellation?"

He laughed. "No. A bunch of stars are called a constellation. There are many different groupings of stars. They're all constellations with different names."

"Oh." She put her fingertips on the end of her nose, her cheeks turning rosy. He recognized the new gesture as soon as he saw it. Embarrassment.

He looked up, smiling. He remembered the word 'constellation' but couldn't find any patterns he knew. Amid great swaths of dancing lights, shimmering anonymously against the deepening plum-colored sky, none had names he could recall.

Unacceptable.

He pointed at the stars straight ahead. "That constellation is Gilligan the Navigator." He kept a straight face to hide the fact that he was inventing facts, letting the words fall. Not even knowing where the words came from or entirely what they meant.

"Gilligan?" The woman tilted her head.

"Yes. That pair of stars are his eyes, seeing the way forward. And those stars making a circle are the ship's wheel, guiding all those who sail on the tides of burning sand."

She pulled his arm around her and settled into his shoulder. "I think you're a poet."

Her words bloomed as a warm spot in his chest. He put his chin on her head and watched the puffs of dust rise as the prow of the ship cut through the sand.

"I know I love you," he said.

He slept with the woman nestled against him on the bench until the sun brightened the room through the window.

He got up. The first box was empty.

The copper rectangle over the second box caught his eye. Yesterday, it had been blank. A simple, plain sheet of metal riveted to the wall. Now, there were pictures.

At the top, he recognized numbers and a symbol: 1/3. On the left, a shape with four sides. He said, "Rhomboid" as soon as the fancy word popped into his mind. The shape was silver, not copper. Below the rhomboid, an arrow pointed down at a stack of shapes, also silver. Next to the silver rhomboid was a pair of sticks and another arrow pointing down to a collection of sticks. On the right, a shape like the bottle of water, a down arrow, and a collection of bottles at the bottom.

He understood.

"What did you do with the packets?"

The woman sat on the deck. "What?"

"The silver packets and things that came out of the box. Where are they?"

She pointed at the sand. "I threw them overboard."

"Oh." He took a deep breath.

"What's wrong?"

He ran his hands through his hair. "You didn't know."

"Know what?"

He led her into the cabin. Showed her the plaque. Explained what he thought it meant.

She put her fingertips on her nose. "Okay. From now on, we'll store them in the bin."

"Promise?"

"Cross my heart and hope to die."

The boat lurched. Dropping forward, they fell into the wall.

They left the cabin and grabbed the railing. The boat accelerated, slipping down a slope.

"Dunes!" He inched forward, the woman grabbing his belt. "I want to get a look." They wedged themselves together in the bow as the boat leveled off and started climbing the next pile of sand. He had the spyglass in a pocket and wrapped an arm around the railing while he tried to get it out.

"Careful!" The woman sat, wrapping her legs around the post of the railing and clinging to his leg with her arms.

He readied the glass as the vessel rose. Squinting through the lens, he couldn't see the ship in front of them. He reasoned it was in the trough between dunes. Instead he saw a glimmering in the distance. He dropped to the deck as the boat tilted over the peak and put his arm around the woman. "Do you want to look?" She considered the railing and the incline as they went up. "Okay. But I'll just sit. Hold me."

He wrapped his arms around her waist. She steadied the spyglass at the crest of the dune.

"I see it!" She bounced up and down where she sat. "What is it?"

"I don't know."

The vessel descended again. She handed the spyglass back. The boat carried them up and down the swells. Each one was a little taller than the last. Finally, the woman raised her hands over her head, trusting him to hold her. "Whee!"

He laughed. At the top of the next dune he could see the glimmer without the glass.

"We're getting closer," he said.

The woman took the spyglass. With the tip of her tongue parting her lips, she focused. "It's a tree!"

At the top of the next dune, he looked again. "Good job, honey."

She put her arms around his neck and kissed him. "You can call me 'honey' all you like."

"Then I will call you Honey from now on."

"What shall I call you?"

"Whatever you like."

She mulled it over. "Seems kind of long, Mr. Whatever-you-like."

"You're teasing me. I like it."

She squeezed tighter. "Good. I'll just call you Mine."

"I like that too."

The rolling dunes continued beneath them. For a time, they took turns watching and waiting. The tree grew out of the sand as if the dunes were pushing it up from below. Mine guessed the tree was at least two-hundred feet tall. The trunk and branches were the same green as the leaves, faceted, catching the morning light and throwing sun-sharp shards to the sky and to the sand and to their eyes. He was sure it must be glass.

Mine got tired of waiting and went to check the box. He timed his walk so the vessel stopped climbing before he negotiated the corner. One unexpected bump and he'd fall off the boat. In the box, there were silver packets and bottles. The plaque had changed again. In the corner "2/3" was engraved and the old shapes had been replaced with new ones. He studied the diagram.

"What took so long?" Honey opened her packet and Mine followed suit.

"I noticed a new diagram on the wall." Mine let the aromas waft up to his nose. "Sausages on a stick. Eggs and bagels."

He took a bite as the boat evened out, heading up the next incline. "Chorizo. It's funny how we remember food so easily."

Honey laughed. "But we can't remember our own names."

They ate. The dunes leveled off, sands flat again. Honey sighed in relief and untangled herself from the railing. "I'll put those in the bin."

Mine handed her his packet and skewer and bottle. "Thank you." He looked at the crystalline tree. The boat would sail past it soon. Honey reappeared.

"We're almost to the tree."

She plopped to the deck.

Mine caught her expression. "What's wrong?"

"I don't understand that stupid plaque."

He put a calming hand on her arm. He didn't admit to getting it already, and easily. He remembered she'd get upset and start to cry if he made her feel dumb. "We'll work it out."

Honey's expression went from upset to fearful. "What's that?"

Ahead, there was a line of rising dust and a thin curtain, sparkling, sparking.

Instinctively, they retreated from the bow, shoving themselves against the cabin wall. He threw his arms around her. A rumbling of machinery sent shudders through the vessel. Honey screamed. He looked through the spyglass.

"We'll be okay," Mine shouted. "I know it."

The boat slid through the curtain. The hairs on their bodies crackled with static. On the other side, a fresh expanse of desert spread before them like a giant blanket of rolling velvet.

Mine pecked Honey's cheek. "We're fine. See?"

Honey tentatively opened her eyes. She inhaled at the view. "Oh." Her voice soft.

The tree dazzled with shattered refractions and reflections, dappling the sand with sharp-edged rhomboids of light.

Creatures swam around the roots.

Honey saw them. "They're alive." They watched the creatures paddle in the sand as the boat drifted on. "How did you know we'd be okay?" Tears stood in Honey's eyes.

"Whoever brought us here went to a lot of trouble." Mine kept his voice even. Humble. "They wouldn't do that just to let us die so soon." He gave her the spyglass. "And the other boat's still ahead of us."

Honey looked through the glass. She pressed herself into Mine's shoulder. "You're so smart."

Mine watched the creatures swimming in the sand. More mechanical clanking and slamming. "I think the curtain keeps those creatures here."

"Sand dolphins?" Honey smiled.

"Maybe," Mine replied.

"Are they dangerous?"

"Doesn't look like it."

Several creatures approached, circling their boat. One raised up to starboard, almost standing on its tail to look at them.

It sang.

It could have been either male or female but Mine thought of her instantly as a girl because she had a curving softness to her body and her song was high and pleasant. She had short, ropy hair that barely touched her shoulders. Her skin was scaly and bony plates curved from behind her neck like an armadillo. Her green eyes had white membranes that slid down in approximation of a blink. She sang as the boat sailed past, then dove into the sand.

Neither Mine nor Honey could remember a real name for them.

"Maybe we never saw them before," Mine said. "We could call them Sirens." He explained the story of Odysseus and the beautiful women who sang to sailors, seducing them with their calls, leading them to crash their ships.

Honey listened with her arms folded over her stomach.

"I don't think our ship can change course. We have nothing to worry about."

"I don't like them." Honey sniffed and disappeared into the cabin.

———

The boat sailed on. Mine watched the sirens swim and play until food appeared in the box but Honey said she wasn't feeling well and stayed in the cabin. The diagram showed what to do with the materials from their meals and Mine gave it a try.

He pulled on the lip of the water bottle as the diagram showed. It unwound into a long, thin wire. He threaded the wire onto a skewer and started to sew the silver packets together.

"What's that for anyway?" The sun was setting, and Honey emerged from the cabin, holding the copper lantern. Her eyes were red.

"I don't know. The plaque should tell us. There's one more message."

She sat down and took the pieces. He'd sewn four of the silver packets into a square. "You're really bad at this." She wasn't teasing but he wasn't blind to the uneven stitches he'd made, and the puckered edges, and he didn't say anything when she started to unpick his work.

"Mine? I don't know why I got upset. Are you mad me?"

He slid an arm around her waist. "No, Honey. You're too sweet."

"Oh." She put her fingertips on the end of her nose. "I'm glad you think so." She cupped his face and kissed him.

"I remember something else about you," he said.

"What?"

He pointed at a collection of stars. "You're named Honey after that constellation. Honey the Seamstress. Those stars are her needle and the stars up there are her wavy hair. But she doesn't sew clothing. She sews broken hearts back together using her hair for thread."

Honey almost cried. The next kiss was longer. She finally sat back. "I remember something about you too. How patient you are."

Honey kept stitching packets together in neat lines. Mine looked ahead through the spyglass. The orange blur in the distance was now a deep, red line. It came and went in seemingly random threads. He wondered what caused it and decided it couldn't be anything good.

Days passed.

At times, they talked about the boat. They wondered how they had come to be here. How the boat worked to move them so implacably over the sand. How food appeared. Why the packets were supposed to be stitched together. Without answers, the topics wore themselves out. Still, Honey dutifully stitched. In between, she took to sunbathing on the deck. Mine studied the sirens and recognized the ones who appeared every day, as if checking on them. They remembered things about each other, now and again. At night, he made up constellations in the scintillating sweeps of stars, told stories about them to Honey, and watched the red line on the horizon grow thicker and angrier.

"Honey! Look!"

The atmosphere was prematurely dark. Massive clouds like black anvils gathered. Flashes of lightning jumped from cloud to cloud as if they were trying to kill each other with jagged bolts.

The next curtain caught them by surprise. Only when they heard the grinding machinery did they notice.

Another moment of electrical charge and they were through. An archway dominated the view in front of them. Black and glossy. Then a flash. "Lightning." Mine gave the spyglass to Honey. "We'd better get inside."

"Wait!" She pointed at the dark sand. Sirens swam in a circle. Like the sand, the sirens were darker here. Someone struggled in their midst.

"Help!"

A man.

He kicked, swimming. Sirens dove in on him.

"They're killing him!" Honey gripped the railing.

Mine calculated the path the boat would follow. "Sit on my legs!" He went to the starboard side of the boat where it was widest and lay on the deck, the upper half of his body hanging over the swirling sand. Honey's weight settled on his thighs.

Only one chance.

The man saw them. He knocked a siren away with an elbow and reached up. Hands slapped together. Mine pulled. The sand dragged on the man's legs. A siren caught him, hissing, yanking. Mine held on. The man flailed at the siren. The siren let go.

Gasping for breath, Mine let the man grab his shoulder to raise himself to the railing. A siren hissed at Mine from the sand, shaking. Moments later, they fell to the deck.

"Thank you," the man coughed. "I thought I was finished."

Mine stood, getting a look at the man. His face was unlined

and pleasant. He wore a cotton shirt and blue satin bow tie. Suspenders held his tweed pants and his shoes were wingtips, perfectly shined.

Mine knew him.

"Are you all right?" Honey brushed sand off his shirt.

"I am now. Those sharks almost got me."

Mine's heart beat in his throat. "I remember what sharks are. These creatures aren't sharks."

The man nodded. "Well, they *are* carnivores. All of them."

"What happened?" Honey asked. "Where's your boat?"

"I guess I fell overboard. My vessel must be far away by now."

Honey laughed. "You said 'vessel.' Just like he does." She pointed at Mine.

The stranger shrugged. One shoulder ahead of the other. Honey laughed again.

"You two should look at the arch," the stranger said. "I found it without equal."

The boat had drawn close to the dark monument. Mine picked out the details. Hundreds of small pillars formed the construction, stacked in columns. The gate was made of bones. Ancient, fossilized, black. Human. He wanted to look away. Couldn't. "What is this place?"

"Study it well. I could mean your survival." The man pointed at a dark shape in the sand, beyond the arch of bones. Mine made out larger angular shapes and smaller round shapes. Dread gathered like an acid pool in his stomach.

He felt Honey's hands on his arms. "Are they dead?"

The skulls were blackened. Skeletal remains draped upon the derelict ship as if on display. The wood rotted. Another ship, half-consumed by the sand, lay to starboard. A decayed hand extended through the cabin door, beseeching.

Lightning illuminated the landscape. There were dozens of wrecks spread over the sand. Hundreds. And corpses.

"Honey? Do you recognize him?" Mine looked over his shoulder. "Where did he go?"

Light exploded, thunder deafening, inches in front of their vessel. The flash of heat and pressure threw Mine backwards. He grunted as he slammed to the deck. He couldn't hear Honey screaming but she was. The belly of the sky ripped open and rain fell in gouts.

Darkness.

———

Mine blinked, his sticky eyes reluctant to open.

"Honey?"

"I'm here, Mine."

"What happened?"

"Lightning, Mine. You were hurt."

Mine rubbed his forehead and remembered. A lot. "Where is he?"

"Outside."

"We have to get rid of him."

"No, Mine. He's helpful. He remembers so many things."

"He's a liar. I think he's killed people."

"You can't know that."

"Don't you recognize him? He's wearing my brother's face."

Honey pressed her fingertips against her nose.

Mine struggled to his feet. Fell back on the bench. Got up again.

Honey read his expression. "Mine, you're scaring me."

Mine staggered out the door. The boat rolled as if the desert felt his anger. The man turned as Mine stepped onto the deck. The silver packets floated behind the boat like a kite, tethered by wire.

The man looked at Mine. "You're quite unlucky, sir. Nearly killed within moments of my arrival. I would have taken good care of her for you." He let go of the wire and the silver kite flew away.

Mine punched him in the face. The man's nose blossomed in blood. He laughed. "Don't be hasty. Let's talk about this." Mine grabbed the man by his tailored shirt, lifting, shoving. Over the railing. The man grabbed Mine. "If I go, you're coming with me."

Mine slapped the man's hand loose. Pushed him back.

"You're not strong enough."

Mine snarled. "I am this time."

A wailing siren arose from the sand, wrapping her arms around the man's neck. His eyes flew wide as she pulled. Mine bent down, lifting the man's legs. He went over, shrieking. In moments, he was swallowed up by the sand.

Honey. Crying. "The silver kite was supposed to keep the lightning away."

Heat bathed Mine's neck and face. "It's metal. If anything, it would draw lightning to the boat." He pointed at the ruined ships in the sand, the blackened corpses. "He killed them."

"It was their fault, he said." Honey wailed. "They were wicked. When they died, their boats went off course. I think we were wicked too. We were wicked, Mine, and that's why we're here. We were wicked, and this is hell."

Mine couldn't slow his breathing. His fists strained at his sides. "I remembered other things. After seeing his face—my brother's face—I remembered you slept with him." Freshly wounded, he wanted to hurt her. He pointed at a patch of sky,

the only patch not obscured by thunderheads. "See that constellation? That's Promiscua the Whore. Named after you."

Mine stormed into the cabin, leaving Honey in the rain.

The plaque was blank. He examined the sides. The corners.
The rivets had been tampered with. Mine pulled on the plaque.
It came loose. He turned the plaque around.

"He said it was blank for a reason." Tears rolled down
Honey's face.

His anger barely in check, Mine showed her the other side
of the plaque. The side that had been against the wall.

Honey wept harder.

They barely spoke. They ate apart. Slept apart. Honey on the
bench. Mine on the floor. On the horizon, the hot, angry line
grew into a wall of red-orange fire, a thousand feet high. They
heard the flames. A dull, constant roar. The flames extended in
both directions as far as the spyglass allowed them to see.

They were heading straight for it.

The boat would only deviate from its course if they died.

They might be dead already.

The third diagram on the plaque had been clear enough.
Two figures protected by a silver shield, standing as fire rained
down. The packets were supposed to save them from the flames.

They'd never have enough packets now. Not after losing the
others.

Mine said, "We need extra packets."

Honey glared. "We only get six each day."

"I'm going to try finding more. Will you help me?"

She folded her arms.

"If we don't work together, we won't survive." Her eyes

were hard but Mine pressed on. "I said things I shouldn't have said. I'm sorry, Honey."

Honey's eyes softened. "I didn't know what you remembered about the affair. And I was afraid to ask. I did break it off with him. I never should have let it happen at all. But I'm the one who ended it." She glanced to the side. Licked her lips drily at the fiery wall.

"Together." Mine said.

They had plenty of wire. Mine had spent days twisting the wire into rope. He wrapped the cable around the post at the center of the rear railing and twisted it tight. He'd threaded the other end through the loops of his belt where the fabric was most sturdy and bound it.

"This boat never stops but it doesn't go fast," Mine explained. "Some shipwrecks are close. I can jump across from the front, check for packets, then jump back to our vessel."

Honey nodded, swallowing thickly.

"Make sure the cable doesn't get tangled. And don't get hurt."

"Okay."

Mine's heart pounded as he stood in the bow, waiting for a promising derelict. The wall of fire loomed larger.

"Here's one." He panted. Climbed over the rail.

Jumped.

The rail hit him in the midsection. He grunted but ignored the pain, clambering over. He dashed into the empty cabin. The owners had jumped off—or been pushed. In the bin, he found several packets. He stuffed them into his pockets and ran out.

His ship had nearly passed. He climbed to the top of the railing and flung himself across the gap. Honey helped him back aboard, his breathing uneven. He pulled the packets out of his pocket.

Seven.

Honey hopped and clapped. "That's more than a day's worth."

"Not enough." Mine recoiled the cable. Honey's mood turned grim, realizing. She started sewing.

Mine plundered more ships but jumping took its toll. He was drenched, sweating, with few packets won.

He'd also found corpses.

On his fourth trip, he missed his target and fell to the sand. He kicked but the deck was out of reach. He struggled to his own boat. Honey helped him up and over the rail.

"You should rest."

"How many?"

Honey showed him the progress she'd made.

Not enough.

The wall of fire seemed twice as close. Twice as loud. Mine used the spyglass.

The ship in front of them was about to hit the wall of fire.

Transfixed, Mine watched. A tiny figure ran out the door and jumped into the sand. Mine couldn't hear any screaming over the monumental growl of flames. The lack of human noise made the scene more terrible. An enormous flare burst ahead of the cabin as their boat entered the flames. The figure swam away from the fire. Heartbeats passed. Mine forgot to breathe. The cabin caught next. The wall consumed the wood as if starved for fuel. The door caught. A second figure stumbled out, covered in sheets of flame. The figure staggered across the deck and fell into the sand as the vessel was swallowed by the hungry orange beast. Pieces of the vessel were caught in the updraft. The body flew up as well.

Mine swallowed thickly. His stomach felt like broken glass as the swimmer fought the current of sand, knowing from miles away it was a losing battle. The flailing figure disappeared. Another gout of flame erupted in the wall and it was over.

He wanted to throw up. No time. He angled the spyglass down to scan the space between their vessel and the wild, raging wall.

He needed another wreck.

Minutes passed. The wall of flame was a mountain.

"Sew them together, Honey." He was resigned. "Make it like a sleeping bag."

Honey looked at the pieces. "We won't both fit."

"I know. But you will."

Honey wailed. Mine raised the spyglass. A boat had drifted off course impossibly far. Honey saw it too. "You have to try!"

Mine nodded. He climbed the rail and jumped. The sand was harder, baked by the heat, and he practically ran across the gap to the deck.

He smelled the bodies before he saw them, the cabin filled with flies.

Nauseated, he held his breath and searched for silver. The woman lay dead on the bench. The man hung from the fixtures in the ceiling. Their packets were sewn into a long rectangle, fashioned into a noose.

Mine went to the man, ignoring the flies that rose in a fitful cloud. He lifted the body to get some slack in the noose.

He felt time escaping. Any moment, the cable around his waist would yank him away. He worked to untie the blanket. Leaving without it wasn't an option. If he didn't get the blanket, he was dead. He heard the cable rasping around the frame of the door. He worked faster. His fingers pinched, grabbed, pulled. His heart hammered in his chest.

The silver slipped free. He clutched the blanket and ran out. Honey on their vessel, sliding away, naked desperation painted on her face. His breathing huffed like rags in his ears. He leapt to the top of the railing. Threw himself toward the vessel.

Toward Honey.

He slammed onto the hard sand. Gripped the cable.

The cable snapped taut. He grunted, feeling like he was being cut in half. The boat pulled him off the baked sand, rolling him into the softer wake. Honey reached for the cable. She moved her arm in a circle, winding the cable around her wrist. Mine shoved the silver into his mouth and started pulling himself up the lifeline. The drag of his weight would be too much for Honey, but she grabbed her wrist with her free hand, using her forearm like a stanchion. She moved to port and braced her feet against the post of the railing.

She screamed his name. Crimson lines flowed down her arm.

Mine pulled. The cable cut his hands, every movement generating agony. Time slowed. Eternity. Pain.

He reached the deck, fingers slick with blood. He breathed deeply. In. Out. In. Out. Honey pulled his shirt, leaving lines of red.

The heat from the wall was intolerable. Mine's lungs burned.

They unfolded the piece of silver blanket.

Still not enough.

"Finish the shield. Save yourself." Mine's voice broke.

"No. Look."

Honey laid the pieces on the deck. "If we stitch it together here, it will make a blanket big enough for us both to roll up in. Remember our honeymoon?"

The memory came. The two of them, wrapped in a quilt. Knowing so little about each other. But knowing they wanted to be together. Smiling then.

Mine smiled now. "Okay."

Honey sewed.

Mine checked outside. The wall of flame dominated the sky like it was falling over on them. The intensity of the heat burned like a living, breathing monster.

He stitched too. Desperate minutes flew by.

Honey said, "If I could change the past, Mine, I would. And I'm sorry. I remember you forgave me."

Mine tried to remember too.

Tears traced lines through the dust on her face.

He kissed her tears.

The vessel lurched sideways. They almost fell. He shoved her down onto the edge of the blanket. Dropped on top of her. Crackling sounds announced the bow meeting the inferno.

They rolled over and over in the silver. Mine pulled shut the gap above their heads and held it.

"I can't remember forgiving you before," he shouted. "But I can forgive you now."

Wood exploded, the bow and cabin wall feeding the conflagration. The side walls erupted next. In moments, there was no sand, no cabin, nothing but the sound of raging fire and a flood of memories flowing back to life. Worlds becoming glass.

Rising.

Anna Marasco is a licensed clinical social worker, which allows a deep exploration of human behavior and emotion. She is also an award-winning author, an international award-winning poet, and a teller of stories—some of them true, most of them not. She knew she wanted to be a writer ever since she rewrote her beloved Momma Cat, into the ending of Jonathan Livingston Seagull, with Momma eating Jonathan in the end. Anna enjoys applying this approach in her life, writing and rewriting sequels until satisfied, often choosing to live in fantasy more than reality. In her spare time, Anna enjoys frolicking with the loves of her life: her horses, Henry and Fancy.

About this story, Anna says: "Inspiration comes in a variety of ways, and, most of the time, the muses are inconvenient and questionable. The idea for this story grew out of my love of history, but really started when I was caught in the cross fire between two separate discussions happening at opposite ends of a table full of writers. The ideas about how clothing played a pivotal role in the Holocaust—particularly, yellow stars and the coats that carried them—stewed in my head, festering until I rewatched a favorite movie, 'Stand By Me.' This story is my version of 'Stand By Me,' set during the Holocaust."

Difficult topics require a skilled hand to tell the story. This is one of those—an achingly touching tale, told with compassion by a writer who reveals the depth of her own heart on the page.

The Stars Are Eyes
Anna Marasco

I

Germany. Winter, 1939. The coldest winter on record for 110 years. At least, that was what the grown-ups told us, but me and Joanie didn't care. Grown-ups just made up dumb stuff so that us kids wouldn't do what we wanted. So we'd listen to them better or some bullshit like that.

The first time I met Joanie, I heard him before I saw him. He was never very good at hiding. A cough shook the dried bushes by the von Dusseldorfs' garden, and I skidded my feet to a stop, straightening the frayed seams on my bottom-layer tweed jacket. I wore two jackets back then, thought it made me look snazzy. It only made me stand out more with my puffed-out sleeves and split seams.

Another cough and rustle from the brush. It had to be one of my classmates pulling a fast one on me. What did fast one even mean? Fast one? I sounded like my pops. The boys liked to play tricks on me. They said I startled easily. Maybe I did, but I wasn't going to let them get me. Not again.

"Aha!" I leaped in front of the bushes and pulled a branch

aside. A little boy crouched between the leaves. He coughed again.

"Oh." I slouched my shoulders, mildly disappointed I wasn't beating the boys at one of their pranks.

The kid stared up at me, holding his breath.

"My name's Arman," I said.

"Meno?" his high-pitched voice chirped.

"What?"

"Meno." He pointed to me.

"Arman."

"Meno."

"Arrrrr-monnnnn," I said, and he stared. What was wrong with this kid? "Never mind." I shook my head. "What's your name?"

"Jonah."

"Joanie?"

"It's Jonah. Jo-nnnahhh."

"Right, Joanie." I liked messing with him. It was too easy. When annoyed, he'd get this curl between his eyebrows like a caterpillar crawled under his skin. He never did get my name right, so why should I say his right?

"I'm not supposed to talk to strangers."

"Right," I said. "And I'm not supposed to be late for dinner, and yet there you are talking to a stranger, and here I am late for dinner."

His little tongue licked his thin lips, and his pale, sunken face narrowed.

"You eaten?" I asked.

He shook his head.

"Aunt Hilde hates scavengers at her table." Aunt Hilde wasn't really my aunt. She just took me in and told me to call her that. She was an old bat that was friends with my parents. How she ever made friends was beyond me.

His eyes widened, or his sockets sucked them farther back into his head. The kid looked like he hadn't eaten for half his life, and he looked four, but I later learned he was six. He was dying, wasting away in front of me. Any opportunity to piss off Aunt Hilde was a good one to me.

"So, you coming, or what?"

He crawled out of the bushes. His head barely touched my hip bone. I was tall for twelve, and he was short for six.

"Whoa." I pushed him back into the brush, dry branches crackling. The yellow star stitched on his jacket's breast pocket stood out like the pimple on my nose. "You can't come out with that. You'll get us both killed."

Tears brimmed his eyelids and stuck in his sunken sockets.

"Come on, Joanie. Don't drown." I peeked over my shoulder and handed him the cross-stitched handkerchief from my pants pocket. "Come on, kid," I said over his whimpers. "You're going to draw a crowd." I called him kid even though I was still a kid myself. But twelve was practically a teenager, and a teenager was pretty much an adult. So, really, I was a grown-up.

"Wait here," I said. "I'll come back after dark."

"It's scary after dark."

"The day's not much better."

"Promise you'll be back?"

"Promise."

"Really?" His words were pleas. He'd been left there. He didn't want to get left again.

"I'll spit on my father's grave before I break my promises."

He smiled, his front two teeth were missing.

Good, I thought. *At least you can't bite me.*

II

Black sky stretched over the town, but Aunt Hilde was still awake. I lay on the roof, bundled in my coats, gaze stuck to the stars, like I did every night. I was never alone under the stars. They were like eyes, but not the eyeball part. They were the sparks stuck in the irises, like the flecks that flickered in my father's eyes behind building tears. The stars were salvation. They saw everything but never passed judgment.

Aunt Hilde's window slid open, and my eyes clicked a quick blink. I wiggled to the roof's edge and peered over the gutters. Aunt Hilde was the only person I knew who slept with the window open in mid-November, probably to recharge her cold heart.

Her light dimmed to dark. It was now or never.

I climbed from the roof to the oak tree and slithered down its branches until I hit the bottom one. The lowest limb was about my height from the ground, making it easy to jump onto and hide behind its browning leaves. I checked my surroundings before jumping to the unshielded ground. Streetlamps reflected off the wet roads, but the buildings cast shadows that concealed my scurrying body as I ran the few blocks to rescue Joanie.

The von Dusseldorfs' bushes sat still. Did the little bugger leave? I'd returned later than planned, but it looked like he'd been there for a while. I didn't think he'd get too far.

I spun a slow circle, checking over my shoulders.

Please still be here, I thought, ignoring why it was so important this kid stayed alive. He was the one who wore the yellow star. He was doomed, but I needed him to live.

A sneeze.

"Joanie," I whispered.

"You came back. You came back. Came back."

"I said I would. Now get out of those bushes. The patrol will be back."

He slid out. Dry branches rustled and broke below his clumsy body. We darted through the shadows, Joanie tucked tightly behind me as I dragged him across cobblestones and gardens.

Boots clicked behind us. We ran faster, our little legs leaping through the dark.

"We aren't going to make it," Joanie huffed as I pulled him by the hand.

"You don't even know where we're going."

"No, but we're going too slow. Going too slow. It's too slow."

"Shut up, Joanie."

Even when he whispered, he was loud. I could've worn my earmuffs and still heard every syllable he muttered. And why did he have to repeat everything?

"They're right behind us." My words slithered in a hiss between my lips.

We slid around the stone corner and scorched rock of the Muellers' old house. The Muellers fled when the patrols burned their house down. They harbored a Jew, and they were fried. That was why Aunt Hilde couldn't know about Joanie, why no one was allowed to know.

The wrought iron fence around Aunt Hilde's house reflected a glint of yellow streetlights—a sight I caught halfway down the block. We were almost home. We were going to make it.

"Are we almost there?" Joanie said.

"Not if you keep talking."

Patrol boots scuffed a clicked stop on the stone. Muffled voices gurgled behind us.

I held my breath in hopes it would hold my thoughts.

Crouched in the corner of the Muellers' old shed, I wedged Joanie behind me, which was now a pile of rotted wood. Lucky we were kids; our short and skinny bodies fit about anywhere, especially Joanie's. He was like miniature doll parts stuck together to make a more awkward, starving doll.

The soldiers stopped at the house, flashlights shining in the blown-out windows. Bats scattered from the chimney. The men mumbled low, turned their backs to us, and walked away, boots ticking like a clock.

Now was our chance.

I flung myself forward, dragging Joanie behind me. We ducked through the shadows and ran through the front gate. I pushed Joanie up the tree.

"No, no, no," he said, his arms flailing, not even grasping at the trunk.

"What the hell, kid? You never climb a tree before?"

His whining echoed, and I threw him onto the lowest limb, the one in line with my head and climbed up beside him, tucking us behind the brown, dying leaves. His breath was warm against my hand cupping his mouth, muffling his whimpers as the patrol marched down the block and turned the corner.

I crawled through my window, then leaned over to tug Joanie up. His eyes were wide as he looked around the dark room. It was the first time I'd seen him look alive and not like a corpse stuck in a shallow shell.

So, I wondered, *how does a twelve-year-old hide a weird, doomed six-year-old in his bedroom at his crotchety fake aunt's creaky house without anyone knowing?*

My eyes darted around the room, searching for the potential hiding spots.

Joanie was a lot louder than I expected. That was probably

why he was left in the bushes. With his chattering mouth, he would've led the whole Gestapo to his hideout. It wasn't even real talk. Most of the time, it was just coos and gibberish. He stood by the window, unmoving, staring at me.

"What are you looking at?" I said.

He didn't blink. He didn't respond. He didn't move.

What was wrong with this kid?

"Come on," I said. I climbed back out the window and reached my hand for him. We crawled farther up the old oak tree and to the roof.

"Lie down." I sprawled out on my back, and Joanie did the same next to me.

"Wow." His words were a whisper, just a breath blown behind his lips.

"I know."

The stars punctured the sky with pinprick embers. Each was a tiny spot like a tear dabbing a page, but all of them together flooded us with light. A police siren whined and wailed down the street like a dying donkey, and Joanie flinched, burying his face in my shoulder. My hand hovered above his body, unsure if I should hug him or pat his head or squeeze his arm. Instead, I showed him the sky.

"That there is Aquarius." I pointed to the water-bearer constellation. "The land used to be really dry, and Zeus put this guy in the sky to pour water out of a gold cup to make it rain on the people below."

Joanie's eyes widened, and his mouth opened to a capital O.

"And right below that is Piscis Austrinus. It's a fish that drinks Aquarius's water. And over there is Grus. He's a crane— like the bird? He eats the stars and poops them out to make more." I made up the part about Grus. Grus never came with a story.

"How do you know? Did the stars tell you that?"

"Sort of. My father taught me about the stars. He said they talked to him. That was why he became an astronomer."

We stayed there, bodies unmoving. The sparks from the stars ignited electricity in us that until that moment lay dormant. The stars were alive, much more so than Joanie or me.

"What's that?" Joanie pointed to the brightest star above us.

"That's Polaris. She's the North Star. We follow her so we don't get lost."

"North Star. North Star. North Star," he said, followed by a whispered, "Meno."

Weird kid, I thought, not an uncommon thought when it came to Joanie.

We fell asleep on the roof, awakened by a morning sun that cracked the stone shingles of the village bordering the horizon. Joanie's head snuggled into my armpit as I held him close, each keeping the other warm. I never had a little brother. It was strange trying to figure out how to take care of one. I hugged him tighter. We were going to make this work. We had to.

III

A month passed. A month of me sneaking half my meals to Joanie in dirty handkerchiefs smeared with smudges and food from my mouth. A month of me shoving Joanie under my bed when Aunt Hilde's footsteps echoed down the hall. I kept a bedpan in the room to save him from wandering, and every night I emptied it in the back garden where the streetlights didn't reach. Aunt Hilde looked for the dog that ruined her dianthus patch for months. It was winter. The flowers were already dead.

Every day, I locked my bedroom door and crawled out my

window to get to school, ignoring Aunt Hilde's shouts for me to use the stairs like a civilized person as I trudged down the walk, even though she wasn't much for civilization herself. Joanie hid in my room like a stray dog until I got home. I treated him as such, too, leaving food around the room for him to find throughout the day like a puzzle. It kept him quiet; at least, I think it must have, because Aunt Hilde never said anything, and every day I came home to find Joanie still there, sitting in the corner or hiding under the bed, his large round eyes lighting up whenever he saw me.

But every night I'd wake up, sweat sticking my pajamas to my skin, because the nightmares were getting worse. They were no longer just the nightmares of my parents' deaths, but now they were dark and vivid dreams of the Gestapo burning down our house to find Joanie, just like they'd burned down the Muellers'. I knew what I was doing. Aunt Hilde didn't. Even though she was an old bat with a croak to her voice and she was mean as a viper rising to strike, she didn't deserve to suffer for my destructive decisions. She made her own bad choices that'd get her in the end, but she didn't need mine as an add-on.

"Stars," Joanie said every night and pointed to the window. We'd crawl to the roof and huddle under a blanket, shivering. He pointed from one constellation to the next, and I'd tell him their stories. Sometimes, I couldn't remember my father's stories. Guilt formed in my body like building water against a dam, leaking slow streaks from my eyes, to disappear like the memories of my father's stories, precious and fading. I wiped my cheeks quick. *Men don't cry in front of men*, I reminded myself.

"It's stormy," I said one night. Rain pattered on the glass. The sky cried like I was crying, but the sky wasn't holding back. "We're not going to be able to see anything."

"Stars. Stars. Stars." Joanie clenched his fists, and his voice raised.

"Hush," I said, slapping my hand across his mouth. "Aunt Hilde is home."

He licked my hand.

"Gross!" I wiped my palm on his shoulder.

"Stars. Stars. STARS," the kid growled like a demon was crawling up his throat.

"Okay. But you have to be quiet."

I sat him down on the bed. What was I going to do? I couldn't procure stars from my butt like a fart. Or could I? There was loose paper on my desk in the corner. I poked holes in some sheets like the constellations—all the ones I could think of.

"You stay there," I said and pointed to him seated on the bed. I flicked the ceiling light off and flipped on my flashlight, sticking it behind the first paper with the holes. Light speckled the wall in front of Joanie, forming Leo the lion.

Joanie clapped. A smile spanned as wide as it possibly could on his narrow face.

"Leo was a godly lion who fell to earth." I tried my best theatrical voice, to be just like my father. His voice boomed low, and he acted out his stories, but he only taught me the tales. He never taught me how to perform them. I had to whisper to keep Aunt Hilde from discovering us. "Leo was eating animals and people in the forest, and there was no way to kill him because his skin was so thick that spears and arrows and weapons couldn't get through his flesh. Hercules came down from the skies and strangled the lion and saved the world, and Zeus put the lion in the sky to thank Hercules for saving everyone."

Telling my father's stories was exhausting. Father told them better. But Joanie's eyes lit up like the stars themselves. How could I refuse that face? Joanie belonged with the stars. He looked at the world like the bad wasn't there. I wanted so badly to do the same.

I flipped through the pile of star charts, flashing each one on the wall and telling its story. When I was done, I handed them to Joanie.

"Meno," he whispered. He spread the charts on the bed and studied each one like he was going to have a test on them, because his life hadn't tested him enough already. "Meno. Meno."

"What?"

"Meno. Meno. Meno." He ignored me and said *Meno* with every page he inspected.

"Meno? That's your word for important stuff, isn't it?"

Joanie looked up at me, not dropping that goofy grin on his face. "Meno." He pointed to me. "Meno." He looked to his charts. He piled up the papers and tucked them next to his spot under the bed before crawling next to them. "Meno."

I never liked the name Meno before, but after this moment, I loved it. It meant I was important to someone. I mattered for first time since my folks left.

IV

A week later, I came home from school and was sure we were done for. I could hear Joanie's screams as I trudged up the walk. We were screwed. I scaled the tree faster than I ever had and crawled through the window. Joanie was in the middle of the room, screaming, fists clenched, and face purple from yelling so loud.

"Meno. Meno. Meno," Joanie screamed.

"Be quiet." I tapped his lips with my hands, trying to silence him. No luck.

He screamed louder.

Aunt Hilde's feet stomped up the wooden stairs. She hadn't made it yet. She was slower in the afternoons, after a few glasses of wine. We still had time.

"Meno. Meno. MENO!"

"Your stars," I said. "Your stars will calm you down." I looked under the bed. No star charts. I flipped back the covers. No cards.

"Where did your stars go?"

Aunt Hilde's footsteps echoed in the hall. I tossed my school bag on the bed and opened it. I hadn't even opened my bag at school and had no idea if it held any paper, but I needed to poke more cards. I had a single second to save us.

Joanie's star charts lay on top of my schoolwork.

"Joanie?" I held out the cards to him.

"Meno." His screaming lips slid to a wide smile. "Meno. Meno." His voice softened, as did his expression. "You needed them too. Needed them too. Need them too."

"You gave me your important things?" A smile crept across my face.

Aunt Hilde's stomps stopped at the door, and my smile slipped away. Her shadow stretched through the crack under the door.

"Quick." I lifted the bottom of the quilt, and Joanie slid under the bed. How was I going to explain this to Aunt Hilde? The doorknob turned. I hopped to my feet and took a deep breath.

"MENO!" I screamed, fists clenched, until my own face turned red and purple.

"What on earth are you doing, child?" Aunt Hilde held her

hand to her heart. Her face contorted into her usual throwing-up expression. She liked her wine, but her wine didn't like her.

"I hate everything."

"Good for you. Now do it more quietly. You'll draw attention and get us arrested. How you came from your parents I shall never know." She pulled her silk handkerchief from her pocket and dabbed her lips like she was trying to hold back the vomit and walked away, clicking the door shut behind her.

"Geez, Joanie." I peeked under the bed. He hugged his star charts to his chest. His eyes were closed tight as he gurgled a light snore. "That was close. Way too close." I pulled the quilt from my bed and wrapped it around his little body. He was all I had in the world. Sure, Aunt Hilde was there, but Joanie gave me hope that maybe the world wasn't so bad after all.

V

"Come on, Joanie." We jogged through the dark streets, hugging close to the shadows and avoiding streetlamps. Joanie kept close behind me. We'd gotten bored of watching the sky above the roof and decided to go on an adventure through the city, racing in and out of buildings and hunting new stars.

"There's Pisces." I pointed up, keeping my voice muffled against my shoulder as I turned my head to Joanie. "And Cassiopeia. And Andromeda."

"Wow. Wow. Wow," Joanie said, followed by giggles.

The wind's cold breath blew, and the streetlights flickered. I tightened my coats around my body. The bulkiness of the two coats made it impossible to button them. I tucked Joanie tighter in his. His eyes stayed stuck to the stars.

"North Star. North Star. North Star." He pointed to the brightest star in the sky as I buttoned him up.

"Yep. Sailors used to follow her so they wouldn't get lost."

"Don't get lost. Don't get lost. Get lost."

"Yeah, Joanie. Don't get lost."

The wind blew again. My cheeks numbed. My lungs burned with the cold. The streetlights flickered, buzzed, sparked, and then burned out, dimming the street to black. I reached my hand for Joanie, but not fast enough. I groped the air. My arms flailed, trying to find him in my new blindness. Nothing.

"Joanie?" I called in a whisper.

No answer.

"Joanie?"

I tiptoed across the street, trying to find my friend, my little brother. The streetlights flickered back on. He was gone.

"Joanie?"

"*Schokolade,*" a man's muffled voice said. "Here, have some."

"*Bringt ihn hierher,*" said another voice.

I peeked around the corner, searching for the owners of the voices so I could avoid them. Two Gestapo stood in their black suits, pointing at the building as they talked. Their voices fell mute to my ears as my eyes sank to the little boy standing in the middle of their conversation. Two soldiers stood nearby, cradling rifles, eyes panning the block. Joanie shifted back and forth on his little feet, munching a piece of chocolate.

"How did you get here, little boy?" one of the Gestapo asked Joanie.

I stayed hidden and searched for a way to save him.

"I got lost," Joanie said. "I followed the North Star like Meno said."

"Who is Meno?"

"Meno. Meno is Meno." Joanie giggled. "I'm hungry. Where's Meno? Meno gets me food."

"Want some more chocolate?" one of the men said. He broke off a piece from his bar and handed it to Joanie.

No, Joanie. Don't take it. Don't take it. Don't take it.

Joanie grabbed the chunk of chocolate and stuffed it in his mouth.

"Mmm," he said. A smile spread across his thin lips.

"Is good?" the other man said. They both looked the same— tall and skinny in their long black coats with the red armband, hiding their Lugers on their belts.

They gave Joanie more chocolate. The silver wrapper caught a glint of a streetlamp.

"This one can eat, Rolf," the non-Rolf one said, a chuckle to his tone. Joanie kept chomping away. What kid wouldn't, though? We never had chocolate. I was jealous and wanted some myself, but not enough to get me killed. I'd seen the men in suits like these march people away.

"I don't want to kill him," Rolf said. His voice was nasally, like he had a cold.

"I do not want to, either, but it is the only option. It's their heads or ours."

"I cannot, Fritz."

"It's them or us. And it's never just us. It will start with our wives, then our children, and us very last. My family does not deserve to suffer. This is how they survive. This is how we survive."

"I know, Fritz, but I don't want any more to die."

"Our families do not deserve—"

"And these people do?"

"Do not look at him, Rolf. It is easier if you cannot see his face."

Joanie crunched his chocolate, oblivious to the conversation being had about him.

Run, Joanie, I screamed in my head. *Run!*

Rolf and Fritz led Joanie to the building behind them and leaned him against it. One held a big gun, not the handheld Luger. It was the size of his leg, thick and black. He pointed it at Joanie.

Get out of there, Joanie! I tried to will him with my thoughts, but he just smiled, eating his chocolate, eyes locked on the chunk of candy in his hand.

The gun's pop lit sparks under the dim light. Joanie's little body was airborne before he fell limp to the ground.

"Joanie!" His name flew from my lips before I could catch it. The patrol turned.

My heart sank the length of my body. They saw me. I ran down the cobblestones in the opposite direction from Joanie. I wanted to run to him, to hold him and hug his tiny head into my chest. But that meant I'd get killed, too, and I'd always been a coward.

The Gestapo feet clicked sharp beats on the stone, and I ran faster.

"You there!" Rolf yelled in his nasal voice, boots pounding the pavement behind me.

My legs pumped faster, feet slapping the ground.

"Hey!" He panted.

"Grab the boy!" Fritz said, his voice booming louder than Rolf's. "Get him!"

The voices persecuted individually, but together their words were like spears being flung at me. They were catching up. They were going to kill me, too.

I tugged my jackets tighter around me, trying to keep them from flapping behind, to keep them from taunting the men to grab the tails. I dove between buildings, as did Rolf and Fritz and new soldiers behind them.

Run faster. Run faster. Run faster. Joanie's voice was chanting in my mind.

Why did you have to wander away, Joanie? My thoughts overflowed like the tears on my face. *I couldn't save you.*

My legs pumped faster. My muscles burned. My vision blurred. I turned into the alley leading to the train tracks and looked over my shoulder. My pursuers had fallen behind. Garbage lined the narrow stretch between stone buildings. Old wooden pallets were piled with broken tree branches. Bullet holes spider-webbed windows. I slid under the pallets, crawled to the back, farthest away from the opening, and leaned myself against the stone of Mr. Armstein's boarded-up pharmacy.

Why did you have to be so stupid, Joanie? Why couldn't you just stay with me so I could save you? I couldn't save you.

My heart carved itself out of my chest in heavy beats, and my stomach gave it a boost. I was going to throw up and I hadn't even had any wine.

The patrol's boots beat past in their jogging parade. I ducked my head deeper into the pile of debris. The railroad tracks peeked through a crack in the garbage. The soldiers ran along it, holding tight to their guns.

Everything replayed in my mind: the sparks from the guns, Joanie's body falling, the last bite of chocolate melted in his little hand. My tears pushed through my held breath. Soft whimpers croaked in my throat, and I cupped my hand over my mouth.

Why did he have to leave? Why did everyone have to leave? And why was I still alive? I clamped my eyes closed, but the tears fell harder.

I crawled out of my hiding place and took off my wool jacket, leaving the more frayed and worn tweed one. I never removed the tweed one. My mother had wrapped me in it before she left on the train with Father. Its tattered threads were the eroded fibers of my short life. At least they were holding it together, barely. Joanie couldn't say the same.

The tweed coat's gray matched the gray spanning the sky as sunrise split the horizon. The stars dimmed like the spark in Joanie's eyes. I brushed my palms across my jacket. My fingers traced the white stitching that attached the faded yellow star, feeling its worn, soft felt. I sucked in a single deep breath, a burn in my lungs. And then I slid my woolen top coat back on.

Gregory Lemon fell in love with stories when he discovered a book of Greek myths in his school library. He fell in love with reading when he read the Harry Potter and Little House series to his five children—twice—each. And he fell in love with writing when he began to write fiction, an escape from the daily emails and technical documents. Greg is a member of The Infinite Monkeys and Salt City Genre Writers Chapters of the League of Utah Writers. When not writing, he is also a member of the Precision Speakers Club of Toastmasters International, where he earned the Distinguished Toastmaster Award. He can be found at www.WriterGreg.com and on Twitter as BookWriterGreg.

About this story, Greg says: "When I finished reading "The Frog Prince" by the Brothers Grimm I thought, "That was weird." What father would marry his daughter to a flagrantly rude former-frog who snuck into her bed? How does the servant not die from having iron bands wrapped around his heart? And still not die when the bands break because his heart swells with joy? Let's not even start on the 'insta-love' at the end of most versions of the tale. I wrote "The Maiden's Request" as my offering to fix all of the 'weird' in the original tale."

A fun thing about being a writer is the ability to put your own spin on a classic story, and Greg's take on "The Frog Prince" is a well-executed retelling of the tale.

THE MAIDEN'S REQUEST
Gregory Lemon

Henrik adjusted the silken robes sticking to his lanky frame. He hated the elaborately decorated silks he was forced to wear in the imperial palace of Chienhu. The wools and leathers of his native Rikenvatten would have been more comfortable, were it not for the oppressive heat and humidity of this foreign country. Servants walking in the hallway bowed to him as protocol required. He tried to ignore the strange looks and suppressed whispers as he passed. He thought after a couple of months the novelty of a Rikenvatten in Chienhu would have decreased.

A crash down the hall caused all heads to turn. A young maid in soiled robes desperately collected the now-empty bowls and food rolling away from her silver tray. Above her, Grand Secretary Li yelled about her clumsy nature.

This was not the first time Henrik had seen the Grand Secretary lash out at servants when there were problems. The louder his shouts, the more likely it was his fault. By his overreaction, it was more likely his failing eyesight that led to the accident and not the maid.

Henrik quickly stepped into a smaller side hallway to escape notice. Pressed against the red wall behind one of the large golden pillars, Henrik watched the Grand Secretary shuffle past, brushing crumbs off his sleeves. Henrik avoided him as much as possible. The Grand Secretary's distrust of foreigners was well known—and Henrik struggled to hide his disdain toward him.

"Hiding from the Grand Secretary again, Henrik?"

Henrik turned to find the princess sitting on a padded bench, rolling a pair of golden meditation balls from hand to hand. His heart skipped a beat at her warm smile. He quickly bowed to hide the color rushing to his cheeks. "Good morning, Princess Jing."

She leaned forward and whispered, "I don't blame you. I try to avoid the old dragon whenever I can as well."

"I apologize, Princess, I meant no disrespect to the Grand Secretary."

"He enjoys finding reasons to complain where none exist. Anything new needs extra scrutiny. You and your horses are as new as they come. He prefers to be carried in his litter, no matter how slow his porters are."

She paused, and Henrik looked up. Once they locked eyes, she continued, "I'm glad that Father likes new things. I have him to thank for our meeting."

Henrik bowed again. "I'm honored by your words, Princess."

"Please, I've told you to call me Jing when my father is not around."

Henrik's heart gave another leap. "I don't know if that would be appropriate, Princess." It was Henrik's turn to lean in and whisper. She leaned forward to accept it. "The walls have ears."

Princess Jing laughed and stood. "And that's why I'm going out to the pagoda by the koi pond. Father said he built it as a retreat from the summer sun. I believe that it's an escape from palace intrigue." She paused to slowly tuck a strand of hair behind her ear. "Would you care to escort me?"

"I wish I could, Princess. I am to prepare the horses and carriage to collect Lady Nevena for tonight's banquet."

She clasped her hands with excitement. "How wonderful! Do you know why she is coming?"

"I do not. A member of the Fairy Council may request anything of any royal across the realms without explanation."

Jing pulled on her long black hair flowing down the front of her white and gold silk robes. "It is wonderful when she comes but her aura wreaks havoc on my hair."

"Your hair has always looked nice." Henrik fumbled the words while studying the patterns stitched on his shoes.

Jing smiled as she tilted her face to keep viewing Henrik's. "Have you met other fairies? Maybe some from Rikenvatten?"

The smile left Henrik's face. "Yes, I've met my share of fairies. More than I care to remember."

Princess Jing tilted her head. "I would love to hear that story, if you would like to share it."

"Maybe another time, Princess."

Henrik held the lead horse's bridle after securing the last of the equipment attaching them to the carriage. Everything was ready for its departure. He brushed the hair of the lead horse to pass the time. His mind wandered to Jing's perfect hair.

Jing was often on his mind. She alone did not treat him as foreign trash who was disrupting honored traditions with these horses. Many in Chienhu had never seen a horse before, but Jing, like her father the emperor, was excited about the benefits horses could bring to their empire. Henrik was grateful that the people of Rikenvatten had a reputation of excellent horsemanship. It made his rapid accession in the ranks of servants smooth, but there were many who resented a foreigner given so much honor and respect.

After weeks of watching the emperor and crown prince receive riding lessons from afar, Jing came close enough to ask questions about the horses. The princess confessed she thought he and the horses were oddities. Henrik was quickly smitten with her beauty. Her raven-colored hair was common in Chienhu but rarely seen in Rikenvatten.

Henrik's thoughts were shattered when Jing appeared, fleeing from the bamboo forest, clutching her hands to her chest and running as fast as her silk slippers could carry her. Their eyes met, and Henrik saw the terror within. She stopped as if to take a step toward Henrik but then continued her panicked flight to the palace. "Oh, no," Henrik whispered. He had a feeling he knew what scared Jing, but hoped he was wrong.

Henrik could not leave his position with the horses until the carriage left to collect Lady Nevena. He watched the palace closely for any sign of what had happened to Jing. After what felt like an empty eternity, the carriage left, and Henrik hurried along the path through the bamboo forest.

The path led to a small pagoda on the edge of a beautiful koi pond. The shade of the pagoda softened the heat as Henrik crossed underneath. It was easy to understand why Jing chose to spend so much time here.

Henrik approached the edge of the pond on the far side of the pagoda. A few feet away, a large flat rock barely broke through the water. He sighed as he ran his fingers through his light-yellow hair. Once he made sure he was alone, he carefully called out, "Frederik?"

A large ugly toad broke through the surface and landed on the rock. Water slowly drained off its wart-covered brown skin.

"The princess ran out of the forest terrified." Henrik sat down on a bench staring at the toad. "Would you care to share anything?"

The toad's small raspy voice scratched through the heat. "I saw an opportunity to break my curse. I was so close to getting us back home."

"That doesn't tell me what happened."

"The princess had some noisy balls and was trying to juggle them. They kept dropping and eventually one fell in. I only asked if I could retrieve it for her."

Henrik leaned forward, elbows on knees. "You actually talked to her? Oh, I'm sure that went over fantastically."

"Well, no," Frederik admitted. "She screamed."

Henrik sat up. "Of course she screamed. She is terrified of the Cursed. Her father has filled her with horror stories about creatures like you. One word and she'd know exactly what you are."

"I'm tired of waiting in this sad insect-ridden excuse of a pond. Scaring her is better than doing nothing." Frederik stretched out his tiny legs and mumbled, "I had to try something."

"You've exposed yourself as Cursed to a member of the royal family. The emperor hates the Cursed. He'll send soldiers to hunt you down."

"I don't think she's going to tell anyone about me. If she does, she'll have to tell them about her promise."

"What promise?" Henrik slowly asked.

"I said I would get the ball for her if she promised to have me as a companion and friend in the palace, let me sit with her at the dining table, eat from her plate…"

"Are you crazy? Do you really think the princess is going to bring one of the Cursed into the palace as a dinner companion? You'd be lucky if the chef doesn't make *you* for dinner. What in the name of the fairies possessed you to bargain with her?"

"Since scaring her didn't work, I was hoping my request would make her angry enough."

"Obviously it didn't."

"True, but she agreed. She said the ball belonged to her grandmother and was recently given to her by the emperor. The embarrassment of losing them would be too much. So she promised me everything I asked for. I figured that when I'm in the palace I could get her really angry and then—POOF —I'm human!"

"She was probably too scared talking with one of the Cursed to know what she was agreeing to," Henrik said mostly to himself.

"Well, it doesn't matter now. After I retrieved the ball, she snatched it and ran away. I would have followed her, but I worried a crane—or worse, the palace children—would snatch me up before I got to her."

Henrik's mind spun with the complications this made in the plans to free his brother.

Frederik's croak broke the silence. "What are you going to do?"

"I don't know. I'll check on Jing and see if she's told anyone."

"Oh, is she Jing now? When did this development occur?" The toad's croak took the teasing tone Frederik's had before the

Curse. Henrik was glad to hear it but was not going to respond to the inquiry.

"You stay put while I survey the damage."

"I won't go anywhere." The teasing tone was replaced by something much more bitter. "Just don't forget about me while you enjoy yourself at the palace." The toad disappeared under the water before Henrik could respond.

After he had bathed the smell of horses away and was again wearing his uncomfortable silk robes, Henrik started wandering the halls, hoping to run into Jing. A nervous excitement in the servants allowed him to pass by without the normal stares. He presumed it was due to Lady Nevena's arrival. Finally, there was someone in the palace more foreign than he.

Of course, the banquet!

Henrik quickened his pace until he reached the open doors to the hall. Servants lined the red walls as the royal family ate at the large circular table in the middle. Henrik slid next to one of the golden support columns for a better view. He hoped to remain hidden and wait for an opportunity to talk with Jing when she left.

Lady Nevena, the Fairy Council member who oversaw the Chienhu realm, sat between the emperor and empress, the highest honor bestowed to a guest. She could have passed for a beautiful dignitary in a simple blue silk robe, were it not for the soft but visible glow from her personage. The only symbol of her Fairy Council position was the simple silver diadem encrusted with aquamarine gems that rested on her head.

The crown prince was next to his father. Jing was next to her mother, looking unsettled as she swished her utensils through her wensi tofu soup. Henrik wondered how much her promise to Frederik ruined her meal.

Jing looked up to see Henrik behind the servants. She tilted her head in an unasked question. Henrik had never been in the banquet hall while the royal family dined, and he guessed she was a little surprised. A small smile crossed her lips, but the concern did not leave her eyes.

Grand Secretary Li entered the hall and approached the aged emperor, failing to keep his hurried pace composed. He gently tapped the emperor's shoulder and quietly relayed a message into his ear.

The emperor whispered intensely, "A what?" The emperor's eyes darted to Jing, who avoided his gaze by sinking lower into her chair. The emperor stiffened into an angry resolve. He nodded, and the Grand Secretary motioned to a servant, who swung the door open.

There on the threshold was the visitor, a large brown toad.

By this time, the whole hall had fallen silent. The only noise in the room came from the toad's approach to the circular table. The tension rose as the emperor stood.

"Stop." The emperor raised his hand. "Are you Kith or Cursed?"

"Sire, with great humility, I am one of the Cursed." A murmur spread through the hall. The toad strained to keep his voice heard. "I assure you, gracious Emperor, I am innocent and mean you neither harm nor disrespect—"

"Your assurances mean nothing. All Cursed claim to be innocent." The emperor's sharp response dripped with hatred. His response dropped to an intense whisper. "What do you want, toad?"

Henrik's muscles tensed. His brother may have caused the

required royal anger, but he feared he may not survive long enough for the curse to be broken.

"Your Majesty, I come to collect on a promise from your daughter."

All eyes in the chamber swung to Jing, who ferociously explored her soup. The emperor turned his head back to the toad. "Explain."

"Earlier today, your gentle daughter was juggling her golden meditation balls at the pagoda in the bamboo forest. One ball fell into the pond, and I retrieved it for her."

"And what did she promise you?"

"She promised that I would be her constant companion."

The emperor turned to the princess. "Is that so?"

Jing's flushed face was near tears as she nodded. The face of the emperor became redder, the silk fan of the empress waved faster, and Jing tried harder to disappear in her chair. Again, Henrik expected to see his brother transform at any moment.

Nothing happened.

The emperor turned to the Lady Nevena. "My Lady, I would appreciate your counsel in this matter. Is this Cursed to be trusted or executed?"

Nevena's fingers traced small, intricate patterns in the air close to her lap. Soon, the fairy stopped and smiled. "Your Majesty, the toad you see before you was once an honorable man. A moment of gallantry against those of ill intent caused him to be cursed. He can be trusted."

"Thank you, my Lady." The emperor turned his attention back to Frederik. "You shall become my daughter's companion." Jing let out an involuntary squeal in protest. The emperor tensed, but continued, "You may enter the palace, but you are not, under any circumstances, to enter her chambers."

"Thank you, Your Highness." The toad shifted toward the

fairy. "Thank you, my Lady. Your benevolence is greatly appreciated."

Lady Nevena nodded.

The emperor swept his hand from Jing to the toad. "Well?"

"Father, no!"

"He helped you in your time of need. You are duty bound to do as you promised."

"But, Father!" He raised his hand to silence her. Jing's eyes swept across the hall, desperately searching for help. "Father, may I request a servant to help care for my new companion?"

The emperor thought for a moment. "You may. Who?"

"Henrik, the horse master."

The old lotus seat cushion Henrik carried down the palace hallway provided little padding. It was difficult to see the warty toad resting on its dusty brown surface. No one could have found a more insulting vessel to carry the newest royal companion.

Henrik was sure the emperor had tried.

The princess and her attendant walked slowly in front of Henrik. Then Jing stopped at a bench and sat. Addressing her attendant, she said, "Please go and prepare my chambers for the night and wait for me there."

The attendant bowed and left them alone.

When she was gone, Jing put her face in her hands and let out a groan of frustration. "Henrik, what am I supposed to do?"

"Princess, I—"

Her face shot up out of her hands, and she yelled, "I forbid you from calling me Princess ever again!" The flash of anger was gone as quickly as it came, replaced by a resigned sadness.

It hung between them like a heavy curtain. After a moment, she gently patted the open space next to her. "Please sit with me."

Henrik sat, subtly turning the cushion and the toad away from her view. No matter how he turned the cushion, the toad shifted to look at the princess.

"My father is furious with the shame I've brought to the palace. That"—pointing at the toad—"is the first Cursed to enter the palace since my father banished the previous Grand Secretary for treachery. He loved him as a son and trusted him like a brother. When the betrayal was discovered, Lady Nevena cursed him to be a golden tree snake, fast enough to flee, but too weak to harm humans." Jing leaned her head back against the wall. "I was young at the time, but I still remember my father's hurt and anger. I never wanted to be the cause of something like that. And that is what I have done tonight."

Her eyes filled with tears as they sat together in extended silence. She reached out and gently took Henrik's hand. She smiled as they looked at each other. "Thanks for listening."

The toad said, "Is there anything I can do to help?"

"You want to help?" Jing leaped from the bench as her tears returned. "Leave! Leave this palace and never look at me again!"

Henrik and his brother barely spoke after entering the servants' buildings. He placed the cushion on the floor of his room and went straight to bed without changing. Visions of Jing running and crying haunted Henrik's attempt to sleep. The desire to fix the harm Frederik's actions caused kept him awake. Guilt mixed into his thoughts because he thought more of Jing than his cursed brother.

Henrik rolled over to check on the toad. The cushion was empty. He shot out of bed and walked quickly toward the palace, searching, hoping he wouldn't attract a patrolling guard's attention. Henrik neared Jing's chambers when a woman's scream startled him.

"Jing!" Henrik rushed to open the door to the chamber. In the dim light from torches outside the window, he only saw the closed drapes of Jing's canopy bed.

"You foul creature!" The toad came flying out from behind the drapes. Henrik ducked and heard a loud thud on the wall behind him, followed by a much larger crash on the floor.

The attendant rushed to the bed and opened the silken bed curtains. She sat and spoke calming words at the princess's side. "My lady, are you all right? What happened?" Fury coursed through Jing's eyes as she pointed to where she had thrown the toad.

Henrik heard shouts from soldiers running along the halls. He turned to see a broad-shouldered man groaning and stirring in the corner. The man's arms and legs fumbled as if he had forgotten how to use them. Henrik grabbed a discarded robe and covered him. "Frederik, you idiot!" Henrik pulled Frederik to his feet. "We need to get out of here, now!"

Jing screamed again. "Frederik? Who's Frederik?"

"He is my older brother," Henrik

The anger on her face became a confused panic as her glare shifted between both men. She whispered to Henrik, "You can't be found here!"

"I did it, Henrik. I broke the curse. We can go home!"

Soldiers burst through the chamber doors. The two men did not resist as they were forced to the ground and tied with ropes.

Henrik and Frederik stood in the middle of the royal court, waiting for the emperor. They were surrounded by palace guards, and their ropes had been replaced with iron shackles and chains.

"You look pretty good, all things considering," Henrik said. "But I still think you are an idiot."

Frederik chuckled as he rolled his shoulders but then winced. "It hurt more to transform this time."

"That was probably the impact with the wall."

Frederik looked down. "Couldn't you have grabbed a man's robe?"

Indistinct yelling could be heard from the hall outside the room. The doors behind them slammed open, and the emperor stormed to the throne. "Are these the foul scum?" he bellowed.

The empress and Jing entered the hall and came alongside the wall. Jing's eyes were red. She looked like she had run out of tears. The empress gently held her shoulders as they stayed in the far corner.

The emperor paced back and forth in a rage. He sized up Frederik and had a new look of hatred for Henrik. Finally, he broke his furious silence. "How dare you enter into my daughter's chambers! You will both be executed for your crimes against the crown."

Lady Nevena entered the hall. Her blue robes glowed brighter in the hall as the servants were still rushing to light candles around the room. "Dear Emperor, I believe you should hear their story before you continue." Her demeanor was calm, but there was radiant authority behind her statement. It was not a request.

"Hear them? They will be executed! Vile scum who were caught with my daughter!"

"I snuck into the palace," said Frederik. "He tried to stop me."

Henrik shushed him.

The emperor's face leaped between the brothers, his family, and the fairy. After a moment of swirling glances, he let out a quick huff and turned to sit on his throne. He motioned for all to take chairs along the wall. The empress and princess took their places in the smaller thrones at his side.

"I will hear you, as requested by Lady Nevena."

Frederik stepped forward, and the guards drew their swords to keep him in his place. "Most honorable Emperor, my name is Frederik. I am the eldest son of King Ulrik and Queen Caroline, Crown Prince of Rikenvatten." He swung his shackled hands to his right. "This is Prince Henrik of Rikenvatten, my younger brother."

The shock of this proclamation spread to all who were in the room. Lady Nevena smiled and said, "Emperor, these men speak the truth and are men of honor, as I stated before."

"Honorable men are not caught in my daughter's chambers!" yelled the emperor. A stern look from Lady Nevena and an increase in the glow of her aura forced him to compose himself. "Explain," he growled at Prince Frederik.

"Your Excellency and court of the Chienhu realm, last year my brother and I were traveling through our kingdom and came upon a gang of thieves stealing from a royal outpost. As I led the charge against them, I was transformed into a toad by an evil fae in their number.

"My brother returned us home, seeking a means to restore me to human form. Those who wished to usurp our family's reign claimed that Henrik murdered me and concocted a fantastical tale to steal the power of the throne for themselves. We both had to flee the country with only our lives until I could be restored. My faithful brother knew I could not survive the coup nor a winter near our native land, so he brought me here, cared for me, and secured service with Your Majesty."

"That does not explain why you committed this treachery against my daughter."

Lady Naveen interrupted, "Breaking a curse, such as this one your Majesty, varies depending on who casts the spell. It appears the fae intended to sow additional harm to Rikenvatten by requiring an outburst of royal anger to break this curse."

Frederik nodded and continued. "We meant no harm to Your Highness, your family, or your empire. We believed many times that the curse was about to be broken. I entered your daughter's chamber in a desperate attempt to anger her. My brother was too late to stop me." Frederik bowed before the Emperor. "I humbly beg your forgiveness, Your Majesty, and yours, Princess Jing. We only request that you allow us passage that we may return to our family in Rikenvatten and clear my brother of the false murder charges."

Jing whimpered. Her eyes met with Henrik's, and they shared a long gaze.

The emperor pointed to the princess. "You think I could so easily forgive you when my daughter is in such a state?"

"No, Father," Jing said. "That is not what I meant. Please do not harm them." She pointed at Henrik. "I... I love him."

The emperor stared at his daughter. "He tends the horses. How could you fall in love with a servant?"

"He's a prince from a foreign land," Jing said.

The emperor's eyes narrowed at his daughter. "Did you know?"

"No." Jing looked at Henrik. "He never told me who he

was, but there always was something more about him that I could not ignore."

Henrik stepped forward. "If it pleases Your Majesty, may I speak?"

The emperor slumped back. "This is madness." He waved his hand, granting permission.

"We are truly sorry for the harm and distress that we have caused. I hid this from Your Majesty and Highnesses so that those who sought our demise would not hear rumors of our location and put your subjects in danger if they followed us here. Our kingdom is in peril from those who would destroy our family. It is imperative that we leave and restore my brother's claim to the throne."

Henrik turned to Jing. "I am sorry that I could never tell you who I was. Your kindness sustained me through this trial. If my kingdom were not in peril, I would ask your father for your hand." Henrik stared deeply into the eyes he had long cherished. "I love you, Jing."

Jing clasped her hands to her mouth and laughed through new tears. She looked cautiously at her parents, then leaped from her throne. Henrik almost lost his footing as she threw her arms around his neck. "I will come with you."

"You will do no such thing!" bellowed the emperor.

The empress reached out and placed her hand on the emperor's. With the faintest touch, his protest was silenced.

Henrik, still in chains, moved so that he could look into Jing's eyes. "Your father is right. You must stay here."

"I don't care," she whispered.

"I care."

"Will you ever return?"

"Henrik the horse master needs to leave. But I will return as Prince Henrik of Rikenvatten and court you properly."

"I don't care what you're called. Just promise you'll come back to me."

"I promise."

Daniel Yocom does geeky things by night because his day job won't let him. This dates back to the 1970s through games, books, movies, and stranger things better shared in small groups. He's written hundreds of articles about these topics for his own blog, other websites, and magazines after extensive research, which includes attending conventions, sharing on panels, and road- tripping with his wife. Join in the geeky fun at guildmastergaming.blogspot.com.

About this story, Daniel says: "I was struggling with an idea for a story to write for this anthology. Then I had the opportunity of writing a review of a horror book and a number of horror movies. I'd also been working on urban fantasy settings and decided to take the two and create my own horror story. The setting comes from my days of riding the bus across the Salt Lake Valley to go to college. My route included going through an industrial area, which was usually quiet when traveling to those early morning classes."

If you routinely yell "don't do it!" to the doomed characters in horror movies, you should know that the character in this story can't hear you either.

LIVING ON THE STREET
Daniel Yocom

Early morning classes sucked, especially in the middle of winter. If John hadn't promised Sandy not to miss class again, he would've stayed in bed instead of freezing his ass off outside before 7:00 a.m. He shivered as he scrunched his head into his scarf and adjusted his orange Broncos knit cap down over his ears.

Snowplows had pushed the ice and snow into a long barricade separating the sidewalk from the street. Icy water soaked into his shoe when he climbed through the pile to get off the first bus, and his toes cramped and ached. This was a horrible spot to catch a transfer and even worse when it was late.

The only thing traveling down the industrial road was the occasional flurry that picked up splinters of ice and stung John's face.

He'd probably freeze to death waiting, then he'd miss the bus, and class. Again.

No, Sandy would see his frozen corpse and drag him onto the bus when it arrived.

A gust of wind ripped snow off the top of the roadside ridgeline and threw it at John with cold vengeance.

He turned away from the wind and saw movement at the entrance of the alley behind the bus stop.

A scrawny dog, no more than thirty pounds, huddled at the entrance of the alley. John didn't dare look any closer. If he did, he'd go over and feed it some of his sandwich. And, if he left his post for even a second, the bus would finally show up. The driver wouldn't see him and would just cruise on by.

No, John's only option was to stand sentinel by the bench and wait. He slipped his thumbs into the straps of his backpack to take some of the weight off his shoulders and paced around the ice-covered plastic bench.

John focused on the street and willed himself not to look at the sad-eyed dog. He couldn't stop himself. Was the stray brown and black, or was it covered in dirt and grime?

The dog stood—on two legs.

John bumped into the bench. Not a dog. A child wrapped in a ratty coat with nothing but a cloth wrapped around its head. They would be freezing. His heart sank.

Shit. This couldn't be happening today. But it was. He had to help. He couldn't be one of those people who just walked by acting like there wasn't anything wrong with what they saw. He'd never forgive himself.

Sandy would understand. She'd have to. Helping a child get off the street in this weather was more important than a geography lecture. He approached the child.

The kid retreated behind a dumpster in the alley. The dim light from the parking lot behind the building cast a small shadow on the ground. Such a small, thin shadow.

John stepped over some newspaper and plastic wrap frozen to the ground and pulled down his scarf. "Hello?"

The shadow froze.

He took a cautious step closer. "You okay? You shouldn't be out here."

The tot peeked around the corner of the dumpster.

John couldn't be sure through all the dirt, but he thought a little girl hunched before him. Most of the homeless people went south for the winter, but the shelter on Fourth Street was still open. He had to get her there.

"Hey." He spoke as soothingly as possible and squatted to her level. "I can help you. You're probably really cold. I know a place nearby where you can get warm food."

John leaned forward to counter the weight of his books.

The girl didn't move farther away, which was a good sign.

John remained still and breathed calmly. The cold air froze his nose hair. John extended his hand and shuffled forward a few steps.

She withdrew down the alley a few feet from the dumpster with a look of fear in her dark brown eyes. No. He couldn't scare her away.

"Hey, wait, I'm John. I want to help you. What's your name?"

The child stopped. John gave her a small smile.

"That's right, I'm not going to hurt you. I bet you're cold and hungry. There's a place nearby where we can get you some warm food and dry clothes."

John took a cautious step. When the child didn't move, he braced one hand on his knee and reached out as far as he could.

The girl jumped at John and made a loud, barking call. Her face twisted into a snarl as she made the noise.

John pitched backward and almost fell. He caught his balance, and in his shock his eyes widened. Children moved all around him. They perched on the fire escapes, more crept in the shadows, and others charged from deeper down the alley.

John blinked. They weren't children. They were monsters with short canine snouts. They wore torn rags over fur-covered bodies.

His scream filled the alley. Adrenaline pounded into his blood as he turned to run to the bus stop.

Two monsters blocked his way. They each raised a weapon, a broken pallet board with nails protruding from the end and a dented metal bat.

His mind raced through the possibilities of how to get away from the diminutive horrors as his feet pushed against concrete. They were two small creatures he could run past.

A growling creature fell on him from above. It bit into his shoulder. Needle-sharp teeth penetrated his jacket, pierced his muscle, and scraped on bone.

Excruciating pain made him twist and throw himself against a wall. He knocked the thing off. He had to run.

The two with the makeshift clubs edged close, feral eyes full of hunger.

He dodged an awkward swing of the bat.

The bat clanged against the frozen cinderblock wall, creating a small hole.

The creature's face twisted into a snarl of hate and pain while its hands worked to maintain a grip on the weapon.

The one with the board swung higher and hit John in the side. A rusted nail punched through his parka and into his flesh. His padded coat absorbed most of the blow, but the nail was a stabbing pain.

Another creature landed on him.

The sudden weight pulled John off balance enough to prevent his immediate escape.

Jagged claws almost as sharp as the teeth ripped off his hat and dug into his scalp. John felt cold air and hot blood in his hair.

The bat connected with John's left calf, tripping him and causing him to stumble.

He bounced against the building, but kept moving. They closed in around him, and doubts crept into his plan.

John opened his mouth to yell for help, but the monster riding on his backpack pulled the scarf into his mouth and gagged him.

Another swing with the board caught John in the right thigh.

He stumbled and rolled along the wall. The nails ripped out of his skin. Burning pain like getting caught on a barbed-wire fence.

He needed to get out of the alley.

Someone would see. The bus would come. They would help.

More snarling and snapping creatures landed on John. Their weight pushed him down. He fought to keep moving his feet forward. His right hand pushing him along the wall.

The bat struck his left shin, metal on bone.

Pain raced through John's toes all the way up his body. He screamed into the scarf. The taste of bile entered the back of his mouth.

More of the hideous things crashed into him from behind and caused his right knee to buckle.

He bounced off of the wall and fell. His hands slammed the cold concrete just before his face would have.

The pitch of the barking rose like an excited crowd near the end of a narrow game.

Tears blurred John's vision as he looked for a gap in their line.

He scrambled on all fours and crawled for his life.

Claws grabbed and dug in everywhere.

They shredded his clothes and sliced open his flesh.

John swung, kicked, and crawled. He reached the entrance to the street and saw the bench.

Splinters showered around him when the board broke over the top of his skull.

John lurched forward, dazed. Every movement agony.

He'd made the empty sidewalk. Frantic, he searched beyond the bench for the bus and hoped the creatures wouldn't pursue him into the open.

The bat struck John across the face. Warm blood soaked the scarf and flowed into his throat.

John gagged.

The monsters rolled him onto his back and dragged him back into the alley. What were they doing? His body stopped responding to his brain as they sank their teeth into his flesh. Overwhelming pain, shock, and horror paralyzed him. They ate his flesh and grinned at him through bloody teeth.

A rumbling bus engine caught John's attention. He wanted to cry out for help, but only a gurgle escaped his lips.

He thought of Sandy sitting by the window, with coffee and a donut for him. Disappointed in him. All because he had tried to help a freezing child.

Teeth tore into John's stomach and ripped him open. Steam filled the air around him and the bitter cold entered his gut. His eyes lost focus as his blood drained.

———

Sandy looked out through the frosted glass of the bus and shook her head. A flash of orange caught her attention. She hoped John waited out of the wind, but it was a child. She sighed. John would give away his winter hat and skip class. Again.

Richard Timothy and the written word have not always gotten along. Growing up dyslexic, reading felt more like a punishment than something to enjoy. Sure, Superman had to deal with Lex Luther, but Richard had to deal with the weekly spelling bee in front of the entire class, and has yet to encounter a more profound evil. Despite this, he's always enjoyed writing stories. When the words didn't come out right, he kept at it until they did, and the more he wrote, the less confusing the words became. He's learned that as long as he keeps writing, he and his dyslexia argue a lot less. To find out what book changed his life, visit him at: www.richardtimothy.com.

About this story, Richard says: "This whole story started thanks to a friend sharing an experience he had with one of his LDS mission companions. After knowing each other only a few days, the guy told him about the night he snapped the neck of his girlfriend's cat just to see if it worked like it did in the movies. It was so unsettling, I had to share it. The main character came about thanks to reconnecting with an old college friend. Through our correspondence I through she could use a reminder of what a bad ass she really is."

There's a gritty, realistic sensibility to Richard's vision of the apocalypse that makes it all-too-easy to suspend disbelief and imagine death creeping toward you through the underbrush—and hope Amy and Flint are looking out for you.

TILTING SCALES
Richard Timothy

I

God, she hated the color green. It was everywhere now. The survivors had even dubbed the endless sea of plant life the Green. Through a scope, Amy scanned the area below. The end of the world was supposed to be anything but this. Cracked, dry landscapes, drought, bomb-pocked, scorched wastelands—any of that would have felt right. But this lush green waist-high-fern-covered bullshit as far as the eye could see—hell no. The end of humanity wasn't supposed to be filled with a nice after-noon breeze at 30 percent humidity and a 20 percent chance of rain. Goddamn eco-friendly apocalypse.

She exhaled through her nose, clearing her mind of any distractions as she studied the area where she'd seen movement moments ago. The sun burned overhead, feeding the Green, and chasing away the shadows.

Flint knelt behind her, whispering, "Where are you looking? I don't see anything. Did you really see—"

She took another deep breath, pushing his voice into the background. Did he ever shut up? So what if it was his first time as a spotter? If he couldn't learn to keep quiet while she was targeting, he wouldn't be back. That lesson had to wait; all her focus and breathing needed to be spot on. You didn't pull off a headshot at two hundred yards without both of those working together.

She snapped her fingers and flattened out her hand. Flint's buzzing commentary halted. Good. She placed her finger back on Bessie's trigger, her lever-action .308 Browning BLR Light-weight, named after an old blues artist she'd listened to with her daughters.

The plants rustled again. She had it. Her breathing, smooth and even. Her eye, refusing to blink. Two leafy boughs parted; a head popped up. The scales in her mind started to fill—one life for many? The scales tilted. She squeezed. Spongy pink-gray clumps and red splattered on the sea of ferns below. The mass dropped.

"Deer." She ejected the empty shell and levered a new one into the barrel. She picked up the used shell and pocketed it.

From the southern edge on the roof of the Natural History Museum, she scanned the open area all the way to the Navigen Pharmaceuticals building. Nothing else disturbed the natural ebb and flow of the Green against the light canyon breeze. At least they'd have some real food tonight instead of something from a box or tin can.

"That. Was. Amazing." Flint paused dramatically between each word.

She rolled her faded blue eyes. "Let the others know what the shot was for and tell them to send a crew out to pick it up before something bigger drags it off."

"But what about—"

She produced her best exasperated sigh, hoping it would register that he was asking stupid questions again. "I'll have them covered. Just keep them on the radio and get them to the right spot. And hurry up."

Flint pulled the radio from his belt and let the remaining three rooftop gun posts know that they'd brought down some fresh meat. Amy made out one "Atta girl" before Flint switched channels to call down to the survivors inside the museum to send out a retrieval team.

Amy peeked over her shoulder at Flint. She didn't want to—mostly—but she hadn't quite reached the no-staring phase.

If the statue of David came to life, aged about ten years, and wandered around without a shirt on, you'd have Flint—fit, sculpted, and smooth. A touch off-putting for a man in his mid-20s. She examined his arms. She hadn't shaved her legs or pits in at least ten months, but even his forearms were razor smooth. If it wasn't for his thick mop of loose curled brown hair—that smelled like papaya—she'd have nicknamed him Al for alopecia.

The crackle of the radio pushed her head back to the task: food. Real food. "They outside yet?" she asked, gripping Bessie against her shoulder as she started scanning for a reason that would require calling off the retrieval.

"They just left." Flint peered over the edge. "Yeah, I got you. Over."

She forced the radio chatter to the background as she swept the area a hundred yards in front of the group. Nothing. She lowered the stock, letting the rifle's weight shift to the strap along her back. Grabbing the binoculars hanging around her neck, she checked on the recovery party trudging through the ferns. The leader, Ernie, made a path with a machete in his right hand, while keeping an old sawed-off double-barrel shotgun at the ready in the other. He never went anywhere without that menace of a weapon.

The man in the middle held the radio to his ear, repeating Flint's directions. The third pushed a wheelbarrow. Once Ernie spotted the splattered mess on the leaves, their pace doubled.

The wail rolled toward them as Ernie's two followers scooped the deer into the wheelbarrow. Shit, a Howler. The cry had a scratch to it, as if the monstrosity had a creature trapped in its lungs and every time it howled the creature inside tried to claw its way out.

Her face chilled as the blood in her cheeks rushed to find a place to hide.

Howlers were what remained of the infected population who hadn't been lucky enough to die. The plant growth that started inside the host hadn't matured to complete the metamorphosis from human to plant. Those caught halfway through the change wanted the pain to end, and consuming human blood was the only thing that would complete the evolution and finally consume the rest of the human host.

Another scream. The scratch in it pricked the base of her skull, like the sound of frost being scraped off the windshield on a February morning. Her shoulders spasmed as the sound shivered down her spine.

The binoculars dropped, slapping her chest and pulling the strap around her neck taut. Squinting, she took in the entire area. She could hear the men's yells intertwined with the howl. There was nothing moving… yet. She couldn't see it, but it was there. Maybe it heard her shot. Maybe it smelled blood. Maybe it was the radio. Maybe it… She shook her head. Screw maybe. Find it. Look for movement. Find it and kill it. The scales had already decided: the Howler had to be put down. It was the only kindness she could offer those infected.

"Come on," Flint chirped into the radio. "You got to hurry. It's coming. Over."

"Where it is?" Amy snapped.

"What do you mean? Can't you hear it?"

"Yes, but where the hell is it coming from? I don't see anything moving."

"I don't..." Flint's voice cracked. "I only heard—"

"I can't shoot it if I don't know where it is. So shut up and help me find it. We've got people out there."

Silence.

"Now!"

Her heart raced, added with the adrenaline; the thump, thump, thump pulsed in her ears. She had to relax. If she couldn't get her heart rate down, she'd miss. If she was calm, the bullet would be calm. Calm bullets killed. Her eye returned to the scope. With each breath, she blew out any stress that remained inside.

In.

Out.

In.

Out.

Rocks crunched as Flint took a spot next to her. Good. It would make his location calls more efficient if he managed to spot anything. She scanned left to right and back.

A flutter. A leaf had just bobbed against the flow. Her eye followed the scope's crosshairs. Air cooled the edges, pushing her to blink. The breathing helped. Calmer now, she watched, waiting for more broken movement.

The bark of a gunshot echoed from behind her. Her trigger finger locked. Another shooter's nest had taken the shot. She watched through the scope as a seagull fluttered out from the location she'd been watching.

Silence followed. She got to her feet and turned to Flint.

He pulled the radio off his cheek, indented where the

mouthpiece had been. He gave her a thumbs-up. "They're okay. They're back inside. So's the deer. Who took the shot?"

She sighed. Rubbing the back of her neck, she gestured behind her. "Based on the echo, probably the north nest. I just hope they dropped it for good." Better they got the kill than her. No matter how many Howlers she dropped, there was always the chance the next one might be someone she knew.

II

Amy chewed on the last chunk of deer meat as her spoon searched for a carrot or potato, something solid to chew. Only broth remained. She downed it and set the empty tin mug on the cinderblock next to her bench. Gamms surprised her when she handed her the mug of stew two days after she'd dropped the deer. A second helping was common, a thank-you from the kitchen to anyone who brought in fresh food. But a third, this was a first for her.

Amy leaned back and looked up at the full moon, her hands resting behind her head. She liked her nest. The museum was three stories high with four protection nests set up on the roof for optimal coverage to protect the survivors who'd made their home inside. Survivors had naturally made their way to the museum thanks to the solar panels and their efficient battery storage. They would keep the air filtration system up and running in case of another pollen attack. Being in an office with filtered air had saved her during the initial attack. She knew it was an attack. The pollen killed humans—only humans. Every other living animal she'd encountered since was completely unfazed.

Being close to the university and hospital kept the ongoing expeditions into the Green a constant reward, especially their latest scavenging trip into the university. They'd found a cache of seismic sensors in the geology department. They'd programmed the sensors to send a location signal for any seismic activity within fifty yards. They'd set up a three-hundred-yard perimeter around the museum a month ago. All testing during daylight hours had gone well.

The museum normally locked down at night, allowing only one access point, which was always guarded. The roof camps were only manned during the day to keep watch for survivors, food, and the occasional Howler. With the increase of Howlers in the area scaring off food, a plan was devised to use the sensors for kill duty.

The buildings had been equipped with military-grade motion sensors and spotlights. A small spotlight in the center of the museum roof, aimed straight up, would turn on for five minute intervals every hour to attract the beasts while the ground sensors identified their locations. When close enough, about a hundred and fifty feet out, the spotlights would kick on, illuminating the area, and stun the creature long enough to take it down with a clean and easy shot. Tonight made it the second night of testing the new system.

As the small spotlight shut off, Amy glanced at the spotters' perch ten feet away. Flint's bare chest gleamed as he rubbed on sunscreen, jabbering about getting a sunburn during a full moon. Her head tilted as she watched. *Is he posing?* And what the hell did he have against shirts? At least he was making himself useful and looking at the handheld, checking for any movement around the sensors.

"Aren't you cold?" she asked. "Maybe you should put on a shirt or a jacket or both. Anything really."

He smiled.

Shit. Should've kept my mouth shut.

He strutted over to the bench and flopped down next to her, too close to be unintentional. "Naw, I'm good. I like the chill. Besides, it keeps me alert for these all-nighters." He gave her a soft nudge with his elbow, pressing it against her right breast.

She was on her feet and away from him, grateful her small frame could go from seated to standing in an instant. She hated being touched. Killing the love of your life to keep his infected self from drinking you dry had a way of doing that.

It could have been an accident. It's just that… nothing about it felt like one. She made a decision. If her reaching over a table could result in a bowl of apples giving her an accidental boob graze, maybe he deserved the benefit of the doubt—just once.

Flint didn't say a word. He just smiled at her and pulled his hands up behind his head. He leaned back, stretching.

She looked toward the abandoned city center. Only blackness. "What do the sensors say?"

Flint unfolded his six-foot frame and walked over to where the handheld was plugged in. He watched her as he lifted the device, his gray eyes reflecting the screen. They flicked down.

"Still nothing." He pressed a small button on the side of the device. "And now if something sets off a sensor, we'll hear it."

She picked up her fleece jacket, navy with a front zipper, and put it on. She and Tom had each earned one the summer they took up hiking—one hundred trails in three months. It was baggy on her, but it was the only thing of his she still had. She leaned down and rubbed her cheek against her shoulder. His smell was long gone, but her cheek remembered the evenings they'd spent outside on a porch bench, watching both kids. She breathed in deeply, trying to fill his jacket just a fraction more, so it looked more like it did when he'd worn it. It and she remained empty.

Flint's fingers slid between the collar and her own skin. He stroked the sides of her neck.

The chunky heel of her boot shot backward, denting his shin.

He screamed and jumped back as she jerked away. She spun to face him, crouching down.

"What the hell was that for?" he yelled, dropping onto the bench and rubbing his shin.

"No touching," was all she could manage. She picked up Bessie from next to the bench, her fingers gripped white, except the one resting next to the trigger.

He raised both hands in the air. "I was just trying to give you a neck massage. You looked stressed. Sorry. I was just trying to help."

Did he just grin? She squinted, trying to tell for sure. Even with the moonlight, she couldn't be certain. She screamed inside. That memory belonged to her—a perfect moment of happiness—and he'd violated it with one uninvited touch. "Don't ever touch me." Her voice was a granite cliff covered by a mile of Antarctic ice.

He limped back to the handheld, head down, shoulders high. "Jesus," he mumbled, "I didn't know, okay?"

He was lying. She'd been in the room when Lance gave him that strict warning. Her stare burrowed into him.

"Okay, fine." He turned from her. "Yeah, he told me. Sorry, I forgot. I'm an asshole."

"Yes. Yes, you are. Now shut up and do your damn job." She lowered Bessie and watched him retreat to his perch. She pushed her hearing out into the darkness, praying for a howl. Killing something would help her get through the night.

III

Amy didn't like to complain. Her mantra was: don't be a little bitch, act like an adult, and figure it out. Considering Flint's uninvited attempt at a neck rub didn't result in her stomping, severing, sautéing, or shooting off his balls, she figured she'd handled the situation like damn Disney princess. The only reason he was still working with her is she believed he'd learned his lesson. A new person might result in her having to teach that lesson all over again.

Tonight, his stupid grin was at a minimum, and most surprisingly, he'd shown up for his shift wearing a shirt—almost. It was one of those black mesh muscle shirts that left nothing to the imagination, but it was still a shirt, damn it. She chalked it up as a win. As dusk faded, he kept his distance too. He kept vigilant watch on the handheld, checking the perimeter for movement every few minutes.

The evening chirped—a good sign. If crickets were predator free, humans should be too. They'd been that way since the Howler was hit earlier that week. The surroundings usually calmed after one went down. The ground team wheelbarrowed the Howler to the burn pit in the museum's parking lot and roasted it the next morning. If they didn't torch it within twenty-four hours, another fern would sprout from the remains.

The thought of the Howlers had her questioning Flint. When the Howlers came, and they always did, how would his scales tilt? She'd survived. Her loving Tom, opinionated Lindsey, and little Margot... She looked to the stars, blinking away the memory. The only way it made any sense for her to still be here was so she could protect others. She needed someone she could trust. It was established that Flint was an asshole. But could an asshole still have your back when it counted? Maybe.

She rubbed some warmth into her legs. She needed more information before she could make her assessment on continuing to work with him. Maybe if she shared something about herself, he'd do the same.

"I grew up on a sheep ranch in north central Wyoming."

He looked up, clearly surprised she'd started talking to him.

"Even though we had hired hands to watch the sheep, my dad made sure we spent our summers working on the range to help keep them safe—the sheep, not the help. Part of the job meant learning to shoot. I think I was five when I shot my first gun. I was ten when I lost my first sheep. My dad…"

My dad was a mentally abusive prick. She thought about changing the subject. *No, keep going.* She wanted Flint to feel obligated to share something personal too, something true. "According to him, I'd taken food out of the family's mouth because I failed to save one stupid sheep." She gripped her knees to stop rubbing her thighs. "When you're ten, it's important to have your dad acknowledge you exist. I promised I'd never miss again. Of course, at ten, I had no idea I'd never be able to keep that promise. Everyone misses. Still, when my brothers used their allowance for the movies or eating out with friends, I spent mine on ammo and practiced shooting. I didn't always hit my target, but I scared plenty of coyotes away. Never lost another sheep to those furry bastards when I was on watch."

She glanced up. Flint stared at his feet, batting around a loose rock. She patted the gun, then she rolled her head from shoulder to shoulder until she felt her neck crack.

Flint's head jerked up at the sound.

"What?" Amy leaned forward. "Something on the screen?"

"No"—he checked the handheld—"nothing. It was the crack from your neck. Reminded me of a forgotten night, years ago."

"What about it?"

The handheld rested next him. He rubbed his hands together. "Truthfully, my first handjob." He seemed to enjoy the look of disgust she gave him. "If it helps, it wasn't the happy ending I was hoping for."

It didn't help. Maybe having him share something personal wasn't the best idea. At least nothing he could say would lower her opinion of him.

He cleared his throat. "I was in high school, junior year, I think. Anyway, Sally and I had just started going out. Decent face, amazing tits."

Amy closed her eyes to keep from rolling them. Douche. It was the end of the world, and somehow guys like this, who probably got off spray-painting boobs on vacant walls, managed to survive. Realizations like that convinced her there was no higher power.

"One night, while her parents were at a movie, she calls me over. We sneak some of her dad's vodka. After our second drink, we end up in her room. I got a good buzz going and figured why not. I unzip and pull it out for the first time. Guess she was feeling it too 'cause soon she's working me like a five-speed manual transmission. Suddenly, a creak on the stairs has me jumping toward the corner of the bed where I'm hidden from the open door. As I'm zipping up, Sally starts giggling, and in walks her stupid cat, a fat gray-and-white tabby. The interruption puts Sally out of the mood, and she heads down-stairs to grab us some sodas."

Amy's mind flashed to a vision of her two girls playing with their own cat, Elwood. The memory warmed her.

Flint clenches a fist. "I'm so pissed I grab the cat's head with both hands. The little shit freaks and sinks its claws into my arm. I give it a quick twist and—crack. Just like your neck sounded. Thing stopped moving instantly, just like in the movies. I had to toss it under her bed when I heard her coming up the stairs." He tilted his head back, and in the moonlight, she could see the toothy grin.

A handful of rocks were flying at Flint before Amy even realized she'd thrown them. "Fuck you!" She couldn't help but imagine a younger Flint holding her little girls' lifeless cat instead of the one in the story. Her hand dug in the loose rocks on the rooftop for another throw.

"What the hell, Amy?" He jumped back and took cover behind the bench.

"You had no right—" A soft beeping stunted her words. It came from the bench seat Flint was hiding behind. Rocks clicked against those on the roof as they slid from her hand. Everything faded except the beep, beep, beep, beep.

"Where?" she shouted as she rushed to the shooting perch, pushing everything else into the pit of her stomach.

IV

Flint grabbed the handheld and studied the tiny screen. "Three-hundred-yard perimeter breach, straight south."

"Activate the motion lights. I can't see shit." They'd only trip on about a hundred feet out, so they had a little time before the movement triggered the lights. She pulled a night-vision scope out of her pack and scanned the area Flint identified. The sound of Flint's feet crunching on rocks closed in. She pulled away from the scope to find Flint standing next to her, looking though his own night-vision scope. Her mind fogged. Too close. He was too close.

She shooed him away. "Over there. Move over there."

He looked confused. "But you said I need to help you spot."

True, but he hadn't been a kitten-killing freak at the time.

"You do. I just need some extra space. Two steps that way." She pointed the direction with her elbow.

He took a half step away. "There. Now let me help find this thing."

Shit. Fine! She hated it, but he was right.

The handheld beeped in quick succession. He checked the monitor. "Shit, that's two more. One more behind the first and the other between the north and west camp."

"Call it in. Get east here, now."

Her mental scales strained. Working with an asshole? Sure, why not? Surviving the end of the world had a way of turning people into assholes. Working with a sexist asshole douchebag? If it meant saving others, sometimes sacrifices were needed. But working with a sexist asshole douchebag who got off by snapping cats' necks in his free time? The jury would have to wait.

The radio crackled as Flint called it in, requesting aid. "I see it," he yelled. "Movement just north of the southern trail."

Her scope jumped to the trail, following it until she saw movement.

"About two hundred feet out. The motion lights will kick on soon. Lose the night scope," she told Flint. She pulled a lighter out of her pocket and thumbed up a flame. Her eyes focused on the light. They needed to be ready when the spotlights came on. She closed her eyes and listened. Something was off. Howlers didn't move in packs. They never had. Plus—it was silent.

A faint howl finally brushed against her ears. "That howl isn't right." She glanced at Flint. She held her breath to keep it from obstructing her hearing.

"Oh God." Flint spun around, hearing it the same moment she did—not a howl, but crying.

"Someone's out there." Flint spoke frantically into the radio.

She needed lights. She pulled off her fleece jacket and threw it over the edge. It waved and descended like a broken kite, but it caught the sensors' attention. The lights kicked on. She spotted the movement in the dark gray beyond the lights and followed it with Bessie's scope. At one hundred feet, Amy saw her. Breaking through the foliage, a young girl, maybe sixteen, ran for her life.

Through her scope, Amy saw the girl's fear.

"North team's on the way," the radio announced. "Number three's headed south. West team has it. Over."

Voices rushed to them from behind as the east team finally showed.

Amy's scope trailed behind the girl. Ferns jerked left and right. The scales began to fill. The girl, alive but scared. An unknown chasing her. Young girls didn't run and cry when nice things chased them. The scales tipped.

Amy squeezed, Bessie flamed and barked. She levered in a new shell and repeated the light show two more times. On the third shot, a squeal of pain filled the night. The girl bolted forward, away from the noise, disappearing into the greenery as she fell. In a flash, she was back on her feet, limping now. Her face contorted in pain as she struggled toward the museum.

"Goddamnit. It's wolves, not a Howler!" Amy yelled.

José, the east camp shooter, appeared and set up next to her.

She didn't know if the first wolf was dead, but its scream filled her with hope. At least right now there was nothing chasing the girl.

"The ground team is out and on their way," a new voice said. Janelle, the east camp's spotter, stood close, holding a radio.

Flint was at the edge of the roof, doing his job. "Thirty yards out and to the right," he said. "It looks like the other one is trying to sneak around to the other side. Amy, you see it?"

As she spotted the second wolf, a familiar howl crept in past the radio squawks and camp chatter—the scratch, the pain, and hunger, all there. A Howler had caught the girl's scent.

The group watched as a ripple of moving ferns leaves raced away from the girl. The wolf's survival instinct had taken charge. Amy shifted her position to watch the direction the wolf was running away from.

The whizzing sound of two ropes writhing together in gravity's grip caught her attention. She looked up. Flint had tossed the emergency rappel rope. He'd already put on his harness and, as soon as the two ends hit the ground, he started to lock in.

"She can't run," he yelled. "I'll get her to the others. Just keep me covered." He hopped off the roof, descending to the ground before anyone could order him not to.

The girl watched him rush to meet her. He scooped her up like a fifty-pound bag of potatoes and slung her over one shoulder as he rushed toward the ground team.

Amy gritted her teeth, pointing Bessie to the location Janelle called out. None of what just happened made any sense. Was it possible that she had been wrong about him? *Focus, bitch. You're working.* She spotted a head bobbing out of the Green.

The Howler dashed toward Flint and the girl. Amy had the piece of shit in her sights. The Howler's head pierced the canopy, showing its human side. The head twisted, revealing a bulging white-and-brown husk on half of its face, like the trunk of a quaking aspen. A sprig of green fern leaves grew out of one eye. The mouth opened to howl again.

Bessie spat. The human side of the Howler's face caved in as white puss sprinkled down on the leaves.

Amy got to her feet and cracked her neck. She looked past José, ignoring his high-five pose, and locked on Janelle. "You should probably get back to your camp. Also, tell Flint if he doesn't bring in my jacket, he'll be rappelling back down there to get it."

Janelle nodded and busied herself with the radio as she and José made their way back to their camp.

"Thank you," Amy called out, hoping they heard her, but realizing it hadn't sounded very sincere. She found that more and more she had to remind herself to use manners when dealing with others. So yeah, good chance she was an asshole too.

She thought about Flint, and the scales in her mind began to bend. Okay, so maybe the prick had fond memories of killing cats. Could have been a one time thing, maybe not. Did she care? No. Because in this new world, no one ever took the express route off a roof in the middle of a Howler attack to carry someone to safety. No one except that creepy son of a bitch.

She picked up the radio Flint had left behind. "Tell my spotter to get back up here. The night's just getting started."

She smiled and settled back down with Bessie. Who knew? With a little guidance, he just might graduate from sexist asshole douchebag to incorrigible asshat.

Joni B. Haws loves to lose herself in stories, both in print and on screen, while lamenting the daily tethers of cleaning and carpool. Her favorite kinds of stories are those that feel real, but aren't, and vice versa. Married to a left-brained accountant brimming with routine and good humor, she has a fair allotment of time devoted to hot baths, belting power ballads, and stocking her Little Free Library. Look for her story "Little Rabbit" in The Hunger: A Collection of Utah Horror, and her non-fiction essay in Utah Reflections: Stories of the Wasatch Front.

About this story, Joni says: "My idea for this story sidled up next to me almost as soon as the word zodiac was mentioned. Being a Taurus myself immediately brought bulls to mind, and I can't think of bulls without thinking about my dad, whose profession was the same as Kyle Farley's is in this story. Though Kyle's personality is not quite like my dad's, I did draw some inspiration from what it feels like to be the progressive kid of a good ol' boy, and let shine through my belief that love conquers all."

There's no bucking bull in this story, but you're going to want to set your expectations aside for this one and just hang on for the ride anyway, because every time you think you know what's going to happen, Joni twists the story back on itself or flips it completely over. Yee-haw!

GRABBING THE BULL
Joni B. Haws

Never say no to a giant. Words to live by, assuming Kyle had more life coming. He wished he could go back in time and give himself that advice, but at the time he thought saying no was protecting his family, not putting them in harm's way. He thought of Jenny and Jacob, at home just an hour away, and fresh tears blazed down his cheeks. What was Jenny doing at this moment? Did that madman have her?

After hours of struggling against them, the ropes binding his wrists left the skin raw and bleeding. With his arms around the metal support beam, he couldn't get to them with his teeth. The giant man, Eames, must be waiting for Jacob to get home from school. *Don't go home*, Kyle pleaded silently. *Stay after for a rehearsal. Go to Jackson's house. Anything. Don't go home.*

But, of course, he would go home. Jenny was holding Jacob's phone for ransom in exchange for a completed World History project. He would be eager to earn it back.

No phone. No way to warn him. Not that Kyle could warn either of them anyway. After Eames had tied him up deep in the recesses of the red-roofed barn, he had taken Kyle's phone and wallet. His wallet containing his driver's license, printed with his address. Eames's final words to him looped in his mind: "It didn't have to be like this."

Kyle screamed in frustration and pulled again at his bonds, but the damn giant knew his knots. His cry was answered by a loud moo, a lowing so deep it resonated in his chest. He glared at this other giant, with whom he shared the barn. She was a beauty, a wonder. She was the reason he was in this mess at all.

Kyle Farley sold bull semen for a living. Like every other Monday, he kissed his wife on the cheek, gave her tushie a squeeze, and climbed into his Ford F-150 to begin his weekly dairy visits. He stopped at the Maverick for a full tank and a Snickers bar. He was tempted to grab a Pepsi but was really trying to lay off the caffeine, his bladder not being what it used to be.

After a quick stop by the Logan office to pick up the aluminum barrel of liquid nitrogen and straws of the merchandise, he was on his way up to Cove, then up through Idaho.

The rearview mirror harbored a stale, lemon-scented pine tree, bleached and crusty. Jacob always insisted his truck reeked, but Kyle couldn't smell it, and he vacuumed it out with meticulous attention after every trip. Teenagers would complain about anything.

"This is our top seller, Blue Star," he told the first dairy owner, who escorted Kyle to his "office," a particle-board desk in the milking barn. Kyle pulled out a magazine bearing his company's logo and tapped a glossy photo of a Holstein bull, its black spots gleaming, ears erect. "Handsome som' bitch, ain't he?" he said in his salesman voice. "Blue Star was sired by Blue Ribbon III and universally improves calving ease and milk production herd-wide. This boy's the James Bond of the bovine world." This seemed to soften the ruddy-faced farmer a bit.

Kyle leaned in. "Spreads his swimmers far and wide and makes some damn beautiful babies. Whaddya say? How many Bond girls you got in your herd?" He gestured to a row of cows hooked up to milking machines, glassy-eyed under the fluorescent lights. One gave a lazy moan.

The ruddy-faced farmer balked at the price, but Kyle reminded him that you can't pay too much for a strong genetic line of producing daughters. After a little more bandying of stats, the farmer purchased two hundred units, and Kyle started whistling the moment he shut the door to the cab he couldn't smell. One of his associates had been trying to sell to this particular farmer for the past several years but had never been able to assuage the man's concerns over price.

Kyle was the best damn artificial insemination salesman in the region and could perform a single procedure in twenty-six seconds to boot, should the need arise. He glanced at the clock and smiled. He'd be in Thatcher before eleven, ahead of schedule.

As he drove, he gave the interior a solid sniff again. He might think that Jacob was messing with him about the smell, but Jenny had confirmed, with a cute crinkle in her nose, that the scent of bovine au naturale had indeed integrated with the upholstery. So why was it cute when she said it, but so frustrating when Jacob did?

"It's Jake, Dad," he could hear Jacob say.

"It's Jake, Dad," Kyle mimicked aloud in a juvenile, nasal tone. He'd named his son Jacob. Jake was a dog's name.

"He's just coming into his own," Jenny would say. "He's finding his place. Please don't push him to find it somewhere else."

Finding his place? Jacob had a place, with a good home and parents who provided for him. He had a place on his sports teams and with the kids at church. If anything, he was wandering from his place, turning mopey and terse or babbling about his nighttime dreams like they were as portentous as Pharaoh's. Kyle would say it was time for Jacob to join the real world.

What he wouldn't say was how much he hated the fact that Jacob had quit baseball to join a ballroom dance team. Kyle had come around a bit when he saw how much physical contact Jacob was making with girls as he twirled them around. He supposed he couldn't fault his son, the sly dog. And, if he was being honest with himself, Kyle actually kind of liked that Argentine Tango. It took a real man not to flinch while a lady threw swift kicks between his legs.

Jacob's obsession with dance was starting to fester in Kyle's craw, however. These new "modern dance" classes just looked like an excuse to pantomime orgies and seemed to Kyle like a bunch of liberal nonsense. He knew there had to be gays in those classes too. Kyle was no bigot; he knew the gays had the right to buy cakes and make their own choices behind closed doors, but they sure as hell better keep their hands off his Jacob.

Kyle glanced at the speedometer and noticed he was going nearly fifteen miles an hour over the speed limit. He lifted his foot off the gas and slid an old Travis Tritt CD into the dash slot. Man, could that guy work magic on a guitar.

The sale in Thatcher was routine, Bill Bateman buying even more units than he had the previous four years. Unlike the man in Cove, Bill had an actual office where he conducted business. The old metal desk was dented, but tidy.

After the transaction, Kyle clapped Bill on the shoulder. "I hope you're telling all your dairy buddies about us. We'll make Idaho a Blue Sire state."

Bill adjusted his manure-stained cap. "I think you've got this market pretty well saturated, Mr. Farley. There is that one farm, though, on the Steele Road, up east toward Lago, that no one seems to remember. I'd forgotten about it myself until I chewed the fat with its owner—somebody Eames—in Preston a few weeks back. Biggest guy I've ever laid eyes on. Geez, if I looked like him, I think I'd have ditched the dairy business and made a million in the NFL." At the mention of football, he gestured toward a photo of a young teen in a red-and-white uniform tacked to a cracking cork board.

"That your boy?" Kyle asked, as he was clearly intended to do.

"Yup. Didn't see much of the ball last season, but I think his time to shine is right around the corner." Bill gave the photo a sharp tap on the word *right*. He turned toward Kyle. "You got kids?"

"No," Kyle answered, feeling immediately ashamed. The lie had just slipped out. He pulled on his earlobe and cleared his throat, changing the subject before he became too flushed. "I don't believe Mr. Eames is on our map. Do you know the name of the farm?"

"Uh, something to do with gold, I think?"

Kyle was eager to leave the scene of his crime and get back to business. This quick sale had him so far ahead of schedule he could easily take the detour up to Lago and still make all of his appointments for the day. Kyle followed the directions Bill gave him: up Trout Creek, then a left onto Steele. The two-lane road meandered along, flirting with the winding tributaries of the Bear River. Summer was filling her dance card, and the field crops carpeted the gentle hills in the green of new growth.

The Idaho skies were their own brand of blue, and Travis Tritt was telling the world to leave the long-haired country boys alone.

Why had Kyle told Bill he didn't have any kids? He wasn't ashamed of Jacob. Was he? He spent the drive going over reasons why he was justified in his lie. It was inconsequential, helped him get back on the road. Besides, a man could love his son without announcing that the boy slid into jazz shoes instead of home base.

Kyle almost missed the turn. Tall conifers lined the road for miles, nearly obstructing the entrance. His only clue was a large mailbox painted a bright goldenrod and emblazoned with an elaborate monogram of GCC. He made the left through the trees to be rewarded with a small sign announcing Golden Charms Creamery. The gravel drive led to an enormous red barn planted on a small rise. Sun-bleached fencing ran up and down hills like the bounding of carousel horses. A few Holsteins grazed within their borders, but not in the numbers Kyle expected.

As he pulled up to the barn, he saw a huge man, sporting western-style plaid and a long red beard, loading boxes into a pickup truck near the sliding doors. Though the truck's body and wheels were as burly as any Kyle had seen, the man stood taller than the cab, well over seven feet tall. Unlike the basketball players Kyle had seen at that height however, this man didn't resemble a bean pole, but a grizzly bear. He had found Mr. Eames.

Kyle parked and got out to introduce himself. The man never even paused in his task.

"Excuse me, Mr. Eames?"

"Yeah." Eames did not make eye contact. His deep voice carried like the ring of a gong.

"Hello, sir, my name is Kyle Farley. I'm a representative of

Blue Sire Breeding. I saw that your sign called this place a creamery. You have your own cattle?"

"Yeah," Mr. Eames repeated, ignoring Kyle's outstretched hand. This would be a challenge.

"You, uh, sell milk, primarily?"

The man finally straightened and sighed. "Artisan cheeses and butters, made in house." He had a slight lilt in his voice.

Kyle came to Eames's sternum. He stared up at deep eyes set into a freckled face as he pulled the folded magazine out of the back pocket of his Wranglers. "Well, I'm sure you're already familiar with the benefits of using the highest quality semen for your herd, particularly if your products are high end. Do you use your own bulls or have you dealt in artificial insemination before?"

Mr. Eames hooked two bratwurst-sized thumbs into his belt loops, his eyes squinting. "Show me what you're selling and be done."

Wow, this guy really didn't shoot the shit. Kyle opened the magazine, set his feet wide, and embarked on a well-practiced spiel about Blue Sire's award-winning bulls.

Eames didn't let him finish. "Nice book report. Go away," he said and started for the barn door.

"Blue Star is our top-selling sire. He is a son of Blue Ribbon III—"

Eames halted with a jolt. He turned his massive frame to face Kyle. "What's his name?"

"Uh, Blue Star?"

A grin broke across Eames's face like a sunrise over mountains. "Come inside and have some coffee," he said, reaching Kyle in two strides and ushering him into the barn with one meaty hand.

Eames led Kyle to a large partitioned room within the barn,

obviously Eames's living quarters. The furnishings were scant but oversized. A worn quilt with elaborate designs of yellow and blue Celtic knots covered the enormous bed in one corner of the room. The walls were bare, save for a calendar tacked to the wall, its April photo showing a close-up of drooping blue-bells. Notes filled the boxes of each date, one circled in blue Sharpie. Today's date.

Eames gestured to the single chair tucked beneath a tall table in the kitchenette. Kyle sat, feeling like a toddler with his feet dangling, the tabletop even with his Adam's apple.

Eames poured a mug of coffee from the heated pot, then laughed to see Kyle in his chair. "Sorry. I'm not much for entertaining. I'd offer you another chair if I had one." Eames pulled a glass pitcher from the stainless-steel fridge and poured a serving of thick cream into the coffee, then offered it to Kyle.

Kyle raised a hand, still perplexed about Eames's dramatic change in demeanor. "No coffee for me, thanks."

"Just as well," Eames said cheerily, sipping it himself. "Only have one mug too. But at least try a bit of my cheese. I've got a batch that just finished maturing." He sliced a thin wedge from the wheel waiting on the counter. Kyle had some lactose issues but knew declining more offers could be bad for business. It was all about rapport.

The cheese, hard, but not crumbly, had a sweet, nutty taste. Its smooth texture coated his tongue in a delightful way. As he chewed, the savory flavor transformed, offering a complimentary tang.

"Wow." It was not a kiss-up wow. He didn't consider himself a cheese connoisseur—he could recognize the difference between cheddar and Swiss—but this was amazing. He finished the slice in three bites, lactose be damned.

Eames leaned against the wall, crossing his beefy arms. "Tell me about yourself, Farley. Are you local? Family? Kids?"

This was the man who had nearly dismissed him out of hand? Kyle thought it odd. Still, he never missed a chance to turn on the charm when a sale was on the line, and he was determined to repent of his answer the last time he was asked about Jacob.

"I'm from Cache Valley, across the border in Utah." He pulled out his phone and showed Eames his home screen. "That's my wife, Jenny, and our sixteen-year-old, Jacob."

Eames nodded. "They're lovely."

Kyle sat up a little straighter. "Jacob's a dancer," he said, defiant against his flushing cheeks. Determined as he was to let his love shine brighter than his embarrassment, the heat beneath his skin was a betrayal.

"Is he, now?" Eames caterpillar eyebrows crawled up his forehead.

The small talk continued. Kyle checked the time on his phone and said, "If it's all the same to you, I'd love to discuss the business at hand."

Just then, a deep, rumbling bellow echoed through the barn.

Eames grinned. "Seems the business at hand would love to be discussed. Follow me."

The barn's interior wasn't open like most of the structures Kyle was used to, but walled off into separate rooms, some of which must be where the goods were processed. Where were all the cows?

Kyle's jaw fell open when Eames led him to the answer. A cow, the color of pure cream, towered above them, at least ten feet tall from the shoulder. Her coat shone with the luminosity of silk, stout horns of what appeared to be pure gold cresting each billiard-ball eye. A rope snaked through a ring in her perfectly pink nose, securing it to a steel frame anchored into the cement bay in which she stood.

Eames crossed to the elephantine animal and rubbed her neck. "This is Bridget."

Bridget lowed deeply, begging to be milked. Eames pulled a Rubbermaid trash can from a nested stack and obliged her. He glanced up at Kyle, who stood agape, while the brilliantly white milk sprayed into the can. "Here's what I propose."

With his butt going numb from the concrete floor and his back aching, Kyle replayed the scene on repeat. He'd given up trying to free himself.

Eames's idea had been pretty simple. Also, completely lunatic. All Kyle had to do was go home, grab his family, and come back so Jacob could dance for some stars in the sky. Then *bibbidi-bobbidi-boo*, Kyle uses Blue Star's sperm as proxy for the "sky god" and gets a "princely reward." Kyle remembered the way his heart pounded when he realized Eames was batshit crazy. The man and his freakish cow were certainly phenomenal, but Eames's story defied the limits of believability. Lots of people made it into the record books without claiming magic, which was exactly what Eames had done.

"I'm flattered that you think my family worthy of such a feat," Kyle had said, trying to placate the insane giant man. "But I've got a schedule to keep, so I think I'll just be on my way. Good luck, though." He'd turned tail, striding to the exit, when he felt Eames's hands around his biceps.

"I have to insist," Eames said, all warmth gone from his voice. "I'll give you another chance to cooperate. I can't stress enough the urgency. I promise it will be worth your while."

"Sir, please let me go. I said I'm not interested. I'm sure you'll find someone else."

"It won't be someone else. And you've seen Bridget. She doesn't let just anyone do that." The vise-like hands around Kyle's arms tightened and lifted him off the floor. Kyle had fallen into surreal shock as Eames tied him up, muttering about how it had to be tonight. After confiscating Kyle's belongings, he had parted, huffing, "It didn't have to be this way."

Daylight was gone by the time Kyle heard a truck pull up, gigantic tires crunching on the gravel. Kyle's blood sounded like the march of soldiers as it pounded in his ears. Sucking in the smell of sour hay and manure, he thought he might vomit. He prayed Eames had returned alone.

A moment later, Jacob's voice called for him. "Dad?"

Kyle scrambled to his feet in a panic. "Jacob! Are you okay? Is your mom okay?" The agony in his wrists meant nothing as he tried desperately to pull away, to run to his boy. He craned his neck as Jacob entered the room, relief hitting his heart like the point of an arrow when he saw that Jacob appeared unharmed.

Eames trailed Jacob, biting his lip. "Jenny is fine. I, uh, did have to tranquilize her though."

Kyle felt his blood turn to venom. "I will kill you!"

Jacob approached Kyle and put a tender hand on his arm. "Dad, calm down. It's okay. It's all going to be okay."

Kyle stared back and forth between his son and Eames, straining to understand. "You're... He hasn't hurt you?"

"Dad, I dreamed him. And her," he said, acknowledging Bridget. Turning to Eames, he said, "She's amazing." Eames beamed, revealing a mouth full of postage-stamp teeth. Jacob turned back to Kyle. "I got home from school, and he was just sitting on the couch. Mom was asleep. He said he had something he needed me to do, but I think I already knew."

Eames strolled over and loosened the knots at Kyle's wrists. "Thank the gods for that. I wasn't excited about bringing him by force." He paled when he saw the bloody lines the ropes had left.

Kyle grabbed Jacob's arm. "We're leaving."

Jacob shook him off. "Bridget's dying, Dad. Her milk is drying up. If she doesn't have a daughter to take her place, no more magic cows. No more magic milk." His face betrayed nothing but utter sincerity.

Kyle's heart fell into his stomach. In the course of an hour, the huge man had hoodwinked his little boy, exploiting his foolish notions of true dreams and fantastic nonsense. He couldn't believe his own son could be so easily swayed by the rantings of a nutjob. The disappointment rang ragged and familiar. "Oh, Jacob."

Jacob's face hardened. He turned to Eames. "Has my dad seen the letter?"

Eames shook his head. "Didn't have it on me at the time." He turned to Kyle. "Look, Farley, I'm sorry if I scared you. I had to get your cooperation one way or another. Please, come let Bridget help you."

After prodding from both Eames and Jacob, Kyle took grudging steps toward the stately beast. The only way he could see out of this now was to go along with it.

"Put your hands beneath her teat," Eames said and began milking. The rich milk flowed over Kyle's hands, over his wrists and forearms. The sting of his wounds immediately quelled. He stared in shock as the angry red lines lightened, healing before his eyes.

Kyle looked up to see Eames, patting Bridget's rump, his eyes reddening with tears. "That's a girl, Bridgie." Eames straightened and looked down at Kyle. "I've been her caretaker all my life. We've been together since before your country was formed. I brought her here with great effort, to hide her from those who would steal her. She is last of a great line sired by Taurus, The Bull, and only Taurus can sire her daughter. But the old ways are lost. The ancient dances died with the civilizations that believed in them. I didn't want to believe I'd ever lose her, that she could be the last." Eames didn't bother wiping away the tears that dripped into his beard. "Her time's running out. She doesn't have long."

He pulled a yellowed envelope, folded in half, from his shirt pocket and worked it in a circle with his hands while he spoke. "Taurus is a being who respects power, grace, agility, passion. The old ones knew just how to petition Taurus through the movement of their bodies. He has so much to survey; we are just specks in his universe. It takes something truly special to capture his attention. It couldn't be just anyone. Several years ago, I got a letter from an old friend, a soothsayer from the old country. I didn't understand it fully until you pulled up to my barn today."

Eames took a letter from the envelope and placed it in Kyle's milk-soaked hands. It was dated April 27, 1928, and contained just two lines of loopy script: *He who brings you a blue star possesses the seed you require. Taurus must be courted by midnight of April 23, 2018, or the animal will perish before the sun rises on the 24th.*

"Blue Star," Kyle whispered. He looked at his wrists and found them unblemished.

"Today is April twenty-third. Tonight is the night Taurus surveys this world, and Bridget doesn't have even one more day left. If she bears the daughter of Taurus, he will prolong her life until his offspring is safely born and weaned. Don't you see? You have come to save us in the eleventh hour."

Bridget turned her head and made a soft mewling sound. As Eames caressed her flank, she folded her front legs and fell heavily onto her side. Great gusts of air escaped her pink nostrils.

Eames turned to Jacob. "Are you ready for the dance of your life?"

Kyle begged Eames to let him call Jenny, but Eames insisted she would still be out cold on their couch back in Cache Valley.

"I'm sure she'll call you when she wakes up," he said. Eames's hair stood out in comical wings from all the times he'd run his hands through it. The scant glow of the half moon could barely be seen through a thick layer of clouds shielding the heavens.

The three of them took turns watching the sky. They couldn't begin until the clouds cleared. Kyle noticed that Bridget's mouth had begun to drip with thick strings of mucus, her breathing increasingly labored. As the minutes passed, Eames became more agitated, cycling between creative cursing, explosive sobbing, and punishing the furnishings. Even Jacob, who had only been friendly with Eames, cowed near the window, not meeting the big man's eye.

What if this whole thing was a bust? Kyle's level of skepticism fluctuated as he ran the situation through his mind, but it was looking more and more like they may really end up with a deceased Bridget on their hands, and then what would Eames do? If he lost control for even a moment, it would only take one tantrum to cause either of the smaller men significant harm.

"Hey, hey," Kyle said, beckoning the other two. "I can see a little patch of sky. I think the clouds are blowing through."

Eames rushed to the window. He actually jumped up and down.

The clock on the wall read 11:43 p.m.

Eames's anxiety had rubbed off on Jacob, who began pacing. "What if I don't do it right?"

Kyle tousled his hair. "You'll be fine. Just, you know, pull out some moves. Do you want some music?" He kept his voice light, burying his own nerves. If whatever Eames thought was supposed to happen didn't happen, what would become of his defunct saviors?

Jacob growled in frustration. "That's all you think this is, isn't it? That's all you think I do? Just 'pull out some moves?' I know you think that dance is dumb, that it's a waste of time. You think I don't notice when Mom comes to my performances alone, the way your mouth gets all tight when I invite you to watch me? Cheering me on didn't seem so hard for you when I was playing your precious baseball."

Here it came. The arguments. The parents-just-don't-understand routine. Kyle rolled his eyes, bringing his palms up. "All right, let's calm down for just a second—"

Jacob's hands pulled at his hair and then exploded from his head with another growl.

Kyle glanced over at Eames with a look that said, "Teenagers, am I right?" but Eames glowered down at him.

Jacob closed his eyes. "When I dance, Dad, it's like my body gets to... to say the things my voice can't. I know I'm a huge disappointment to you, but this actually matters to me, no matter how much you make fun of it." Tears escaped the corners of his eyes. "I'm sorry I can't be what you want me to be. And I don't know if I can be what you need me to be, Mr. Eames. I'm just..." But he said nothing more. He didn't appear to know just what he was.

Kyle felt gut-punched. His son stood sobbing a few paces from him, vulnerability rolling off him in waves. In that moment, Kyle saw him with fresh eyes. The concern on Jacob's face held a mature kind of gravity, his frame lithe and tall. When had his boy grown so tall?

Eames stepped back toward Bridget and rubbed his hands along her neck. She responded with a soft moan.

Kyle's feet carried him to Jacob, where he pulled him into a fierce embrace. "You are my son. Athlete, dancer, those things don't matter. I was wrong to make you think they did. I am proud of you, Jacob."

"It's Jake."

Kyle shook his head a little, smiling. He pulled away, holding his son by the shoulders. "I am proud of you, Jake."

Jake's eyes shifted to focus on his father. "Yeah?"

"Yeah."

Jake turned to Eames. "Let's do this."

They ended up in the open pasture, listening to a silence too eerie for a wakening spring countryside. Clouds still blanketed most of the sky, but Eames was able to point out the constellation Taurus to Kyle, the top half of it at least. Eames nodded encouragement to Jake, who had stripped down to jeans, his pale torso blue beneath the moonlight.

"We're out of time," Eames said. "You must begin."

Jake's movements began reserved, unsure, but not embarrassed. He appeared to Kyle to be trying out certain sequences of movement, sometimes repeating bits of improvised choreography. Kyle dared not close his eyes, but he swallowed every heartbeat, willing his son to perform.

And then, like a lightning bolt, Jake transformed into a calligraphy of dance. The hairs on Kyle's arms pricked as he watched his boy expand into elegant lines. Flexed feet and jerking arms sang dissonant notes in the air, then melted into honeyed melodies of smooth, fluid motion. The dance appeared as a story to Kyle, and the story spoke of quiet pain, restrained rage, and powerful strength. Somehow, it spoke of love and forgiveness. It said things to Kyle's heart that he had no words for, plumbed depths in him that had never been reached. A glorious ache filled his throat. It took his breath away.

By the time Jake stilled, his chest heaving, both Kyle and Eames were biting back sobs. Kyle embraced his son again. As if awaiting applause, they all looked to the sky. Were the stars of Taurus shining brighter than they had been a few minutes ago? Kyle couldn't be sure, but he found them now with ease. The three men breathed in the electric tranquility.

Eames turned to Kyle and clapped him on the back, nearly knocking him off his feet. "Now for the easy part, right?" He looked like a man afraid to exhale.

Back in the barn, Eames instructed Kyle to perform a standard insemination on Bridget, though it felt far from standard to Kyle. It took all three of them to coax her to her feet, and Eames stood close, whispering near her muzzle. Kyle's long plastic gloves weren't quite adequate protection, his left hand inching along her rectal wall, guiding the vaginally inserted tube containing Blue Star's sperm in the other hand. What was normally a wrist-deep procedure had him swimming in Bridget up to his shoulder.

Eames chuckled and called her a good girl as Bridget's sphincter rebelled, releasing a foul load that spread across Kyle's neck and back before plunking down the steps of the ladder. Kyle cursed, and Bridget cursed back, but he finished the deed in less than two minutes.

After being hosed down, he asked, "How will we know it worked?"

"Let's see," Eames said. He pulled a bucket from a shelf, blowing into it to remove any debris. He held it beneath one of Bridget's teats and milked. Out spurted a brilliant, shimmery liquid, reflecting the harsh lamplight.

"Is that—?" Kyle asked in disbelief.

"Gold," said Eames, grinning, and then he began to laugh, setting down the bucket.

It was odd to see a giant giggle, odder still to see him begin bouncing around in a pointy-toed jig, one arm curled up over his head. The Farley men dropped their jaws in unison. Eames bent at the knees and picked them up, one in each arm, and spun in circles. After setting them down, he picked up the bucket, filled it, and handed it to Kyle. "For you. For your services, and all the trouble I put you through." He turned to Jake. "Thank you, Jake. You are an amazing young man."

Kyle and Jake were back on the road by 1:00 a.m., Kyle wet-haired and wearing one of Eames's T-shirts like a dress. Eames had said they might even make it home before Jenny woke up. Kyle had thumbed the screen of his phone as Eames returned it to him, noticing that Eames had entered in his contact information. "In case you need any artisan cheeses or butters. Good for what ails ya," he said and winked.

Now, as father and son drove down the dark roads of rural Idaho, Kyle reached over and put a hand on Jake's shoulder. "You really were magnificent, son," he said. "I had no idea you could do those things. What were you thinking about while you danced? Girls?" he joked.

Jake smiled a little and rubbed his neck. "Actually, Dad, we should talk…"

Laurie Heath has been a belly dancer, burlesque dancer, and knitter. She loves asking "What if?" and discovering where the answers might lead, knitting a story out of the tangled webs of dreams and questions. She loves inspiring women to be fierce and live with passion, whether it's through dance, writing, or some other form of expression. When she isn't writing short stories or poetry, she is cooking up delectable dinners (especially pasta), crafting, traveling with her partner, Craig Kingsman, or hanging out with their cats, Mystery and Mayhem. You can follow her adventures on Facebook or on Twitter (@writinglaurie).

About this story, Laurie says: "I was participating in an A-Z short story challenge. For the 'E' week, I thought the word 'egg' could provide an interesting jumping-off point. While thinking about different types of eggs—fish eggs, ostrich eggs, frog eggs, and chicken eggs—one of my favorite childhood television shows popped into my head: 'Mork and Mindy.' In it, the alien, Mork, arrived on Earth in a giant egg. I thought, "what if an egg just appeared in some small town tomorrow?" I started writing, and over the course of three evenings the story grew and evolved, pretty much the way 'The Egg' metamorphoses in the story."

How do we react when something unusual happens? And how long does it take before the unusual seems commonplace? "The Egg" challenges not only our sense of wonder, but our awareness of the world around us.

THE EGG
Laurie Heath

John Cade noticed it before anyone else, large and conspicuous, sitting on the corner of Oak and Vine. It resembled a giant golden fish egg. It gleamed with slimy iridescence and looked like it would burst any moment.

"That wouldn't be a good thing." Andy Jenkins eyed the giant globular thing.

"You just don't want that to spill out on your picture-perfect lawn," Abel Cade said, secretly relieved it sat closer to his neighbor's house than his own.

At first no one got near it, let alone touched it.

Leave it to teenagers to goad each other to do what no one else would.

"Do it, Zach!"

"No way. Mom will kill me," Zach said.

"You're saying that because you're chicken shit," John said.

"Whatever. You're chicken shit." Zach crossed his arms and stared at John.

"Okay, I'll do it for twenty bucks from each of you." John Cade smiled. He felt the most affinity for the thing he discovered and wouldn't mind making a little money off his buddies.

"No, you won't," Zach said. "You'll get in trouble."

John shrugged. "So? How about it? Twenty each. Then I'll put it on YouTube."

They wrangled John down to fifteen dollars each. Thirty bucks? Not bad.

John pressed one hesitant finger against the orb and held it there for several long seconds before he said, "It looks slimy, but it ain't."

Dr. Perkins pulled over in his BMW. He heard about the strange object's appearance from a patient and eagerly closed his office doors to take a look for himself. He paced around the orb, sidling between it and Andy Jenkins's fence. He pushed his glasses up the narrow bridge of his nose, as if that imbued him with more authority. "It can't stay out here. Someone could run into it or steal it."

"You just want to take it to your office and make an experiment of it." Andy Jenkins thrust an accusatory finger at the doctor. "Yeah. You want your name in the news for discovering this… this egg!"

"It's just as likely to be something toxic. It ought to be quarantined," Dr. Perkins said. He turned toward Andy. "I'm surprised you want to keep it so close to your home. This could be ground zero for an epidemic." Dr. Perkins's voice pitched higher when his authority was questioned.

By day's end, Mayor Cindy Marshall decided not to move the egg at all; she blocked off the perimeter with cement barricades that stood like chess pawns on the sidewalk.

Onlookers stood, shocked that all the noise, scraping, and vibration of the forklift didn't crack the egg or, worse, smash it beyond recognition, but Larry Hanks was the forklift operator, and no one knew their way around construction equipment like Larry.

Mayor Marshall hoped to keep the egg secret, but it's

impossible to keep a three-foot golden orb out of the public eye. John Cade and every other kid posted selfies with the egg on Snapchat, Instagram, Facebook, Twitter, and a half dozen other social media apps, hours before the announcement was made about the peculiar object on the corner of Oak and Vine. Even adults, who ought to know better, couldn't resist talking about the most exciting thing to happen to the town in fifty years—since the time when J. Edgar Hoover's car broke down at the edge of town and was towed to Simpson's Auto Shop.

A few news crews from the bigger cities flocked to the town to do stories about the egg. That's what everyone called it in town. Over the course of the week, it looked less like a fish egg and more like a regular fowl egg. It became ovoid and opaque.

Those were words several reporters used in their stories. It grew, and the tip of the egg peeked over the top of the neighboring plastic picket fence.

The following week, Dr. Perkins invited some colleagues to examine the egg. They claimed to hear a heartbeat. Several of them also claimed to see some sort of figure within the egg when a beam of light hit the egg just right, but since the mayor forbade any invasive tests or transporting the egg even temporarily, that's all the information they could glean.

In a month's time, the egg swelled to the size of some of the adults and teens. The egg's fame brought some popularity to the town. There was a definite uptick in business at the local fast food chains and the diner. Even the old Sleep Over Motel's sign lit up NO VACANCY, which to everyone's recollection was a first.

Someone decided to put up a webcam so everyone could see it no matter where they lived, but it was only available from sunrise to sunset—it was a cheap webcam. Andy Jenkins didn't like it one bit, but he didn't try to dismantle it. More likely he just wanted something else to grouse about.

By the middle of the second month, most of the locals had grown weary of the attention the egg brought to the town. Exhausted by the strangers asking the same questions over and over and even more tired of the transient sales people hawking cheap wares with the golden egg shining proudly from their carts.

Some townspeople, no doubt spurred on by Andy Jenkins, started thinking the massive egg was more of a public nuisance than anything else. It was all idle talk, not worth picketing or coming to blows.

"It has to be a publicity stunt of some sort."

"Doubt it. No one could make something that weird."

"It's in the way."

"Jonas nearly smacked into it on his trike. The little guy snuck through those useless barriers. I grabbed him just in time. Can you imagine what running into that thing would do to a child?"

"If it topples over and cracks open, there could be trouble."

"Whatever was in it probably died weeks ago. That's probably why it changed the way it looks."

Mayor Marshall, to her credit, ignored the gossip. She convinced the town council to post a security guard near the egg at night. "There's enough traffic during the day to keep it safe," she reasoned.

The fact of the matter was, as the days went by, some of the townspeople started to feel less awed by the egg and more fearful of its presence.

"A thing like that has to be Satan's doing," Kayla Jenkins told Annette Goynes over coffee. Her eyes widened. "Do you think this is the beginning of the Apocalypse?"

"Could you imagine?" Annette sipped from her steaming cup. "Something like that starting in our little town."

"Well, it ain't the most God-fearing place," Kayla sniffed with righteous indignation. "Look how many people don't attend Bible study or go to church. And then there's that gay club they just had to allow in the high school."

"True, true. At least we'll be saved." Annette indicated herself and Kayla with her half-eaten scone before taking another bite.

"And we'll pray for the rest of them."

Kayla Jenkins and her husband paid little attention to the egg— certainly not enough to notice hairline cracks appearing near the top of it. But then again, neither did anyone else who frequented the area since the mayor ordered the itinerant salespeople hawking egg souvenirs to move at least two blocks from where the egg stood. Maybe Sara Fisher noticed the cracks. She threw a ball for her dog to fetch, and it struck the egg. She retrieved the ball with a great deal of anxiety and ran away, dragging her poor dog home by the collar.

If the webcam ran at night, grainy images would have shown the hairline cracks deepening. It looked for all the world like porcelain, dropped and glued back together except for a tiny missing chip at the very peak of the narrow end of the egg. It would've been clear that the egg was undergoing another metamorphosis. The security guard didn't notice the changes happening within the egg because her seven-year relationship was shattering. She was having a text argument with her boyfriend. She left her post at sunrise, eager to return to her apartment and toss her now ex-boyfriend's things out in the rain.

It was a dreary Sunday morning. Anyone who wasn't getting ready for morning service remained tucked in their beds, oblivious of anything happening at all. Around 10:00 a.m., when the tempest battered the small town and congregants at the church raised their voices in song, a luminous finger reached out of the chink in the egg.

Andy and Kayla Jenkins and their neighbors could have had front row seats to the event they had waited for since the egg appeared if they had stopped on their way to church or thrown open their curtains and blinds while enjoying their morning coffee or tea.

The glowing finger hooked itself around the edge of its fragile home and wiggled at it like a loose tooth in a child's mouth. The webcam caught all of what follows, except, of course, what the early morning fog and condensation obscured.

The finger became a hand, shedding its own light on the task of tearing away bits of the egg. Soon, a pair of very bright hands made quick work of dismantling the narrower end of the egg. The bedraggled head peeking out from the top of the egg didn't seem at all concerned by the rain.

The being took a human form, soaked hair clinging to its body, black iridescent feathers newly fledged glued to its androgynous form. It emanated enough light to put the LED street lamps to shame. Keen hawk-like eyes surveyed the dismal surroundings while its hands furiously continued to break away the confines of its shell.

Thirty minutes passed. The top half of the egg littered the walkway, street, and Andy Jenkins's lawn. The rain slowed and the clouds broke, allowing a hint of daylight to shine through—enough to illuminate the shards of shell so they looked like broken abalone. Still, no one noticed what had emerged in their very own town.

It stretched its magnificent arms, too bright for anyone to look at, and spread the oil-slick wings, beating them as a great bird might beat away water after being in a birdbath. The wings shimmered with their own aurora borealis as they dried. The magnificent creature shook water from its head, grinning with delight at every simple movement it made.

Just as people started leaving the church, they noticed a luminous figure with dark wings wheeling and darting in the sky.

"That's a strange bird."

"No! Look, it's someone!"

"Is he—she—*it* naked?"

"Don't be silly. Must be a flight suit. Some sort of experimental glider."

"That's no glider. It's wings!"

It left its witnesses wondering far below as it surged upwards, giving the onlookers the impression of a strange eclipse, the luminous torso blocked by the wings and then torso blocking the wings.

Higher and higher it surged, becoming a new star in the broad daylight before flickering out completely.

Norm Jenson is retired, and grateful for the added hours available for reading and writing—his wife claims he reads books like most people eat potato chips. He is a fan of Lydia Davis's stories, Louis Jenkins's prose poems, and any well-written mystery, and subscribes to the notion that there are good stories everywhere which he prefers to read and write in bite-size chunks. When he's not reading or writing, he enjoys a nice game of chess, an evening with Bach, Mozart, and Beethoven, and birding with his sweetie and lifetime partner, Gail. His book, Mostly Anecdotal: Stories, is available on Amazon.

About this story, Norm says: "An Old Man Meets a Dragon was born out of thinking about the obligation one feels when a friend invites you to the launch of his new book, to the debut of his band, to the opening of the play in which he has a starring role. You may not be a fan of the genre, but that's what friends do: support one another. You may even learn that something you didn't think you cared for is not so bad—and maybe even pretty good."

They say you can lead a horse to water, but not make him drink—and in this story, Norm leads an equally reluctant reader to explore beyond his comfort zone, with amusing results.

AN OLD MAN MEETS A DRAGON
Norm Jenson

I went to an author's reading the other day, a celebration of his new novel. He sat between two towers of books—copies stacked on either side like a gate swung open to allow entry to his tale. I sat while he read, trying to discover why anyone reads fantasy. I tried imagining dragons dripping from the towers and a raiding party of orcs—short, nasty, brutish, like wild pigs—at a dragon's barbecue, but it didn't work.

It was boring, the bit he was reading. I was startled by the snort of a snore. Was it the old man seated beside me? His chin rested in his wrinkled hands, his pale blue eyes focused on the author. He seemed alert, but if not him, who had made the noise? He turned to look at me, and the author, still reading, was also looking at me. The king had just banished someone from the kingdom—an innocent, I thought, but I couldn't be sure.

I'd come to the reading with good intentions—a promise to my friend John—trying to keep an open mind, and yet my literary smugness was smeared on my face like cream cheese on a bagel.

It was as I'd expected, all dragon and no fire.

Being at the end of an aisle, I rose and left the reading. As I reached the front of the store, another stack of his books, festooned with dragons and gleaming swords, waited. I turned. The fans and the author and the dragons were all staring at me.

Remembering John and feeling the judgmental glares, I took a book from the stack, paid for it, raised it above my head, and tipped it toward the crowd in a little wave. At home, I placed it comfortably on the shelf, knowing it would never be read.

He told you I'd be comfortable on the shelf. I'm not. He didn't even bother to tell you my name. I have one. A good one: *Fire Dance*—a title full of promises of adventure and wonder. It might not be great. It's not *Dune* or *Catcher in the Rye*, but it's worthy. It's not that I thought I'd be famous. I never sought a World Fantasy Award, a Hugo, or even a Nebula, though one would be nice, but I am not a waste of time. I thrill and chill and excite and marvel, but only if I'm read.

But here I sit, lodged between John Updike with his pretty sentences and Raymond Carver with his tales of suburbia— nothing but pedestrian literary hoopla.

I've never had anyone turn a single page, and all because some tottering old man went to a reading and, after falling asleep, sashayed out the door—but not before buying me and holding me above his head with a little "See, I'm a good guy to buy your crap" wave to my author.

They get to a certain age, the old farts, and they become rude and impatient, and they don't care. He was just another grouchy old man with a sense of entitlement worn like a skunk wears his stripes. It's genre envy through and through—him with his literary nose held high.

But he forgets that I am a book of fantasy. He forgets that

the rules are different. He forgets that reality is not what it seems. I ask him, "Hey, old man, have you ever felt dragon breath?" I ask him, "Are you ready to die in the night when the dragon's fire consumes you and your literary snobbery?" Already Mr. Updike is complaining about the heat and Mr. Carver is looking to a cathedral for consolation.

I promised my friend John I'd go to the reading and listen to Parker—or was it Percy?—read from his book, *Fire Dance: Book I*, a story of dragons and a king and a princess in need of rescue. There was a twist: the princess was from the twenty-first century. Something about a time-travel mishap or maybe a wormhole, but her boyfriend finally figured out what happened and traveled to rescue her.

I'm not a fan of the fantasy genre, but my friend was sure this author and this book would change my mind. We met at John's favorite coffee shop, Caffeinated, a few days after the reading. He was already there when I arrived. I picked up a cup of French roast and joined him.

"Well," he said, "great, huh?"

John is my friend—my best friend. "Well…," I replied.

"Don't tell me you didn't like it." He raised his eyebrows. "When I read it, I couldn't put it down. I loved how he…" He stopped, took a deep breath, and waited.

"No, uh, I liked it, and the crowd at the reading was certainly enthusiastic," I said.

He looked at me askance, trying to decide if I was sincere. Wanting it to be true, he quickly convinced himself it was.

"And Parker, great, huh?"

So it *was* Parker.

John smiled, sat forward, and looked at me. His chocolate brown eyes sparkled. "The way he reads his work."

"It was... He's focused, and nothing—nothing—gets in the way of his storytelling."

John turned and looked at the door. Smiling broadly, he cocked his head and waved.

"Hey, Parker, come and meet my friend. He was at your reading. He bought your book and was just telling me how much he liked it."

Parker looked at me like I was an orc at a dragon's barbecue. "You read it?"

I glanced at John. "Oh, yeah."

"It didn't... put you to sleep?"

Somewhere in the back of my mind, I heard a book laughing at me. Perhaps I deserved it.

Multiple award-winning author, Scott E. Tarbet writes with great gusto in several speculative fiction genres, sings opera, teaches middle school, loves Steampunk waltzes, slow smokes thousands of pounds of Texas-style BBQ every summer, and was married in full Elizabethan regalia. He makes his home in the mountains of Utah. Follow him online at scotttarbet.timp.net.

About this story, Scott says: "'Deathstalker' is the origin story of a deadly adversary in the "A Midsummer Night's Steampunk" universe. Until now, all the uses of Doctor Lakshmi Malieux's mind- and body-altering technology have been benign, even altruistic. But now, preceding the beginning of the second novel, she is away from her Bombay leper colony hospital, and a misguided lab assistant experiments on an arachnid he should not: a deadly Deathstalker scorpion."

For readers who missed the heyday of Saturday afternoon creature features, Scott has kindly revived the genre. For the rest of us, you're gonna re-live some memories with this one...

DEATHSTALKER
Scott E. Tarbet

A flash of blue light, intense, searing, blinding, burning. An alien sun pierced each of my six eyes, reaching through into my head, turning my brain inside out, shaking it like a mongoose ragging a dying cobra. Bright. Too bright. Pain. Brighter even than the yellow desert sun I always hid from, deep in a stolen burrow or under a rock.

Another agonizing flash, this time red. I twisted one way, then the other, frantic to escape. My claws snapped up in front of me, my three pairs of legs scrambling. Above my head the needle-pointed stinger at the end of my slender, segmented tail glistened with a drop of deadly venom. But there was no predator to fight, no prey, no shelter, nowhere to run. I was surrounded in every direction by transparent walls, just taller than I could reach.

Danger loomed. *Hand,* said a distant, panicked part of my brain. *Human.* The deadliest enemy of my kind. How I understood this I did not know. The brown hand grasped my glass prison, and it tilted, rose into the air. But the human had made a fatal mistake. The thumb gripped the top edge of the prison, just within my reach.

I struck. The stinger plunged, withdrew, plunged again.

Three times I stung, faster than thought. There was a high-pitched scream of agony, and I was falling, my container turning over and over in the air.

Shards of glass burst in every direction when it hit. I felt sharp slivers ping off me. My carapace seemed somehow thicker, impervious. I scrambled away across the floor. The human, enraged with pain, stomped after me. But my mind seemed faster than my legs. I spun, and as the bare, brown foot came hurtling down to crush me, I met it with my upraised stinger. The foot smashed down on top of me, pinning me to the ground, but to my surprise, when it withdrew, the human bellowing with new pain, I was uninjured.

How could this be? I should have been crushed, lifeless. Instead, I turned toward the human who towered so high above me, claws and tail poised. Again he stamped on me, again I anticipated his move. Again I buried my stinger in his flesh.

Again he screamed with pain, and now I could feel the thud of running feet, coming from somewhere far away. His screams became gasps as he fought for air against the rising tide of paralysis from my venom. He fell to his knees, futile fingers scrabbling at his throat.

I had to find darkness. I had to find shelter, hide. I had to calm my swirling brain, sort out what had just happened. There —a cabinet door, with a tiny gap at the bottom. Perfect. I ran, forced my way beneath it. Just enough room. Blessed darkness. Transparent shapes loomed around me in the gloom. Later, I would understand that this cabinet held beakers, specimen dishes, test tubes, other lab equipment, but as yet I had no names for the objects that filled my world.

Terrified, I swiveled to face the door, every nerve quivering.

In the room outside, excited voices exclaimed over the

fallen human. More running feet, more voices. Silence, then high, keening wails.

A tremor ran through my body, and my own paralysis overcame me. I was rooted to the spot, unable to move. I felt a split open in the front of my carapace. No! Not now! I knew this sensation: I was about to molt. I would be vulnerable, defenseless. This molting was not as it had always been before. This was sudden. No time to prepare, hide, secret myself away.

But it would not be delayed or denied. I shuddered, twisted, pushed. So fast! This molt was happening in a few agonizing seconds, not the usual hours.

The old carapace suffocated me. I felt entombed in the sarcophagus of my own body. Out! I had to get out! I shook, strained, fought to breathe.

With an audible crack, a split appeared. My head shot forward, my slender claws emerging close behind. I writhed, twisted, fought, landed on my back. My newly emerged legs unfolded from my belly and waved feebly in the air. I lurched to my feet. My tail lashed, twisted. At last I threw aside the old shell.

Somehow, I knew this had happened before, and I knew this time was different. I did not yet understand how I knew.

The transformation continued, but I was not to wait long hours for the new carapace to harden, for the legs to strengthen enough to bear my weight. It happened in seconds. I rose to my feet, flexed my legs and the segments of my powerful tail. I felt new strength surge through me.

I had doubled in size. And there was more. Some part of me understood that I was different—stronger, faster, more—what? —intelligent? Yes. I understood things I had never understood before. If I did not yet know who I was, I knew what I was, the perils that faced me, something of what it would take to survive.

Most important, I knew that I was far from safe. The humans would soon be searching for me. But unlike the ignorant lab assistant who had dropped me, and then tried several times to kill me, they would be prepared. They would come with thick leather boots and gloves, with poisons and clubs. They would be intent on killing me. I would not allow that to happen.

Hunger stabbed at me. The molting transformation needed its fuel and had left me hollowed out and shaky. Food. I had to find food.

I crept toward the cabinet door. The gap beneath it, which had been barely large enough to allow me to squeeze through, was hopeless. Now that I was twice my previous size there was no chance of escaping that direction. I began a circuit of the cabinet, looking for a hole, a crack—any way out. Hunger gnawed, pushing its way forward until I could think of nothing else. I had to kill, had to feed. Nothing else mattered.

Halfway across the back wall, I halted. There was a scrabbling noise ahead of me. I took several steps, and heard the scrabbling continue, stop when I did. Something alive shared the cabinet. Hunger flared again, filled me with urgency. I charged ahead.

I was much faster than the mouse. I was on it in seconds. My tail, longer than the rest of my body, flashed forward, lashed out with the deadly stinger, penetrated the hindquarters of the fleeing rodent. I stopped, waited.

It did not take long. The mouse ran only a few more steps, then its legs refused to move, and it collapsed. It trembled, gasped, heaved, then stopped moving. Through the floor of the cabinet I could feel the rapid patter of the beating heart gradually slow, then stop altogether. I advanced, held it steady with my pincers, and began to tear off and devour chunks of flesh.

New energy and strength burned through me, ignited new pressure. I could literally feel myself expanding, pressing outward against this carapace that was only a few minutes old. It was agony. How could this be? What had happened to me that had accelerated my normal growth from months to minutes? And not only normal growth, which was incremental. This growth was... logarithmic.

Where had such a word come from? A few minutes earlier my brain had no language at all, only instinctual urges to feed, flee, fight, procreate. What had happened to me?

By the time I finished consuming the mouse, which only took a few minutes, another molting was upon me. By the time the second molting of this young day was finished, with all its thrashing about and crashing of glassware, I had again doubled in size.

And now the next phase of my life began. As I stood trembling, spent, knowing that I must kill and eat again immediately, I became aware of a voice outside the darkness of my cabinet.

"Hello?" The voice was human, female, and young. It seemed to be coming from directly outside the cabinet door.

"Hello? I need to talk to you. I know you are frightened—I would be too—but I can help you. I can explain what has happened."

Talk to me? This human wanted to talk to me? Why would she? And why would I want to talk to her? In the heat of my anger, I saw my stinger whipping forward into her flesh, just as it had with the lab assistant.

Then I realized, with a start, that I did understand her, that her words were more than menacing noises to me. I dimly remembered hearing human speech before, when I had been lying in wait beneath a pile of machine parts, which was crated and shipped from my desert home to... to wherever I was now.

I remembered being blinded by the light of the crate being opened, blinded and frozen with fear long enough that I heard a shout of alarm from the humans and felt myself swept into the specimen dish prison. I had not understood the speech of the humans then, had not known the noises to be speech. But now —now I understood this female plainly.

"Leave me alone," I said. In the darkness of the cabinet, I recoiled in fear. I spoke? I was conversing with the human? My mind reeled. How could I understand? How could I form human speech?

"I want to help you," the human said. "What was done to you was wrong. The person who did it was experimenting with things he did not understand. He used machines he had seen used, but he used them incorrectly, with far too much power, far too close together. He wasn't supposed to even turn them on. He was wrong. I am sorry."

"He hurt me," I heard myself say.

"I know he did, and he has paid a terrible price."

"He hurt me," I repeated.

"But he will never hurt you again. He is dead."

I realized she meant that my venom had done its work. Dimly, the memory came to me of the mouse, of stinging it to death, devouring it, the strength and power and growth surging through me. Before today, that mouse would have been five times my size, and I would have been lying in wait for the occasional small insect to blunder into range of my sting. Now the thought of the dead human, already made tender for me by my venom, tugged at me.

"I am hungry," I said.

"I will see that you are given food," said the female human. "But Akshay did not realize what he had done. He did not mean to hurt anyone."

"He tried to kill me. I had to sting him many times to make him food. I am hungry."

"Let me help you. Let me explain what happened and how we can help you."

"What did you do to me?" I asked.

"Akshay exposed you to the blue diamond rays of a machine that fortified your mind, brought it to its full potential. Then he exposed you to the ruby rays of a different machine, which accelerated and strengthened the processes of your body, made you stronger. Just how much stronger, we do not yet know, but he overdid both. The power was unregulated, far too high."

"And so I understand your speech," I said.

"And you yourself can speak," she answered, "and think. Reason. Remember. Before the two treatments, none of that was possible."

I could barely recall, a mere hour before, resting and waiting in the dark of the machinery crate. Life was the instinct to lie still and wait for food. There had been no memory, no anticipation of anything beyond the next meal. Now, everything was different.

"What is this place?" I asked.

"You are in the laboratory of Doctor Lakshmi Malicux at the leper hospital in the city of Bombay, India."

The names meant nothing to me.

"You are Doctor Lakshmi Malieux?"

"No. Doctor Malieux is away. She is my godmother. I am the daughter of her childhood friend. My name is Pauline Spiegel. I am visiting here, recovering from injuries I sustained last Midsummer Night's Eve."

"Your name is Pauline Spiegel," I said slowly. "I do not have a name."

"No," she answered, "but you are welcome to choose one for yourself."

"What am I?" I asked. "You are human. I am not."

Pauline Spiegel cleared her throat. "No, you are not. You are a new type of being, one of many who have been made thinking, reasoning creatures by Doctor Malieux's machines. We call you micromechs."

"What was I before?"

"I do not know," she said. "I have not seen you, but I am told you were some type of scorpion."

Far above my head I heard the chirp of a cricket. I tensed. A cricket! My favorite prey before today. I paused, realizing that I understood the speech of this food.

"I have seen his kind before," said the cricket. "He is from the desert of Syria. He is a scorpion, all right. A deathstalker scorpion."

"The deadliest scorpion in the world," muttered the human.

"Come down from the ceiling, food," I said. Hunger pushed at my mind again.

"My name is Cobweb," said the cricket, ignoring my demand. "I too have been exposed to the lights, but much more carefully than you were."

The food was taunting me.

"We are all friends here," said the cricket. "We help Doctor Malieux and Miss Pauline in their work."

"Be careful in there, Cobweb," said the human.

The food laughed. "He was much more dangerous to me when he was smaller," said Cobweb. "Now he is ever so much bigger. Slow and clumsy. I doubt he can climb these walls at all. I am quite safe."

The food was making me both angry and hungry. She thought I couldn't climb? I would show her I was a good climber—one of the best. I edged toward the wall, as silently as I could. But I realized that even I could hear my footsteps now. I was not accustomed to my new size.

The cricket laughed again. Staring up into the darkness, I could make her out on the ceiling, directly above the door of the cabinet. She thought she was safe up there in the darkness. But my eyes were perfectly attuned to hunt her. I would eat her.

I rushed forward, intending to run up the door and sting her to death before she realized I was even coming. It would have worked before these last two moltings.

But I was too heavy. I hit the door. The spines on my front feet dug into the wood, and I was on my way up. Unfortunately, my speed and unaccustomed bulk pushed the door open.

Suddenly I was again out of the darkness and into the light. I was momentarily dazzled, awkward, my middle and rear legs scrabbling for purchase on the swinging door. I fell backward onto the floor of the laboratory.

Above me the cricket shrilled an alarm.

I scrambled to my feet.

The human towered over me, startled into immobility. It was only then that I realized the true extent of my own metamorphosis. An hour before I would not have been as long as the human's little finger. Now I was longer than her foot.

My hunger and my anger were spurred by my new strength and speed. Before she could react, I charged. She jumped back with a cry of fear. I had her. I threw myself at her, tail whipping forward.

The world went into slow motion. I could see the needle-sharp point of my stinger hurtling toward her leg, a drop of my deadly poison glistening at its tip. It would bury itself halfway between her ankle and her knee. Before she could react, I would sting her again and again, as I had the lab assistant. And this time, I would feed. This human would be food.

The needle flew through the stocking that covered the leg. But then everything went wrong. My stinger bounced off. I struck again and again, with no effect.

The leg was metal.

Abruptly I became aware that the air above me was alive with diving, buzzing insects and birds. None of them were food. All glinted with bright metal, some glinted with gems.

I whipped about with my tail and my pincers, but these demon micromechs were too fast and too agile. There were too many of them. They would distract me with their diving attacks, and soon the human with the metal feet and legs would do what the fleshy feet and legs of the assistant could not: she would crush me.

I turned and ran. The open door of the laboratory loomed, and I sprinted through it. A knot of humans watching from the end of the hallway screamed and scattered. I bolted past them, out the door, and into the darkness.

In the score of sweltering days and sultry nights since then, burning hunger has been my constant companion. But human prey is abundant in the slums of Bombay. I feast, rest, molt. Feast, rest, molt.

Soon I shall arise. No more will I cower in darkness. I will return. Pauline Spiegel, my enemy, will kneel. And she will be consumed. Humanity will kneel.

C.H. (Charlie) Lindsay is a writer, poet, housewife, and mother, but not necessarily in that order. She has spent thirty years as an event planner, organizing and running numerous science fiction, fantasy, and horror conventions. She spent a decade acting in musicals, is a member of several national writing organizations, and is a founding member of the Utah Chapter of the Horror Writers Association. Mostly blind due to a degenerative eye disease, she collects print books for her library and audiobooks for herself. She also runs a fleet of online, text-based roleplaying simulations. She lives in Utah with her "seeing-eye husband," and two cats, who also consider themselves to be children.

About this story, Charlie says: "I grew up on fairy tales, mythology, and fantasy books. I love happy endings, but my stories tend to gravitate more to the dark and twisted. In researching this story, I was intrigued by the myth of Krotos, the son of Pan, who was placed in the heavens as a reward for his service to the Muses. He is my inspiration for 'Sagittarius Rising.' More specifically, I wondered what might happen if someone wanted to bring him back. I was also drawn to the idea of someone who paints nightmares before they happen in real life. I blame the fairy tales."

If, after reading this story, you find yourself looking askance at paintings—or your own doodlings—don't blame Charlie. Blame the fairy tales.

Sagittarius Rising
C.H. Lindsay

A burned and dismembered body rose from a pile of rotting leaves, the parts clinging together like pieces of a morbid jigsaw puzzle. Where there were gaps or missing pieces, smoldering internal organs glowed dark crimson.

Maya studied the canvas on her easel, dabbed her brush in ultramarine blue and burnt umber, and added shadows to the eye sockets. Was it enough to give the illusion of unlife? She tipped her head to one side and considered the painting for a moment, then added another shadow. At first, she'd been afraid to paint the images that haunted her dreams, but now she found a perverse pleasure in the macabre.

"Oh my. That's gruesome," a woman announced loudly from the doorway.

Startled, Maya's hand jerked and smeared the paint across the eye and nose sockets. "Hi, Peggy." She didn't need to turn around to know it was her best friend. Peggy lived across the street and often dropped by to chat, but hadn't for a few weeks so Maya could get ready for her exhibition. "I'm painting nightmares. What's up?"

"No wonder you keep your lights on."

"I did at first, but now I paint at night and sleep during the day." The smear gave Maya an idea. She carefully repaired it so the face looked like it was fractured and set her brush in a jar of solvent before turning to face her friend. "What can I help you with?"

Peggy wrapped a strand of her long blonde hair around her finger as she stared at the canvas. "Did you hear the news?"

"No." Maya looked at the unfinished painting and sighed. She really wanted to get back to work, but she should at least talk to Peggy for a bit. "I just got back last night and started… this."

"That's right." Peggy turned her attention back to Maya. "Your exhibition. Congrats. I read opening night was a success." She grinned. "I also saw pictures of you and your boyfriend online."

Maya wrinkled her nose. "Nikos is not my boyfriend." Because it took forty-five minutes to drive down the mountain to the nearest city, Maya scheduled her meetings with her agent and accountant so she only had to go to town once a month. She and Nikos tried to get together on those days, if he wasn't busy with his job selling home security systems. "I've only been out with him four times in the past six months. I really don't know him that well."

In an attempt to shift the conversation, Maya said, "My new paintings are actually selling better than the old ones did."

"That's great." Peggy looked back at the painting and grimaced. "I still like your fairies better. Sorry."

Maya would have agreed with her six months ago, but these new paintings fed her dark muse and gave her a drive to create like never before. "You said you had news?"

"Oh, yes." Peggy turned back to Maya, her smile disappearing. "It's been crazy around here. Four college kids were camping nearby, and they left their fire burning when they went into their tent. The tent caught on fire. Another camper heard them all screaming and called for help, but all four kids died."

"That's terrible." *And familiar.* Maya glanced across a row of paintings on the wall. One depicted a fire-blackened forest with four burning figures dancing through the ashes. She felt sick to her stomach. "No," she whispered. The painting was too different. It was just coincidence. She turned back to Peggy. "When did it happen?"

"The night before last, while you were away." Peggy saw the image of the four dancing corpses, flames encircling their bodies. "Oh my. Another nightmare?"

"Yes, I finished it last week. Four fire elementals celebrating a burned-out forest," she insisted.

"Didn't you tell me Nikos introduced you to this type of art?" Peggy asked.

"Yes. Why?" Maya met Nikos at a lecture in town. They started talking about art, and he suggested she try doing darker works. But what did that have to do with the kids?

Peggy shook her head. "Just a silly notion. Never mind."

Maya pointed to a sculpture on a small pedestal in the corner. The nine muses danced around a satyr. "This is new," she said, changing the subject again.

"Where'd you get it?"

"Nikos took me to the Greek Festival before the exhibit opened, and I bought this. The muses are supposed to bring me luck."

"Ooh, how pretty," Peggy said, examining the sculpture closely. "So, now that you're not bogged down getting ready for your show, want to come over for lunch and gossip?"

Peggy's gossiping was how Maya got most of her news, especially about the tiny canyon community of Aspen Hollow. Normally, they talked, ate, and watched a movie. Maya's stomach did a guilty flip-flop because she knew she should say yes, but she'd spent four days in town for the exhibition and she was anxious to paint. "I'm really sorry, but I can't right now. I know, I owe you a dozen lunches, and I'll make it up to you, but I need to finish this and get some sleep."

Peggy's lip trembled, and she looked hurt for a moment, then forced a smile. "I'm the one who should apologize. I forget you artist types dance to a different piper than the rest of us." She looked at the painting again. "I think I'll tell Don about this."

Don was a neighbor and the sheriff of Aspen Hollow. "What? That one of my paintings bears a slight resemblance to what happened?" Maya said, rejecting the suggestion. "It doesn't mean anything."

"I still think he should know about this new painting. I told him about the others."

Maya wanted to object, but it would only make her friend more determined.

Peggy hugged her and headed out the door. "Call me when you come up for air—and don't take too long."

Maya let out a long, slow breath. Why would Peggy think Don needed to know about her paintings? At least he hadn't come to see them, so he obviously didn't think there was anything peculiar about her work. The tension in her body eased as she picked up her brush. It took an hour before she deemed the painting finished. Only then did she let herself go to sleep and dream.

———————

Maya watched the waterfall do a slow ballet off the cliff. The beautiful spot fueled her productivity. She had done so many sketches, mostly of the gorgeous surroundings, but she couldn't keep herself from adding a splash of blood to the rocks or a foot poking out of the pool at the base of the waterfall. Then the sun dipped lower, and she lost the perfect light.

She carefully put her sketchpad and pencils in her backpack and hiked quickly down the mountain, eager to be back home before it got dark. As she approached Aspen Hollow, she caught the smell of smoke. Not the clean, wood smell of a campfire, but the pungent, bitter smell of something that should not be burning. She scanned her surroundings and saw the smoke. A house? She picked up her pace, her heart pounding in her ears.

She ran past a large pine tree and saw flames scurrying across the roof of the old Granger house, threatening to jump to the forest beyond.

Maya meant to go past the house to get help, but a cry pierced through the crackle of the flames. She slowed and looked at the windows. Had she really heard someone?

An old woman waved from a partially boarded-up window on the second floor. "Help!"

Maya looked at the roof. If there were any chance of saving the woman, she'd have to act fast. She ran into the house and up the stairs, covering her mouth with her arm as the smoke grew thicker and praying she'd made the right decision.

"Let me out!" the woman screamed as Maya ran into the room.

The heat in the room intensified. Maya held out her hand. "Come with me. I'll get you out."

The woman turned, her eyes red from the smoke filling the room. "No! You can't. It's too late."

"It's not too late." Maya's eyes burned, and tears ran down her cheeks from the smoke, but she couldn't leave the woman to die. She had to do something.

She took a deep breath and prepared to dart across the room and grab her, but the old woman's eyes changed to match the fire that surrounded her. Two satyr horns thrust out of her skull. "Krotos comes for you, my dear. Embrace the fire and your destiny." The woman burst into flames and disappeared.

Panic rose like bile in Maya's throat. Had the woman just turned into a demon? Maya screamed and turned away, stunned and shaking. Smoke burned her lungs. She coughed and pulled the collar of her shirt over her mouth and nose.

Heat struck her skin like a heavy weight as she hurried to where she thought the door was. The floor gave way beneath her, and she fell into a pit of fire.

She woke gasping and choking, the lingering smell of smoke still in her nostrils. It took several deep breaths to calm her pounding heart.

She went into the bathroom and drank a glass of water to soothe her scratchy throat. That was the first time a nightmare had addressed her directly. She shuddered and turned on all the lights on the second floor. Then she went upstairs to put it on canvas and work through her fear.

Red-orange flames climbed toward the half-boarded-up window like fiery roses through thick smoke. The old woman stared through the pane; her eyes burned the same color as the flames around her. Two red horns protruded from her forehead, their tips coated in blood. One hand reached out in invitation.

"I think I like the other one better," Peggy said, motioning to the four figures dancing in the flames.

Maya turned and looked at the painting as Peggy pointed and nodded. "I think I do too." The nightmare still unsettled her.

Then she saw the sheriff standing behind Peggy and frowned. "Hi, Don."

"Afternoon, Maya," he said, nodding his head in greeting. "Peggy's worried about your nightmares. She insisted I come talk to you."

"*Insist* is a little strong," Peggy said, looking guilty. She was twisting and untwisting a strand of blonde hair. "I just thought, after yesterday, that he should have a look for himself."

Maya pursed her lips and turned back to her canvas to put her brush in the jar of solvent and bite back an angry retort. "They're just nightmares," she told Don when she turned back. "Have a look for yourself."

Don walked down the row of paintings, carefully looking at each one.

"That one," Peggy said when he stopped in front of the four fire elementals. "That's the one she painted before those kids died."

Don turned to Maya. "What was the nightmare?"

Maya sighed. "I was walking in the woods and heard a strange noise. I went to see what it was. There was a clearing burned out by fire. Those four fire elementals were celebrating the destruction."

"Nothing else?" Don asked.

"No." *No kids. No tents. Just the four elementals.*

He nodded. "What about this guy, Nikos?"

Maya looked sharply at Peggy. Exactly what had she told Don? "He's just a guy I met at a lecture. We've gone out a couple of times."

"He told her to paint this stuff. She never had nightmares before that," Peggy added.

"Do you think there's a connection?" Don asked Maya.

"No. He suggested it, yes. But I'm the one who gave it a try.

He's asked about my paintings, and he came with me to my art exhibition, but he has nothing to do with the nightmares."

Don nodded again. "Okay. Thanks."

"That's it?" Peggy asked. She waved her hand around the paintings. "But what about these? These are her nightmares."

Don looked at the art and back at Peggy. "What am I supposed to see in them?"

"I don't know. Something."

"There's nothing here but dark art," Don said. "I might even buy one."

Peggy frowned. "I don't understand this either, but something's going on. Maya wasn't psychic before. Now she's painting these horrible things *before* they happen. And talk to that guy, Nikos. He gives me the creeps."

"Maybe I will, but I think it's more that her paintings are giving her nightmares and this psychic thing is just a coincidence. The mind has its own way of dealing with stuff like this." He smiled at Peggy. "Come on, I'll let you fix me dinner."

He took Peggy by the arm and led her to the door. "Nice work, Maya. We'll see ourselves out."

Peggy looked back at Maya, clearly wanting her to say something.

"Feed him," she said, trying not to smile. It was a relief that Don didn't take her friend too seriously. "It's the least you can do after dragging him over here for nothing."

"Wasn't for nothing," Don said, flashing a smile. "I got to see your studio."

"Fine," Peggy said, finally giving up. "Talk to you later."

Five days later, Maya was working at her easel when her phone rang. She glanced out the window. The shadows in her yard indicated it was late afternoon.

"Maya?" Peggy sounded like she was crying.

Maya set her brush down. "What's wrong?"

"The police were just here. Don... Don's dead."

"I'll be right there." Maya dropped her brush in the solvent, put her shoes on, and ran across the street to Peggy's.

She found her friend sitting at the kitchen table, staring at the wall, the phone still in her hand. She looked gaunt and withered.

Maya sat down and squeezed her hand. "What happened?"

"Somebody killed him and cut up his body." She began to cry again. "The police found him in a shallow grave. Burned." She looked at Maya, not caring about the tears that ran down her cheeks. "All I can think about is your paintings."

It felt like an accusation. That her art was the reason Don was dead. But it couldn't be her fault. "They know it's him for sure?"

"They found his wallet near the body. It was covered in his blood."

Maya hugged Peggy, and they both cried.

"How did the police know to talk to you?" Maya asked when they were both calmer.

"He told his buddies about me. I guess I'm the closest thing he had to family," she said, starting to cry again.

Maya filled a pot with water and put it on the stove to boil. "Who would want to hurt Don?"

"I don't know. The police think it was because he found a lead on the murders of those kids. The ones in the tent. Don said it wasn't an accident. They asked me if I knew anything. But I don't."

Who would set fire to a tent full of college kids? "What made him think it was murder?"

"He was investigating a couple of hiking accidents. He found something that connected them to the fire, but he didn't tell me what." Peggy shook her head. "I wish I could help them find who did this." Her lower lip quivered.

Maya brushed the tears off her cheeks. She was shaky and still couldn't assimilate what happened. She prepared two cups of strong, sweet tea. "Drink this."

They finished the pot of tea in silence, both lost in their own thoughts. Slowly, they began to talk about Don. Maya knew Peggy was feeling better when she pulled out a jar of cookies to munch on. When it grew dark, Maya stood and stretched. "I'm staying here tonight, but I need to go home for a few minutes. I left my brushes soaking and I need to lock up the house. Come with me?"

Peggy nodded and followed Maya across the street.

They were still a little jittery when they walked into the house, so they turned on the lights and checked the first floor. "I'll wash out my brushes if you'll check the second floor."

Again, Peggy nodded.

Maya ran upstairs, put away her paints, and began to wash out her brushes. She heard something and glanced over at the muses sculpture. The satyr was looking at her. She blinked and looked again. "Maya," it spoke in a deep baritone grumble. "You have served your muse well. As a reward, the gods have chosen you, and soon I will come to claim that which is mine."

The stress was getting to her. At least she hoped it was just the stress. "I'm losing it." Nightmares were one thing, but this was too much. She took a slow, deep breath and looked back at the statue.

"I am Krotos, son of Pan. Together, we shall reclaim Mount Helicon and restore the muses."

"No," Maya screeched. This was not real. Panicking, she dropped her brushes on a towel and ran downstairs.

"What happened?" Peggy met her at the landing. "I heard you shout something."

"Nothing. I'm hearing things." She sounded a little hysterical to her own ears. "Let's go back to your place and watch a movie." Anything to get her mind off death and statues.

Peggy looked at Maya hesitantly. "Okay." They turned out the lights and locked the door.

They watched *Singin' in the Rain* and *Young Frankenstein*. Movies that were supposed to make them laugh. But both failed miserably. At least they distracted them for a few hours.

The next day, they worked together, pulling weeds and trimming the roses in both their gardens. Talk was minimal, but getting back to familiar routines helped them both start healing. Don's next-door neighbor stopped by to offer condolences as he also had a visit from the police. He invited Peggy and Maya to dinner. They spent a pleasant evening smiling at the antics of his three small children and talking about anything but what happened.

Thoughts about Don's murder crept back in when they walked into Maya's house for a cup of cocoa. Peggy stopped at the kitchen table and picked up a rose. "Funny. This wasn't here when we left. Was it?"

Maya looked at the bloodred rose in Peggy's hand for a long moment, her weight shifting uncomfortably from one foot to the other. She'd never seen a rose that shade of red. She locked the door. She knew it. How did it get there? "Maybe Nikos snuck in and left it there as a surprise?" she lied.

She recalled the satyr's words and ran upstairs toward her studio, toward the statue. She heard Peggy following behind her. She stopped on the second floor. There on her bed, another dark red rose lay on her pillow. She picked it up and turned to Peggy, not sure what to say.

"Nikos sells security systems, right? I'll bet he wanted to tell you he was thinking about you."

"I'm sure that's what it is," she lied again. A rose on her doorstep was sweet, but one on her pillow—creepy. Someone had been in her bedroom, touched her things. The rose in her hand shook. She placed it behind her back to keep Peggy from noticing. Together, they checked the rest of the second floor. Nothing else was amiss.

Maya slowly climbed the stairs to her attic studio. At the top, she came to an abrupt stop.

"What is it?" Peggy asked, coming up behind Maya.

"All the paintings have been rearranged," Maya said. She pointed to one painting of a sculpture made of burned hands and feet. "That was in my supply closet."

"Would Nikos do something like this?" Peggy asked.

Maya had no idea. She shook her head, grabbed her cell, and dialed 911. "I can't stay here tonight. Can I stay at your place?"

Peggy nodded. "Sure. I wouldn't want to stay here either. And I could use the company."

Maya knew Peggy was thinking of Don. Her friend didn't need this on top of everything else. She paced while she talked to the sheriff's office. She couldn't help feeling violated.

While Maya was on the phone, Peggy searched, but found nothing else out of place and no sign anyone had broken in.

"The police will be here in an hour. Will you wait with me?"

Maya asked. She didn't want to be alone and she didn't want to leave the house until the police arrived.

Peggy looked at the paintings again and nodded. "Just not up here."

They went back to the kitchen and made cocoa while they waited. Maya pulled out a package of Scotch shortbread to go with it.

When the police arrived, Maya offered them cocoa, but they refused. They looked around, took pictures, and asked questions.

"There's no sign of forced entry," one officer said. "You say nothing was taken?"

Maya shook her head. "Not that I noticed, no." It sounded like she had a creepy stalker, which didn't make her feel any better.

The other police officer nodded. "We'll come back in the morning and have a look outside, then file a report. With no real evidence, there's not much we can do. But with what happened to Don, Peggy's connection, and her house being right across the way, we'll be on the lookout and will send a car through the neighborhood a few times tonight. We're all real sorry about what happened to him. We're gonna find the sonofabitch."

Peggy choked back tears.

Maya knew she couldn't expect much more. She was grateful they'd come all the way to Aspen Hollow. "Thank you." Having the police look around helped her feel better, but she still felt like she was on the verge of losing it again. A statue had talked to her. What was next? She glanced at Peggy, who looked pinched and ashen. "I'll be across the street if you need me," she told the officers.

One of the officers looked at the notes he'd taken. "We have your cell number. We'll call when we're on our way."

When they were gone, Peggy and Maya locked up.

For Maya, tonight held a feeling of menace in the darkness, augmented by the smell of a fire somewhere. The two women jogged across the street to Peggy's place and locked the doors.

A clap of thunder woke Maya a few hours later. Normally, she loved a good thunderstorm, but not tonight. Not when she no longer felt safe.

The floorboards outside the guest room squeaked. "Peggy?"

No response.

"Is that you?"

The door slowly opened, and hooves clattered across the wooden floor and paused as the door closed again.

Lightning flashed outside her window, illuminating the figure of a satyr approaching. He was singing softly. She didn't recognize the language, but it was haunting.

Maya wanted to scream, to grab something as a weapon, but she felt fuzzy-headed and lethargic.

He stood over her, reeking of burned leaves and rotting meat. "I want you, Maya." His voice was deep and oddly accented. It was the same voice that spoke to her from the statue. He put his hands on her shoulders and pushed her back against the pillows. "The gods have chosen, and I approve."

A nightmare. It had to be a nightmare. She told herself to pull away, but she just lay there, watching him.

The satyr looked deep into her eyes as if reading her soul. He looked pleased. "Your paintings speak truth, even if you do not." He let go of one shoulder and sang again, mesmerizing her as he carved a pattern over her heart with his fingernail.

A sharp, searing pain burned through her skin and into her

heart. The heat intensified, spreading rapidly as it consumed her. She cried out, but he silenced her with a passionate, suffocating kiss.

His mouth tasted like meat that had begun to ferment, his tongue like a salty slug. Her mind screamed at her to fight, to get away, but her body wasn't listening. The painful fire that still burned through her altered as her body began to respond to his touch.

He grinned as if aware of her mental struggle. "Your fight is futile. Even your body recognizes Krotos as its master."

Krotos again. Her mind recalled something she had read once about the muses. Had Krotos served them?

He ran a hand across her womb. "You will bear me many fine offspring."

"Never," she managed to say, her teeth clenched as she fought her body's response.

"You cannot fight your destiny."

Like hell she couldn't. "Watch me."

He ran a finger across the painful mark he'd carved into her skin. "You are mine. I will always find you."

"Maya? Did you have another nightmare?" Peggy asked, knocking on the door.

Krotos looked deeply into her eyes again. "Next time, you will not resist me." Then he waved a hand in the air and disappeared.

Peggy opened the door. "What's going on?"

Maya's chest still burned where Krotos marked her. She closed the neck of her nightshirt to cover the wound. "I don't know." She turned the switch on the bedside lamp, but it failed to come on.

Peggy tried the switch on the wall. Nothing. "Must be the storm."

"Do you have a flashlight?" Maya asked.

"Yeah." Peggy left and returned with a large flashlight. "You all right? Did you have a nightmare or something?"

"Yeah." Maya took the flashlight and excused herself to the bathroom. She looked in the mirror and unbuttoned her pajama top. A symbol of an arrow with a cross on it had been scratched into her chest, leaving an angry red welt around the broken flesh. *Not possible.* She called Peggy in. "Do you see anything?"

"What is that? When did you get a tattoo?" Peggy looked closer. "It looks like it might be infected."

A tattoo? He'd permanently marked her. "What is it?"

"You don't know what your tattoo looks like?" Peggy's eyebrows rose high as she glanced between Maya's face and the tattoo. "Wait a second. I've seen that before."

"When? How?" Maya tried to calm her breathing.

"Remember when I was big into horoscopes? I know I've seen this before. I'll be right back."

Maya went back to the bedroom and sat on the bed, her legs shaking too much to stand.

Peggy returned with another flashlight and a big hardcover book with a tattered dust jacket. She flipped the pages and pointed at the symbol: the same one on Maya's chest, an arrow with a cross on it near where the fletching would be. "There it is. It's the symbol of the archer, Sagittarius. Why would you get a tattoo of that? Aren't you an Aquarius?"

"Yes." Maya rocked back and forth as she stared at the symbol. First, the nightmares and the long hours at her easel, then Don's death and the break-in, and now this.

She put a hand on the mark. It still hurt. "Would you believe I woke up with it?"

It sounded insane. But then, having a satyr carve a tattoo

into your flesh with a fingernail sounded pretty crazy too. *I'm going nuts*, she told herself. There had to be a plausible explanation, but she couldn't think of one.

Peggy gave her a concerned look. "Come on. I need some cookies and you need some antibiotic ointment."

In the dark kitchen, Peggy poured two glasses of milk and opened a package of chocolate chip cookies. Then she pulled a tube of antibiotic ointment out of the medicine cabinet she kept in the cupboard next to the sink and handed it to Maya. "Want to talk about it?"

Maya stared at the pattern the flashlight made on the ceiling for a long moment before answering. "Not tonight." She wasn't ready to talk about it, and she doubted Peggy would believe her.

"Does it have something to do with Nikos?" Peggy asked.

"Maybe."

"Thought so."

"Let's talk about gardens instead," Maya suggested. As she hoped, Peggy talked about what she wanted to do in her yard over the next few months.

Maya eventually went back to bed, but she did not sleep well.

"Did you have any more nightmares?" Peggy asked when Maya walked into the kitchen.

"No." She didn't want another conversation about satyrs, nightmares, or anything else. She just wanted to go home and work. Painting allowed her to think. It gave her clarity, and right now, she needed that more than anything.

She glanced out the window, surprised that it was so late in the morning. "I thought the police would have called by now."

Peggy set Maya's cell phone in front of her. "They did. You left this in the kitchen last night."

"Why didn't you wake me?"

"You looked terrible last night, so I met with them and let you sleep. I wanted to ask them more about Don, anyway."

Maya was both irritated and grateful. "Did they find anything?"

Peggy shook her head. "Just our footprints. There was no sign that anyone had tampered with the windows or stood in the bushes. I'd have woken you if they found anything."

Maya sighed. It was what she expected. She wondered if Nikos was the creepy stalker type after all. When she went home, she would put a bell on the door, just in case.

"The cops were nice." Peggy paused. "I asked if I could help organize Don's house and take anything that I'd given him. You know, as a memento. Since it's not a crime scene and the police have already looked inside, they said I could, as long as there was a police officer with me." She looked at Maya. "I'm going over in about an hour. Want to come?"

Maya considered going along, but now that she felt more like her house was safe, she really needed to go back and spend time in front of a canvas. Besides, Peggy would have someone with her. She shook her head. "I'm still too worked up over the roses and need to paint for a while. How about I do that while you clean and I meet you back here tonight?" She still didn't want to be alone after dark.

Peggy frowned, the sadness evident in her eyes. "Will you be okay?"

"As long as you come with me to make sure the house is still secure," Maya said. "And I'll be back around dark. We can watch more movies."

"Okay," Peggy replied reluctantly. "Oh, I almost forgot. You remember that smoke we smelled last night?" When Maya nodded, she continued, "There was a house fire on Lone Pine Road. An old lady left a candle burning."

An old lady? "Is the woman okay?"

Peggy shook her head. "They think she died in her sleep."

The news struck Maya like a physical blow, and she felt shaky. She had to think and she had to paint. Maybe, when she could wrap her brain around what was going on, she could talk it over with Peggy. But right now, she needed the clarity that came from her work.

The blackout was over, so they turned on the lights as they checked the house. Everything was as they'd left it. The roses were a little wilted, but they hadn't been moved. Maya threw them in the trash as she said goodbye to Peggy. She bolted the door, hung some bells on the knob, and went to her studio.

Burnt umber highlighted the figure of Maya as she reclined on an ornate lounge covered in rose petals. She wore a white Grecian gown that draped over one shoulder, leaving her tattoo clearly visible above her heart. She smiled at Krotos, who stood before her on his shaggy goat legs. He wore a Greek fustanella kilt and held a single dark red rose that dripped blood onto her gown. In the background, the constellation Sagittarius filled the night sky.

When the painting was finished, she wondered what the meaning behind the strange image was. Regardless, she would hide it away in her closet when it was dry. This one was not based in a nightmare, like the others; but then, neither was Krotos. It was definitely not something she wanted anyone to see.

A hand on her shoulder made her jump. "Your wish is my command," Krotos whispered in her ear.

"No."

She turned to face him. He no longer smelled of burned leaves and rotting meat. This time, he smelled of the deep woods and musk, with a touch of something sweeter underneath. It made her feel light-headed.

"I chose you above all others." He put a hand on her tattoo. Heat raced through her heart and loins. "The time has come." He spoke words she could not understand, but they drew her to him. She sucked in a deep breath. His scent filled her with desire. Her heart pounded as she slowly rose to her feet to embrace him.

"You must give yourself to me," he whispered.

Her mind screamed "No!" but her inner voice was distant, and her body would not listen. She said, "Yes."

He pulled her against him and kissed her. His scent and the feel of him made it impossible for her to think clearly. "Now, say the words."

"What words?"

He put a finger under her chin and lifted it until her eyes met his. "Say: I give myself to you, body and soul."

She got lost in his gaze for a long moment. There was something at the back of her mind she needed to remember, but it eluded her.

"Maya. Repeat after me: I give myself to you."

"I give myself to you," she repeated obediently, and her tattoo began to burn again.

"Now, say: body and soul," he urged.

There was something she should do, some reason she should resist, but the thought dissipated like morning mist.

"Maya. Say the words."

Oh, yes. "Body and soul."

As soon as she spoke, the tattoo seared through her body and branded itself onto her heart. The intense pain made it hard to breathe.

"And now, give to me what you promised." Krotos picked her up in his arms and took her to bed.

When she was alone again, she curled up in a ball and cried, mortified at what she'd done and ashamed of her willing participation. She desperately wanted to hide from everyone, especially herself. She couldn't face Peggy. Not yet.

After a while, she fell asleep and dreamed of finding a cave in the woods. It was hidden between a large scrub oak and a clump of aspen, not far from the trail to the waterfall above Aspen Hollow. In the chill of the night, a light and the smell of a campfire beckoned.

She squeezed through the narrow entrance, scraping her shoulder. The passage turned sharply and opened into a rectangular cavern of rough limestone. A gas lantern hung on the wall, illuminating a sculpture crafted of a dozen burned hands and feet. From the center of the grotesque display, a blackened skull leered at her. The similarities to the painting she'd hidden in her closet startled Maya, and she bumped her head on a low-hanging rock.

Her head throbbing, she stumbled deeper into the cavern and toward a fire on a stone altar at the far end. Something on the altar was burning. At first she thought it was an animal, but as she got closer, she realized it was too long and lean.

No. Not a body. A rising panic choked her. She had to escape.

She turned to run, but a hand came out of nowhere and grabbed her shoulder, stopping her cold.

"It's too late," a male voice whispered. "The final sacrifice is complete. Now you must fulfill your destiny."

The voice sounded familiar. Before she could turn to see his face, he pushed her toward the fire. As they got closer, she could clearly see that the sacrifice was human.

Beside the altar sat a table holding a large bowl half-filled with blood. A head floated in the center, with only the forehead and long blonde hair visible on top. It was Peggy.

"No!" She wrenched out of the man's hands to run away, but all went black.

She woke up screaming.

"Peggy!" She had to make sure her friend was all right.

She hadn't intended to fall asleep when Krotos left, but she wasn't thinking clearly at the time. She pulled on her clothes and ran across the dark street.

The lights were on in Peggy's house, and the door wide open, but there was no sign of her friend. She grabbed a flash-light, left on the kitchen counter from the blackout two nights before and rushed back outside to check the yard.

She found a wadded-up piece of paper by the corner of the house and picked it up.

When she smoothed it out and looked at the photograph, her stomach twisted into knots and her heart pounded. It was a sculpture made of burned hands and feet exactly like her dream. The blackened skull in the center grinned maliciously at her. *This can't be.* She dropped it as if it were covered with maggots and ran to the backyard. "Peggy!"

She bumped into a blood-spattered table pushed up against the siding. Blood dripped onto the grass, and she saw a gore-covered knife.

She cried out, her mind reeling.

The wind shifted, and the smell of burning meat and hair from the barbecue pit made her sick. She approached with a hand on her roiling stomach. A body stretched out over the fire. "No." She began to shake uncontrollably as she recognized Peggy's burning body.

The nightmare could not be real. Was she going insane? Maya dry heaved. *I have to get out of here. I have to stop this.* Peggy could not be dead.

Almost blinded by her tears, she ran toward the front of the house... and crashed into Nikos.

He grabbed her arms and held her steady. "It's better this way. She would have ruined everything."

His voice was the one from her nightmare. "What's better? Peggy's dead."

He sighed, clearly displeased by her tears. He pushed her into the backyard, where the smell of burning flesh choked her again.

Nikos spun her around and shook her. "You need to understand. I found some of the Greek demigods in the stars. They're real. The ancient Greeks knew them, and flourished. We need to bring back their art, their philosophy, their way of life, and for that, we need their gods."

She stared at him, dumbfounded.

"I picked Krotos from Sagittarius. He served the muses. That's when I realized what I had to do. I made sacrifices to him to get his attention. Eventually, he spoke to me. He agreed to help restore the muses. But he wanted more. He wanted a future. He needed you."

"Me?" her voice squeaked. Nikos was insane. None of it made sense. Was that just his excuse for being a serial killer?

She played along and nodded so she didn't end up like Peggy.

"I knew you were the one. A gifted artist, a beautiful woman. And you had the Sight—although you didn't realize it. You're a muse's dream. Krotos's dream. You see his visions, and you paint. You make them happen."

No. It wasn't true. She had nightmares, but Nikos made it all happen: the kids, the old woman, Don, Peggy, everything.

"I set you on the path to discover your true potential. And you did. You inspired me. You are my muse."

She wanted to scream at him, to kick him. Instead, she looked at Peggy's body and hated Nikos for what he had done.

"It was her fault," Nikos said, following Maya's gaze. "She sent her boyfriend after me."

"You didn't need to kill her," Maya said, unable to keep the words inside.

"Yes, I did. You can't truly give yourself to Krotos if you have someone else, a friend like her who will keep you away from him. She was in the way."

His grip on Maya loosened, and she pulled away, but he caught her by one arm. "I did this for you. For both of us. You should be grateful."

"Grateful?" she fumed. "You're a psychopath."

He backhanded her across the face. She stumbled backward and slammed against the bloody table. He glared at her as he approached. "Their deaths are your fault. I won't let you ruin this for me."

There were no words to express what she thought of him. "Go to hell." She grabbed the knife, still sticky from Peggy's blood, and stabbed Nikos in the neck.

He struggled to pull out the blade, and she ran into the house, grabbed Peggy's car keys, got in her car, and sped out of

Aspen Hollow. She blew through both stop signs and didn't slow down until she was a mile outside of town. Shaking uncontrollably, she pulled over.

It was not her fault. Still, she should have sensed that Nikos was crazy. She should have stayed with Peggy last night. Instead, she followed the path Nikos had laid out for her. She had given herself, body and soul, to Krotos.

Her tattoo burned, and she put a hand over it to try and stop the pain. Was he calling to her? Sooner or later, Krotos would come for her again. And she could do nothing to resist him.

But she would not think of that now. There would be plenty of time for regrets and remorse later. Right now, she had to stop Nikos from hurting anyone else and clean up the mess she'd made.

"No." Her hands tightened on the steering wheel. She couldn't drive thirty miles to the police station. That would give Nikos time to get away, to hide. She had to stop this, stop him, right now. She turned the car around and sped back.

Nikos was not at Peggy's. A trail of blood led across the street and into Maya's house.

She slipped inside and grabbed a cast-iron frying pan from the kitchen. She slowly followed the blood trail up the stairs, her heart pounding in trepidation. She paused on the second floor, although the drops continued. He was in her studio. *Damn him.*

She crept up the stairs, afraid to breathe too loudly, and peered into the room. Nikos's back was to her. Her paintings were lined up along one wall, and he'd lit several candles. He chanted something that sounded like Greek.

The words tingled up her spine, and she shivered. Whatever he was doing had to stop.

She took a deep breath for courage, lunged into the room,

and hit him on the back of the head with the frying pan. He fell, hopefully unconscious, but she didn't care if he was dead. She paused just long enough to make sure he was out, then set the frying pan aside and headed for the row of dark art.

She quickly took the five paintings directly related to Nikos and laid them side by side. She poured an entire can of paint thinner over them. Once the solvent soaked into the paint, she would rub the canvases with a cloth until the images were unrecognizable. There would be nothing left for Nikos, and her paintings would never hang in a shrine to his crimes.

"No, you can't destroy them," Nikos said as he got shakily to his feet. "Those are my reward. My future."

She hadn't hit him hard enough. She swallowed her panic and faked a confident smile. "Too late."

Nikos stared at her. "It doesn't matter. Destroying your work won't change that you foretold the sacrifices. You made me as much as I made you."

No. The thought of Nikos using her gift, her art, for his own warped purposes, and then blaming her, was unbearable. She grabbed a candle and held it up. "Stay where you are or I burn them." She did not want to burn down her house, but she was not going to let him walk away without paying for what he'd done—one way or another.

Nikos paled. "You wouldn't dare."

She moved slowly toward the door, hoping to lock him inside until she could bring the police. "You killed my best friend. I have nothing left," she said, throwing his words back in his face.

He raised his hands and stepped out of her path to the door. When she was safely past the canvases, he lunged at her. "I'll kill you for this."

Terrified, she thrust the candle in his face, splattering it with molten wax. He roared in pain and rage but continued to block her escape. Getting the police was no longer an option. Only one of them would walk away.

He tried to tackle her, but she kneed him in the groin and pushed him as hard as she could. He tripped and fell onto the paintings.

Before she could have second thoughts, she tossed a candle onto the painting next to him. With a *woommff*, the paint thinner burst into flame, engulfing Nikos in fire.

She ran down the stairs as he screamed. On her way out, she grabbed her cell phone and left him to his fate.

By the time Maya reached the front yard, the entire third floor was ablaze.

She collapsed onto the lawn and dialed 911 and told the dispatcher what happened.

Nikos was dead. It was finally over. Tears of loss streamed down her cheeks. But his words still echoed in the back of her mind: *"You made me as much as I made you."*

The door to her house slowly opened, and she panicked, thinking it was Nikos.

"Maya, come. Live with me among the stars." The deep, rumbling voice of Krotos came from inside. "Together, we shall await the right time to return and restore the muses."

Her tattoo blazed white-hot, but with her art gone and Nikos dead, his words no longer had the power over her they once did.

She now had a choice. Stay and be afraid of inspiring another Nikos with her dark, twisted imagination, or go with Krotos.

But that would be a cold existence. The Greek gods were not known for their tenderness or fidelity. And when he tired of her, he would leave her to a half life among the stars.

She looked at her house, at the smoke and flames. Everything was gone because of Nikos. She would not let him control her destiny. She took a deep breath and made her choice.

She would make a new beginning, a new future. She would find a way to use her art for good. For Peggy.

She looked at Krotos in the doorway, his hand outstretched to her. It was all she could do to stand up to him. "No."

"Maya, I am your destiny. You will come with me." Her tattoo seared through her like a branding iron. Her knees buckled, but she turned and stumbled away from him. Away from the darkness.

This was Nikos's nightmare, and she would not become another of his victims.

Eventually, she would remove the tattoo from her flesh, even if she could not remove it from her soul. She would never be free from Krotos, but she would paint a new future for herself. She put a hand on her womb. Regardless of any consequences of the past few days, she would live.

The weeks of stress weighed heavily on Maya. The police, the reports, Peggy's funeral, moving away from Aspen Hollow and into the new house. Starting over. After a few days back at her canvas, she found peace. She had completed two paintings and almost a third.

Maya carefully layered a mixture of yellow ochre and white over raw sienna to highlight the golden Peggy-fairy. Her butterfly wings kept her just out of reach of a puce Nikos worm as she valiantly defended a bush of bloodred roses. This one was for Peggy.

Maya looked at her nearly empty wall of new art: two Greek myths where Nikos was being punished by the gods. In one, he plunged from a cerulean sky, his Icarus wings melting from the heat of Apollo's sun. In another, a tormented Nikos lay chained across a boulder of blood red and sap green. A giant eagle tore out his liver. In the background, Krotos played the panpipes.

She had yet to find where she wanted to go with her art. Regardless, with each new painting, she returned Krotos to his place in mythological history, and his power over her faded. Krotos would forever stay in the stars where he belonged.

Her future—and her destiny—were once again her own.

Scott Bryan is the author of the upcoming Foresight Chronicles series and so spends a lot of time as the scribe for a three-hundred-year-old vampire child, sharing tales of her endless battles with Dracula across history. He also searches the Multiverse, looking for fascinating narratives to share with this world. He's met lost fantasy creatures, demonic beings, time travelers and Multiversal agents, each of whom have offered him stories to tell. When not creating worlds, Scott generates technical drawings, enjoys life with his wife and children, collects stories and figures of heroic champions, and walks his fierce warrior Chihuahua. You can find him on the web and see what he's currently working on at night-children.blogspot.com.

About this story, Scott says: "I'm into a lot of fun concepts, such as super heroes, classics monsters, and time travel, but ones that always comes to the forefront are multiverse stories. As a chronicler of the Multiverse, I've seen plenty of strange versions of Earth. The setting for this story, World X2604, counts itself among the more tragic. Populated with talking humanistic animals, rather than making jokes and living a cartoon life like the inhabitants of similar worlds, this one is tormented with constant war. The Mammalian Forces have been fighting the Marine Marauders for over a hundred years. The real story is on the front line where brave soldiers like Joe the Fire Monkey face horror every single day."

The best advice for reading this story is to throw away all of your preconceived notions, go along for the ride, and if the starfish start flying, run for cover!

MONKEY FISH
Scott Bryan

Sweat pooled on the back of Joe's thick, furry neck. He gently brushed the trigger of his Fire-Bomber 2000. Not hard enough to actually set it off, but just so he would be ready if they emerged from the deep.

He'd practiced using the weapon for months. The days of setting his tail on fire were long past him. He knew everything there was to being in the Fire Monkey Battalion. He should be ready. And yet Bill's words kept echoing in his mind. "Training is not fighting. Wait till you're actually out there. That's when you'll know."

The Mammalian Forces liked to employ bulls as drill sergeants due to their tendency to force their will on smaller animals. Bill had proved that stereotype true, but it was his mentorship, his willingness to look after Joe, that allowed Joe to feel any sense of ease.

But now, Bill was miles away and Joe stood with his feet planted on the eastern shore, his Fire-Bomber 2000 tight in his hands, his eyes fixed upon the endless ocean in front of him. It was vast and full of danger, and he was at its edge.

As monkeys go, Joe was screwed.

"Remember your training, soldiers," his commander roared. "Fire the moment you see their stinking scales!"

Joe wouldn't move his gaze for anything in the world, but he knew what Commander Leo Thickmane was doing. He could hear his leader's calculated footfalls in the sand behind him, a lion's proud gait.

Temporary courage washed over Joe at his leader's very presence. "You've trained for this. We have the advantage. The Marine Marauders may have confidence, but they will be out of their depths. Teach them to stay where they belong."

Thickmane strode down the beach among the thousands of animal soldiers. Joe listened as the mighty lion urged on the troops. His borrowed courage left with his commander, and Joe blinked to keep the sweat from dripping into his eyes and stinging them again. Thickmane could inspire a sloth to run a marathon, but that didn't mean it would beat a cheetah. Monkeys were built for the entertainment industry, tree house maintenance, and the service sector—but war?

There wouldn't be a Fire Monkey Battalion if this terrible war hadn't lasted this long. So many already lost.

He absently lifted his left foot and scratched his butt, not losing his perfect balance.

"Uniform riding up again?"

It was Cecilia, his crab friend. She worked hard as an infantry assistant. After the life her species endured, her willingness to serve came as no surprise.

"No," he replied. "Just getting tired of all this waiting. I have lost track of how many hours we've been standing here."

"Well, it's better than the alternative," she replied, pushing a water bottle to his lips with her claw. He took a sip from the plastic straw. She continued, "They're devils. The minute they rise from the deep…" Thick apprehension covered them both. Her tiny eyes swam in fear. "Just be careful, Joe, okay?"

"I will." He returned his gaze to the sea as she moved on to the next soldier. Cecilia was a nice girl. She insisted on helping, even if she wasn't a mammal.

She was not alone. A lot of refuge crabs and lobsters supported the cause as a way of saying thanks for their new lives of freedom. Some served as a way to get revenge for their former slavery and abuse. As the only survivor of her family, Cecilia had lots of reasons and Joe respected every one.

His heart sprung into his throat when the alarm went off. The time had come.

A great surge of water washed past his toes, sending icy prickles up his legs. Instantly with the water came a swarm of razor-sharp starfish engulfing the troops. Savage pain tore at Joe's furry arms and legs before he could even move.

Joe instinctively leaped into the air, making most of the living projectiles miss his wiry form. Once firmly back upon his feet, he let out volleys of fire toward the attack. That's when he saw them.

He'd spent ages training and viewing footage of their fish foes. Despite all that, he was unprepared.

Instead of just seeing large, bubble-like eyes on the sides of the heads, bodies covered in multicolored scales, and flat fins that lightly reflected the light, he saw an army of monsters.

The bottom half of the creatures were indeed fish-tailed, but the top half revealed fur, two front legs complete with hooves, and heads that could only be a fellow mammal: goats.

Joe heard a voice shout the obvious. "Capricorns! They sent the Capricorns first!"

Each monstrosity had a starfish launcher strapped to its back and each wore a wheeled harness that allowed these denizens of the deep to travel on land.

Joe used his natural agility to avoid as many starfish as possible, but every once in a while one would draw blood, causing a yelp of pain to escape from between his lips.

He knew the stories—many innocent goats stolen from their lives as simple farmers, never to be seen again. Terrible fables spread through the land about horrible experimentations under the foreboding sea.

Those stories were clearly true. Joe watched the blank stares of the attackers. He took a deep sigh and said a soft prayer for the lost souls he faced now. He squeezed the trigger, sending forth a jet of fire against the coming horde.

The beach fell to chaos as soldiers he'd known for months died around him. Shouts of anger and fear deafened his ears. The once-bright sand grew thick with mixed blood of mammals and fishes alike.

The undersea warriors had emerged. Fish fought his fellow troops with swords and projectile weapons made of choral. It was unnerving how easy it was to bring so many living creatures to death.

A stray starfish punctured the hose on his Fire-Bomber 2000, rendering the weapon useless. "Oh crap! Oh crap!"

His long fingers grappled with the harness across his chest. He'd seen the training videos, heard the stories. He had to get rid of the weapon—the pressure was building up inside, and it would soon explode.

A scream of desperation left his lips as he tore it off and chucked it away. He shielded his face as it exploded in the horde of approaching fishes.

Sea daggers hit the sand inches from his feet.

He drew his pistol. If he could just get to the outpost behind him, he could rearm.

He bounded up the beach, over to the piles of dead. He made quick time until his foot caught on a broken, bloody shell and he fell face-first into the sand.

"What? Who?" He couldn't stop himself from seeing her lifeless body. Cecilia's blank eyes stared off to shores unknown.

The sound of crunching sand made him spin. He fired his weapon, seeing his attacker's large bubble-like eyes.

Terror. Loss. The look in his enemy's eyes felt entirely too familiar as he fell onto the beach.

The enemy raised his own gun in a flippered hand.

It went off with jet of salt water and shards.

There was sadness with fear in the fish's eyes as Joe felt a sharp pain in his chest.

He fell to his knees and looked down at his now blood-washed uniform, feeling the wet spread over him like sadness.

A wave reached up to his knees and retreated.

The enemy collapsed beside him, a mortal wound sinking him to the sea-washed sand.

The adversaries' gaze met, locked, and faded as both died in the space between wet and dry, water and earth, enemy and friend, united in death.

Terra Luft shaped her unique imagination with Stephen King books and her mother's discarded romance novels, which explains a lot. An overachiever by nature, Terra tackles every project with coffee and sarcasm, and believes rules exist to be broken. She works full time by day and writes by night, fighting to maintain an often elusive work-life balance thanks to her inability to say no. A member of both the Horror Writers Association and Sigma Tau Delta International English Honor Society, Terra gives back to the writing community through the League of Utah Writers, where she currently serves as the Infinite Monkeys Genre Writers Chapter President and Conference Committee Chair. She lives in Utah with her husband and two daughters, the ghost of their naughty dog, and a cat who stole her heart. Find her rantings on life and writing at terraluft.com.

About this story, Terra says: "Dissolving Echoes grew from visions of a character based on the astrological aspects of Leo—the tarot card Strength and the phrase "I will." This moment-in-time came directly into focus, a woman facing her own mortality who chooses to act, no matter how futile. Her illness is dire, yet her spirit is unbroken, her will unbending even as her past echoes into the present, deepening her resolve. Having survived a very real brush with death myself, the character reactions were influenced by my own fight—to survive, to thrive—even in the face of the unknown."

If you have ever been on a train and caught a glimpse of events through an open window as you pass by, you've experienced a slice-of-life story. In Dissolving Echoes, Terra leaves the "window" open for a little bit longer, providing a larger glimpse into her character's world; but like that train passenger, leaves us with an ending that will be unique to every reader.

DISSOLVING ECHOES
Terra Luft

Pain could be medicated, but she ached deep down at the foundation of herself. Aches like this needed mind work and Zen states, which she couldn't achieve right now no matter how hard she fucking tried. Neither meditation nor medication touched this ache.

Miranda unfolded her legs and, tucking a stray curl that had escaped the mass atop her head, reached to the side table and switched on the radio. If she couldn't clear her mind, maybe filling it could distract her from her dark thoughts. And the ache.

She didn't have a diagnosis. Months of hell and still nothing but a battery of tests to rule out possibilities, leaving her like a pincushion. The waiting drove her crazy.

She felt herself shutting down. Inexplicably, systems and senses decayed, organs coming next, yet no mention of why or how long it would take. Their only answers: pills and time, like either gave her a fighting chance.

She didn't want her usual NPR; she needed music. The kind that would fill her with energy at every drumbeat. Bonus if she could sing along to lyrics that spoke to her soul. Even better, heavy guitar riffs. The kind that could carry her away like the old days when her brother's band played in the garage, her sitting on the old leather couch in the corner. Experiencing the sounds, not just listening.

Bangle charms dangled from her wrist, clanking amid the bottles, knocking two of them over with a muffled rattle of pills as she reached across the table. Dead soldiers, now lying between one of her sketchbooks and watercolor pencil sets. She ignored all of it. She had abandoned the artistic distraction weeks ago after it lost its effectiveness. Like everything else.

The rock station at the end of the dial didn't let her down. Familiar beats flowed out. She turned the volume up loud enough the neighbors would complain. Fuck them.

Leaning toward the tall speakers, head back, eyes closed, she let the guitar chords pound her ears, pushing everything else out of her mind. She sang along like a lead singer, not a karaoke wannabe alone in her apartment. She lost herself to the music in a way she never could while meditating, try though she did. Song after song sang back to her. Music had always been her escape.

"This is KYFM, Aurora's home for new rock, like this one from Dream Rage. Enjoy." The DJ's voice resonated welcome even while breaking her trance.

A new song—heavy on guitar, just what she needed.

The music mesmerized. Nothing she'd heard before, but familiar all the same. Moments of silence between the beats, spaced just far enough apart to build power into the music. When the lyrics started and that voice—dripping with emotion from the first notes—took the music beyond being a mere song, it spoke to her soul. Helpless but to listen while it transported her. Beyond her pain. Beyond her fears. It reminded her of childhood nights spent in the garage, hanging out with her homework just to be near... him.

She was fourteen—a child, her whole life ahead of her—when her brother first brought Ian home. Whenever he was around, she lingered, knowing one day they would be together. She felt the promise as a certainty, an inevitability she could take for granted like the sunshine and the schoolyard grass. It took two years for him to notice her and finally agree. She gifted him her virginity at sixteen and cemented their future together. Or so she thought.

The chorus brought her back from her memories.

I know you have arrived
Nothing more to say
But I love you.
Life for me
is lying with you
In the shadow of a tree.
Beyond the edges, reality
Branches grow unevenly
Much like you and me.
It's true I still love you
I'm not coming home
Please forgive me
Is this a dream

On the second repeat of the chorus, she recognized those words. They were her words, her lyrics, *her* creation. How…?

With the recognition came the knowing. Why everything about the music was familiar. Those long-ago garage days rushed back to her mind.

That thieving bastard.

She closed the hundredth page match from her Google search with an aggressive mouse click. It distracted her from the new ache in her side and hip. Research counted as meditation, didn't it? Consuming, like the welling anger barely kept beneath the surface. She didn't have much to go on. The DJ said the name of the band was *Dream Rage*, but nothing came up besides new-age crap about dream interpretations or bands with *Rage* in their name. She tried calling the station, but after multiple attempts and busy signals she'd given up.

"What are you obsessing about now?" Cami said, startling Miranda.

"God, you scared me." Miranda felt her heart pounding in her chest—a normal reaction for once.

"How long have you been sitting there?" Cami walked into the breakfast nook that had morphed into their office.

Miranda looked up from her laptop. She didn't know what time it was, so she couldn't honestly answer. "I just sat down a few minutes ago."

"Then why does it look like you haven't showered, and the coffee pot is full but cold?"

Damn. Cami could read a room. Miranda sensed writhing tendrils snake up her back, clawing, grasping. Pulling. Focused on not crying out in pain, she ignored Cami's question. She was close; she could feel it.

She did lament the coffee though.

"Seriously, Miranda, you need to eat. You know what the doctor said."

"I know how to take care of myself."

"I'm not so sure. You have that look in your eye when you start a project and I don't see you for days."

"What look? I don't have a look," she said, eyes now averted. It hurt that Cami didn't think Miranda could take care of herself. What did the doctors know anyway? Other than some fatigue and an abnormal blood test, she was in perfect health—or appeared to be. Her repressed pain screamed through her subconscious, willing to be acknowledged. She refused it.

"You say that, but this is the same way you were about that waterfall last summer."

The waterfall was both an artist's dream and an activist's nightmare. She'd had to save it from the despicable company upstream threatening to destroy it.

"You're wrong. This is nothing like that." A stray hair fell from Miranda's messy bun with the shake of her head. She tucked it behind her ear where it wouldn't tickle her cheek.

"You can't even stop whatever it is to look at me while we have a conversation."

Miranda looked up and met Cami's eyes. "Sorry, I didn't know trying to find where I can see a new band I heard on the radio was going to cause such a commotion."

The look of confusion that crossed Cami's face gave her much satisfaction. Miranda raised an eyebrow and silently challenged her to press the subject. It wasn't any of Cami's business anyway.

"A band? You let an entire pot of coffee go cold because you're researching a new band?"

"I was meditating this morning—doctor's orders and all—and heard it on the radio. They were amazing." She looked back to the computer to hide the half truth that Cami would have seen otherwise.

"You know that's a contradiction, right? If the radio was on, how were you meditating?"

"It wasn't working, so I turned on the radio, if you must know," she said, unable to keep the smile from her voice. Leave it to Cami to focus on the details.

"You're incorrigible. You know meditation does wonders for your blood pressure, but only if you actually do it." Spoken like the true yogi she was.

"You do you, and I'll do me," Miranda said, not looking up.

Cami laughed. The floorboard between the hallway and the kitchen creaked, signaling her departure.

Alone again, Miranda typed the name she'd been avoiding in the search engine: Ian Smithson. Her hand hovered over the enter key. Her insides clenched, protesting.

She'd forced herself to stop typing those letters together years ago and had been successful. Not because she had finally put him behind her, but because nothing came up. The search had become fruitless.

Seeing his name again, the cursor blinking at her, daring her to hit enter, unnerved her. Especially with the sound of his voice still echoing through her mind from this morning.

She already knew he had grown up in Denver, been the lead singer of her brother's band, and a constant in her adolescence before disappearing. She didn't know where he'd gone or why he'd abandoned their dreams—their plans—of a life together. Never a word. He'd just vanished. It haunted her and her relationships ever since. A fear of intimacy that led, she was sure, to her current undiagnosed death spiral. No one had said it yet, but she felt where her body was taking her. An unexplained end, a sudden stop. Abandonment, like Ian's, but this time of flesh.

Did her stolen words that he'd turned into lyrics have something to do with it? She wouldn't know unless she violated her rule not to search for him.

Enter.

A skeleton Wikipedia article, clearly written by a groupie fangirl, tied him to his new name, Ewan Danger—which explained why she hadn't been able to find him before. She followed the internet bread crumbs with growing apprehension and anticipation.

His band was indeed called *Dreem Raage*, employing a ridiculous misspelling that had thwarted her previous searches. They were touring the club scene with another band she'd never heard of. An amateur photograph next to the tour schedule showed his unmistakable half smile below eyes she remembered losing herself in. Age had changed him but not significantly.

Memories jostled at the edges of her mind, waiting to rush in and take her back to those long-ago days—their promises and potential.

She noted concert dates in cities she could drive to and plotted their reunion—one that ended with her serving him papers for copyright infringement. She could taste the vengeance.

It wasn't all she could taste. His lips on hers, a combination of mouthwash and cigarettes. His hands in her hair, on her body—

He had abandoned her and their life plans. Facts didn't change. She knew. Parallels and experience—hopeless and lost. Parallels echoing through time and circumstance.

The pressure spread up her back and entered her neck, stopping just short of her skull. Wrapping as if taking root. That was a new one. It fueled her affirmation. She refused to surrender.

If her mystery illness and the unknown future it held had given her anything, it was the conviction to act quickly. It would be a pleasure to derail his life like he'd done to hers so long ago.

Rachael Sparks is a writer and freelance illustrator who is married to a mechanical engineer who keeps her firmly grounded in the logical while she explores the whimsical with her art and writing. She has two girls and two boys who remind her that play and imagination are essential, especially as an adult. A jack of all trades, her artwork encompasses just about any medium you can imagine. She has been printed in the Warp and Weave anthology journal and is currently working on a dystopian cyberpunk trilogy, "Dragon of Heaven - Angel of Earth." See her latest artwork and short stories at www.patreon.com/rachaeljsparks.

About this story, Rachael says: "I wrote this story one night while staying up with the baby for hours, listening to Ray Bradbury to pass the time. It came to me all at once in a sort of daydream, and my imagination just took over. Because I wanted to retain a sense of the dream-like qualities of this piece, I had to resist explaining away too much. By the time I was done, it reminded me of the first time I had seen Fantasia. I loved the way those artists took an emotion and gave it a world to stretch its wings in!"

This is one of those stories that encourages the reader to find someone else to read it aloud so they can close their eyes and simply immerse themselves in the imagery. If you must read it with your eyes open, don't rush through it. Take your time, and let your senses carry you along.

BLACK AND GOLD
Rachael J. Sparks

My feet beat the earth as I ran through the woods, feverish and out of breath. Nothing could stand in my way as I ran from death. Or toward it. Either way, I could not turn from the path. Was this moment even real?

Animals of every kind filled the woods behind me, but not the friendly creatures from my childhood. These jagged shadows charged among the undergrowth, barreling toward me in a rush. Bears and deer and foxes and skunks and birds of every size and insects and snakes and rabbits and mice and badgers. Shadows of my former friends, mindless and stampeding. They pushed me toward death, threatening to rend me limb from limb.

Ahead, a yawning pit opened in the forest floor like a gaping wound in the flesh of the earth. No light penetrated the rip. It was a hungry maw destined only to swallow, always swallow. When the bees had vanished ages ago, many animals had starved to death. The chasm was a materialization of the aching that had taken over our forest.

I stopped just short of the edge, my wild heart pounding against its cage. Glancing over my shoulder, mad beasts poured over the horizon. Studying the chasm, there was no escape. It stretched for miles in either direction. I turned to face the animals again. Somehow, they had flashed ahead and were right on top of me. I threw my arms in a cross before my face, ready for impact.

But the animals paid me no mind. They threw themselves into the night of that void behind me and tumbled away into space without hesitation. Creatures great and small, falling to embrace the eternal dark. A cold chill flashed across my skin, and suddenly I knew there really was no bottom, for not one sound escaped the canyon as they fell. Instead of death cries, a deep silence fell.

Rank upon rank of creatures brushed past me, quite close now as their numbers increased, threatening to take me with them in their inconceivable hunger for that blackness. Fighting against the press of bodies, I knew I had to escape. I glanced up and around. Perhaps the trees could offer me refuge.

I jumped, clawing at the gnarled trunk of a tall pine, fighting against gravity. Moss and sap ground into deep scratches along my arms as I slid back down again and again. I couldn't reach even the lowest branch.

I spied a large black bird winging my way. Not knowing what else to do, I leaped for the bird and caught him by the foot. His momentum carried me off my feet and into the air. I pulled him close and in a moment... ate him mid-flight.

A terrible sickness and aching filled my belly and spread through the rest of me. Curling into a ball as I fell, black feathers sprouted across my face, chest, and back. Thin bony plates of ebony armor covered the skin of my still-human body. Sharp talons tipped my fingers and toes. A long feathered tail twitched in the airstream behind me.

How much of me was bird and how much of my original

body remained? I couldn't tell. Enormous black wings sprouted from my back, ripping through my shirt like paper. The wings immediately started pumping, instinctively flapping hard to bear me up again. I narrowly missed the yawning chasm and flew on, leaving the nightmare behind.

The ground fell away fast, and I pressed onward. A massive dark mountain crouched against the skyline. It drew me toward it. I hoped to find some answers about what sickness had been eating my forest. As I got closer, a deep rumble coalesced from the mountain. A premonition raced across my skin like an army of spiders. I could do nothing to stop what would happen next.

Another rumble and the mountain's heart exploded in a gush of flame and dark clouds erased the horizon. A wave of black soot painted the forest. Fire and lava poured down in all directions, the brightest shade of red I had ever seen. Molten rubies stood out against the darkness like the glittering blood of ancient stars.

Trees erupted into flames, the bright tongues eating away at the place I called home. The few animals that had escaped the madness of the chasm were now taken by the heat of the inferno. An anguished cry ripped through me at the sight of it. I could not land, could not save them. I flew in helpless circles, screaming like a forlorn eagle. It was over in an instant, my family destroyed before my very eyes. I could not bring myself to believe it.

All lay in darkness now: the trees, the plants, the ground, the sky. I whirled around, surveying a land I had known as intimately as my own body. Trees stuck up at odd angles, charred to their cores. They jutted across the barren landscape like so many bones in a burned carcass.

Heart aching, I reached out with my mind, searching across my beloved valley. Searching for... I don't know what. Some sign of hope, maybe. A vacant stillness filled the land, and I could scarcely breathe for fear of shattering the fragile remains of this place. My eye caught movement, sending my heart fluttering in surprise. I flew down, carefully landing among the wreckage. There, in the tendrils of smoke and ash, I spied a tiny bird. A puff ball, really. It was utterly black, like everything else in this place.

I held out my hands, and the thing hopped lightly onto my fingers. I caressed the fluffy chick and was astonished to see the black wipe off at my touch. The tiny bird was a brilliant and shining gold underneath. I carefully cleaned the rest of him off, going slow, taking my time lest I disturb this small wonder. His coat shone like a living treasure. The sight of it filled my eyes with tears, and my heart beat steady and strong. I knew what I had to do.

Lifting the creature to eye level, I silently thanked it for its gift and swallowed the tiny bird whole.

A violent shudder passed through me, and my wings shook back with a snap, all melancholy gone from me in an instant. Straightening in resolve, I looked to the mountain that had stolen my home with a single sweep of its fiery, unforgiving arms. I sprang with a mighty leap to the skies. The gold of the tiny creature worked its way through my veins, washing me in a cold vibrancy like mint and spring water.

My wings lengthened, growing impossibly long and thin. The dark feathers lightened to a shimmering silver. Tiny beads of icy water formed along the blade of my wings. A fine mist fell from my feathers, and I sailed out over the valley, watering the forest with my cool, soothing rain.

Everywhere the water touched was cleansed to its core. The gentle voice of the pouring water quieted the phantom screams of the dead where they echoed brokenly in my heart. The charred wasteland was washed deep in its soul. A great muddy river filled what had once been the canyon of shadows, covering the place where my animals had fallen like the fresh dirt of a grave.

When my work was finally done, the place seemed less empty. It seemed... simply bare, like a stone washed by the river. Brushing my face, my hand came away wet with grateful tears. A deep cleansing sadness took me. Soon, all would be well.

My moment had come.

I flew as high as my wings would carry me, beating hard to escape the cloud of ash brought on by the mountain's explosion. Reaching the pure light of the sun, I let its rays fill me. I took in as much light as I could possibly take, and then I soaked in even more. My body thrummed with the energy of light. Folding my wings, I gave myself to gravity.

I fell toward the very heart of the forest. At the center of a small clearing lay a large flat rock like a wide table. The impact of body and stone was absolute, more lasting and real than the bonds of birth and death. My body was now totally devoted to the earth. From the place where I broke her open with my own flesh and blood, a crystal spring slid out upon the ground. The water bubbled up bright and merry as a newborn babe. It clattered over stone and root, spreading every which way until the streams touched every part of the valley.

And everywhere the water passed, new life began to push through the wet ash. Tender shoots of grass grew, yellow-green and delicate but also impossibly strong. Better still, flowers sprouted in every color and shape imaginable, cheering the land. But best of all was the return of the bees. The scions of the earth, guardians to all living things. Nothing could survive without them, and their appearance allowed my spirit to rest once and for all, knowing my forest would be saved.

They were the secret keepers. They would hold my story in the glistening halls of their geometric cathedrals.

In black and gold, my spirit would live on forever.

Justin Matthews is a stay at home dad who turned to writing as an alternative to banging his head against the wall. Since he learned to read, he devours books and gleans inspiration from multiple genres—from fantasy to crime to horror to even a few YA gems that he reads "to make sure they are okay for the kids." He finally decided the stories cluttering his mind needed to be put to paper and either given to the public or burned quietly in a back room. Check out his wild ramblings and "Stay at Home Dad" stories at catharsisofbogue.com.

About this story, Justin says: "'Death with a Vengeance' was the result of a disturbing dream that I had—one about waking up dead. It became an exploration of my fear of drunk drivers and what it would feel like to not only drive drunk, but actually kill someone as a result, and then be haunted by the memory. The story went from a wild mess to an actual horror story thanks to some great editors and readers. Of course, ghosts still don't exist, except in my head."

This story taps into guilt at the deepest level—and gives a whole new meaning to the phrase "what goes around, comes around."

Death with a Vengeance
Justin C. Matthews

Death and disinfectant filled my nostrils as blackness receded and bright fluorescent lights assaulted my eyes. I heard water dripping nearby. I turned my head and saw stainless-steel tables, one topped with a human shape covered with a sheet. *Where am I?* It looked like the morgue on CSI. *Why can't I feel my arms or legs?*

I sat up and didn't feel the familiar weight of my body. I turned to get off the table, but somehow spun too fast, fell toward the floor, but then fell upward and floated toward the ceiling. I looked down and saw *me*, lying on an autopsy table, broken and battered.

I stifled a scream, staring at my blood-matted hair and jagged shards of bone showing white through lacerated skin. Holy crap, I was a spirit. A disembodied ghost. I... I was *dead!*

I jerked as the door opened. An old man with horn-rimmed glasses entered and approached what was left of me. He took a clipboard from under his arm and fished in the pocket of his lab coat. He retrieved a cheap ballpoint pen and scribbled on a form. He scratched the stubble on his chin, donned a pair of thin surgical gloves, and let out a deep sigh. He turned on the morgue's dictation machine and began his task: my autopsy.

"Poor schmuck," he mumbled, as he used a large pair of shears to cut off my torn and bloody clothes. I began to tremble and shrank back to a corner of the ceiling as the coroner made the first line of the Y incision. *What happened to me? How did this happen? Why am I hearing strange laughter in my head?*

As I watched the coroner go about his work, I concentrated, trying to remember all of the events that led to this. Memories flashed, tumbling over each other in their bids to be seen. I replayed them slower and slower until they made sense.

———

"Fine, Mara, whatever you want," I said to my wife when she told me she was leaving for good.

"It's not like you listen to me. Jason does. He is better than you at so many things it's not funny. You can't hope to compare," she said.

"Fine, Mara, whatever you want," I repeated, draining the glass and reaching for the Jack Daniel's bottle. "I'm not fighting for you anymore. Take your boy toy and your crap and go. And don't come crawling back in a week when he's had enough of your BS and dumps you on the curb. I'm done and he will be too."

"You pathetic, drunk jerk. Go ahead, have another. Why are you even bothering with a glass? Swig it out of the bottle, you lush. No one cares about you. You have no friends, no family, no one. Especially not me. You're such a pathetic loser."

"Just get the hell out," I said quietly. She picked up her bag and left for good this time, slamming the door on the way out. I poured another drink.

I didn't want to be alone, but I couldn't stand to be with her, either. I didn't care anymore, not about her, or me, or life in general. I had to get away. Jack was the only friend I could count on now. Somewhere in the Old No. 7 label lay the answers to all of my problems. "It's me and you now, Mr. Daniel." I saluted the bottle with my glass and drained the contents.

The next day was bleak. She was still everywhere. Her broken hairbrush in the bathroom trash, the smell of her on what was once our bed, the feel of her in the kitchen she had designed. It was only a week to my birthday, and I'd be celebrating without her for the first time in eight years. I'd show her. I didn't need a drink, and I didn't need her.

I spent most of the day in my safe spot—Toby, the stained recliner I'd owned since college—napping off my hangover and wallowing in memories and self-pity. I'd show her.

The clock on the wall ticked away the hours until well after the sun had gone down. "Ha, I win," I said finally. "Made it all day without a drop of alcohol." I'd earned a drink. I went to the cupboard where I kept my supply of Jack. Empty save a note from *her*. It read, *Jason and I will enjoy every drop you can't have.* She'd left a kissy mark in the red lipstick she knew I loved at the bottom. Damn her.

It was only 10:00 p.m. I grabbed my keys, a jacket, and headed out into the frigid January night. I drove *Betty*, my rusty Buick Skylark, to a local dive bar called Nick's.

I pulled into a parking space a few feet from Nick's welcoming pink neon sign and walked through the door that promised solace.

After hanging my coat by the door, I threaded my way through the crowd of locals and habitual drunks. I claimed one of the well-worn stools near the end of the bar. The bartender came over and asked, "What'll it be?"

"Whiskey, double, neat. Jack if you please." I laid my Visa on the bar. "Start a tab, brother."

He smiled and took my card, turning to retrieve a tumbler and a half-full bottle. He poured with a flourish. I thanked him and picked up the glass, staring into the amber liquid for a moment before tossing it back. "Bless you," I said to the glass as the familiar fire began to build in my belly and fill the void inside.

The bartender smiled, maybe he thought I was talking to him. "Another?" he asked.

I nodded and set down the glass.

He poured again. "Woman troubles, I'm guessing."

"What else?"

He smiled again.

I got the feeling he'd seen this before.

"Be right back to top you off," he said and went to fill another order.

Over the next couple of hours, alcohol and questions filled me. Was there something more that I could have done with Mara, to keep her? Did she want to try for me? Did I even want her anymore? *Why am I even bothering? Why is the guy at the end of the bar singing at the top of his lungs? Maybe I should have another drink.* Or water. Water would be a good idea. Jack would be better. *I should slow down before they stop serving me. What is with all of this crap my life has become?*

By the time the bartender shouted for last call, I'd finished off the bottle of Jack and a few beers to boot. I was ready to go. I stood to leave, grabbed the bar for support, and waited for my head to catch up with the rest of me. I was drunk. Tomorrow I would remember why I had been drinking. Jack got me through tonight, and he'd be there tomorrow. I did know one thing: I needed to walk home.

I staggered to the door and shrugged into what looked like my coat. I steadied myself against the doorframe for a moment and walked out into the January night.

I made it ten feet out the door before I tripped and fell to the freezing cement. The cold seeped through my coat as I lay there. It felt good for a few minutes, even when Nick's other patrons walked around me, shaking their heads in disgust. I needed to get warm. I needed to get home. I got to my feet and saw my car. I would be okay, I just needed some heat. No driving, just heat.

I stumbled to the driver's side and pulled out my keys, only dropping them twice before I got the door open. The odor of stale French fries and old pizza wafted from the interior as I sat down heavily in the driver's seat. I inhaled the familiar smells, trying to keep from adding vomit to the dirty beige upholstery. I started the car and turned on the heat.

"Betty, Betty, Betty, Betty, warm me up, baby," I said, waiting for the vents to blow warm. I should clean her up. Maybe trade her in for something made this decade. Betty II. *Good, heat's finally coming. All will be well.* I got warm and started to get sleepy. I needed to get home. *I feel better now. Hey, I could drive. Betty knows the way.*

I shifted into reverse and started to back out into the street. "C'mon, Betty, let's get home," I said. "Shift into drive, go slow, we can do this." We started down the street, slow at first, and then faster. "We *can* do this."

I turned up the radio and concentrated on the road. I passed cars, honking at the slow ones that barely seemed to move. I squealed my tires around corners. Who put that statue in the middle of the street?

I ran straight into it, breaking it free and flipping it up onto my windshield and then over the car. My heart skipped a beat and I slammed on the brakes, instantly sober for a second. "Oh hell," I said. "What just happened?" I already knew. That wasn't a statue.

I began to tremble. The car grew smaller. I couldn't get enough air. My chest felt clamped shut. I pushed the gearshift into park and clawed at the door handle. I had to get air. The door opened and I leaned out, sucking in the cold morning, trying to calm down. I looked behind the car, at the still figure lying in the road. *Oh dear Lord, please let them not be dead. Please, please, please.*

I got out of the car and stumbled to the person in the street. It was a man. *Don't touch, just look for breathing.* I held my own breath as I looked for telltale steam coming from his mouth. *Is that steam there? Did his chest just rise or am I imagining it?* A pool of blood started to grow underneath the man. *He has to be dead, he has to be.*

"What have I done?" I yelled into the night. This was serious trouble. I killed a person. I shouldn't have been driving. "But he just jumped out in front of me," I muttered, and then words began tumbling over themselves. "I was driving just fine. It wasn't my fault. I killed a man driving drunk. I'm going to jail. I don't want to go to jail. I can't go to jail. I'll be there for years. What am I going to do?"

I began to gulp air, trying to think clearly through my whiskey haze. What had I done? I looked around and didn't see anyone else. I made my decision. I turned and staggered back to the open door of my car. I fell into the seat, slammed the door, shifted to "D" and stomped on the gas.

Tires squealed; Betty shot forward. Manslaughter. Driving under the influence. Leaving the scene of an accident. It was only a life sentence if I got caught.

I made it the remaining three blocks home without incident.

I pulled Betty into the garage, hoping none of my neighbors had seen me, the dent in the hood, or the cracked windshield. I reached up and pushed the button on the visor, closing the overhead door. "Sorry, Betty, you're staying here until this has blown over," I muttered, closing my eyes as I tried to figure out what to do next, and slowly faded into unconsciousness.

I woke up later, shivering in the cold driver's seat, key still in the ignition, radio still playing. At least I had shut the motor off. Sunlight was just beginning to stream through the lone window in the garage. I squinted at the light reflecting off of dust motes and the huge crack in Betty's windshield. *Damn. It really happened. I hit someone last night.* I felt nauseous. I started to shake. I still had enough of Nick's whiskey in me to be relieved they hadn't found me yet. I moaned. *A man—I'd hit and killed a man.*

I staggered into the house, aiming toward the stairway and my bedroom. I climbed the stairs, undressing and dropping clothes with each step. Once in my room, I tumbled into the unmade bed, and seconds later passed out again.

I didn't move until late in the afternoon when the sun shone through my bedroom window and onto my face. I felt terrible. My head throbbed, like tiny men with sledgehammers were beating on the inside of my skull. I made my way to the bathroom and looked at myself in the mirror. My eyes were beyond bloodshot, they looked… haunted.

I put on the robe I'd left crumpled on the floor and started to brush the taste of the bar out of my mouth. I looked into the mirror again and hated what I saw. "You bastard," I yelled and punched the mirror, leaving my knuckles bleeding and a myriad of accusing faces staring back at me. I had checked. He wasn't breathing, was he? He was bleeding. He was dead. No one saw me, did they? *How am I going to live with myself? If they catch me, how am I going to deal with jail? Is it as bad as the movies make it out to be?*

I picked up the cup next to the sink and filled it with water. I needed some aspirin. I tried to swallow a sip, and my stomach protested. I needed to find something to eat first. I headed downstairs.

The empty Jack Daniel's bottle sat accusingly on the table when I entered the kitchen. "No!" I yelled at it, swinging and knocking it to the floor. This was the last bottle I had when Mara left. Still, I needed food. I opened cupboards at random, looking for something that didn't make me want to vomit. The only thing remotely edible was some cold cereal that had lived in the pantry for years. At least the milk in the refrigerator wasn't expired. *Thanks for that, Mara. You always did take care of me. How am I going to take care of myself now? I screwed up the first day.* I poured a bowl of cereal and headed to the living room. Toby welcomed me like the old friend he was and reclined obligingly as I picked up the remote. Pretend everything's fine; eventually, it might be.

I started eating the stale cereal as I turned on the TV and flipped channels until I found a rerun of *The Munsters*. Classic comedy would help. I ate and tried to laugh at the corny jokes, until a commercial for the news came on. "And coming up on 2 News at Six, how a pet parrot saved his owner's life by calling 911. And police are looking for help in finding the person responsible for a fatal hit-and-run last night. We'll see you at six."

My jaw dropped and the spoon froze halfway to my mouth. My hunger evaporated, breath catching in my lungs. I began to quiver. My heart pounded in my chest. I had killed someone. I had left him to die. I was a killer.

Still staring at the television in shock, my spoon lowered slowly as thousands of fleeting thoughts crashed through my numbed brain. *What should I do? How am I going to make this go away? Should I just turn myself in?*

I didn't move for several moments. The phone rang and I jumped, spilling most of my cereal. It rang again. "Damn!" I struggled to get out of Toby and the dripping milk mess. Another ring. My heart tried to beat out of my chest. *I need to get this milk cleaned up, the answering machine will get the phone.*

As I got a dish towel from the kitchen, the phone continued to ring. And ring. Where the hell was the answering machine? Did freaking Mara take that too? "Stop it," I yelled. Another ring. Finally, I reached for it.

I picked up the receiver and hoarsely whispered, "Hello?"

No answer.

"Hello?" A recorded message began to play, offering me a limited time discount on vinyl siding. "Damn computer, I'm on the Do Not Call list!" I slammed down the receiver.

I sighed deeply, and the phone rang again.

"Damn telemarketers."

I answered, but before I could yell "I don't need any of your crap!" I was stopped short by a mournful wail on the other end.

"Hello?"

Silence.

"H—hello? Who is this? Hello? Hello?"

No answer, save the sound of distant breathing.

I slammed the phone back onto the cradle. Damn prank callers.

I half-heartedly looked back to the cereal bowl in my hand

and the puddle of milk in Toby, not to mention what was on me. I grimaced at the mess.

The phone rang for a third time.

I snatched up the receiver, shouting, "Leave me the hell alone!"

A menacing laugh greeted me.

My mouth went dry. "Who is this?"

More laughing. Finally, a ghostly echo said, "Good. You should fear me."

"Wha—"

"Yooooooouuuuuuu killllllled meeeee!"

I let out a scream and dropped the phone and the cereal bowl to the floor. I ran upstairs to my bedroom.

Under the safety of my blankets, I could still hear the voice, the accusation, "You killed me!" Over and over again. At some point, I passed out. Thankfully, when I came to later that evening, all was quiet. I made my way to the bathroom and refused to look at myself in the shattered mirror. I could hear the voice in my head and it wouldn't leave. I needed to go out and get some air. I changed out of my clothes, ripe with the stench of spoiled milk, and went downstairs.

I saw the mess I'd left. I needed to go outside, but I had to clean this up first. I turned off the television and hung up the phone before wiping up the spilled cereal and sweeping up the broken bowl.

This wasn't helping. All I kept thinking about was how I needed to tell someone. But who could I tell? It couldn't be the police. I couldn't just go up to a random person and say, "Hey, guess what? I killed somebody with my car last night." The police were looking for me. The thought had me hoping they would just break down my door and get it over with.

The phone rang.

I froze. I wasn't going to answer.

It continued to ring.

Ten times.

Eleven.

Twelve.

"Okay, okay," I shouted and picked up on the thirteenth ring.

Please let it be another telemarketer. "Hello?"

"Murderer. Bastard. YOU KILLED ME!" The voice lowered to a menacing growl. "I will be with you. Your death awaits. Your soul is stained. Fear my wrath." The line went dead.

My hand couldn't hold the receiver steady. It took both hands to get it hung up again. Guilt overcame me, and bile rose in my throat. The voice was in my head, repeating *murderer* over and over again. My stomach lurched. I cursed and ran toward the sink, vomiting out what little I had in my belly.

I wiped my face and headed to the front door. I looked out of the small window. It was dark. I could go outside and get some air, get away from the phone. I turned the lock and then the knob. The door wouldn't open. I tugged with all of my strength, but it wouldn't budge.

I ran to the garage door, not wanting to see my car, but needing to get out. It wouldn't open either. *I'm trapped. I'm trapped in my home with nothing but that damn voice.*

The phone rang again. I didn't answer—instead, I tore the cord out of the wall and threw the infernal machine across the room. Even though the phone sat in broken pile, I could still hear the voice, now coming from everywhere, accusing me over and over.

"Leave me alone!" I screamed at the walls. "Leave me the hell alone! Let me alone, damn you!"

Three days passed in much the same manner as the first. The voice kept coming. I tried several times to sleep in Toby, but the voice would reach an unbearable volume, shouting, "FAILURE. WORTHLESS DRUNK. KILLER." I couldn't sleep. I couldn't hear anything beyond the voice. I was too scared to eat. I couldn't escape, I couldn't shut out the voice.

By sunset of the fourth day, I was exhausted and starving. I huddled on the floor—not even Toby could give me solace. I was muttering to myself, mimicking the voice and laughing after every word, "Me. Drunk. Killer."

Finally, I stumbled toward the stairs and my bed. I needed sleep. I climbed the stairs on my hands and knees until I reached the top, where I collapsed. I managed to drag myself to my bed and drop into it.

The voice came again, this time in a booming thunderclap. "MURDERER, I COME FOR YOU."

A long high-pitched scream erupted from my throat. I turned toward the door as it flung itself open. Through the door, accompanied by an icy wind, floated the spectral figure of the man I'd killed.

Silence filled the room. He smiled wickedly and raised an ephemeral finger at me. I scrambled off of the bed, backing away from the ghost.

I backed into the wall and started sliding toward the corner. The ghost cackled and threw his arms wide. What had been a solid wall was now empty space, and I fell backward through it.

I dropped the twenty feet to the ground, screaming until I hit. Sharp pains accompanied snapping noises in my chest and arm. A few ribs had broken for sure, along with my left arm. I groaned in agony and stood. At least my legs still worked.

Gritting my teeth and cradling my broken arm, I ran from my house into the surrounding darkness. Every time I looked over my shoulder, all I could see was the ghost, shadowing my every step.

I broke through some bushes and stumbled onto an unlit street, stifling a scream as another jolt shot through my arm and ribs. I recognized the street. Ghostly tatters of yellow police tape materialized, hanging from trees lining the road.

I stopped and stared at the asphalt. As I looked, an irregular dark stain appeared. Blood. This was the place where I had killed. I fell to my knees as the shade caught up with me. Vomit rose in my throat.

"Hmm, this looks familiar," he shrieked and floated toward me.

I forced myself to stand. *Keep running.* I had to get to a hospital. I could confess and end this madness. I ran again, darting around cars and trash cans, cutting through yards until I came to the middle of another street lit by a few dim lights. *Which way to the hospital?*

As I turned left, the voice that had harassed me for days went silent. Just down the block, tires squealed as a pair of headlights streaked around the corner. I froze in the bright white beams. The engine revved, the car wove back and forth; the driver was drunk. Time slowed, an instant seemed an eternity, but I couldn't move. I was going to die.

I screamed as the steel bumper crashed into my legs, snapping them both. I flew over the hood, my shoulder going through the windshield before I rolled up and over the roof, and finally slammed to the cold pavement. My whole body was on fire. Pain was the only thing I knew.

As my eyes dimmed, I saw the driver's door open. A man got out, stumbling toward me. He babbled and cried. I exhaled for the last time, crushed and bleeding on the street. Killed by a drunk driver.

I floated in the morgue, watching the conclusion of my own autopsy.

A calm voice said, "Hello, Murderer."

I whirled about to see the spirit that had chased me.

"What more do you want?" I asked. "I'm dead, you should be satisfied."

The ghost rested a hand on my shoulder. "You are not finished."

"What?"

"The only way to move on is to complete the cycle. I killed while driving drunk. You killed me while driving drunk. I led you to your death from a drunk driver. I can now move on. And you—"

He pointed to a spectral phone that appeared on the wall. I was pulled to it as he dialed a number and handed me the receiver. "It's your turn for justice."

The phone rang and a tense, male voice answered, "Hello?"

I couldn't speak.

"Hello," he said again.

I could only breathe into the receiver.

"Damn prank callers," he said and hung up.

"Was that the guy who hit me?" I asked.

The spirit nodded.

I was to torment this poor soul in the manner I was tormented. I was to ensure the man would be dealt his death in the same way I was.

"I can't do it." I recoiled and let go of the phone.

The phantom smiled and began to fade as he called out to me, "You must. It's the only way to end the anguish and reach the other side."

I didn't want to torture this guy. Why didn't he deserve a break? I didn't want to cause trouble, I just wanted to be left alone. It had just been an accident, hadn't it?

I looked down again as the coroner pulled a white sheet over my corpse, covering my face. Why didn't I get a break? Why was my body lying there atop a stainless-steel slab and not at home, getting drunk? Anguish set in as I pictured what should have been my future. I would have changed. Life would have gotten better. I would have gotten over Mara. Got a new car. Stopped drinking. Helped others. All of that and more was gone forever.

Rage filled me then. Rage at myself for being so stupid in so many ways. Rage at losing my wife. Rage at my drunken driving. Rage at the world for not helping me, even if I hadn't asked. Rage at the man who had taken my life by making the same stupid mistake I did.

A desire for vengeance filled me to bursting. I didn't want to be stuck in this world as a wraith. I wanted to move on. I *needed* to move on.

With purpose, I returned to the ethereal telephone and dialed the only number I knew. My victim answered.

I laughed in anticipation of justice, of revenge.

"He—hello," the man said.

"Hello, Murderer. You killed me. This is just beginning," I whispered, and hung up the phone.

J.T. Moore writes magic with diversity because everyone deserves to be the main character. She wanted to see more POC protagonists in speculative fiction, so she decided to write them herself. Her mystic lineage shows itself through the silver streak in her hair. She looks for wonder in the world and knows she can always find it in the pages of a good book. J.T. celebrated the completion of the Ray Bradbury Challenge, 52 Stories in 52 weeks, with a loud scream, wine, and the conviction that she can pursue her dream. She is an active member of the League of Utah Writers Speculative Fiction Chapter and the Utah Horror Writers Association. You can find her on Twitter @jtmoore487 and on her website: jtmoorewrites.wordpress.com.

About this story, J.T. says: "This story began as part of a '52 stories in 52 weeks' challenge, and turned into a day in the life of someone who didn't fit in. You can't be serious all the time, and I wanted to have fun with this tale, to add a little weird to balance out the grit. To ask; how does it feel when you realize you are finally where you need to be? The idea stuck with me and I'm still wondering what adventures lie in his future."

A fun thing about urban fantasy is that almost anything goes—and this story certainly tests that "rule" to the limit!

MY NAME IS JOHN
J.T. Moore

I grabbed the back of his neck between my jaws and crushed, cleaving his head from his undead body, my half-form giving me the extra bulk needed for the task without ripping through my purposely baggy clothes.

One less vamp to worry about.

The drunk girl he'd been feeding on was slumped against the wall, dazed. I spat out as much of the putrid blood and flesh as I could, gagging at the smell. I've always hated that sickly sweet rotted-meat stench. I took a few extra minutes behind a dumpster to resume my human form before I went back to the young woman. After calling a cab, I dug through her purse to find her address to give to the driver. I looked around, pretending I had a right to be doing what I was doing. It would be just my luck to save this woman's life, then get arrested for mugging her just because my skin was a darker shade of tan.

She became more lucid as we waited for the taxi.

"Eat some protein, in whatever form you take it, with a glass of orange juice when you get home. That will help get your energy back," I told her.

"What happened?" she asked.

I thought for a minute about how to answer that question and drew a blank. Avoiding situations like this was what kept me off the supernatural radar, and that's the way I liked it. Finally giving up, I said, "I just saved you from getting all your blood sucked out by a vampire. You'll feel better after you eat." With that dazed look still in her eyes, she wouldn't remember what I said anyway.

I gave the cabby her address and instructed her to go straight home. At my own car, a black Mustang that had seen better days, I pulled out the bottle of Listerine that I always kept in the glove compartment and rinsed twice. The burn gave me a feeling of being clean, and the whiskey I was going to get next would take care of anything else.

Scorpion's Tail was the name of the bar. It was a dive, but the drinks were strong, and they let you drink in peace as long as you didn't cause trouble. The music was loud, the people louder. The bouncer was back at the door again after being conveniently lured away by the vamp's human decoy. Nothing he could have done anyway. I sat at the bar again, easier access to the bartender. Tables were full; they were not hurting for business.

The musky smell of wolf and something else I couldn't describe, almost feral, passed under my nose. Not what I needed tonight. I pulled out my phone. The best fuck-off ever invented. I'm a lone black wolf, disowned by my pack and cut off from my family and any potential mate. To them, I am not a real wolf. After one whiff of me, they would assume I was easy prey because I didn't smell like a typical predator. Many had died because of that assumption. They knew I was not from the local pack.

I wasn't from any pack. Not anymore. I'd been discarded long ago, like a piece of trash, for not being enough.

I downed my double shot of whiskey and felt the burn in my stomach, the taste of the vamp finally washed from my mouth. I turned and watched the wolf walk towards me. Dressed casually in jeans and a button-down shirt, he looked to be in his early thirties but could have been closer to seventy. Werewolves were ageless and dangerous. He ignored the admiring looks of the women as he sauntered over and sat on the stool next to me.

"I saw what you did to that vamp out back," he said. "I've been after him for days. Thanks for that." He must have caught the tangy scent of aggression mixed with surprise off my skin because he laughed. "No games." He held both hands in the air. "I don't have the time or the energy for bullshit. My pack has enough trouble with demons and other monsters terrorizing this city. We don't need any more complications."

"That's a change." I turned on my stool to face him. "So you came over here just to thank me?"

"Yes and no. I've heard about you, and I know some people you may enjoy meeting." He held out his hand. "I'm Ben. Come on over to our table. I'll pick up the tab, and you can meet the rest of my pack."

Walking to the table, I saw the oddest assortment of people ever assembled. They definitely did not look like my idea of a werewolf pack. Ben introduced me to all five people and gave a short bio for each of them. There was Tina, a nymph with tree allergies; Peter, a zombie with a heartbeat; Rayven, a witch who said her spells backward; Dean, a vampire who fed on other vamps; Colin, a clumsy elf; and our host, Ben, a cat/wolf shifter.

It was an AA meeting for supernaturals.

I fit right in.

"Hello, my name is John. I'm a vegetarian werewolf."

A chorus of voices answered. "Hello, John."

Sariah Horowitz graduated in archaeology but she thinks of herself as Archie Oogly's Ex (Archaeologist) because no one will pay her to play in the dirt, so she explores the world on digs, in books, and in her writing. While on her digs, she imagines fantastical situations that could happen with a little magic in the mundane world. She is a member of the League of Utah Writers. Dig up more of her writing at sariahhorowtz.com.

About this story, Sariah says: "All my inspiration starts with the question: what if? Such as, what if magical species had a problem with relationship or life in general? The other inspiration is making mundane situations magical. Swimming is the closest to flying I'll ever experience. The sensation of floating without harness or machine is amazing, yet fleeting. I began wondering what would a flying creature think about swimming. What if she had once been able to fly, but this is the only way she could fly now? How did she become wingless? How would she cope?"

While the possibility of waking up wingless is not something most of us can relate to, traumatic injury and the resulting changes in the course of one's life are not exclusive to the realm of the Fey.

WINGLESS
Sariah Horowitz

The swimsuit fit better without my wings. The turquoise violet color had complemented those appendages perfectly, but without the competition, the fabric seemed overbright, too gaudy. Hands on hips, I estimated how much my figure changed during my extended recovery. I seemed slimmer. So that was two positive things about being wingless, I supposed. My hands dropped to my sides. I tried to find another, but failed.

The scars on my back began to itch again. They felt longer, now that my back was exposed. The one-piece swimsuit, designed for a winged Fey, provided a long open back to accommodate all kinds of wings without misshaping the rest of the garment. But, of course, that was no longer an issue for me. To be honest, I didn't need any of my old clothes anymore. Without wings, what was I?

Certainly no longer a true Fey.

I went to the window. Through the blinds, the lush green of ivy-covered guest cottages lined the cobblestone paths of the spa grounds. I could see patrons walk past my window on their way to the dining hall or the pools. The Department paid for our stay, as I was injured on assignment. Tarry accepted without consulting me. I knew they were trying to help and I'd heard this place was highly rated, a relaxing retreat, but being here felt like banishment.

The spa was built near the sea and took advantage of natural hot springs. From what I'd seen, it was a nice place. This hide-away was built for the entire magical community with all entrances on ground level. I don't believe I'll ever be accus-tomed to doors being on ground level. Walking was my only way in and out of buildings now.

I swallowed the lump in my throat. For a brief second, I wished for Feyterra and its familiarity, but just as quickly dismissed the idea. I can't go home. Returning to Feyterra as a non-flying Fey would destroy what little self-confidence I had left. I couldn't imagine taking the mundane access route used for children and mutilated figures like me. The thought of my mother seeing me broken and useless would break my heart. No, going home wasn't an option.

Some guests passed the window. They wore long kimono robes in a variety of colors. It matched the Asian-themed motif of the spa. Fashion seemed easily interchangeable between realms. I had bought our robes in Kyoto during an assignment two years back, so Tarry and I ought to blend in nicely with the other guests. Tarry claimed his kimono made him look short. I was not a fan of the baggy clothing either, but at least I could walk around with my back completely covered and not draw unwanted attention.

My kimono lay on the top of my open bag beside the window. I held it up to the light. Orange and violet swirled together across the silken surface. Beautiful. My wings had been those colors. I would never again see those colors flash in the mirror, or worry if my clothes clashed, or hide them when we were undercover in the human realm.

I ran my finger down the blinds, closing them with a rattle

like playing cards. How could I adjust to losing part of me? I glared at the fabric in my hand. One snap of my fingers and the color would change to black or green or any other color I wanted, but my fingers stayed still. The healers said I needed to face my scars, physical and mental. Maybe this was my first step.

I sat on the bed, allowing the wall around my memories to fall.

Tarry and I were delegates, sent from the queen herself to report on happenings in magical communities in this district. The job, however, was a cover. To the magic community, we were Tarragon and Ardeth Frais-Vered de Magnolei, part of the Department of Magic and Human Affairs. Behind the facade, we were part of a group protecting human children from smugglers—code name Fairy Godparents.

Most Fey I knew dealt with romance, but our small undercover group handled more serious cases. Most of Tarry's and my job seemed to be ticking off the Veredan and other guilds who considered humans as nothing more than breeding stock. The downside to having powers and millennium-long lifespans meant lack of fertility. Add that to centuries of fighting with each other and all magical species had population problems. Solution: mutate human children to grow into the surrogate mothers of the next magical generation.

Humans have no magical genetics, but if exposed as infants, they mutate and become magical beings. This allowed them to produce a desired pure magic offspring. However, these mutations often resulted in horrible side effects, and children who didn't have the proper traits were often terminated. With the decline of humans willing to trade their children for spells or wealth, the demand for children was filled by smugglers. Buyers ranged from the elf clans to the vampire dynasties. Girls were preferred because they adapted easier, and smugglers would do anything to obtain them. Our last mission had been to prevent one of these harvests from happening.

I pressed my face into the cool silk of the kimono. The memory of that night played across my mind like a stranger's nightmare.

We were almost too late. Two kidnappers were about to take off with a baby when we arrived. Tarry tackled one, keeping him from using magic. The thief holding the baby slipped out a window and took flight. I followed.

Car headlights darted below, and phone wires threatened to entangle me.

I closed in.

I could use magic, but he still had the girl. I could miss and hit her.

Power tingled at my fingertips, and I threw an energy blast over his head. He dodged, but the force hitting the building pushed him off course. I closed the gap between us. He turned, smacking me with his wings as he blocked the girl from me. Frantic flaps steadied me. He rose higher above the buildings.

Kicking off a windowsill, I launched myself after him. In a few wing beats, I was yards above the buildings, feet away from the bastard. I double punched him in the shoulder, sending him reeling into a light post. I drew closer.

He slowed and faced me, hovering just beyond my reach. A sick smile spread across his lips, exposing mossy teeth. He held the baby out toward me. Winked. And released her into the night sky.

The screaming baby plummeted toward the street below.

His laughter rang in my ears as I dove. My wings tunneled against my back, causing me to rocket toward the pavement. The wind carried me and the baby's scream closer together. My fingers touched her clothes, and I grasped what I could. I pulled her to me. There was no time to pull out of the dive. At my speed, stopping was out of the question.

I rolled, putting my wings between us and the asphalt, and slid the entire length of the street. Tar and gravel peeled my skin away easily like rusted rakes. My nerves and voice screamed in agony. Then all went black.

Technically, the mission was a success. The two intruders were arrested, the ring busted, and the tiny baby girl safely returned home. Everyone told me what we accomplished was noble, and I knew they were right. But it was hard celebrating when my life consisted mainly of hospital beds and surgeries.

My fingers clenched. The success had cost me. My wings had protected me and the child from the street, but still almost killed me.

Wings are easily infected and shredding them across the asphalt destroyed them. By the time I was found, my shredded wings were infected. There had been only one solution.

Apparently, they botched the amputation and attaching fake wings would be pointless. I hoped to never meet the doctor who performed the amputation. I wouldn't be responsible for my actions. Margot, the head healer, explained to me the day I was awake enough to comprehend the news. The next day, a letter came from Feyterra thanking me for my service as a delegate but I was being replaced as a Fey representative. They didn't say it, but I knew the reason; I couldn't represent Fey as a wingless.

My life was now in limbo. I had no reason to stay in that realm and no reason to go back to Feyterra. The Godparents told me I was welcome, but I didn't see how I could be of any use. Chasing flying bad guys on foot was pointless. Hiding in an office was not me. Life looked bleak. I was alone in this.

I wiped the tears away with the back of my hand. My eyes still stung from nightly cries, and they would never ease up if I didn't get a grip.

I stood, pulling the kimono on, the cloth flashing in the vanity mirror across the room. I met my red eyes in the reflection. The woman in the mirror seemed to dare me to turn away like I did every time I saw my reflection. I had managed to avoid mirrors and window reflections for several days. I couldn't do it forever.

Now was as good a time as any to face my fears.
I turned slowly and let the robe fall partially off my shoulders. My back shone moon pale against the bright color of the garment. Even when my wings had been exposed, there hadn't been much of a chance for sunlight to reach the skin through the wing slits in my clothes. Now the smooth pink skin was marred by two angry red scars where the skin was pulled together over the shoulder blades. Even with the best plastic surgeon, they stood out like ugly knife gashes on my back.

The door opened, and I saw Tarry in the mirror. For a moment, he was the Tarry I remembered—full smile lighting his face as if waiting to tell a joke. He froze, the smile vanished, and his eyes looked past me to the mirror reflection of my back.

Despite the many reassurances that my being wingless didn't bother him, the look in his eyes said otherwise. My heart cracked, and I bit my lip to keep it from trembling. His eyes shifted to my face, his expression changing to concern.

I shrugged the robe over my shoulders. Turning my back to him, I picked up my brush and started after the tangles. "Trouble with our reservation?"

"No, the front desk was swamped. Looked like a shifter family reunion."

"Is the full moon this weekend?"

"Don't know. I didn't check." Tarry ran his hand through his disheveled black hair.

"Keep doing that and you'll look like you have dead grass for hair," I told him.

His smile didn't reach his eyes. "I'd need to be blond to pull that off."

"All right, then grass with squid ink spilled on it." I laughed, but the joke was weak. He was the wise guy and usually had a quick comeback. But he only looked more uneasy.

I pulled a hair elastic off the brush handle and tried wrapping it around my thick hair. In my agitation, I only succeeded in pulling a small clump of my hair out. "Ouch!" I slammed my fist on the vanity. The hair-tie skidded on to the floor.

Tarry picked it up. "Here, let me."

Unable to think of a reason to refuse, I stood silently as he ran the brush through my hair and worked the strands into a single braid.

"I asked at the front desk about pool hours," he said. "They're open late because of the nice weather."

"Thanks." I watched the reflection of him work my red locks together with ease. I envied his long fingers. In no time, a long braid hung down my back, and he wrapped the elastic around the end.

I expected him to walk away, but he stayed, hands resting

tentatively on my shoulders. Standing motionless, I enjoyed the light pressure. This was the closest we'd been in weeks. He always seemed to have an excuse to stay away, something about "not wanting to hurt me." I missed having him close.

"Ardeth."

"Yes?" I tried to meet his eyes in the mirror.

He stared intently at the vanity. "You're beautiful."

I wanted to believe him. Needed to believe him. But doubt crushed my thoughts. Having wings was everything to a Fey. Everything to me. Losing my wings was like losing a piece of my identity. I stood out like a spotless ladybug.

I told myself I didn't care about my looks if Tarry was at my side. All I wanted was my joking husband back. The Fey who would make everything all right with his lighthearted manner, silly quips, and easy smile. But I didn't have him. He couldn't even look at me. How could I be beautiful if he couldn't even look at me?

His lying hurt more than the asphalt.

I pulled away. "I better hurry if I want the pool to myself. I want to go while everyone's at dinner."

He didn't stop me. Didn't even call out to wait for him.

I slammed the door and stormed away.

Why was he acting like this? One moment he called me beautiful but the next won't spend any time with me. I must be more repulsive than I thought.

Paving stones in soft grays and moss green showed the way to the pools. The flow of traffic headed for the main hall. A flow of patrons of a variety of skin tones, hair colors, and vibrantly colorful robes. I had to travel against the current. Even with my back covered, I felt exposed. The other Fey flew between buildings and those who walked let their silken appendages drape behind them like glorious capes.

No one stared outright, but I felt their eyes on me long after I passed. They had to guess my race and wonder why I didn't flash my wings like the others. I had to check my thinking. This was stupid. Why would they care about my back? But maybe they heard about it. I was a diplomat. What if someone recognized me?

Foolish, I chided myself. This kind of thinking was ridiculous and unproductive. Still, I refused to meet anyone's gaze. Finally, I reached the entrance to the pools. Slipping through the gap in the hedge, I closed the gate firmly behind me.

Hot springs welled up in crater-shaped pools. Rising steam created a comfortable, enchanting haze. I found stacks of towels beside each pool, a good thing since I forgot to bring my own. In the center of the yard stretched a long rectangular pool. The smooth glass surface reflected the mountains adjacent the resort. Along the different levels of rock stood tall stalks of bamboo and bushes of fragrant flowers blooming year-round. Even the smell of the sulfur was toned down to a light egg scent. The elves had outdone themselves.

I draped my kimono over a bamboo rack beside the gate. Ignoring the inviting warmth of the smaller pools, I went to the large rectangular one. I came to swim. I stood at the edge, wondering why I hesitated. My insides clenched as I realized—I usually had to choose to let my wings drag behind me or collapse them against my back.

I took a deep breath and dove in before the pain prevented me from swimming at all.

The shock stole my breath and made me smile. Cold water has always been my favorite.

The silence of the depths thundered comfortably in my ears. I dove deeper into the water's embrace until I touched the bottom.

I crouched, then rocketed back to the surface. Water peeled away my hot emotions and gave me only peace.

Gone was the humiliation of being wingless. Gone was the restraint of the land.

I flew again.

My head broke the surface. The air tasted fresher after my submersion. Swimming had always been my escape. Growing up, the other Fey thought I was crazy for going to the lake to swim. It was cold and big, and none of the other children wanted to go with me. None except Tarry. He claimed he was protecting me from monsters lurking in the deep.

We all knew there were no monsters in the water, but I hadn't questioned him. Not until we were teens did he find courage enough to tell me he came because he liked me. He didn't enjoy water as much as I did. Now that I thought about it, the only time he had been completely submerged was when he slipped on a rock in the lake and pulled me under with him.

Remembering him coming up dripping and blushing like a sunset made me laugh. He had always been there for me. According to the healers, he'd refused to leave my side until I had come out of the coma and even then, he had been reluctant to leave.

Yet, even with his devotion, he had become distant, as if he were afraid of breaking me. Losing my wings must have been a real shock to him. My heart skipped a beat. What if he left me over this? No, if he wanted to leave, he would have done it already.

But the idea lingered.

I'd heard of couples splitting over a partner's inability to fly, or walk, or see. Why would Tarry be any different? Perhaps he pitied me or felt obligated to stay. I pushed the thoughts back.

Tarry didn't waste his time. If he had wanted out, he would have done it a long time ago.

I treaded water, making small waves as my limbs churned beneath the surface. Being weightless reminded me of flight. In school, we did water exercises to prepare us for when our wings came in. Flying and swimming were so similar. Diving in the pool was like riding an air current, rising to the surface was pushing against the drag of the wind, and floating here was almost like being suspended in the clouds.

I put my face back in the water, my limbs relaxed, rising to the surface, hanging suspended in the liquid wind. With my eyes closed, I could imagine soaring on the wind current. The pool's depth impersonated the vast emptiness of the night sky. The ripples whispered like the breeze in my ears.

Arms grabbed my middle.

Water rushed my eyes and mouth, making me splutter. I was dragged out of the pool and thankfully released.

I lay on my back, coughing and collecting my senses.

The uneven stone ground prodded my unprotected back, reminding me something was missing. Tears of fury and pain joined the droplets on my face.

I struggled to sit up.

Panting breaths alerted me to someone kneeling next to me.

I wiped the water out of my eyes and found myself face to face with my outraged husband.

"What are you thinking? Are you trying to drown yourself?" He was in his orange swimming trunks, his brown wings fully exposed. His narrowed eyes stared into mine.

I glared back. "Mind your own business!" His accusations lit the resentment festering in me for weeks. "You can do what-ever you like. You have wings."

I was up for a fight, but his face suddenly became unnaturally passive.

"What were you doing?" he asked.

"I was flying, if you must know." I folded my arms. "Water is my sky now. Is someone going to come and take that away from me too?"

He recoiled as if I'd struck him. He stood, taking a step away from me and collapsed his wings against his back, hiding them from my sight. "I thought you were trying to kill yourself."

My anger faded. I didn't want to hurt him. I tried to smile. "Dying isn't on my agenda. Why would I kill myself when I have you?"

His eyes glistened, and he looked away to hide the tears. "Live for yourself, Ardeth. I'm not worth it."

My insides twisted. Was he trying to tell me something? "Why do you need me? Are you still mine?"

Silence.

"Tarry, what's wrong?"

"Nothing. You just scared me, that's all."

"No, that's not all. I know there is more. You call me beautiful, but you won't look at me. We don't spend time together anymore. What's wrong? Tell me."

He looked away.

"Tell me."

Silence.

"Tarr—"

"It was me. I cut off your wings."

I froze. "What are you talking about?"

He looked up. "I cut off your wings," he said it slowly, emphasizing each word. "I ruined your life."

This wasn't computing. "You weren't the one who did this

to me. Poison from the asphalt and creeps who steal little girls did this to me. Not you."

He took a step back. His words finally sunk into my numb brain. It couldn't be true. My back throbbed at the thought. "You cut them off?"

He glared at the pool's shimmering surface.

"How?"

He addressed the water. "Good thing the baby was with you. The way she screamed the stars heard it. By the time we found you, though, it was almost too late. Rampion and Teazel took the girl and that parasite back while I waited with you." His voice was forced calm. "You were burning with fever. Not moving. Your wings were skinned down to the framework. Black tar and gravel covered what remained of the colors. Blood ran into the gutters, carrying shreds of rainbow skin with it. I didn't need to be a healer to see your circulation slowing by the second. Even if I borrowed the winds of the universe, I couldn't have gotten you to the healer in time. I made the decision. I took out my knife and I... I..."

I clasped my hand over my mouth. The scars on my back throbbed. My entire back ached. Imagining his knife slicing through my flesh made bile rise in my throat. I swallowed twice. My throat felt dry, but I had to ask.

"Why?"

"I couldn't watch you die." He raised his head, and I saw the fear of that night reflected in his eyes. "I took your wings so you wouldn't leave me." His gaze dropped. "Selfish, I know, but there it is. It doesn't seem to have worked though. You're tearing yourself apart. All because of what I did to you."

My mind spun faster than my wings ever had. My husband removed my wings, stole my ability to fly, and left me deformed.

But with the exact same action saved my life. All so we could be together.

Tarry straightened his shoulders. "I understand if you hate me. Tell me to leave, and I'll go."

I stood and took a step toward him. He stiffened, closing his eyes in anticipation of a strike. It stabbed my heart to see him like this. I turned away.

"Is that your answer?" he said quietly.

"I need to think." I snatched up my kimono and fled through the gate.

I didn't know where I was going. Eventually, I found myself on a ridge looking over the grounds. In the distance, beyond the drop of the spa, the town of Compass Point took up the rest of the land toward the sea. Heavy clouds gathered over the horizon. My emotions churned like the distant waves. I sank down on the grass and collected my thoughts.

Knowing the truth should have caused some sort of relief. But it didn't. I hated not knowing who had done the operation. Now that I knew, I felt worse. The one person I trusted the most was the one to make me a wingless.

My finger clenched around the grass, ripping it up out of the ground.

Tarry's face flashed across my mind. The expression of pain when he told me. Unable to look at me since I woke up from my coma.

My throat tightened.

He was the one tearing himself apart. Were my actions ruining things? I didn't know what to think anymore. The pain and confusion left me numb.

Unbidden, a memory invaded my unguarded mind. I'd been laying in my bed, sedated, partly awake. Angry voices came from outside my hospital room door. I recognized Tarry's voice along with the main healer, Margot. The pain relievers left me unable to move and in a semi-conscious state but didn't inhibit my hearing.

"You said there would be a chance," Tarry said.

"A chance, yes, but I wasn't certain," Margot said. "I've asked the professionals."

"She has to get prosthetics. She needs them."

"There's nothing to attach them to. The way they were cut off left nothing for the prosthetics to attach to and be functional."

There was a long silence.

"The way they were cut off," Tarry repeated. His voice was barely audible.

Margot said something else, but I couldn't hear her. Footsteps retreated down the hall, and I heard the hinges on my door squeak. A moment later, the chair beside my bed creaked, Tarry's warm hand caressed my hair, and I heard a shuddering gasp of a sob.

"I'm sorry. I'm so sorry," he said over and over.

Why hadn't I remembered that until now? I hugged my legs tighter to my chest and stared at the blurred image of the ocean before me.

The light slid behind the clouds and faded altogether. A cold chill puckered my skin, and I pulled my robe tighter around myself.

Something draped across my shoulders. I looked up and found Tarry standing over me, dressed, his hand lingering on his coat over my shoulders. Our eyes met, and I managed a small smile.

We walked back in silence. I couldn't find any way to voice my thoughts.

Back in our room, the silence continued.

We prepared for bed, retreating to opposite ends of the room as we changed into our night things. I slipped into my night-gown, the silky material snagging on my still-damp hair. I didn't realize how many of my clothes had open backs. Adjusting the ankle-length dress, I sat on the bed and watched my husband prepare for bed.

The routine was the same—brushing teeth and similar chores. The same things as always, but I couldn't stop staring. His wings, collapsed and folded tight against his back, reflected the room's light in flashes.

It was hypnotizing.

Rising from the bed, I walked behind him, barely aware of my actions. He didn't stop me, only turning his head in surprise when I put my hands on the smooth coloration on his back. On his wings.

My fingers found where they overlapped, and I gently pulled.

Realizing what I was doing, he relaxed and allowed me to unfold them to their full length. They draped against his back, smoother than finest silk yet stronger than leather. They were earth colored, resembling a brown moth wing pattern.

I rarely studied them up close before. Flecks of blue and green danced along with light streaks of gold glistening in the lamplight. I pressed my face into the warm, soft membrane and stroked them lightly with my fingertips.

I looked up to see his eyes watching me in the mirror. My cheeks burned. I stepped in front of him to use the sink.

Staring in the ceramic bowl, I began to untangle my hair from the damp braid. As I shook my hair out, it fell and covered my back in a cherry-colored wave.

I was about to turn when I felt the warmth of Tarry's body

close beside me. Both of us stood there, unsure of our next move.

His hands slid down my back until they almost touched my scars. My skin tingled at his touch. His fingers caught in my hair, and I jerked my head. His hand retreated, but he didn't move away. We stood like this, waiting for the other to move.

I didn't dare meet his eyes in the mirror.

I reached up and moved my hair out of the way and draped it over my shoulder. His touch returned. His hand slid from my back, down my side, and found its way to my middle. The other joined until both arms were securely around me and his chest pressed against my exposed back. I leaned into him, safe and familiar.

I looked up into the mirror, and our eyes met. Words were useless. I turned my head toward Tarry, and our lips met.

We stood together with his wings rising protectively over us both.

Watching scary movies through split fingers terrified Caryn Larrinaga as a child, and those nightmares continue to inspire her fiction. An award-winning mystery, horror, and urban fantasy writer, her debut novel, Donn's Hill, was awarded the League of Utah Writers 2017 Silver Quill and was a 2017 Dragon Award finalist. Caryn lives near Salt Lake City, Utah, with her husband and their clowder of cats, in a ninety-year-old house with a colorful history, and its creaking walls and narrow hallways often send her running (never walking) up the stairs. For free short stories and true tales of haunted places, visit www.carynlarrinaga.com.

About this story, Caryn says: "Like most of my stories, 'A Friend in Need' was born out of anxiety. Someone asked for a small favor, but circumstances prevented me from doing it. My friend didn't mind. Everything was fine. All the same, I worried about the unintended consequences of my inability to help. Then, because I'm an omni-directional agonizer, I imagined the worst thing that could've happened if I had helped—getting stuck in traffic, running out of gas, being captured by demons... you know, normal stuff. And it's better those catastrophes happen on the page than in my life, so here we are."

With a slow build-up and a lovely twist, this story has the feeling of a modern-day Twilight Zone episode—but with no split-finger viewing required.

A FRIEND IN NEED
Caryn Larrinaga

The impossibility exhausted me. She couldn't be there.

But in defiance of all logic, Emily lurked in the corner of the classroom, trying to catch my eye from behind Dr. Radcliffe's desk. It took effort to ignore her, to block out the stare that burned into my forehead in a way it had never done while she was still awake.

I refused to look, choosing instead to focus on the half-empty can of Super Energy Blast at the edge of my desk.

"She's not here," I muttered to the can. "She's not here."

The repeated mantra didn't do any good. Emily remained, her brown eyes wide and unblinking, same as she'd done for the past week. No matter where I was, no matter what time of day… if I got tired enough, she'd be there. Chugging energy drinks bought me a couple sleepless days and nights of peace, but the caffeine crash loomed right around the corner. The fatigue pressed down on me like a weight—God, I wanted to close my eyes. Close them for a minute and rest…

"Still with us, Annie?"

My eyelids snapped open at the sound of Dr. Radcliffe's voice. She frowned at me from beside the whiteboard.

"Sorry." I cleared my throat and stretched in my seat, then

grabbed my pen and tried to copy the chart Dr. Radcliffe had written while I'd been dozing. I welcomed the distraction from Emily's gaze, and I took care to write my notes, including more details than I'd ever done in four years of college.

"As you can see, the grading is very straightforward. If you get your senior projects in on time, follow the formatting guidelines, and stay on topic, there's no reason you won't pass. See me during my office hours if you have additional questions. Class dismissed."

There was a loud scraping of chairs as the other students in my advisory group packed up their things and left the classroom. I stuffed my notebook into my messenger bag, hoping to sneak out while Dr. Radcliffe erased the board, but when I raised my head, she was already standing at my desk.

"Do you have a minute?" she asked.

"Sure." I tried to make it sound casual, like I had no idea what she wanted to talk to me about, but the spike in my voice betrayed me.

Dr. Radcliffe half-sat on the desk across from mine and looked at me for a few silent moments. I ran my hands over my head and straightened my ponytail, hoping I didn't look as disheveled as I felt. I showered at least twice a day in my bid to stay awake, but my old routine of straightening my hair and picking fun, layered outfits had long since fallen to the wayside in favor of hair ties and whatever T-shirt smelled cleanest.

At last she spoke, tilting her head toward my energy drink. "Doesn't seem to be working."

"No, not really."

"Listen, I know you've got a lot of finals to study for. And I can't imagine what you must be going through since Emily…" She trailed off and pursed her lips. "Well, I'm extending the deadline on your senior project. Why don't you take summer semester to wrap it up?"

I shook my head. "You don't need to do that for me. I'm fine."

"I really think you should. It could make—"

"No." The booming volume of my voice surprised me. I lowered it to explain myself. "I appreciate your concern, but I don't want to delay my graduation."

Another semester here would do me in. I couldn't take the stares from my classmates, the pity from my professors. Emily was the one who'd gotten sick, not me. She was the one who wouldn't wake up. But nobody was trying to help her; they all seemed focused on me.

I didn't get it. I wasn't Emily's only roommate. I wasn't even the one who'd found her and called the paramedics. I wondered if Zuri's professors offered to extend deadlines or waive assignments. Knowing Zuri, probably not.

"I'll have my project to you next week," I said. "Same as everybody else."

I zipped my backpack and stood. I felt Dr. Radcliffe's eyes following me out of the classroom, but I didn't turn around. Her gaze was a hell of a lot easier to ignore than Emily's.

A vicious funk greeted me when I opened the door to our apartment. I glanced at the Jenga tower of dishes piled in the sink, thought about washing them, and opted to open a window and air the place out instead. Cleaning was one of many things I'd avoided since the paramedics had wheeled Emily away, and Zuri was too busy with Student Council activities to care that I wasn't pulling my weight. That, or maybe she took the same kind of pity on me as everyone else and just wasn't bitching at me about it.

I shoved an empty pizza box off the couch and stretched out across the soft cushions. It was easier to ignore Emily out here than in our bedroom. In there, she stared at me from the hundreds of selfies and group photos we'd taken together over the last four years. Out here, she only stared at me from the corner where Zuri kept her yoga mat.

"Hey, Emily," I told her. "I know you're a figment of my imagination, but I'd still appreciate it if you'd let me squeeze in a nap before chem lab."

She mouthed something in return, but I couldn't hear it. I could never hear it. The words were probably random song lyrics or something else my brain was too worn-out to process in any healthy way. Maybe after graduation, when there was more space in my head, I'd finally figure it out.

A light hum filled my ears. I felt the forceful tug of sleep on my eyelids. My body, impatient for rest—deep, quality rest—tugged me deeper into the cushions. I closed my eyes and hovered briefly on the edge between consciousness and noth-ingness.

"Annie!"

Emily's voice slapped the buzz of sleepiness from my mind. It'd been exactly twenty-eight days since I'd last heard it. When I opened my eyes, she wasn't skulking in the corner anymore. She kneeled beside the couch, eyes frantic and cheeks flushed.

I scrambled to sit up and backed away from her, pulling my knees to my chest and trying to retreat as far back into the cush-ions as possible. I trained my eyes on the ceiling fan and whis-pered my mantra, "She's not here. She's not here."

"Annie, I'm here!"

"She's not here. Not here. Not here." I shook my head and pinched my arms and legs. "I'm dreaming. Wake up!"

"Look at me, Nan!"

I hated that nickname. Emily only used it when she was trying to nettle me. Out of sheer reflex, I turned my head and shot her a glare. Her eyes went wide, and words—finally audible after so long—spilled out of her mouth at light speed.

"Listen! You're awake, and I'm here!" She glanced down at her chest, which was translucent enough that I could see the pile of unwashed clothes behind her. "Or I guess part of me is. My body's still in the hospital. But I hate it there, Annie! Please, help me come home!"

I stared at her, really looking for the first time in weeks. "Is it really you?"

She tried to grab for my hand, but she passed right through my body. "Yes, it's me. I've been trying to talk to you for days." A tear rolled down her cheek. "I can't believe you can actually hear me."

My brain imitated my car's engine in the dead of winter, half starting and then choking out. Again and again I turned the keys, trying to process what the hell was going on here. Emily, in our living room, talking to me...

But it couldn't be real. *She* couldn't be real.

I'd seen her the day before in her hospital room, tubes and wires coming out of her throat and arms. She'd been skinnier there, thinner than she looked now, with limp, stringy hair and skin the color of ash.

"You're not here," I whispered. "You're in a coma. You're sick—"

"I'm not sick!" She reached for me again, then seemed to remember that she couldn't touch me and dragged her hand down her face instead. "That's why I need to get out of there.

The doctors will *never* be able to help me. It's not an infection or a fever."

I'd never seen that desperate look in her eyes before. Even when she'd been stressed or sad, there'd always been a light, a hint of a smile waiting to be coaxed out by a good joke. I'd never imagined she could look so frightened. My chest constricted. This was something I *hadn't* imagined. This was real. Emily—my best friend, my confidante, the person who'd gotten me through every failed test and bad breakup—sat here, translucent, asking for my help.

I straightened up. "Okay. If you're not sick, why are you in a coma?"

"It was a demon."

"A demon?"

Under different circumstances, I would've laughed. On a normal day, Emily might have been rehearsing for an audition or playing a practical joke. But I didn't think Emily would've stalked me like a living ghost for the past week just to prank me, so I had to take anything she told me at face value.

Which means, I realized, *that she's talking about an honest-to-God actual demon.*

I struggled for words. "I don't... I don't know how I can help with that."

Emily's face was still flushed, but now that I'd agreed she was, in fact, somehow visiting me from the confines of her hospital bed, her pupils had grown still, and she looked less like a desperate addict jonesing for her next fix. "There's a book in my desk," she said. "Get it. The last page has everything you need to know."

"Okay, I'll be right back."

As much as I loved Emily, my self-preservation instincts wouldn't let me stand up, walk by her, and then turn my back to her to go down the hall. Instead, I climbed over the back of the couch, like a weirdo, and shuffled out of the room in reverse, not turning around until I entered our bedroom and closed the door.

As I'd expected, the wall of selfies assaulted me. I froze, staring at them. Emily was everywhere—smiling, laughing, sharing her brilliant light with the world. I didn't want that light to go out forever. I balled my hands into fists and marched across the room, letting hundreds of pairs of brown eyes follow me to Emily's desk. I hadn't touched so much as a pencil on it since she'd gotten sick—no, since she'd been *taken*—but now I rifled through every stack of paper, upended every drawer in search of whatever book she'd been talking about.

It only took me a few minutes to completely empty the thing, but after the final drawer had been pulled free, I panted for breath and rested my hands on my knees. The only books I'd found were textbooks, and the last pages of those were appendixes and glossaries. Nothing in them suggested, "Hey, I can help with this demon problem."

"Dammit!" I banged my fists on the desk, and something landed on my foot—a small, brown book that barely filled my hand when I picked it up. I ran my thumb down the empty spine; there was no title, no markings at all. Just smooth, faded leather. I pulled back on the pages and let them flip past me. Neat, cramped handwriting filled each page.

"A journal," I muttered.

I knew it wasn't Emily's. She always said journaling was too much work, but she kept a diary in her own way. She had accounts on every kind of social media and busily photographed and posted the most mundane details of her daily life, especially if she encountered a stray animal or a particularly cute cup of coffee. Plus, her handwriting was a loopy, messy half cursive that was a headache to read. Whoever wrote this clearly took extra effort to make sure it was legible. It looked like it could have been typed, except for variations in the print size and the occasional inkblot.

The book was short, and it didn't take long to flip to the end. A perfect circle filled with odd shapes and symbols took up the entire last page. Most of it didn't make any sense to me, but a few looked like stick figures and stars. Below the circle, there was a drawing of a single lit candle, beside which were thick, block letters spelling: TRANSIET IN TENEBRAE.

Still examining that final page, I opened the bedroom door and went back to the couch.

"Where the hell did you get this?" I asked.

There was no answer, and Emily was gone when I raised my head. I sighed. Searching her desk had gotten me so keyed up, I could've run a marathon. I was more awake than I'd been in almost a month, and she only appeared when I was beat. I'd have to wait until the high of excitement wore off.

The stink from the kitchen sink wafted over to me, pulled by the breeze from the open window.

"Might as well wear myself out," I muttered, turning on the faucet.

"This is a nice surprise." Zuri stood in the doorway with her hands on her hips and surveyed the apartment. "No dishes in the sink *and* I can actually see the floor?"

"I aim to please." I lay stretched out on the sofa, taking up all three cushions beneath my softest fleece blanket. I'd put the little brown book in my pillowcase for safekeeping. I could feel the ridge of it through the stuffing in my pillow.

She crossed the room to perch on the arm of the couch, took the mug out of my hand, and sniffed it. "Chamomile? Did you finally sell your stock in Super Energy Blast?"

"Just trying to relax." In truth, I was trying to bring myself back to the brink of falling asleep. The tea, the blanket, the home shopping channel that played on the TV—they were all part of a strategy that didn't seem to be working. Had I known this whole time that wanting to fall asleep was the secret to staying awake, I would've saved a fortune on energy drinks.

"I'm glad." Zuri's voice was soft, and she reached down to squeeze my foot. "I haven't wanted to say anything, but I've been worried about you."

I clenched my jaw and said nothing, despite the torrent of angry responses that flooded my mind. Zuri, like everyone else, was more worried about me than Emily. Like everyone else, she professed concern but didn't do much more than talk about it. But if I told her how I felt, we'd get into an argument, and the adrenaline would keep me awake. So I lay there, staring at a spinning silver bracelet on the television screen, and kept quiet.

She sighed and set the mug down on the coffee table. "I know you think it's pity or something, but it's not. I miss you, Annie. You've been different since Emily got sick."

"She didn't get sick." I couldn't help it; the words leaped from my mouth. "She was taken."

"What are you talking about?"

"Nothing."

She slid off the armrest and rounded the couch to kneel in front of me. Her eyebrows were drawn together so tightly that, for a second, I thought she was angry. But when she spoke, her voice was as gentle as always.

"Okay, tough talk time," she said. "I've been trying to figure out how to have this conversation with you for weeks, but I couldn't find the right words. Well, screw the right words. Annie, you need help."

I narrowed my eyes at her. "Help?"

"You're not processing what happened to Emily in a healthy way. There are grief counselors—"

"Grief? She's not dead!"

"Well, she might as well be!" For the first time in the four years I'd known her, Zuri raised her voice to a near shriek. She grabbed one of my hands in both of her own, and her eyes filled with tears. "Don't you get it? She's probably never going to wake up. Every day she's in that coma, it's less and less likely she'll come back to us. We have to let go."

I yanked my hand out of her grasp. "Let go? How can you say that? She's our friend!"

"She *was* our friend. That's what I'm saying. Since the moment the paramedics wheeled her out of here, she's been gone. Can't you feel it?"

"Feel what?"

"She used to fill this whole place with light and energy." Zuri looked around the room with flat, sad eyes. "I can't feel her here anymore."

"Maybe you can't, but I can. I've seen her." Would she believe me if I told her Emily had been kneeling in exactly the spot Zuri now sat, just hours earlier? "I've talked to her."

"Oh, Annie." She sat back on her heels and let her hands fall into her lap. "Why didn't you tell me it'd gotten this bad?"

"When could I have told you? You're never home."

She pursed her lips. For a minute, I thought it was over, that I'd won this argument. It was a good thing too, because I was starting to shake and I knew I'd already undone all the work I'd put into relaxing.

"I'm sorry," she said. "It's hard, being home. You weren't

here when I found her. You get to remember her the way she was at breakfast, happy and bubbly. But every time I walk into this room, I see it all over again. The furniture was everywhere —even the rug was rumpled up by the TV—and she was just laying there." She pointed to the space in front of the fireplace. "It looked like she was sleeping, but when I checked for her pulse, there wasn't one. I thought she was dead. I can't remember calling 911, but I remember sitting there with her cold, still hand in mine."

I stared at her. She'd never talked about it before, not like this. To be honest, I hadn't been able to bring myself to ask. I didn't want to think about it. It was bad enough that Emily was unconscious in a hospital bed without dwelling on what put her there.

Zuri was right: I was lucky. I didn't envy that memory. Maybe Emily was lucky too—lucky I wasn't there and wasn't haunted by what I'd seen. I was able to be here, to see her.

I considered telling Zuri what I'd found and including her in the plan to bring Emily back, but her red-rimmed eyes and slumped shoulders made me suspect she needed sleep even more than I did. Guilt twisted in my stomach. I'd been so wrapped up in my own sadness that I hadn't been paying attention to hers.

"Can I get you anything?" I asked. "Want some of this tea?"

"There's only one thing I want," she said. "I want you to get help. I want you to be able to move on."

"Okay," I said. Compared to what I faced with Emily, Zuri's request was nothing. "I'm guessing you already have the name of somebody you want me to see, right? I'll call them tomorrow and make an appointment."

Zuri's eyes widened. "Really?"

"Really."

She jumped forward, pulled me into a tight hug, and whispered in my ear, "Thank you."

"Why don't you go lie down or something?"

She pulled away from me and shook her head. "I've got a planning meeting for the graduation concert. It's going to be really nice. They're going to dedicate a song to Emily." She ran the middle finger of each hand under her eyes, brushing away gray lines of running mascara. "I'm going to splash some water on my face and head back to campus."

While she cleaned up in the bathroom, I snuggled back down into the blanket and yawned. If she was that happy getting me to agree to see a counselor, I couldn't wait to see her face when Emily woke up.

───────

After Zuri left and the sun began to set, I felt the familiar weight of sleepiness pressing down on me. I blinked, and when I opened my eyes, Emily stood in front of the fireplace. She was more translucent than before, and I could see every detail of the picture frames behind her.

"I found the book," I told her.

Her eyes lit up. "I knew you would."

I sat up and leaned forward with my elbows on my knees. "So how does this work? I read the words and you wake up?"

She shook her head. "I wish it were that easy. You need to stand in the circle, hold the candle, and speak the words. That will connect us, so you can pull me out of the darkness."

"The darkness?"

"I don't know how else to describe it. It's where he's keeping me. It's so dark here, so empty. I want to come home!"

I wanted to jump up and hug her, then remembered I couldn't. "It's okay, Em. I'm coming for you."

"Please hurry." Her form flickered, fading like a candle about to go out. "It's been nearly a month. I don't have much longer."

"What happens when—"

She disappeared before I could finish my question.

"Shit!"

I dived to the side and retrieved the book from my pillowcase. The circle filled with odd symbols waited for me on the last page, but it was barely four inches tall. Emily said I should stand inside it. I needed to draw a much larger version, plus find a candle somewhere. Swearing under my breath, I dashed into the kitchen and started rummaging through our junk drawer. There, among the rubber bands and spare charging cables, I found a candle shaped like the number two, left over from Emily's twenty-second birthday a few months before, along with a small box of matches.

"Aha!"

At the back of the drawer, my hand closed around a cold metal tube. It was a giant, black magic marker, the kind Zuri used to make posters for Student Council events. I had everything I needed, except somewhere to draw the circle.

I crossed back into the living room, twisting the marker between my fingers and racking my brain for something I could draw on. Regular paper was too small. Zuri might have some poster board in her room, or I could check the dumpster for an old cardboard box. Or to hell with it, I could draw on the floor. We'd lose our deposit when we moved out after graduation…. Maybe I could cover it with the rug.

It wasn't even a rug, really. It was a thin piece of carpet the previous tenants left behind. I lifted the edge and saw a curved line, delicately carved into the scuffed hardwood beneath the rug.

It looked like a piece of a circle.

I dropped the corner back down with a slap, dragged the coffee table out of the way, and pulled the rug over the back of the couch to fully expose the floor. I was right; it was a circle. The carving was faded, but some parts stood out clearly, especially in the lower-traffic areas like where the coffee table normally sat. There, I could easily make out a figure encased in a star that matched the last page in Emily's book.

Did she draw this? I bent down and ran my thumb along the edge of the design, feeling the smoothness of the floor that was barely marred by the shallow carving. It seemed old, like years of feet walking on top of it had sanded down the ridges and made the lines less severe. No, she hadn't carved it, but maybe she used it. I stood and walked forward, wondering how many of her steps I was retracing.

The instant my feet hit the center of the circle, the little hairs on the back of my neck twitched. I was close to something powerful. I suddenly wanted to leave the apartment, find Zuri at her meeting, and never return. I certainly didn't want to light the candle that threatened to slip out of my sweaty fingers, and the thought of speaking those foreign words made bile rise up in my throat. But when I closed my eyes, I saw Emily's fading figure and heard her plea for help.

She was depending on me. She'd stood by me for four years —four years of roller-coaster emotions, insane workloads, and living on a shoestring in the hopes that we'd have a better future. Now all she needed from me was one thing—one small thing, really: to swallow my fear and stick to the plan—so she could have that future.

I gulped down the stomach acid, struck a match, and lit the

candle. Holding it above my head, I spoke the words from the book, "Transiet in tenebrae." When my mouth closed over the final syllable, the candle blew out and the lights went dark above me. The room was lit only by the full moon shining through the open window. As I blinked, it began to fade until I stood in a blackness so complete that I couldn't make out my own hand in front of my face.

"Emily?" I whispered. My voice was strangely muffled, as though I was talking through a pillow. "Are you here?"

No reply. I wanted to vomit, faint, and run away all at the same time. Just as I was deciding that option number two was the best choice out of those three, a glowing orb appeared in my peripheral vision. It was moving, growing larger... or coming closer. It was hard to tell which. Soon, the light of the orb filled my entire field of vision, and what I saw inside made my heart swell.

"Emily!"

She lay on the floor of the orb, curled up in the fetal position. Unlike when she'd appeared to me earlier that day, this version of her looked like the one that lay in the hospital bed: thin, wasted, her normally curly hair matted against her forehead.

"Emily!" I shouted again. "I'm here!"

She opened her eyes and lifted her head, squinting at me from inside the glowing ball. "Annie? Is that you?"

"Come on," I told her. "I'm taking you home." I reached forward to grab her hand and yank her out of her prison. As my fingers neared the edge of the glowing light, Emily's eyes widened. "No!" she shrieked.

But it was too late to stop my momentum. I touched the orb and it exploded, blinding me with a flash of lightning and deafening me with a roar of thunder. My legs buckled beneath me, and I let out a cry of pain, echoed by Emily's screaming. The light faded... faded... faded... into nothing.

Emily didn't have long. Soon, I knew, she'd become like the dozens of other husks in the orb with us. They'd been people, once. Now they looked like set pieces from a horror film about a mummy's tomb.

I'd spent days pounding at the glowing haze that surrounded us. It looked like little more than smoke, but was as solid as steel. I was too weak for that now, too weak to fight. Instead, I sat on the floor of the orb and stroked Emily's hair, listening to her ragged breathing.

Through the haze, I could make out Zuri sitting on the couch in our living room. She hugged a pillow to her chest and cried, her tears spilling onto my fleece blanket. My heart ached for her, for all of us, but there was nothing I could do. The demon had already taken my form, following Zuri and haunting her at her most exhausted. Soon enough, she'd find the book, and she'd already seen the carving. Twice.

Emily was too weak to answer my questions, and I wondered what form the demon had taken to lure her here. Knowing her, it could've been anything from a scared puppy to a perfect stranger who needed help. No wonder she'd been the first to go.

And soon, she really would be gone.

Then I'd sit here, alone, until Zuri fell for the demon's tricks. At least when that happened, I'd have someone to stroke my hair while I withered away in the darkness.

A lifelong bookworm, Jenn Adams has been writing stories since she was in kindergarten. She lives in Utah with her four kids, working in tech support by day and writing and editing by night. She graduated from BYU with a degree in English linguistics and a minor in editing and has worked as an editor for two magazines. Jenn has won several writing awards, including first place in a first chapter contest. She enjoys eating ice cream and sipping sauvignon blanc while trying not to think about the eventual heat death of the universe. You can find her at authorjennadams.com.

About this story, Jenn says: "This story was inspired by real events. It's not autobiographical, but I've been in Tanya's shoes. The bills are piling up. The stress is real. The kids need things. The night before I started my current job, there were teenagers in the grocery store acting silly when I wasn't in the mood for it, and I sat down and started writing. I stayed up until 3 in the morning to get the first draft down on paper because when the muse is talking, you don't go to bed even if you really could use the sleep."

One of the handful of stories in this volume focusing on mothers' sacrifices for their children, Jenn's story carries us deep inside the everyday, desperate choices that are sadly all too familiar.

FISH OR CHIPS
Jenn Adams

Tanya pushed her cart slowly through the breakfast aisle, calculating how much cereal she could buy with the money left in her food budget.

Roughly, she decided, none.

Still, cereal was Bethany's favorite food. Tanya looked over the offerings, mostly sugary crap and air. She wanted to squeeze in at least one cheap cereal option for her kids this week, but she refused to buy puffy garbage at five dollars a box. Her eyes landed on the Malt-O-Meal—healthy, tasty, and best of all, one box went a long way. Maybe it tasted bland, but it was the best deal, and they could always sweeten it up.

She knew they were almost completely out of toilet paper, but it was so damn expensive. Three passes down the aisle later, she had the absolute cheapest TP per square in her hands. Maybe it was time to get a bidet—one of those cheap toilet attachments, of course. She smiled, imaging her kids' reaction to that idea. Her phone dinged. Tanya pulled it out of her pocket to read the text:

Don't forget to buy another goldfish to replace Poseidon.
You promised.

She *had* promised. She remembered Hunter's sad eyes when Poseidon died and left Ariel alone in the tank. She'd told him she would buy his fish a new friend. Tanya sighed. At least fish didn't cost too much. Still, all of these not-too-expensive items added up.

A group of giggling teenage girls turned down the aisle ahead of her, one of them with a paper grocery bag over her face with the words "For Sale, $5" written on it in Sharpie. One girl with long blonde hair walked ahead of the others, her phone aimed back at her friends, recording. Another girl with a short brunette pixie cut pointed her phone at Tanya.

"Will somebody please buy my friend?" the blonde girl cried. "Please. She's only five dollars."

Tanya glared at them. "Stop being fools," she said, shaking her head.

"We're putting you on YouTube," the girl with the pixie cut said, laughing much louder than necessary.

"Put this on YouTube," Tanya said, flipping them the bird.

The girls burst into laughter before retreating to some other part of the store.

There was no real danger of their idiotic video going viral, so what did it matter? And even if it did go viral, what did it matter anyway? YouTube or no YouTube, her life was going to suck, and then she would die.

Tanya pushed her cart over to the pet aisle and eyed the goldfish in the tanks. She picked out one that looked strong and healthy and fished it out of the tank into a baggie along with a scoopful of water.

"Let's get you home," she muttered, tying the baggie shut.

She set the fish in her cart next to the large bag of potato chips she'd been craving. The chips stared back, taunting her. After all the things her children *really needed*, she just couldn't afford to buy something she merely wanted. Defeated, she lifted the chips out of the basket and placed them on the shelf next to a box of doggie biscuits.

Tanya's phone dinged again and her shoulders slumped.

What now? She closed her eyes, leaning heavily against the cart for several moments. "Lord, give me strength," she murmured before pulling her phone out of her pocket.

Another text from Hunter:

I need you to get me a flash drive.
Mr. Clark says we have to have it for our next assignment or we could fail the class.

"Dammit," Tanya said, louder than she meant to.

I don't know where I can get the money for the next rent check, the microwave quit working last week, and now his damn teacher has the nerve to require me to buy a fucking flash drive and threaten to fail Hunter if he shows up without it?

No. She wouldn't do it. She *couldn't* do it. How could she afford a flash drive?

Fuming, she turned the corner and nearly ran her cart into her next-door neighbor, Meredith.

"Tanya. Hi. How *are* you?" Meredith sounded much too chipper for a dreary Tuesday evening like tonight.

Tanya opened her mouth to give her usual, automatic response to that question: *I'm fine.* But the words wouldn't come out.

I'm fine. It was almost always a lie anyway, but today it was too much.

I'm fine? The lie was too big. She shook her head and closed her mouth. Her eyes shifted to the floor—the dirty, sticky floor.

It seemed fitting, given her mood.

"Oh, no. Is something wrong?" Meredith asked.

Tanya stood, not moving. Not responding. She turned inward.

Yes, something's wrong. Her eyes stung. She felt herself flooding, a barrage of unwanted thoughts pummeling her heart and mind. *My whole life is wrong. My children's father ran off on us three years ago and I've been working two jobs ever since, just trying to scrape by so we don't all end up homeless. I wish I were dead and I probably would have tried to get there by now if my kids weren't depending on me.*

Tanya shook her head again, blinking hard. She wouldn't say the words out loud, of course. She hadn't told anyone that much truth in years.

"Well, listen, honey, if you ever need anything, you just ask, all right?"

"You don't have a flash drive, do you?" The words tumbled out of Tanya's mouth before she could stop them. She cringed. She didn't want to owe anybody anything.

"I think we just might," Meredith said, sounding pleased as punch.

That's a stupid saying, Tanya thought. What did punch ever have to be pleased about, except never having bills to pay?

"Let me ask Adam when I get home and I'll let you know, okay?"

"It's no big deal, really," Tanya said, backpedaling. "You don't have to do that."

"No, I insist. I'd love to let you borrow one if I can find an extra for you."

"Fine," Tanya agreed just to get out of the conversation. Maybe borrowing one item from her neighbor would be fine. It was just one stupid little flash drive, after all. She forced a smile and made her way to the check stand where a cashier with a fake smile rang up her groceries.

Tanya perused the magazines on the rack as she waited, finding her horoscope in one and reading it while the cashier robotically ran her items over the bar code scanner.

Pisces: Now that Mercury is in retrograde, start looking for love because it is all around you. Don't be afraid to go big and be bold. Tell that special someone how you feel. Take a chance. Now is the time.

She scoffed and dropped the magazine back on the stand. What utter rubbish. Nothing fit her life less than that horoscope did today. She looked back at her cart and watched the fish swim back and forth in the baggie. Pisces. That would be a great name for a fish.

The cashier added the fish to her total. "That'll be $96.52," she said in a monotone voice. She examined a chipped fingernail while Tanya slipped her card into the chip reader and waited.

"Sorry, your card's been denied," Jill said.

"What? I should have at least that much," Tanya protested. She knew she didn't have much more than that, but it should have cleared.

"I can take some things off if you want," Jill offered. She started to lift an item back out of the plastic bag on the turntable —Bethany's Malt-O-Meal.

"No, not that." She selected a few items instead and asked Jill to try the card again.

It still didn't clear.

Oh my god. I hate my life.

After two more humiliating rounds of *What Food Can We Really Do Without This Week?*, Tanya's card finally cleared for

$59.34. If she hadn't been out of money before, she was definitely out now.

The cashier took all of Tanya's unbought items and tossed them into another cart. Tanya walked away from the check stand with her purchases, if not her dignity, and made her way outside. Rain fell from the sky in sheets.

"Of course it's raining," Tanya muttered. "That's just perfect." She felt the cold cut through her thin T-shirt as she hurried to her car and tossed the grocery bags into her trunk. Rain raced down her neck and arms, soaking her. Tanya slammed the door and started the car. Shivering, she looked at the gas gauge. It needed to last till Thursday. The heater coughed and wheezed. She waited to make sure it was going to work before moving.

Pisces swam happily in his baggie in the center console as Tanya navigated through the parking lot. She took her time, making sure she had a wide enough opening in traffic to get out onto the slippery road safely. The last thing she needed right now was to get into an accident.

She approached the freeway overpass, picking up speed as she reached for her phone to turn on some music, when a passenger in the car coming toward her leaned out the window and waved a hand at her.

"What the hell?" Tanya was saying, just as something exploded on her windshield.

Tanya yelped, jerking her head back instinctively, as if the object might break through and smack her in the face. Instead, it ran down the windshield in trails of yellow and white goop.

"Is that an egg?" she asked, astonished. "Oh, no, you didn't," she yelled, flipping a U-turn and slamming her foot on the gas pedal.

Her wipers smeared the egg around on the windshield, so

Tanya rolled down the driver's side window and stuck her head out into the damp night to see the road ahead. She was gaining ground on the offending car. Tanya laid on the horn, tailgating the other car and honking long and loud until they finally pulled over.

She grabbed a Post-it pad and a pen from the center console and wrote down the license plate number, then walked up to the car and knocked on the driver's window.

The girls from the store, the brats who threatened to put her on YouTube, sat in the car. The brunette with the pixie cut kneaded the steering wheel with her hands, the blonde sat staring straight ahead from the passenger seat, and another brunette with hair to her shoulders sat in the back, chewing gum.

"It looks like no one wanted to buy you," Tanya said to the young girl dryly. The girl rolled her eyes, saying nothing.

"Do you know that throwing eggs at a moving vehicle is a crime?" Tanya asked. "You could obstruct the driver's view and cause a wreck."

"Lighten up, lady," the blonde said, tossing her hair.

"Lighten up?" Tanya asked, raising her eyebrows and glaring at the girls. "Lighten up. Let me tell you what I'm going to do instead." Tanya put a hand on her hip. "I want to see your license."

"You can't do that," the blonde protested. "You're not a cop."

"Like hell I can't. Show me your license."

The driver fished it out of her purse, looking embarrassed, and handed it over.

"Olivia Smith," Tanya muttered, looking from the license to the girl to make sure the picture matched. "Looks like you're"—she did a quick calculation in her head—"just barely sixteen." She sighed and gave the license back. "You could really hurt someone, maybe even kill them. Do better." She turned without another word.

She got back in her car, jotting down the girls' descriptions on the Post-it before looking up the local police office on her cell phone. She called the number and described everything to the officer who answered.

The windshield wipers worked their way back and forth, mixing the egg and rainwater together and making a nice goop on her windshield. She looked for the ice scraper to see if it would take that mess off her windshield, but as she reached toward the floorboard, she noticed the baggie missing from the console and Pisces spilled out on the floor.

She sagged against the car seat. The baggie lay broken, with Pisces motionless on the muddy passenger-side floor mat. Pisces died without anyone noticing he needed help. Died because everyone else was too distracted and worried about their own stuff. No one saved him. No one saw his desperation or frantic gasping. He died alone. He never even made it home.

She gripped the steering wheel and screamed. *Those girls could have killed me.* She wished they had.

"Stop it," she whispered to herself, clenching her hands into fists.

She wasn't going to think that way.

Flipping the car back around, Tanya shoved the awful thoughts aside. She squinted through the blurry, egg-smeared windshield. She allowed her eyes to stray to the freeway overpass ahead and fixate on the support beam.

What if those stupid girls did cause her to swerve into something? What if they did kill her? What if the egg on the windshield caused her to crash now? Her kids would get the life insurance payout she set up for them. Her pointless, useless life would be over, and her kids would have everything they needed.

Anything could happen out here in the rain.

She slowed down and flipped another U-turn.

Anything.

She drove back to the store parking lot.

Her hands shook.

Tanya unbuckled her seatbelt, rubbed her hands hard against her legs, gathering her nerve. She wanted to write notes to her kids, to tell them how much she loved them. But she knew she couldn't. Not if she wanted it to look like an accident.

"Okay, Tanya, you can do this," she said to herself. "Everyone will be better off when you're gone. It's scary right now, but it'll all be over in an instant."

She put the car in gear and got back on the road. She accelerated hard, exceeding the speed limit and then some.

"Lord, please let me die and not be paralyzed," Tanya yelled, aiming for the freeway overpass support. She would hit it in about ten seconds.

The phone began to ring, startling her. Tanya glanced at the phone in the console, where Pisces used to be. The words Oakville Police glowed back at her from the screen.

The thought flashed through Tanya's mind that they knew what she was doing and would tell the insurance company her death was a suicide. Her kids would get nothing.

She gasped and veered the car sharply to the right. The car hydroplaned and she spun. She stomped on the brake pedal, mashing it to the floor, her screams echoing through the vehicle.

The car hit the curb, flew over the sidewalk, and careened across a muddy field. The old car plowed into a fence, finally stopping her tailspin through the vacant lot. Her forehead smacked against the window with a thud.

Tanya sat locked in that position, her hands in a death grip on the wheel, her foot still locked on the brake, every muscle in her body quivering. Tears rolled down her cheeks, her ragged breathing the only sound in the car for several long moments after the phone finally stopped ringing.

Tanya glanced out the windows, watching for cars, trying to figure out if anyone saw what happened. When she felt in control enough to move, she peeled her fingers from the steering wheel, noticing how much it hurt to move, how every muscle ached. Shaking, Tanya picked up the phone. One missed call. One new voicemail. Tanya opened the voicemail and hit Play.

A cheerful voice came through the speaker. "Hello, Tanya, this is Officer Dalton. I just wanted to let you know that we found the vehicle in question and we gave the driver a stern warning. I did have one other question for you, so please give us a call back at your convenience. Thanks again, and have a pleasant evening."

Tanya could hear herself laughing as the message played. None of this was funny. But still, she laughed. She felt completely out of control.

Her phone dinged, and Tanya took a ragged breath, wiping the tears from her eyes. She opened the message from Bethany:

Mommy, when are you coming home? I'm hungry.

Tanya swallowed hard. Bethany waited for her return. Counted on her coming home. Her kids could get by without money, but they needed their mom.

She thought about how close she came to never getting that message. More tears slid down her cheeks and she wiped them away, suddenly restless. She pictured Bethany and Hunter running out to help her with the groceries. She wanted to get home and hug her babies. To be with them, tonight and always.

I'll be there soon.

She hit send on the message, then opened the door and went to the passenger side, where she gathered up the dead fish and buried him below the surface of the mud. She threw some left-over McDonald's napkins down on the floorboard to soak up the water. She'd tell the kids she wanted them to help pick out a new fish next week.

She opened the visor mirror, smoothing her hair down to cover the bruise forming on her forehead with a sigh. Her words to Olivia came back into her mind: *Do better.*

"You give damn good advice," she said to her reflection in the rearview mirror before driving her car away from the banged-up fence. She needed to get home.

Talysa Sainz is a young adult fantasy author who believes life's deepest truths can be found in fiction and magic is as essential to life as breath. Reading and writing give voice to her soul. Talysa works as a freelance editor and spends her free time working at the library and volunteering for the League of Utah Writers. Always fascinated with the structure of words, she studied English Linguistics and Editing at BYU. Talysa loves exploring mountains, eating chocolate, collecting nerdy jewelry, and having pun wars with her geeky husband, and writes in the rare moments her kids are quiet. You can find her author website at www.TalysaSainz.com and her editor website at www.TalysaSEdits.com.

About this story, Talysa says: "The zodiac symbol for Aquarius, the water bearer, conjured for me an image of a pregnant woman who held the power of the ocean within her womb. I wanted to express the frustration a woman has when her life literally and metaphorically revolves around protecting other people, and how trapped she can feel. I wanted to explore characters who each believe they are holier than everyone else, despite their actions. I wanted to portray the juxtaposition of the sacredness of motherhood and the depravity of murder, and how people try to protect the sanctity of life in different ways."

Talysa's story vividly illustrates that, despite our best efforts, we never really know what we're truly capable of until we're put to the test—or what the consequences of those actions may be.

THE WATER BEARER
Talysa Sainz

Kala put her hand under her bulging belly and knelt between two unmarked graves at the back of the cemetery, pushing her long black hair out of her face. She lay flowers over one large mound of dirt before putting the rest on the smaller, child-sized mound beside it, and a seashell in between. Only Kala knew who rested in these particular graves—the husband and son of her best friend, Sama.

"Again?" Chief Tomo, Kala's husband, pulled her up by her arm. "You need to stop coming here. People are noticing."

"I don't care." Sama's body had washed up on the island shore two years ago. The priests burned her body for bringing the curse upon herself and her family. Her husband and son were lucky—they were stoned by the village in front of the temple and granted shabby, unmarked resting spots. Kala twisted out of her husband's grasp.

Chief Tomo struck her across the face. Pain blossomed across her jaw and cheek.

"Feel fortunate you are with child, or you would have it worse." He sighed and put his hand on her back to lead her away. "The priests are beginning to question if you can handle being the wife of the chief and mother to the future chief. Once

I have an heir, your role here is… less vital. You know what the priests will do."

Another death threat. It was far from her first, but it would be her last.

"Sama was not a traitor."

"She could have cursed the whole island."

Kala suppressed her retort. The curse of the Creature was pure superstition. The Creature, Kamanu, was the god of the island. The curse, however, was a lie told by the priests to control the people. She wanted—*needed*—to free them. It was her fault that Sama took the risk and swam into the ocean that day, after she caught Kala wading in the water one night. It was her fault that Sama's body washed up on shore and that her husband and son had been stoned. Kala had carried that guilt ever since.

But no more. Today, she would seek vengeance for Sama and cleanse the island of the superstition of Kamanu's curse. She would destroy the wicked priests and the Creature too, if necessary. So she had seduced Priest Nilo. The daughter she carried was fathered by him, not the chief, and thus possessed the Power that ran in the blood of the Creature and every priest he had chosen to carry out his will.

She had stolen the summoning ritual scroll from the temple while Nilo was distracted. The summoning ritual, which the priests had been too terrified to use in centuries, required the blood of one who carried the Power spilled over the altar on the day of sacrifice. Every full moon, the priests sacrificed an animal from the island as a tribute to Kamanu. But today, *they* would be the sacrifice. She intended to summon the Creature. Either Kamanu would bless her daughter or he would die.

"Sama brought her death upon herself," Kala said. A part-truth. "But Mino and Tito did nothing wrong."

"We can't risk spreading the curse."

"I think burning Sama's body was extreme enough."

"Obviously not." The chief picked up the incriminating flowers and ripped them apart. He threw the shell into the distance. "Let's go." He led her away, and as they left the cemetery, he beckoned forward the priest waiting nearby.

Priest Lano began digging up little Mino's grave.

"What are you doing?" Kala cried out.

"Protecting the future of the island," came the gruff voice of the priest as he smiled wickedly. "Even those distantly touched by the curse have no place on our island."

Kala lunged at him, but Chief Tomo held her back. "I told you people were noticing. You have the privilege of being the wife of the chief. You need to be better."

"Privilege is just another name for obligation." Kala pulled away from his grip.

His voice became dark again. "I may not have the Power the priests do, but I am still the chief. If I hadn't spoken up for you, you would have been damned for your association with Sama and stoned as well. You had better learn to appreciate me."

She would appreciate him in his death. His title would give her daughter the chance to rule. His death would allow for new changes, new laws. Her daughter's Power would ensure that nobody challenged her. And the death of the Creature would mean no more priests.

Kala stirred the rest of the poisonous lacas berries into the tea. "She's almost ready to come out," she said, as her husband paced the stone floor inside their hut.

"Yes, yes," Chief Tomo replied, looking outside to the canal.

The canal ran past the temple through the middle of the village and across the island—connecting the ocean to the people, draining away the evil and leaving food and life. Since the ocean was forbidden to them, the ancestors built the canal for fishing. "Hopefully it will wait until the canal dispute has been resolved. We can't afford to get distracted right now."

A distraction. That was how he viewed her baby girl. The people had been arguing about the lack of fish in the canal for three months. She doubted the elders would reach a decision anytime soon.

Kala felt strong feet kicking her ribs and steady hiccups coming from within her womb. This was the last full moon— the last day of sacrifice—before her daughter was due. This was her last chance. She only had the Power as long as her child was inside of her.

Shaking only slightly, she handed the cup of tea to her husband.

"I'm going to walk to the temple," she said.

"Again?"

"Another prayer for our baby."

The chief sipped his tea. "This is cold, again."

Kala stiffened. Would he refuse the drink? One sip wouldn't be enough. She had used all her berries and didn't have time to get more.

Chief Tomo sighed and took a large drink from the cup. "Never mind. Give my regards to High Priest Ziko."

"Yes, of course." She squeezed his shoulder one last time. She would not miss his dismissive words or abusive hand. His death was necessary. Her daughter would be free to rule without the deliberate ignorance that constrained the Chiefs of the past. Kala heard the reassuring thud of his body hitting stone as she left.

Her walk to the temple only encouraged her. She passed several villagers on her way and stopped to talk with them. She loved the people; they were all her cousins, whether related or not. There was more distance between her and them since Sama's death, but she didn't blame them for stoning Mino and Tito; she blamed the priests. She'd been working to repair the distance since her baby began growing inside of her.

Her aunt and several cousins stopped her under the palm trees to ask about the chief and the baby. Not her. Never her. If they knew the father of her child wasn't the chief, but the priest she had poisoned eight months before, her family and friends would not only ignore her, they would kill her. She was grateful to enter the shadow of the temple and walk up its stone steps.

The ancestors built the temple to worship Kamanu, the Creature, the god of the island. Kamanu blessed the land but cursed the ocean, forbidding all from entering his domain. If you gave yourself to the ocean, you gave yourself to the Creature. Occasionally, Kamanu would rise from the depths and choose a new priest at birth by leaving his mark on their forehead and his Power in their blood. The priests were the enforcers for the island; their word was law. They were allowed to do anything they wanted except enter the ocean. Even the holier than thou had to follow that rule. They were also forbidden from fathering children. It would be blasphemy for a priest to pass the Power to a child. Only Kamanu could choose a worthy vessel.

Kala pondered the images carved into the stone walls, reaching inside and out, on every step, every tower, telling the stories of the island—both the history of the people and parables to keep people in bondage. Over the main entrance was the largest carving of all: the Creature. He was as tall as five men, with the scaly skin of a fish, webbed feet, and tentacles bursting from his body, weaving through the other stories. Large red gemstone eyes, the color of blood, depicted death and damnation.

Kala shuddered at the thought of facing Kamanu, but she could put it off no longer. Steeling herself for what must be done, Kala entered the temple. Stories surrounded her on the walls and ceiling, and she remembered the first time she heard the tales of the Creature.

Long before destiny had selected Kala as the future chief's bride, Kala learned the stories from Sama. Sitting on the shoreline, close enough to hear the waves break, Sama would tell the stories from the temple walls. Kala would listen while she played with Sama's beautiful brown baby boy, finding new sea shells he could give his mother. The flecks of blue in Sama's bright amber eyes danced as she excitedly told stories about the sea. Sama loved the ocean, and Kala loved her even more for it.

One night, Kala had snuck to the beach, knelt, and prayed. "Kamanu, will I be cursed if I enter the ocean? Is the great ocean truly evil? Will I die if I leave the island for the waves?"

The wind spiraled around her, and her inner strength intensified. She walked to the water's edge and let the tiny wavelets tickle her toes. She looked up at the sky, waiting for something grand, something supernatural to happen. Nothing came out of the water or the sky or the land behind her. She was fine. She removed her dress to keep it from getting wet, pulled her long hair into a knot on top of her head, and walked farther into the water. She felt the sand sink under her feet and moved forward into the cold waves until they splashed over her shoulders. She whispered another prayer and sank into the water completely.

The ocean threatened to carry her away, but Kala kept her feet pressed into the sand to keep her balance.

Kala was not afraid of the curse. She was afraid of death, and like most of her people, she had never learned how to swim. She left the water feeling stronger, more capable, and with a secret that would change her. She put her clothes on, wrung out her hair the best she could, and went home. It would not be the last time she went into the ocean.

Kala wished she could sneak to the ocean once more before fulfilling her plan, to feel the chilling embrace of the waves that had so fortified her resolve. But as the wife of the chief, she was watched too carefully. If she were caught, the consequences would be dire. Images of being burned alive or stoned in front of the temple came to her mind.

Light danced amidst the stories on the walls and carved stone idols behind the altar, changing colors as the sun moved higher in the sky. Priests gathered for the monthly sacrifice, always at noon at the sacred altar in the center of the temple, which sat in the middle of the valley at the center of the island. Over the altar, the temple opened to the sky.

A man in stiff red robes stepped next to her.

"My husband gives his regards, High Priest Ziko."

"Oh, Kala, your beauty grows as the child inside of you grows. The day must be close. Soon, our next great chief will be free of his vessel and ready to greet his people."

Ready to greet her *people,* Kala silently corrected him. The Power kept her particularly self-aware of her own body and the baby's body within. And Kala was more than a vessel. She was a hero.

"Nurse Bida says within two weeks," Kala said. She didn't like lying. What she said was partially true—Nurse Bida had given Kala her due date—but Kala knew that if her plan was successful, the baby would come much sooner. She nervously patted her belly.

"I'm sorry Priest Nilo will not be there to comfort you on your special day. I know you two were close." The silver-blue mark of the Creature on the priest's forehead shone in the light from a window.

"Mm-hmm." Kala looked down in mock nostalgia. The high priest had no idea just how close she and Nilo had been. As soon as she had conceived and felt the Power running through her veins, she had poisoned him. As he died, she confessed everything—the whole truth, for once. Their affair had lasted ten months and three pregnancies, pregnancies she had quickly ended with doses of lacas berries. She could not—would not—bear a child from the chief, an heir without the Power.

The high priest went on, "I haven't wanted to rush you, but the time is soon at hand. Have you thought more about who you want with you during the birth?"

She had been avoiding this topic, undesirous to tell more untruths in the temple, but telling a lie was the least of the sins she was about to commit. "Yes, I would love it if you would be my birthing priest."

"I would be honored. Come, let us discuss the birthing rituals in privacy."

He led her to a room in the back of the temple. It was simple, almost bare—walls of stone the same as the rest of the temple. A wooden desk sat in the middle of the room, with a stone cup on its corner. Two chairs stood on either side of the desk.

She had been in this room once before. After Sama's body

washed up on shore, Kala came to the high priest for help. "I can't do this," she had cried. "I can't marry the chief."

"But you must." High Priest Ziko had let Kala cry for a short moment before patting her back and offering a prayer. "Oh, Kamanu, our God, have mercy on the island for Sama's sins. Keep the people safe from the curse Sama brought on herself and her family."

The scrape against the floor as High Priest Ziko drew out the chair for her pulled Kala out of her reverie. She gripped the sharp obsidian blade in her pocket. She had made this dress specifically to hide the weapon.

"Have a seat," he said.

Kala eyed the chair. It felt like her body only wanted to sit these days. But once she sat down, it would be infinitely harder for her to get up and act. "I've been sitting all day. I need to stretch my legs." Another lie. She had walked to the cemetery and back this morning. Remembering the destruction of the graves, Kala tightened her grip on the knife.

"Well then, I won't dally. I'll get the records."

The high priest turned and rummaged through a basket on a shelf. This was the moment she had been waiting for—a chance at surprise. A quick death meant a quiet death, less fighting back and less blood on her dress when she met the other priests at the altar.

Deep breath.

Kala felt the unearthly Power flowing through her blood, and with it, the urge to rule, to conquer, to kill. But she refused to give in to those urges. She knew her daughter would be just as strong and resist as Kala did.

She was meant to do this. She was the first female to have this Power. No matter what choices had led her here, Kala needed to carry out her plan to protect her daughter. If the priests discovered the baby girl possessed the Power, they would murder her at once.

Deep breath.

Kala took the blade from her pocket and stepped close to the priest. Raising it over her head, she slashed the high priest through the throat from the side. His body barely made a sound as it slumped to the ground.

She wiped the blood from her blade on the priest's robes. Much easier than the first priest she had killed. She had hesitated then, spilling the lacas berry tea three times before finally giving Nilo the deadly cup. This time was much quicker, much less painful, for both of them.

She slid the blade in her pocket, careful not to cut herself on the edge, and stepped out of the room, shifting the tapestry behind her to cover the door. She went back to the altar, where the priests bowed their heads, waiting for the high priest to lead the sacrificial prayer. A sleeping monkey lay bound on the altar.

Nilo had explained to her once how they tied the animal up the night before the sacrifice letting it struggle through the night to wear itself out. They wanted the animal docile when they murdered it. But was it really more empathetic to calm the beast before the slaughter? More lies, betrayal. Killing for food may be necessary, but this torture was not.

Anger burned through her, flaring the Power to life. Kala struggled but let the surges go. She would not hesitate to kill these men, but it would be by her choice, not the Power's. The cruelty of the island's priests astonished her. Even with the inhuman urges flowing through her, she had more heart than they did.

Kala stepped up to the altar. One priest looked at her. "Is the high priest coming? Noon approaches."

"He'll be with you in a moment." Another part-truth. The priest bowed his head again and closed his eyes in preparation.

Deep breath.

Kala sliced into the priest's neck, just as she had with the high priest. Before his body hit the floor, she sliced the neck of the man next to him.

Priest Lano, the last priest alive, stood up and tried to stop her, but she stabbed him in the chest—once, twice, thrice—and the bloodlust within her fought for control.

Lano grabbed her wrist and wrestled the blade, her only weapon, from her hand and threw it across the floor.

Kala still had the Power, but she feared losing control if she used it. She would not give in to the bloodlust the priests used to control the people; she was better than that. She needed to use her human strength, which was lacking these final days of pregnancy.

Kala pushed herself into Lano's arms, hoping her weight would throw him off enough to distract him while she ran for the blade. He fell backwards, but she tumbled down with him. The priest scrambled to his feet, calling for the high priest as he ran for the back room, worried about his missing leader.

Lano was cornered. Kala grabbed the blade and tried to rise, but she was like a turtle on her back. She rocked back and forth, side to side, until she built up enough momentum to turn over and lift herself up.

Deep breath.

She was running out of strength. She moved as fast as her swollen ankles would carry her. She found the last priest on his knees, crying over his fallen friend.

"Why are you doing this?" he asked. "Did the chief make you do this?"

Of course. It wouldn't occur to anyone that she might be

making this decision for herself, that she could know best, when she was clearly inferior to the chief and the priests. The insult fueled the bloodlust, and Kala finally released the Power.

Hesitation and worry fled her body. This was what she was meant to do. With inhuman speed, Kala jumped forward and stabbed the last priest in the heart. Grabbing the stone cup from the desk, she held it underneath the priest's weeping wound.

The baby kicked Kala in the ribs, as if she, too, knew her time had come. "We are almost there, my darling. The Creature will soon be destroyed. And you, little Masa, will rule with the wisdom that has been unavailable to me."

Kala returned to the altar, set the cup down, and freed the poor monkey. Saying the sacrificial words, she poured the priest's blood over the altar.

The temple rumbled; the earth shook and broke apart beneath it. A pool of water rose around the altar until it sank completely under a flow of ocean waves.

For a moment, silence.

Apprehension crawled over Kala's skin. If Kamanu blessed her daughter, Masa would be accepted by the people. If he didn't, Kala would have to kill a god.

From the water emerged a head, the same mix of green, blue, and gray of the ocean at night. The Creature rose from the pool, eyes closed, arms folded over its chest. Familiarity tugged at Kala. Though less exaggerated than the carving on the temple wall, the Creature was terrifying—twice as tall as Kala, slimy tentacles crawling from its back, sharp scales and claws and talons everywhere she looked. The Creature opened its eyes and stepped from the pool onto the floor of the temple. Kala tried to keep her heart steady.

But the eyes… The bright amber eyes of the Creature were unnerving. Their flecks of blue made Kala fall to her knees.

It was Sama.

Kala gasped. How could this be?

A deep ache pulsed from Kala's belly. The child was coming —now! Kala's heart raced as her body tore open. The Power ripped the baby from her womb. As the Power inside her drained into the child, Kala fainted.

When she awoke, she lay on the stone floor in a pool of her own blood and birthing fluids. The Creature—*Sama!*—was on the other side of the pool, wrapping the baby in a silvery blue blanket. She kissed the child's forehead, and the Mark appeared on the baby's skin. "You will be safe," the Creature whispered, laying the baby down, "for you are the last."

Kala lifted herself to her knees and tried to stand. Her body was weak, and she was losing blood, but she managed to struggle to her feet. She took one step towards her baby, her daughter, her Masa. The Creature turned her head toward Kala. In a moment, the Creature stood before her and wrapped itself around her.

The Creature sucked the life from Kala. Everything in her weakened and faded. As her strength flowed out of her and into the Creature, a glowing figure appeared a few feet away.

Dying, Kala watched the glowing figure grow in substance until it was more like a solid mass of cloud than wisps of smoke. The apparition wore the same dress Sama wore the last time Kala had seen her, the day she jumped into the ocean.

Hanging on to her life by thin vines, Kala felt the Creature drag her across the temple floor and into the pool. For the first time, Kala was in the ocean completely. She wasn't touching earth below; she wasn't in the air above. Her suspension in the water lasted but a moment before the Creature brought her head above the surface and sucked the last bit of life from her. Her vision went black.

When light returned, everything was bathed in a reddish hue, and the room had spun. Kala stood where the Creature had been, at the same time seeing her motionless body floating in the water before her. She looked around, but the Creature had vanished.

Panicking, she tried to ask the spirit Sama for help, but no words came out. Sama smiled sadly, a single tear sliding down her face before she again became white, ethereal wisps and entered the sky through the top of the temple.

A deep instinct inside of Kala enticed her to the water. Resisting, she turned to her daughter and tripped over her own tail. She used her tentacles to crawl to her baby and gave her a simple kiss on her forehead, where a second silvery blue mark appeared. Drained of strength, Kala descended into the ocean she had always longed for, more a part of it than she had ever hoped.

L.D.B. (Lisa) Taylor is a lifelong reader and writer. The author of five independently published books, Lisa's short stories and articles have appeared in print and online publications. She blogs (occasionally) at ldbtaylor.com and writes (daily) from her oversized, perpetually dusty home in the hills. Represented by Rena Rossner, her latest manuscript is pending publication. She appreciates wit, chocolate, hot tea, cool mountain evenings, kindness, travel, and books by the score.

About this story, Lisa says: "'Lilith's Ale' began with the idea that everyone experiences a Before and an After. How we savor the Before! That delicious feeling of being on the verge, of becoming, of a long-desired journey just begun. But the After, there all chances of fresh adventure have been spent. To be caught in the After drives you wild with fear. Making you believe that where you are, is where you shall remain. And yet... India and Jenny's twined stories trickled through both places, as water seeps between stones, eventually transforming them."

There are stories that are a simple retelling of events, and there are those that reach inside you and make you live them along with the characters. This powerful tale is one of the latter.

LILITH'S ALE
L.D.B. Taylor

"They have beene shut up in prisons and dungeons...
allowed onely a poore pittance of Adam's Ale, and scarce a
penny bread a day to support their lives."

-William Prynne's
The Soveraigne Power of Parliaments and Kingdomes, 1643

There's always a Before and an After. Though most times we work to assure ourselves we're living in the Before, because admitting the opposite is just too painful to bear.

Living in the Before allows a person a sense of freedom— the illusion of free will. No matter how muddled the Before becomes, it still holds a promise of light, of living through and traveling on, of becoming more. Envisioning that one fine day, you'll finally become the person you believed you were always meant to be. That faith helps forge a path across those long passages of dark times. Through times full of fear and dread.

Moments when the night's silence is broken by a rapping at the window, sending you scurrying to the deepest depths of your closet, rolling into a tight ball. One fisted hand pressed to your mouth until the knocking, and the ragged breathing behind it, thankfully stops. Allowing you, at last, to fall asleep with one eye open, wrapped in an old coat till morning.

Little India Martin had known such times all too often.

How many nights had she spent squeezing her eyes tight in her closet depths? Whisper-praying so hard and thick with need, her small hands clenched together so tight they were forever after scarred with nail marks. Thin slices of purple crescent.

Other nights, when the knocking never came, she whispered out her prayers, crawled beneath the bedclothes, and switched off the light, doing her utmost, iron-willed best to ignore the shadows dancing on the walls. Dark, lithe shapes beckoning to her with long, wavering fingers, sharp nailed, red tipped. Whisper-praying herself to sleep, India ignored the soft voices inviting her to "Get on outta that bed and join us!" Join them in their revels, their fun. Slide the casement aside, step down through the night air, rush through the darkness to dance the dance of wicked and the damned.

Blessed as few had ever been was India Martin. She was quite a talented girl. Her Grandmother Anna had recognized it first. Proclaiming, "India holds more blessings in her little finger than I ever did in my entire body." And she'd laugh, blue eyes sparkling while India's mother, Jenny, looked on, her thin lips twisting, telling India this was something she didn't enjoy hearing and didn't want to hear again.

India's mother had no blessing, not the slightest whiff. Jenny couldn't whisper-peel the flowered paper from the bathroom wall or eye the living room rug, convincing it to shift a half centimeter to the right. Things India had done as a baby, intu-itively and with no forethought at all.

Letting India know at least one thing in this world was certain: her mother was jealous of her. As jealous as a woman can be of someone who has what she's always wanted. Some-thing Jenny had spent nights mourning the absence of, long desperate years clawing after. For wasn't it true, wasn't it the god's own truth, that all Aldridge women were born with the blessing? Be it the ability to turn withered roses fresh, light a candle with a breath, fetch a raven to do their bidding, or make the man they fall in love with remain caught within that love till they chose different. Every Aldridge woman throughout memory and beyond had some bit of blessing—all but one.

The Passing Over, Grandma Anna called it, shrugging her small round shoulders. Looking away, changing the subject. "No one knows why, it just happens. Sometimes the blessing skips a generation. Why I've heard some consider the Passing Over a blessing in itself."

A blessing? Jenny thought, nearly crying aloud, glaring at her mother. White-knuckled she bit back the words she longed to shout, "Look at you! Just sitting, staring out the kitchen window. Talking to yourself really, not even caring whether I'm here." Jenny grit her teeth, steeping in anger. Unaware of the dark fingers folding over themselves, one dancing layer at a time, closing around her throat. Unaware of her pulse slowing, her body becoming cool. Never even noticing her hair change, fading from strawberry-blonde to palest ash.

"Perhaps India's your blessing," Anna had continued, easily murmuring the words forever regretted. Watching the oak planted by her great-grandfather Willum dancing in the new autumn wind. Its limbs twisting about one another like embracing arms. Like writhing snakes. "With a gift as strong as hers, well there's no telling what she might do."

What she might do, Anna's words cast the final sliver of metal binding Jenny's heart, kicking up a furious, whirling storm in her mind and souring her stomach. In that moment Jenny Aldridge Martin knew the Passing Over was nothing less than a curse brought on by India's mere existence and her mother's acceptance of it. She began hating them both as only a woman overlooked and forgotten can hate.

India was three years old the first time Jenny tried to kill her.

Maybe most three-year-old children wouldn't notice their mother leaving them down by the river. Maybe Mama just wandered off, or maybe they wandered off—something three-year olds are wont to do without supervision. But India sensed Jenny's intentions. She meant to abandon her. Right there, by the deepest part of Sacer River, where it meandered along around that first rocky turn, swirling blue with foaming white peaks. The exact spot Josiah Blake had drowned himself after Sarah Bedlow refused his hand. Instead choosing to marry a man from up north with money and land and better prospects. Hushed voices claimed Josiah's body, or what was left of it, floated there still one hundred years on, clutched by twining grasses, caught fast in the deep water.

Little India saw Josiah there and knew her mother may as well have thrown her bodily in, tied heavy about the waist with ropes and rocks to weigh her down—none of that bobbin' back up like a cork foolishness—as to abandon her right next the river that late November day. Sneaking off when India's back was turned. Telling her daughter, "The prettiest rocks are just there, beyond the water's edge. See 'em, Indy? Sparkling in the sun. Just step on down, don't be afraid."

She wasn't. Even though she saw Josiah's hollow eyes staring up at her through the water, his open mouth whispering, telling her not to get too close. *Stay back, little girl, don't meet a fate like mine.* She listened to her mother's footsteps, sprinting stealth through the woods behind her. Echoing faint and fainter as India crouched down upon a rock outcropping, staring straight at Josiah's sad, wavering face, spreading thin and wide across the river's surface, so deep was he caught and held.

India hugged her knees to her chest and remained in place. Not moving an inch until hours later, beneath the light of a waxing Mourning Moon, Grandma Anna found her. Exclaiming with relief and dismay that India should have wandered off, *ah but now I've found you!* Wrapping her tight in a quilt and plump strong arms, carrying her home to hot cocoa, warm pajamas, and a soft bed. Singing her the cradle songs they both loved best as Jenny sat before the sitting room fire nursing a gin and tonic, wondering exactly when her life had gone wrong and avoiding her mother's eye.

Three years to the day she tried again.

Now, India was six. A big girl in the first grade. She had been reading for almost four years—a fact her grandmother hadn't ignored. Raven Cottage's library was deeper than most would have imagined. Grandma Anna was proud of that library, intent on India enjoying every classic of children's literature she could lay her hands on. Keeping all of the Aldridge Family books, their soft leather covers hand tooled and bound, aside until just the right time. Until she knew India was ready.

Jenny ignored Anna's library, walking right past it as though it didn't exist. As if somehow that particular doorway had sealed itself, refashioning into a dun-colored wall undeserving of a second glance. She had taken to sitting on the back porch, listening to the frogs and crickets serenading from Blokan Pond, chain smoking, smashing out the butts on the concrete porch floor. These days she drank bourbon straight up. Sometimes from a glass, more often from a thick mug enabling an easy grasp when her hands became too shaky and her vision blurred. Some evenings she found the cigarettes hard to light, the lighter flame wavering this way and that as she stared down two, often three cigarettes at once. Those nights she'd decide to take her chances and light the one in the middle. It usually worked.

Jenny, who had been the most popular and pretty girl in her high school, who'd had 'Most Likely to Marry a Movie Star' printed beneath her picture in her senior yearbook, sat alone night after night on a tobacco and ash-stained slab of concrete, stewing in her hatred for her mother, plotting ways to kill her only child and then get the hell away. Toward the sea maybe, for doesn't salt water renew and rekindle? Perhaps by the sea she could find some way to breathe once more.

Other women would have blamed their ex-husbands. Other women, particularly those with Jenny's long lineage of strong Aldridge ancestors with a penchant for revenge would have hunted Clancy Martin down, pummeling him till his lifeless body lay blood soaked and rag edged.

It's what Jenny's mother, Anna, would have done. As well as Jenny's grandmother and every grandmother before, back to Maran Herrick herself, who had landed on the eastern seaboard three-hundred years before with only a wailing infant and a dead husband to her name.

But the Passing Over had left Jenny blighted. Extinguished was the sweet, hot fire flaring within every descendent of Maran Herrick down through the generations—male and female alike. Leaving Jenny weak and angry and, "Oh, so ripe for the picking."

Jenny concocted a new plan. One that didn't rely on her daughter's clumsy curiosity and the swift currents of the Sacer River. Following the river's betrayal, Jenny chose a blade.

Clancy's hunting knife, left behind the December night he'd packed his bag and fled, his motorcycle blasting away in a thick mix of exhaust, smoke, and fear. Leaving Jenny standing in the middle of the icy road in her thin cotton nightgown looking the barefoot, desperate fool she'd been.

Six years on she was no fool, or so she hoped. So she told herself while sharpening the knife just as Clancy had shown her back in high school. He'd taken her squirrel hunting and they'd slept beneath the stars in the bed of his daddy's pickup. Six years on and she was a grown woman with little life behind and seemingly no life ahead unless she grabbed it for herself and took it.

"There was no Passing Over," Jenny told herself, spitting on the whetstone, sliding the blade's edge back and forth. "My blessing was stolen. Siphoned right outta me and into that child. How could Mama call it a blessing? Why it's not even a child at all… it's a curse. A changeling."

Watching the reflection of her lips move, weirdly angled in the gleaming blade, Jenny's green eyes shone. "Sapping me dry since its first breath, maybe even before. Was this why Clancy left?"

"Mama's the fool for not recognizing what *it* is. She can't see the truth, but it's there." Jenny tested the blade with a finger. "I have to stop it, before I'm nothing but a dried-up shell waiting to be crushed. Splintered shards, scattered and swept away by the winds."

Streaking back a clump of lank, greasy hair Jenny opened her bedroom door, slinking silently down the hall toward India's room. Turning the handle, oh so quiet, into the room she slipped. Pressed thin against the wall, watching her daughter, *the changeling*, asleep upon her bed. Her long dark Aldridge hair splayed across the pillow in tangles, pale skin shining in the moonlight, lashes fluttering as her eyelids rolled in dreams.

And so vile was Jenny's sour rage, so determined her mind, she felt no remorse, not a second's hesitation as she moved toward the bed in her stockinged feet. Raising the knife, her twisted lips almost smiling she gazed down, envisioning the thrust, the tiny cry, the blood, and oh the sweet, sacrosanct silence to follow.

India's black eyes snapped open. She watched as Clancy's hunting knife curled around itself, liquid and quick as a snake set to strike.

Before Jenny could scream, before her lips could even part, or her mind realize what was about to happen, the knife, quicksilver and boiling hot, shot toward her throat. Wrapping itself around her dry skin, sinking in and plunging through. Coiling about her vocal cords, fusing them into stiff bands motionless and silent.

India's eyes closed and she dreamed on. The vines outside casting dark, dancing shadows upon her window.

Jenny remained bedridden for weeks.

Anna dosed her with herbal teas, savory broths, hot spiced poultices—every remedy she could recall, every receipt her great-grandmother's books contained.

But Jenny's voice was gone.

It had fled upon the night sky, or so India believed. She imagined it whisking away, white feathery wings sailing silent through the moon-cast shadows of her room while the world slept and the house dozed. Even Jenny's raspy snores disappeared. Collected and tossed out along with the nagging words, the cutting remarks, the sarcastic cooing India had tried to ignore whenever her grandmother showered her with love and affection.

For longer than she could recall, India had heard her mother's thoughts, and she feared Jenny's heart was colder than the deepest river stone. India supposed Jenny never really loved anyone but herself, and wondered whether even self-love was possible with an embittered spirit so thin and crackling dry.

When Grandma Anna questioned her about that night, sideways-like and tricksy, *oh she knew those tricks!* India opened her eyes wide, wrinkling her small brow, claiming she recalled nothing as Anna watched with that look she took on when the need arose. Her dark eyes delving into the depths of India's mind, deeper than any person ought to be able to. After several long moments of eyeing India, Anna finally smiled, handed her a gingerbread square, and bid her to go on out and play.

But India remembered everything. She recalled the metal blade glinting in the moonlight. Her mother looming just above her, set to plunge the sharp, gleaming tip into and through India's own heart, (not river stone, as Josiah Blake's had become, but formed of flesh and blood, beating fast). She remembered the way her eyes seemed to snap open on their own as she lay frozen, caught up within a fierce, unyielding power. Holding her breath, waiting to see what would happen.

Surely it was all a dream, seeing the knife's blade as it melted and stretched. Half spellbound and wondering whether or not she still slept, India's eyes followed the blade's wavering, lingering dance. Watched its final plummet into and around her mother's throat. Heard Jenny's long exhale, a whispered sigh, as she crumpled to the floor. And then, knowing somehow that Anna had appeared, imagined her in her long nightdress with tumbled hair flying.

Rushing past Jenny, lying still and staring upon the floor, Anna scooped India from her bed sheets just as she had from the damp river rock, and tucked the child into her own bed, still warm. Touching a hand to India's closed eyelids she had murmured a few words—an old phrase which India knew by heart—that caused her pulse to slow and send her into true slumber.

Only then did Anna attend to Jenny. She had heaved her daughter's limp body from the floor and eased Jenny back along the hallway, with Jenny simultaneously groping for and swatting away her mother's hands. Smoothing her sheets and tucking her in, Anna lay a white vinegar and rosemary-soaked cloth upon her forehead. Calming her frantic eyes with loving words only a mother could say:

"You tried it again, idiot girl!" Her grey hair, unloosed from its usual French twist, hung wild about her shoulders, her black opal eyes shone hard at Jenny through the darkness. "You tried it again you stupid, stupid girl—and this time you got what you deserved!"

Jenny twisted in the bed, attempting to wrench her arm from her mother's grasp, but of course Anna was stronger than that.

"Can you speak at all?" Anna asked. Biting her tongue, trying to control her rage, to remember this foolish woman was a child of her own body. Knowing what the answer would be.

Grimacing, Jenny clutched her throat, glared at her mother, and shook her head.

"Well, I suppose it'll be quieter around here from now on," Anna said, unable—and unwilling—to keep the ire from her voice. Grimacing, Jenny closed her eyes, forcing herself to lie still, breathing slow.

"Oh yes," Anna whispered, anger encircling her own throat like a vise, turning her voice husky, her mouth dry. "Act calm, my darling girl. Sit tight while I dose you and we both pretend you're on the mend."

Jenny's eyes shot open.

Nearly quelled by their stark, bloodshot fear, Anna forced her voice to steady before continuing on. "Oh, my girl, we both know you'll never mend. You've been broken for too many years. Though goddess knows I'll try, I fear I'll never be able to undo the harm you've done to yourself."

Jenny glared at her mother though her thin lips quivered. A fine film of what could almost have been tears coated her eyes and Anna's heart lurched, her words caught in her throat.

"Will you finally be able to cry then?" she whispered. "Now that you've sacrificed your voice. Will you be able to cry as you've never been able your whole life long?"

"Will I be able to cry?" The words sliced into Jenny's mind. For tears were as alien to Jenny Martin as the ability to love true.

As a child, Jenny had tried to cry. Had pinched herself hard, held the rankest of onions right next her eyes, read the saddest books, watched the most heartbreaking movies. The ones all the other girls at school described as absolutely heart-wrenching and the saddest thing they'd ever seen.

But the tears never came. No matter how long she forced herself to mourn over the loss of her father, to brood over the birth of the unwanted daughter, or relive Clancy's abandonment. No matter how often she whispered *Unworthy* into the mirror. Knowing anyone as weak as she had been was forever damned. Doomed to wish and yearn with empty hands and darkened heart.

No. It was impossible for Jenny Aldridge to cry, try as she might. Though she could attempt to murder her own daughter for the sole sin of existing and hate her mother for her ability to love them both more easily than taking breath.

The days passed. Anna threw out every package of Jenny's cigarettes, poured each found bottle of bourbon down the kitchen sink, tossing the empties with a satisfying clink into the recyclable bin. She dosed Jenny with remedies over two centuries old, fed her plain, wholesome food, forced her to drink water and milk and fresh squeezed orange juice. Watched her daughter's wan face fill in, her sallow skin take on an almost healthy glow she began to recognize some semblance of the girl she had raised in this mute, bitter woman.

Once or twice India snuck just within Jenny's doorway. Silent, her dark eyes veiled. Watching her mother stare, unblinking, at the empty wall opposite her bed.

The sight of her was enough to give anyone the creepin' willies.

India had decided to steer clear of the whole mess. Early on, Anna made some mention of India's going to stay with an unknown and unheard-of aunt, but India knew that certainly wasn't going to happen.

The last few weeks had been the best of India's young life. With her mama cloistered in her bedroom silent as the grave, India had free run of the house. She watched TV till well after ten p.m. whenever she wanted. Ate dinners of macaroni and cheese with potato chips and salted chocolate chip cookies for dessert, without Mama's warnings that she'd grow fat as a cow. She lounged, blanket-wrapped, in the backyard hammock, reading by the hour, and not one person hollered at her. Not a soul told her to get busy and clean her room or go to bed, even though it was still light outside. Whatever could grandma be thinking? Trying to ship her off somewhere to miss out on all her new-found freedom?

As far as India was concerned, Mama trying to kill her had been the best thing that had ever happened.

Until the voices returned. She had thought them finally gone. Those soft, oh-so-inviting voices beckoning to her from her window in the night. It had been years since she'd heard them. Years since she'd turned her back and closed her eyes, wishing them away. Hard wishing that had been, more difficult than anything she'd tried yet. Still she believed she had done it.

She'd been wrong.

She heard them, low at first, cat-calling after her as she tried to read or sleep. Growing bolder, venturing into the daylight and tagging her footsteps as she walked home from school. Whispering from behind the radiator, the pipes beneath the sink. Calling to her from the sidewalk cracks and the boggy bit near the garden's eastern edge where even the ravens refused to venture.

"Come play with us," they whispered, their lithe shapes flitting across the grass, the kitchen linoleum, the honey maple of her bedroom floor. Their words coiled after her, pulling her from sleep. "Join in our dance, you know you want to! Don't you wish to be wild and free? As we are? As your mother was?"

India's eyes flicked open. "My mother?" Ah, this was new. They hadn't used this tack before, mentioning someone else. She had believed only they and she existed in their world. Rising up on one elbow she watched the thin shadows writhe, crisscrossing over her bedroom floor as their words intermingled.

"She turned her back on us. She left us. But you won't do that, will you India? No... You're too strong. Too kind. Why, look what you've survived!"

Ice trickled down her spine; India knew the "she" they spoke of was her mother. Watching them narrow, bunch, then slip beneath her bedroom door, she knew the shadows were dancing down the hallway, making their way into Jenny's room.

Narrowing her eyes just so, India saw through both their closed doors. Seeing the shadows slanting tall and dark upon Jenny's walls, she recognized the fear in her mother's frozen, unblinking eyes as the shadows teased her. Whispering their cruel, tormenting words. Wrapping their thin, dark fingers about Jenny's wrists and ankles, creeping along her arms, stroking the side of her face, leaving it smudged with bits of glowing ember and trickling white smoke.

"Grandma doesn't know," India spoke out loud to herself. Thoughts bombarded her. How could Anna, strong as she was, not realize her own daughter was caught fast within the shadow people's bonds? Wound, as a spider rolls its prey, in a luminescent skein of viscous words and dashed hopes. Her very spirit lifted from her piece by piece.

"No wonder she hates me." India felt tears in her eyes. "She thinks I've done it—but it was them—long before me. I've done nothing," she whispered, wiping the wet from her cheeks. "But I can. I will."

The next day Jenny was worse. Her pale eyes, once described as bewitching and luminous, remained constantly open, refusing to blink. Her lips, called dewy by her class's self-proclaimed poet, and juicy by Clancy after just the right amount of whiskey, were swollen and chapped. Patches of dry skin blotched her face, and her wavy hair, no matter how often Anna washed it with rainwater and chamomile, drying and fluffing it carefully afterward, remained lank and greasy, clinging to her scalp and neck.

Five months to the day of Jenny's silencing, India watched from the hallway as her grandmother hung a painting discovered in the attic during one of her clearing raids.

She'd taken up these raids, so she told India, as a way of clearing out her mind as well as this magpie mess of a house. "A body's gotta keep busy. Work's good for the mind and soul."

And India had bitten her lip, surprised by Grandma's lie. "She knows me better'n that. Is she so scared of Mama's silence?" India knew Grandma was actually searching for anything, a bit of paper escaped from one of the Family Receipts books, a clouded spice bottle containing precisely what was needed, a soft-edged, encrypted postcard from Niagara

Falls, containing some clue of how to find and recapture Jenny's flown voice.

Far at the attic's western end, behind a stack of *Good House-keeping* magazines, a vintage trunk filled with contents so dubious Anna kept it double-locked until she found time to go through it properly, and a tandem bicycle belonging to Great Uncle Julius—who may just return home to retrieve it, one never knew—leaned a large rectangle wrapped in brown paper and thick with dust. It was a landscape, the last painted by Jenny's father, Augustus, the summer before he'd died.

Anna's fingers grew warm the moment she spotted it. Humming to herself she carried it downstairs, disposed of the paper, polished the wooden frame till it gleamed, and carefully dusted the canvas as India looked on. Then she hammered a nail into the wall opposite Jenny's bed and hung the painting at eye level, adjusting it till it was more or less straight. Sitting down next to Jenny, Anna smoothed back her hair, squeezed her hand, and enveloped her in an uncharacteristic long embrace, staring into her open, dry eyes with a mixture of love, pain, fear, and—even the most generous are cursed with some —regret.

But this only lasted a second.

"I'm going into the garden," Anna said, addressing neither Jenny nor India. Seemingly speaking to the air as she walked past India toward the kitchen. India clung to Jenny's doorway, still watching her mother's open eyes, thinking "they're gonna dry up and fall right outta her head." Pondering what the proper reaction would be should that horror come to pass.

"I'll be back in a few minutes. Be a good girl, India Martin," Anna called, her voice sounding oddly far away, as India sidled fearfully into her mother's room. It was overrun with shadow people. Dark shapes undulating around Jenny's bed, reaching out for her, caressing her face.

But Jenny didn't notice them or India. Jenny saw nothing but the glorious, serene landscape opposite her, and a semblance of faint rose seemed to light her pallid cheeks. Wrenching her gaze from her mother's eyes India stared at the painting and caught her breath.

It was perfect. Though she'd never been west, she knew it was the Pacific. Inviting, blue waters, the sun above obviously setting, settling itself. Tucking its rays just beyond the horizon before sighing and sinking from sight.

Grandpa Augustus created those rays with bold streaks of yellow and red blended with burnt umber and mixed grays. Shallow, azure waters trickled and flowed across long stretching fingers of rock. The painting appeared so peaceful and calm, it seemed so real that India was half reluctant to touch it, certain her hand would feel the wet. More than half fearful the salt crystals, for she felt sure they were why the water sparkled so, would encase her fingers. Hold each one tight, draw her in.

India blinked. The shadow people shifted their attention to her, moving in close. Salt spray lit softly upon her face and she licked her lips. Touched her dampened fingers to her mouth, tasting the salt. Inhaling, she smelled the brine of the sea.

"You think to save her?" The sneering voices surrounded her, their laughter curling around her ears, weaving up through her hair, and attempting to overwhelm the ocean's soothing song. "You can't, you can't! She's lost. But you..." The voices drew closer, paper thin fingers sliding sharp against her throat. "You're ours for—"

India slammed her eyes shut and pushed at the voices harder than she'd ever dared push before. Shoved at the voices, those dancing shadows. *My eyes will start to bleed,* she thought. *My head will pop, my heart will squiggle right outta my chest.*

Still she pushed and shoved. Thrust her will at them. Ignoring the throbbing behind her forehead. Piling wish after wish upon the purifying ocean waters, savoring its sharp salt taste. Not Adam's Ale this, but the fallen Lilith's, filled with acrid bitterness. Its sour, earthy flavor one of life and death, and moving on.

India clung to her wishes, her mouth parched from the sea's brine until finally, long minutes later, the voices grew faint and fell away. In their place echoed the faint cry of gulls and the rhythmic dance of the sea.

Opening her eyes, India found Jenny smiling at her and caught her breath. Every trace of the iron threaded bitterness had gone. Jenny's smile was true, lit by the soft eyes of a mother, glowing warm. And *oh what would Grandma Anna say?* Jenny's eyes glittered, brimming with actual tears, their wavering paths shining silver as they trickled down her cheeks.

Inhaling deep, India smiled back. Then, reaching down through all her blessing, she gathered it up and pulled it close. Whisper-wishing her mother toward the painting. Watching Jenny rise from the bed, her long nightdress swirling about her as though already caught up on the outgoing tide.

Jenny thrust her dry, shaking hands toward her daughter as she passed. Grasping them India held tight, pressing them to her heart. And for a moment one heard the other's thoughts.

I'm sorry... The apology made India's chest ache as she watched tears slide down Jenny's cheeks.

It isn't an ending. India's thoughts filled both their minds as she felt her mother's hands became smooth. Turn taut as the salt water lifted her, replenishing her spirit. *Nor a shrive. There is no penance. It's a starting over.* She was surprised by her own words, though she knew they were true. *When we meet again, it'll be different. So many things will have changed by the time I head west.*

So finally, Jenny's journey began. And India? Her light filled the room.

Before Anna returned from the garden, fresh bunches of basil lying damp in her basket, Jenny had already completed her passage from the Before into the After. Her face still wet with tears, she alighted soft within a golden hued world of absolving waters. Where only sweet ocean song whispered into her ears as she began anew, seeking her own blessing. Safe in the knowledge that Afters are meant to be shared.

Some Aldridge women, it was said, could dance upon sea waves when the moon and tides were just right. Some could lift into the clouds with a silent whisper. Some cured the deadliest illness with a prayer and a kiss; some struck down the strongest man with a single glance.

India Martin could do all these and more, before she was ten years old, such was her light and her power.

Though even the most blessed among us don't always recognize the Before and the After. Can't see just where it is they are, how they came to be there, or how they'll move on. It's a rare talent, living in the Present; rarer still to find it fine.

To feel certain you'll become the person you were meant to be. Certain the After will arrive in its own sweet time with a soft, silent rush, a breath of chill air, a whirling dance of mist and rain.

Just as it should.

Jenna Bowman has been telling stories as long as she can recall, and hasn't stopped writing since the day she learned how to put words to paper, and is now an author of fantasy, romance, space opera, comics, and more. Under the names J.C. Archer and J.C. Bond, she dabbles in other genres when the Muse insists. In the real world, Jenna is the "chief everything officer" at Rose and Arrow Creative LLC, and when she's not writing, she can be found making custom journals, turning pens, or creating other art. She is an Asian drama, YouTube DIY, and CW/DC superhero show fan, a comic book lover and proud member of the Blue Lantern Corps. She also plays several instruments, sings, and writes music.

About this story, Jenna says: "I was inspired to write "Grandma and the Wolf" by a combination of two 'what-if' ideas floating around social media about the legend that gets used in the story and the need for more atypical hero types. I feel this story kind of turns the Red Riding Hood story on its head, and the heroine is certainly atypical. I'm planning to write more with Pat in the future, because there is a whole world of family and the fantastic to be explored here."

Fairy tales offer so many opportunities for looking beyond the traditional children's story. Jenna's version provides a fun spin on the tale, with a little cross-genre mixing of mythologies that's sure to please.

GRANDMA AND THE WOLF
Jenna Bowman

Patches of silver light on the ground, mottled by shadows, shifted every time the cold wind blew the branches of the trees above Pat's head. She concentrated on the path ahead of her, feeling out every step instead of trusting the unreliable light of the full moon. She moved as silently as possible through the layer of fallen red, gold, and brown leaves, listening for the mournful howl of a wolf.

In all her sixty-one years, she had never come up against a foe this devastating. True, the toll on the nearby homes hadn't been as bad as it could have been. A few unfortunate family pets had died, and some poultry and rabbits. No human lives had been lost so far, and she hoped to keep it that way. But the personal cost of this matter continued to rise steadily with each sighting of the monster that had stolen her teenage grandson, Blake.

She flexed her arthritic fingers, aching from the combination of the autumn chill and the evening's earlier effort of loading silver shot into shells. She'd discovered over the years that a shotgun was far more effective than silver bullets in a rifle. The hardness of the metal wore down rifle bores, rendering them less accurate, but it made great shot pellets. With luck, the gun she carried would be unnecessary, but fortune favored the prepared.

Pat shook her head as she continued to walk, a tired chuckle escaping despite her efforts at quiet. It had been difficult to convince her grown children that she should go alone; they thought she was too old for this, and either wanted to go with her or stop her from going at all. Her daughter demanded explanations. Her son tried to block the door, claiming she was too old to still be doing this. It was her daughter-in-law who finally realized that Pat was her son's best hope and convinced her husband to stand down. Pat had been surprised by her endorsement. The younger woman had never been her best friend. A decent daughter-in-law and a wonderful mother. But never Pat's friend. That might have changed tonight, but there was no time to dwell on it now.

She would still have a lot to explain when she returned, but for now her focus was on finding Blake and bringing him safely back.

A howl echoed off the foothills, drawing Pat to the present. A grim smile spread across her tired face as she whispered, "Got him."

She turned in that direction, picking up her pace a little. It would do no good if she hurried and tripped on roots or dips hidden by the moon's mercurial shadows. But she knew which way she was headed now, and that helped.

It was impossible not to recall so many other nights like this, where Pat stalked the creatures of darkness to keep her home and her people safe. Nights lit by the silver moon and filled with the wonder of the world beyond the understanding of most. Harry, right there next to her, matching her stride for stride, making sure her back was covered when they fought a particularly nasty creature.

For forty-odd years, Harry had been her constant companion, from before they married right up until the day two years ago when the cancer took him. She had learned to adapt, to get on without him, to continue to protect their home from the dangers of the supernatural. But tonight, more than ever, she wished that he was at her side to face this particular challenge. She could really use his calming influence as she searched for their grandchild.

The ground began to slope upward, and that particular sensation of the hairs rising on the back of her neck, and the headache-like pressure at the back of her skull, told Pat she was closing in on the monster. In fact, she knew this particular path very well. She had often brought Blake here when he was younger, to enjoy a picnic while both his parents worked. Her heart raced faster as she approached her quarry.

The trees opened up before her, leading into the clearing. This time of year, this time of night, the well-worn summer haunt of the locals should have been deserted. It was not.

On the far side of the clearing, a hulking black figure crouched by a lone picnic table abandoned to the season. As Pat stepped into the moonlight, the monster rose to its full height, towering over the table, and turned to snarl at her. Its fangs glistened with saliva, its long muzzle wrinkled as it bared its teeth. The eyes glowed red against its black fur.

Pat's heart rose up into her throat as a cold lump.

She took a deep breath to steady her shaking body and tried to ignore the six-inch claws on the lupine monster's hands and feet. She could not show fear, even though the beast likely smelled it on her. It would be much simpler to use the silver shot she had loaded earlier and be done with it, but this time it was only a last resort, and one she was reluctant to employ.

"There's an old...," Pat began. The words caught in her

throat, and she started again, this time with a stronger, surer, clearer voice. "There is an old legend about werewolves. A few legends actually, but two that come to mind just now."

The monster stalked across the clearing toward her, nose twitching as it paused a couple of times to sniff her out. She held her ground, even though the primal urge to turn and flee back into the trees grew stronger by the moment. She had never been this afraid in her life, even in the face of more terrifying creatures, like the manticore that came prowling around just after Blake's fifth birthday.

She slid the backpack off her back, forcing herself to pry her grip from the shotgun and lay it down on the ground. Instead of the gun, she now held the bag and reached into it. In slow motion, not wanting to provoke the beast by startling it, she brought out a pair of jeans and a pair of socks, holding them up so the werewolf could see that she held no weapon. Not a threat. She prayed to the Powers That Be that this was the wolf she hunted and not another. Where there was one, there might be more, but the fact she found the wolf *here* gave her hope.

"One of these legends says throwing the werewolf's clothes at it would cause it to turn back into a human." She tossed the jeans toward the wolf, followed by the socks. Both landed in the dirt several inches from the beast.

It snarled at her again, but lowered its head to sniff at the clothes. Was there a hint of recognition in those glowing eyes? She withdrew a pair of sneakers, Blake's favorite red Chucks, and dropped them to the dirt at her own feet. They might be needed in a minute. She hoped. She didn't see any changes happening just yet, but she hadn't expected the clothes alone would do it.

"The other is that if someone who loved and trusted the werewolf called it by name, the curse would be broken, the werewolf would regain its mind, and it would be able to change back into human form." She was shaking terribly. She had seen this accomplished once, many years ago, but the circumstances had been different. She was no sorceress, and she did not know if there was enough power in simply reciting the legend to trigger the magic.

She took another deep breath, and her hand twitched toward the shotgun on the ground. She clenched her fists to try to control the shaking as the werewolf moved away from the jeans and started toward her again. No! This was going to work. It *had* to. She refused to use the shotgun and made the choice to trust in love instead.

Pat met the werewolf's red eyes as she pulled a black, well-worn T-shirt out of the bag. And the corners of her mouth twitched upward in spite of her fear.

"So, Blake Watson, it's time for you to put your darn clothes on and come home," she said, trying to sound as normal as possible. "We're all worried about you, especially your mother." She threw the shirt right into the wolf's face. It should buy a little more time for the change to happen.

The werewolf growled and clawed at the shirt, ready to charge at her, but already the hulking black form was shrinking and growing lighter in color. Pat held her breath as the claws and fangs lengthened and fur sprouted again, as if the werewolf fought with the boy inside.

"Come on, Blake. Come back to us. Please," she whispered.

The wolf howled, a sound of pain that tore at Pat's heart, and the fur vanished in a *poof* of shed hair. The dwindling form of the werewolf morphed back into the body of her grandson. He still snarled at her as he stumbled forward, but this time with the irritation of a fourteen-year-old boy. A cold and naked and angry boy.

"Dammit, Grandma, don't look!" Blake snatched up the jeans and turned his back to her, equal parts embarrassment and indignation.

Pat breathed again, letting out the heavy tension and dropping her hands. She turned her back and leaned up against a tree. She didn't think she could trust her old knees to hold her right now as she whispered a soft prayer of gratitude to the Powers That Be for bringing her grandson back to her. Her brilliant, wonderful, unlucky boy.

It was only a moment later before he came around the tree, fully dressed this time, and hugged her, uncharacteristically quiet and on the verge of tears. "Thanks, Grandma. I thought I was doomed."

Pat dropped the bag, wrapping her arms around Blake and holding him close, comforting the scrawny youth. "I wasn't going to leave you to that sort of fate."

"But... how did you know what to do?"

Pat grinned as she released her grandson. She gathered up the bag and the shotgun, then gestured to him to start back down the familiar path toward home.

"Your grandma has a few good secrets. I'm sort of what you might call a badass." She laughed and squeezed his shoulder. "It's a long story, for a place where there is light and hot chocolate and maybe some of those cookies I baked this morning."

"Like your kitchen?" Blake liked to act grown up most of the time, but right now he seemed very much a young child— lost and scared and in need of his family.

"Exactly like my kitchen." Pat laughed again and fell into step beside him on the path. "Come on. Everyone is waiting for us there."

As they continued on their way home, she heard the howl of another wolf deeper in the woods, farther up the mountains.

Blake shivered, and she put an arm around his shoulders. No doubt whatever infected him was still out there... but that was work for another night. She wasn't as young as she used to be, after all. Soon, she would need to train a replacement and maybe even retire. But tonight, Pat would rejoice in this victory and celebrate with her family.

Tomorrow, she might start letting Blake in on the old ways and her secrets.

Rashelle Yeates is a horticulturist and loves growing plants as well as seeing them grow, especially in their native habitats. An ongoing love affair with cameras—having three different ones not including the one on her phone—allows her to take all the different plants home with her. Her love of traveling leads her to visit as many places as she can, with five of the seven continents caught in her view finder, and she plans to capture the last two as well. She enjoys experiencing the different cultures around the world and bringing those differences to her writing. You can find her and her photos on Facebook.

About this story, Rashelle says: "This story was inspired by all the role-playing games I have played over the years. Many of my characters are druidic types who generally have an animal companion of some sort, and another of the players in my group plays a lot of wizards with familiars. These animals come into play a lot, and I started to wonder what it would be like from the animal's point of view. This story is how I picture an animal becoming a familiar."

Writing from the point of view of a non-human character is quite a challenge. Rashelle does an admirable job with this birds' eye view of life on the wing.

FLYING FREE
Rashelle Yeates

I spotted the mouse hiding in a clump of wildflowers as I completed my second circle. Stupid little creatures think they can get away from me, but I'm fast, faster than they know. I circled again just to show it I had no interest in its hiding place, although my whole attention was on it. There could be more than one, and I didn't want to scare them away because I would be back for another meal later.

Satisfied that my intended meal was alone and blissfully unaware of me, I changed the angle of my wings and dove, dropping below the tops of the trees, silent and deadly. I watched through eyes narrowed against the wind as I got closer and closer to the mouse. I was almost upon it before it saw me, squeaking out a warning before dashing from its hiding spot and scurrying toward the trees that would hinder my flight.

I stretched out my talons. The mouse had no chance. My right talon dug deeply into its small body as my wings brushed the top of the wildflowers. My parents had taught me the ways of hunting before sending me out to find my own territory, and I pulled up sharply, landing, and quickly killing my prey. After getting a firm grip on the now limp body, I sprang upward, carrying it to a branch high in a nearby tree, where I could eat in safety.

I don't like staying too long on the ground. There are many strange creatures lurking there and flying high lets me stay far away from them. I love to fly. I am the king of the sky and none can touch me when I'm soaring above.

The mouse wasn't enough. I needed something more. I could go a long time between meals, but I didn't like to. I would have to look beyond this area, though, because the panicked squeaking of the mouse had warned all the other animals. I would not find anything to hunt here during this light time. There was plenty of light left; I could find another mouse, ground squirrel, or rabbit elsewhere.

As I headed away from the area, I thought it would be a nice place to make my own. There were plenty of animals and the trees were tall. I hadn't come across any signs that another had claimed it. Yes, it would make a nice home.

I put off hunting and went exploring. If I was going to make this my home, I had to be sure there were no others that would fight for it. I went high, not wanting to scare away any of the small animals I planned on hunting on the way back. There were many along the way, and I noted where to find them.

A group of trees, that grew so close together there was barely enough space for me to fly between their branches, stood in the middle of a field. I liked to challenge myself, although my parents often warned me against it. They said it would only lead to hurt. I had scraped the feathers on the tips of my wings a few times, but that didn't stop me from trying again. I took up the challenge of winging my way through the trees.

I wove in and out of the branches, going faster than I should have and pushing for more. A few times a stray branch caught the edge of my primaries, forcing me to pull my wings in tighter and take a different path, but I emerged whole on the other side. There was a large tree, perfect for perching, in the middle of the field I came out in. I turned sharply, intending to circle my way to the top, and didn't see the two-legged creature standing next to the last tree until it stepped out from the shadows. Its upper paw glowed as it threw something in my path. I tried to avoid whatever it was by flying up and away. It hadn't felt like I flew through anything, but I wanted to be sure. I settled on the top branch of the tree, looking for the two-legged creature, but it was gone.

I preened through my feathers looking for any signs of what the creature had thrown at me, but thankfully I didn't find anything. Having had enough exploring for this light time I pushed off of the branch intending to hunt and return to my nest.

The two-legged creature had unsettled me so much I couldn't concentrate on hunting, so I rode the air currents back toward my nest. But the longer I flew, the more tired I felt, and my eyes kept wanting to close. I needed to make it back to a safe place, but was beginning to worry about how much longer I would even be able to fly. It was good that I was close to my nest, because I had to force myself to stay awake and on the right air currents. Why did I feel this way? I had flown farther on different trips and never been this tired. I felt like I was trying to fly through the water that came from the sky.

My wings didn't work right to slow me down and I came into my nest too fast. There was nothing I could do except prepare for the collision. I landed hard, my talons twisted and feathers ruffled. I wanted to panic, but was too exhausted to even do that. My eyes refused to stay open now that I was back in my nest and my body wouldn't do anything I told it to do.

This wasn't right. Uncomfortable and not able to change my position, my eyes closed and everything went dark.

Opening my eyes, I looked around in disbelief. It was dark. When had it become dark? It didn't feel like I had slept that long. I untangled my talons, hopped around my nest a few times, and fluffed out my feathers making sure my body responded the way it should. Nothing seemed to be damaged, but my stomach churned like I had eaten a bad piece of meat, although I had not eaten anything after the mouse.

The ball of warmth in the sky had gone to bed while I was sleeping. That never happened. What was going on? Had I flown through whatever it was that creature had thrown? I preened through my feathers again trying to find any trace of something unusual, but there was nothing.

Trying not to panic, I reminded myself my nest was at the top of a tree that had long, prickly needles and was not easy for those two-legged creatures to climb. My parents had told me stories of hatchlings taken from their nests never to be seen again. But I wasn't a hatchling. I was safe. Wasn't I?

I called out my frustration in a harsh scree, and the night animals went silent. They weren't used to hearing me, but I had slept through the light, wasn't tired, and felt very uneasy. I always slept when the ball of warmth slept.

The churning I had felt upon waking was spreading through my body. I tried to clear it by shaking my body and flapping my wings, but the strange sensation wouldn't go away. It started in my middle and spread throughout the rest of me, changing to a buzzing as it settled in my head. I wanted to cry out again and again in frustration, but now that I was more alert, I didn't want to be noticed by the creatures that moved in the dark. The most dangerous were two-legged, but all of them make me wary.

I moved around my nest trying to get comfortable. I might not be able to sleep anymore but I couldn't see well enough to risk flying.

It was going to be a long dark time.

I preened for a long time, straightening my feathers from the rough landing, before tucking my head underneath my wing. I would rest until the ball of warmth returned, even if I didn't sleep. My head continued to ache, the buzzing growing so bad I wanted it all to end. There was something strange going on here, but I couldn't find it in me to care. I just wanted the pain to stop and this weirdness to go away.

I woke with a start. Looking around, I tried to find what woke me, but I was alone in my nest. Thankfully the buzzing in my head had faded while I slept—though it was still there. I felt like myself again. The ball of warmth was high in the sky, higher than it had ever been with me still in my nest since I was a hatchling.

Hopping to the edge, I stretched fully, feeling the light wind push playfully at me. I was stiff from staying in my nest for so long. I dropped from the edge of my nest and the wind rushed up and slid over me. After only a few wing-beats I glided away. It felt wonderful and made me happy.

I was very hungry, so I headed toward the field where I caught the mouse during the previous light time. As I flew across the field, the faint buzzing from before changed to a whisper in the back of my mind. It didn't hurt, but it was annoying. I couldn't figure out what it was saying although it seemed like it was trying to tell me something. I didn't want to listen, so I pushed it out of my mind and concentrated on finding my next meal.

I changed my direction, turning toward a different area I hadn't explored, knowing I might go hungry if I passed up an easy meal in the field of mice. But I needed to find larger creatures that would sate my hunger longer. A rabbit would be perfect, they were fast, but weren't as tricky as those squirrels that burrowed underground.

It takes concentration to look for food, and I was glad, for it forced me to put everything else out of my mind. I liked hunting for the larger animals. I glided high in the sky until I spotted a group of rabbits clustered in a field. They were closer to the trees than I liked, but I decided to go after one anyway. The rabbits stopped as my shadow passed by them, and I flew away so they would not run too soon. When I turned back, I came in low, closer to the ground. I winged my way around bushes and large boulders, keeping my focus on the rabbits. As I swooped over the last boulder they finally saw me and scattered at my approach, bounding away in different directions.

That one—the one that ran away from the trees—was mine. With a few adjustments, I dove for it, but the rabbit jumped high and in the opposite direction. I used the ground to push myself back into the air, and with a few wingbeats I was headed in the right direction, gaining on it. I grabbed at it as it jumped over a rock and only caught fur. But my attack forced it deeper into the field. The rabbit angled back toward the trees and right into my path. I snatched it as it jumped and I landed hard, digging my talons in deep. It wiggled against my hold, trying to get away, but its struggles only forced my talons further into its flesh. I could feel its racing heartbeat and waited until it stopped moving before looking for a branch where I could eat. I pushed off and was headed for a nearby tree when the whispering in my head increased.

I felt drawn toward the whispers.

The insistent pull made my talons spasm, making it hard to keep my meal in my grip. I wanted to fly fast and far in the opposite direction, but I was also curious to find out what could draw me in this way. Maybe if I found out what was causing the pull, I could stop it. Clutching the rabbit tightly in my talons, I turned, following the direction it wanted me to go.

I experimented with the feeling while in the sky. It was pulling me in only one direction, and every time I veered away, the call grew stronger until I turned back toward it.

I hadn't traveled very far when a small field came into view. There was a two-legged creature standing in the middle of it. I didn't know if it was the same creature from the light time before for this one had no glowing light around its paw and I didn't get a good look at the rest of it. I flew higher, keeping the creature in sight while making it more difficult for it to see me. As I passed overhead, the sensation pulled me back down, toward the creature.

I didn't like or trust those two-legged creatures. I called out a warning to the other creatures in the area as I continued to circle the field. I discovered that the whispering faded if I stayed close by, but every time I tried to fly away it demanded my return. I didn't want to stay. I wanted to be as far away from the creature as I could, but the draw on my body wouldn't let me leave.

The fight exhausted me. I was hungry, and I wanted to eat before I grew weak and dropped my meal.

Spotting a high, sturdy-looking branch, I landed, keeping the two-legged creature in sight. I ate as the creature watched me with eyes the color of the moss that grew along the edge of the river. I studied it, with its odd, long brown fur sprouting from the top of its head. The fur moved more freely than my feathers with each gust of wind or movement the creature made, although it didn't move much. I was too unfamiliar with the two-legged creatures to know if it was the ball of light that caused the strange glow around the creature's head or if it was the same kind of glow that had been around the other's front paw.

I stayed long after my meal was finished, determined to outlast it. I also didn't want the feeling of being out of control and too tired to get back to my nest, as after the previous light time's hunt, to return. Thinking about it made me angry enough to scream out directly at the creature.

It finally moved, not away from me like I expected, but not toward me either. That didn't make me happy.

I stared at the creature as the whispering in my head became something I could understand.

"I am a friend. We will be good friends. We will make a great team."

The refrain repeated over and over.

I didn't want to be its friend. My parents had taught me that the two-legged creatures were never friends with my kind. They always took and took. Was this what happened to those of my kind that went away with them? Had they been called against their will to be friends? That wasn't going to happen to me!

My will was great. I wasn't going to give in to the whispers. I could outwait that creature in the field. I was safe in the tree. It couldn't get to me.

As I stared at it I wondered what it would be like to be stuck on the ground. It was hard to imagine. To never know what it felt like to soar through the sky. To not know how the wind caressed my feathers and carried me wherever I wanted to go. I shuddered just thinking about it.

That creature wouldn't stay here long would it? Whenever I flew past others if its kind, they were moving. This one didn't seem inclined to move though. It—he—stared at me.

How had I known it was male?

I half spread my wings in challenge. He was no match for me. We would settle this my way. He couldn't best me. I was king of the sky.

He didn't move.

I wanted to rake my talons down his face. He should have flinched back like the animals did. They were smart to run from my wrath. Why would I want to be his friend if he wasn't as smart as the animals?

I spread my wings to their full extent, sure he would give in this time. I was shocked and yet intrigued when he didn't. He continued to look at me, his arms relaxed at his sides, waiting. I didn't know what he was waiting for, but I had had enough. I didn't want to look at him anymore. More than that, I fiercely wanted the sounds in my head to stay away.

Pushing off from the branch I flew fast at him, aiming for his face. Eyes are very vulnerable and make excellent targets. Extending my talons, I prepared to shred his face.

He didn't flee as I expected. Raising his arm, he held it out at his side just like a branch. Was he serious? Did he really think I wanted to use him as a perch? I wanted him to leave me alone.

I changed my direction at the last moment, afraid he would use something to capture me. I passed so close to him I felt my longest feathers brush his face as my talons raked his arm. That would get my point across. He would leave me alone now, or I was going after his eyes next.

I winged upward hard and fast before circling a few times

waiting to see what he would do. I saw that he cradled his injured arm, but otherwise he hadn't moved. After that warning he was still going to wait for me to come to him?

Ridiculous.

As I circled, I saw a small family of mice close to him. They weren't afraid; he stood so still he had become part of his surroundings. I had never seen that before. The two-legged creatures always moved and made noise that scared away most of the prey.

The whispering was gone, but I knew this wasn't over. I thought my attack would convey my feelings, but he didn't seem to understand. Silently, I glided away.

———

The moment I opened my eyes, the whispering started again, louder than the previous light time.

"We are friends. We will be a great team. I forgive you. I know you are afraid."

The voice rang clear in my head now, no more buzzing. It was easier to bear and harder to ignore. I thought the creature must be standing at the base of my tree speaking up at me, but when I looked over the edge of my nest I didn't see him. He was persistent, I gave him that much, but I wouldn't give him any more.

I meant to go hunting, but found myself winging toward the small field, wondering if he had left to take care of his arm. I didn't want to wonder about him but couldn't stop myself. His ability to stay still as I approached him was unnerving. Nothing stayed still when I attacked them. They always ran, or at least tried to.

He waited in the same spot, as still and calm as before.

Slowing my approach, I circled. I was curious. Would he do the same as before? Raise his arm for me to land on? This time I wasn't sure what I would do if he did. To my own surprise, I wasn't angry anymore, but was intrigued by his manner. He didn't frighten any of the other animals in the field. When I looked around, I saw even more small animals and not just mice.

He wasn't afraid of me and I wasn't sure I liked that; however, I wasn't afraid of him either. In the past, I had been taught to be leery of his kind and to stay away from them. As a result, I had not learned much about them. Now I found myself wanting to learn about them.

No. Not them.

Him.

I wanted to learn more about him. I flew past him before climbing higher and staying near the field, keeping him in sight. He hadn't raised his arm. Good. I didn't want him to think I came so easily to call.

I landed on the same branch as the day before and observed him. His arm was bandaged. I was happy I had marked him. He would carry that mark for the rest of his life as a reminder of my anger. There was a glow surrounding him that might have been a reflection of the sun, but it was different than the first glow. I preened through my chest feathers, happy I didn't see the same type of glow on me.

I wiggled, getting comfortable on the branch. I was hungry but not hungry enough to go off and miss what he was going to do, or how the small animals reacted to his presence. The whispering in my mind no longer bothered me. The thought crossed my mind that not being bothered by it was wrong, but I couldn't find it in me to care.

The man stared up at me. His face calm, no hint of what he

was thinking. Something told me if I really wanted to know I could find out. The whispering would tell me, but only if I opened myself up to it. I was curious, but I wasn't ready for that.

Neither one of us moved for a long time. I pretended to ignore him a few times by working on my feathers, but always kept him in sight. The sun reached its zenith before I moved. Soundlessly I pushed off the branch heading toward him like the day before, the only difference my speed. I winged slowly toward him, circling a few times before moving in close.

I was pleased when he raised his arm, not as confidently as yesterday, but still steady. Back winging, I prepared to land on his arm when I realized what I was doing.

I was going to let him touch me. What was wrong with me? I back winged harder changing direction, going fast and high, trying to clear my head.

The sky usually helped settle me, but it didn't work this time. The whispering changed, speaking different words.

"We are friends. We will have many different experiences together. We are a team."

I stayed high. I didn't want to listen. I fought to force the whispers out of my head, but they wouldn't go away, no matter what I did. They kept speaking those words, as well as promising all kinds of different adventures and challenges.

Slowly, I glided down. I refused to admit to myself that I was heading back to the man. I took up my perch on the branch once again. Too agitated to settle I shifted from talon to talon with my wings half open ready for flight. Why was I changing?

Looking at the man, I saw the smile on his face. Shaking my head, I knew it wasn't a smug smile and having that knowledge confused me even more. I knew he was pleased with my resistance. The whispering told me other details, but I didn't pay attention to them. There was a definite glow about him now and this time it was the same as before.

I was afraid.

I didn't want things to change. I wanted to be the king of the sky, my only concerns what I would eat that day and keeping the area I claimed. I had a feeling I would never again be satisfied with that simple life.

I pushed off from the branch, flying as high as I could, as fast as I could. Maybe this time I'd be able to put everything else out of my mind. Maybe I would be able to stop the whispering and the wondering.

No longer able to see the man in the field, and barely able to make out the individual trees, I could go no higher. It took a lot of effort to stay that high and I remained up there for as long as I could, my wings straining, hoping it would work.

It didn't.

My mind wouldn't shut off. I kept wondering what the man thought of my actions. I also thought a lot about experiencing those different things and challenges the whispering promised. I no longer cared about being the king of the sky in this place. I no longer worried about finding my next meal.

I drifted down, discouraged at my failure. It occurred to me I was thinking more than I ever had. I knew it had to do with the whispering, which whispered no more.

The voice filled my mind as I circled closer to the man. I couldn't think past it, and as the ground became clearer I gave in.

I shortened my circles as I drew closer to the man, knowing I would accept his arm. I had changed too much to go back to the way I was. There were too many thoughts in my head.

His impassive face showed no triumph at my capitulation. He held his arm up for me and I landed gently, keeping my talons from damaging his skin again. I was sorry for having harmed him before, but he shook his head as if he heard my thoughts and spoke aloud, "I will heal, winged friend."

I knew that voice. It was the one that had whispered to me over the last two days.

He caressed my chest feathers with a finger while looking into my eyes. "I am Hilen. And you are," he turned his head sideways studying me, "SkyKing."

I liked the name. It fit. I am the king of the sky. I puffed out my chest, happy. I stayed on his arm as he walked out of the field, Hilen continuing to stroke my chest feathers.

We were going to be great friends.

Jared Quan is a video game addict and writer published in genres ranging from spy thriller to horror/supernatural to fantasy comedy. He has extensively served the writing community as President of the League of Utah Writers, board member of the Cultural Arts Society of West Jordan, Grants Director of the EMAA, Executive Director of Big World Network, Chair of the West Jordan Arts Council, and Recruiting Chair of the AITP Utah Chapter, and was recently given the President's Gold Volunteer Service Award for his extensive service to the writing community from 2015 to 2017. He lives in Eagle Mountain with his supportive wife and five children. Shoot with him under his gamer tag and twitch channel, Resadur164.

About this story, Jared says: "I have recently found a special place in my heart for writing Twilight Zone-style stories, with unpre-dictable twists. I wanted to write something that would get people to really think. This was derived from many first hand experiences I have had in the corporate world, where perception is the reality, and situa-tions are often not what they seem at all. I also drew from a massive pool of experience playing 'First Person Shooters' to help set the framework for this very adventurous, and action-packed story. Ping me if you ever want to get together for some FPS."

To meet him, Jared seems like a nice, friendly fellow. After reading this story, you'll have to agree that he hides a wicked sense of humor behind that cheerful smile.

LAST OUTPOST ON THE ZOMBIE HIGHWAY
Jared Quan

Kevin Gossamer raised the binoculars to his dark blue eyes and searched the killing ground. The bodies of the last zombies he'd taken out the day before lay in the snow, a faint dusting of white covering their gray flesh.

Dozens of frozen corpses littered the foggy mountain road leading to the Stairs Station Hydroelectric Power Plant. On the ridge overlooking the winding road, Kevin kept low, his white camo blending him with the snow. His rebreather mask hid puffs of white breath from rising and revealing his position.

Kevin adjusted the mask out of habit. He hated the masks. *Why do we even wear these uncomfortable things?* They didn't protect them from toxins in the air, and a cloth would work perfectly fine—maybe even better—to conceal the tiny white puffs of their breath.

Kevin's spotter, lying beside him in the shallow pit they had dug, made a hissing noise. "Movement, bottom of the hill," Scott whispered.

Thick fog blanketed the distant position down the mountain as Kevin searched with the binoculars. Dark shapes shifted in the haze, but he was just out of range to count how many or see if they were living looking for sanctuary or a swarm of dead looking for flesh. He reached for his radio with numb fingers.

"Bastion, this is Hanzo, over," Kevin said though his rebreather. "We spotted something moving at the base of the hill, but I don't know what. Visibility is bad, under three hundred yards. Request to redeploy forward, over."

He took another look through the binoculars, but the fog hid whatever was coming up the mountain.

"Copy that, negative on the redeploy. Let 'em come to you, and tell me before you start shooting at anything this time, over."

Kevin grimaced at the exchange. He blamed the radioactive fallout for eroding his common sense and his frequent lapses in judgment. He was still unsure why he chased off the last group that could have resupplied them. His stomach and Stokes reminded him often of his mistake.

"She was never going to let us move farther down the mountain," Scott said, not taking his eyes from his large spotter scope. "Not after you disobeyed her last time."

"Hey, focus on what's out there."

"I can't tell if they're advancing. Maybe it's just the fog shifting?"

Endless minutes of watching the bank of white mist wore on Kevin. The clouds above thickened and choked off the fading daylight as evening approached. His eyelids drifted shut. His head dipped down into the snow. So comfortable. The cold didn't bother him.

Scott elbowed him hard in the ribs. Kevin's eyes shot open, searching for targets.

"You're losing it, man," Scott said.

Kevin tried hard to remember the last time he had slept in a warm bed. He shot a glance down at the outpost, thinking how ironic it was that they were protecting a source of power, but weren't allowed to use any of it to keep warm.

"I see something," Scott said, "by the first turn."

Kevin searched and saw movement. "Contact, west," he said into the radio and adjusted the binoculars. "Damn, just a couple of deer. Sorry, over."

"I could really go for venison right about now," Scott said, touching his empty stomach.

Kevin's hunger gnawed at his own belly. Starvation was their greatest enemy. They needed to replenish their stores. He couldn't stand the frozen and rotten food they had, but he suppressed his gags and ate it.

Fog swirled around the deer, enveloping them for a moment before they raced up the mountainside. Kevin followed them with his binoculars and thought about switching to his rifle.

If they weren't running, he thought to himself.

"Contact, west," Scott said into his radio.

A dozen indistinct forms raced up the road. The dense fog made it impossible to tell if they were human or zombies. Kevin removed the cover from his white TAC-338 sniper rifle and tracked them through the scope.

"Hanzo, are they friendly, over?" Stokes asked, her voice crackling.

"Can't tell," Scott said. "They're running straight."

"Bastion, I'm going to fire a warning shot," Kevin said, "to see if they react, over."

"Negative, negative, we can't spare the ammo," Stokes said. "We'll handle them on the road."

The unknown fast movers ran in two separate groups with about six feet between them. That's when it dawned on him.

"Going hot, only the back eight are zombies," Kevin said.

"Roger, target lead z, red shirt, running left to right, two hundred and seventy-five yards, wind three quarter value, push one left," Scott said.

"On target."

"Send it."

Kevin smiled as three of the zombies came into line with each other. The crosshairs on the scope settled on the lead zombie's head.

He squeezed the trigger and was rewarded with the crisp sound of the bullet exiting the weapon. As planned, three zombies collapsed to the ground with a bloody splatter. The bitter smell of gunpowder caused him to redouble focus.

"Good hit. Three down," Scott reported on the radio.

Kevin slid the bolt back and forward, loading a new round into the chamber. He snapped off a second shot. Two more tumbled to the ground.

"Scratch two more," Scott said. "Houston, we have a problem. One broke off from the chase group. It's headed our way."

"Take care of the stray," Kevin said. The lone zombie left the road and ran up the hillside toward their position on the ridge. Had it seen them or was it drawn by the sound of the gunfire?

"Maximum effort," Scott said. He raised his M16A4 suppressed rifle. The zombie climbed toward them over the rocks like an insect. A single shot, and the creature collapsed, its arms splaying and leaving the outline of a twitching zombie snow angel.

"Nice shot."

"Thanks. I'll be here all week."

"Bastion, the last two are yours, over." Kevin reloaded.

"Roger that," Stokes replied.

Kevin watched the humans and zombies race toward the large sandbag defenses flanking the massive main gate surrounding the outpost. Fire spit from one of the watchtowers, where Stokes was positioned. The unmistakable sound of 5.56 ammo rounds echoed through the canyon. The two remaining zombies were neutralized.

The friendlies made it into the compound through the main gate, which cracked open only for an instant. A moment later, Stokes's voice came over the radio. "Hanzo, both of you get in here now. We have a situation, over."

"Roger that," Kevin said.

"Dude," Scott said. "What do you think is up?"

"Does it matter?"

"Nope."

Kevin and Scott kept low and exfiltrated down the back side of the ridge as the sky darkened. He sank into the snow to his waist in some places but followed the shortest path down to the power station. He ran his hand over the top of the snow.

"That's pure snow, man," Scott said. "Do you know how much that's worth on the open market?" He let out a short laugh.

"Pure, right," Kevin said. He reached down deep in the snow and retrieved a handful of gray sludge that wouldn't stick together. How radioactive was the ash? He didn't want to think about it. "Wait, is that line from an old movie?"

"I think so? How do I not remember that?" Scott asked. "Sometimes it feels like I need to defrag my hard drive, you know?"

"Don't worry about it. It'll pass. We just keep surviving." Kevin realized he had said that phrase so many times.

"Yeah, nothing kills us," Scott said. "We do the killing."

A chill went through Kevin as he thought of what they had done to survive—so much violence and death. He couldn't even remember it all. He didn't want to. He wrung his hands. What was he forgetting? Something important.

"Halt! Identify yourself." The sentry guarding the main gate had a deep voice, and it startled Kevin from his trance.

"It's me, Hanzo. Stand down, Brady." Kevin lifted the rebreather mask a little. He shook his head at his friend. Was he losing his mind too?

"Yeah, yeah, of course. Hey, Hanzo. Hey, S-Scott? Scott. Yeah, come on in." Exhaustion coated every word. He waved them to come, swaying as he did.

The two moved toward the security fence, each step heavier than the one before.

Almost back to base, or home, or whatever this hell is, Kevin thought. *What a waste.*

Brady's head dropped and jerked up. He raised his weapon. "Halt! Identify yourself!"

Kevin's hands flew up. "Brady!"

Brady flipped off the safety, his trigger finger squeezing. Kevin's legs gave, and he ducked. It was too late.

Click.

Click. Click, click. Click.

No ammo.

Kevin jumped to his feet and rushed the guard. "What the hell, you son of a—"

Scott grabbed Kevin from behind and pulled him away.

"Oh my God!" Brady said, dropping the rifle, looking at the weapon, afraid. "I could have killed you guys… I'm so tired. I keep blacking out, and when I come to, I have no idea where I am. What the hell is wrong with me?"

Kevin relaxed. Scott must have noticed the tension drop because he let go. Kevin knew how Brady felt. Everyone had been showing signs of exhaustion. They had been running hot with too few for too long. "Get your ass on the horn and get a replacement up here and get six hours of rest. You dry fire on another one of us, you might not get up next time."

Brady nodded and fumbled with his radio as Kevin and Scott walked past.

"Only time I've ever been grateful we're low on ammo," Kevin said.

The main gate opened just wide enough for the two of them to enter. Kevin glanced past the closing gate to where they would have been lying, torn apart, bleeding out or dead. He paused for a moment.

"Would it have been so bad if we'd been killed back there?"

"What?" Scott asked.

"I mean to finally be done with this nightmare, you know?"

"Dude, what's wrong with you?"

"The same thing that is wrong with all of us."

"Hey, the first rule of fight club is…" Scott paused. "How does it go again?"

"Don't talk about fight club."

"Really? Are you sure?"

"Come on. Stokes is already pissed."

They turned a corner beyond the guard shack and approached the power plant building. The strong scent of BO and filth carried on the breeze. A small group of anxious newcomers stood on high alert. Their eyes darted as if they expected an ambush at any moment. Kevin had to play it cool, or there would be a bloodbath. He'd taken care of worse situations before. That's why Stokes called him back.

"Well, you took your sweet time," Stokes said. She held a heavy bandage on the leg of an unconscious woman with a bullet wound. A huge puddle of blood expanded on the frozen ground, soaking into the snow. Stokes must have accidentally shot her.

"Where's Mercy?" Kevin asked. He set the sniper rifle against the wall and knelt beside Stokes. He peeked at the bandage.

"She's up the mountain," Stokes said. "We need to deal with this. Scott, go grab a stretcher. We need to get her inside."

"Yes, sir," Scott said.

"What was that?" Stokes asked.

"I mean, yes, ma'am." Scott offered a shaky salute before he ran into the building.

"So, what's the plan?" Kevin asked. He looked at Stokes. Her blue eyes were confused and uncertain, as if she had forgotten what was happening. She scrunched up her face, as if she were trying to remember something on the tip of her tongue.

Kevin realized he needed to take command, handle the negotiations, and get the newcomers sorted out. "Right, which one of you is the group leader?"

The three people looked at each other. One of them pointed at the unconscious woman, whose skin had gone gray. "She was, before your goddamn commander shot her."

Stokes looked to Kevin as if he had the right answer. "It was an accident…," she said.

"Brilliant," he said with heavy sarcasm. "We'll get her inside. No reason to leave her bleeding out in the snow."

"I've been putting pressure on the wound and waiting for your slow ass to get down here, so I…" Stokes's words drifted off. "I just need to… think for a moment…"

None of it mattered. The woman looked dead. Snow already coated her body, and the wound was fatal.

Kevin felt for a pulse in her neck. It was slow and fading. Things were going to escalate quickly now. "Damn it," he shouted. *I have to control the situation. Remember, they're in our court now.* Kevin looked up at the man in a gray ski cap with ear flaps, then dropped his gaze. "She's not going to make it."

"Don't you have a medic or doctor?" ski-cap man asked. "This is a military outpost, right?"

"We've made the call, but they're up the mountain. She's lost too much blood. She'll be gone long before they get here," Kevin explained. "I'm sorry."

Ski-cap man looked his friends, a stout man wearing camo Carhartts and a tall, thin man sporting a patchy rust-colored beard.

"What now, Pete?" Camo-Carhartts asked.

Kevin could see the anger building in them. "Listen. Pete, right?"

Pete nodded.

"Kevin." He gestured to himself. "I am sorry. We all are. I promise we are here to save people, and we've saved a lot—but not all." He looked back down at the near-dead woman. "I'd call it an honor if you'd allow me to get some shovels and help you put your friend to rest after you've said your goodbyes."

"Damn it," Pete said. "We never should have come here. How many people can this place support?"

"Not very many. We're almost at full capacity," Stokes said. "I'll call up the mountain to the commanding officer and have a group escort you up to where the rest of our people are, if you want. We can figure it all out."

Stokes still seemed a little out of it, but at least she could snap off the same speech she'd given many times before when new arrivals made it inside the fence.

"That sounds like bullshit," Pete said. "You don't have the

resources to deal with a bullet wound and yet you want us to believe there are people up the mountain?"

"Look, I understand you're upset right now. You lost a friend, but please, you need to calm down." Kevin rested his hand on the Glock 9mm in the holster on his hip. The strain in Pete's voice was bad news.

Pete surprised Kevin by raising his hands. "We aren't looking for trouble. We're just looking for safety—like everyone else."

"Well then, you have to trust us. We could have killed the lot of you on the road," Stokes said.

"You killed our leader, asshole," Pete said.

"It was an accident," Stokes said.

Pete glared at her.

"Please listen," Kevin said, trying to defuse the situation. "You asked about our capacity. How many more do you have in your group?"

"About sixt—" He looked down at his dead leader. "Fifteen. In three vehicles."

"I'm going to have to call this in to command," Stokes said. "That's a lot of people. Wait here." She removed her hands from the woman's leg. Only a trickle of blood escaped. There was almost nothing left.

Scott exited the building and walked over to the group. "So, what's going on here?"

"Where's the stretcher?" Pete asked.

"What're you talking about?" Scott's confusion caused the three men to shift uneasily and glare at him. Pete turned away and used a handheld radio.

"Hey, come over here for a moment," Kevin said, pulling Scott away from the group.

"What's up, brother?" Scott asked.

"I'm running low on ammo. I need yours."

"Anything for you, Chief." Scott handed over his pistol mag without hesitation.

"Thanks." Kevin slid the mag into an empty pocket. "Now get up on the roof."

"You got it." Scott walked back toward the building, stopped for a moment, turned with a look of bewilderment on his face, but then continued.

"What is wrong with your man?" Pete asked as he stepped closer. His smelly breath caused Kevin to pull away.

"F and F. He's fried and fatigued," Kevin said.

"Fatigue? Your people are comatose standing at their positions," Pete said.

"Look, we've been pulling twenty-four hour security since this mess started. We haven't got much food. We're barely hanging on, but we're going to help your sorry asses. Now, please step back."

Pete retreated a step.

"It's almost dark," Kevin said. "We should get you settled down for the night. Let's go inside."

"Not until the rest of our group gets here," Pete said.

"When your group comes, their vehicles are going to draw a swarm of attention. It's almost dark, and we don't have night optics. We're almost out of ammo, so we can't give proper fire support for long. Better to wait until daylight when we have better visibility."

"No deal," Pete said. "You can keep shooting long enough to get my people inside."

"Maybe," Kevin said. "If we get hit by a giant mob that followed your people up here, we're going to get overrun. Even if we had the ammo, our soldiers are in bad shape. We need to wait until morning. Bringing your people now is too dangerous." He glanced at the other guards in the towers. They looked worse than usual, barely standing.

"Let's talk about dangerous," Pete said. He and his two companions drew pistols hidden in their jackets.

Kevin raised his hands. He quickly shook his head to signal for everyone in the towers to stand down. It was always better this way—to make them think they were in charge. "Take it easy. We can work things out."

"You will help our people come up to the outpost—tonight," Pete said. "Or we will kill everyone up here and do it ourselves."

"Yes, sure. Just lower the weapons," Kevin said. "There's no need to threaten anyone. We want to help. We want to get everyone up here. We need reinforcements if any of us are going to survive the zombies." It wasn't a complete lie.

They lowered their guns. A little. Stokes returned from the radio room.

"See, we can all be friends," Stokes said.

Pete called his group again on a small walkie-talkie and told them to roll.

"Stokes, their group is going to need fire support," Kevin said.

"Okay, prep the team," Stokes ordered.

"What did the mountain say?" Kevin asked quietly.

She simply shook her head.

"Don't get any funny ideas," Pete said. "James, Greg, take Natara's body into the building, then sweep it. Make sure there is no one hiding inside."

"How are your people coming up the road?" Kevin asked.

"Three-vehicle convoy," Pete said. "A Humvee and two diesels. They're rolling now."

Kevin picked up his radio. "Team, it's been a while since

we've seen serious action against a swarm, but it's time to lock and load. Three friendly vehicles are coming. They're going to have zombies all over them. Make every shot count."

The radio crackled with confirmations.

"Pick your shots. We don't need to run out of ammo today," Stokes added.

Kevin walked to the ladder ascending to the roof. Pete followed him.

"With your pistols, you'll be more effective here on the ground," Kevin said. "Take out any that come at the gate." He knew it wouldn't be that simple to get Pete off his ass, but he had to try.

"I go where you go," Pete said.

"Roger that." Kevin carefully ascended the icy ladder to the rooftop, where Scott was already in position.

"Damn fog," Scott said as he looked down the mountain. "We won't see them until they are right on top of us."

"This is going to be fun," Kevin replied as he set up the bipod on the TAC-338 sniper rifle.

"Honzo, how are we looking?" Stokes asked over the radio.

"All set up here. The firefight will probably be white knuckle." Kevin scanned the road. "We'll only be able to get a couple of rounds off before they're too close, over."

"Use flares," Stokes said, "and keep the good stuff for when things get interesting, over."

"That is why you get paid the big bucks, over and out."

Kevin walked to the far end of the roof where the M224 mortar waited in readiness. He took off the barrel cover and knelt beside it to adjust the settings.

"Scott, what's the farthest we can see out there?" Kevin called.

"I can make out position three," Scott answered.

"What does that mean?" Pete asked, still holding his weapon at the ready.

"We have presighted the road," Kevin said. "We know the exact ranges to hit several positions. Do you mind putting the gun away? You aren't going to need it."

"Just pretend I'm not here," Pete said.

"Right." Kevin adjusted the mortar and set two shells next to it. "Mortar is set," he said into the radio.

Kevin walked back to his sniper position and lay down behind his rifle. As he looked through the scope, he found the closest wind sock that had been deployed forward to get his bearings. After a moment, he adjusted the scope to the new conditions.

"Contact, west," Scott said into the radio.

"This is where it gets interesting," Kevin whispered.

The lead vehicle's lights could be seen just before it emerged from the dense fog. Kevin swept the area, looking for any signs of zombies, but there were none.

"Pete, do you know how to use a mortar?" Kevin asked.

"Never used one before."

"Well, it's pretty easy. Drop one of the shells into the tube, fins down, and don't stand over the top of it."

"Doesn't sound hard."

"It isn't unless you need to adjust it, but you won't." Kevin could see a second set of headlights from a much larger vehicle pushing through the fog toward them.

"Should I do that now?" Pete asked.

"Yes."

Kevin heard the crunch of Pete's boots as he walked back to the artillery, then the telltale sound of a deep thud, followed by a quick pop as the flare headed to its destination. Pete ran back to the sniper's nest.

"Flare up," Scott reported.

The hovering bright light melted away the fog enough to see the second and third vehicles, as well as the mob of zombies that poured from the trees and surrounded them.

"I estimate three dozen," Scott said.

"Not anymore," Kevin said as he took aim. The undead grouped tight. Fish in a barrel. The first shot tore through three heads, before it veered right, removing the arm of a fourth. He realigned, another shot. The bullet stayed true this time. Six went down; four would not get back up. The next shot hit low, bowling a group down. One head looked like it split as the group tumbled.

"Daaamn, Kev. Hell yeah." Scott reported back to Stokes, "Twenty-five still up and in pursuit."

"The rest are too spread apart to waste ammo on, over," Kevin said.

"Roger that. We'll prep to take them on the ground, over," Stokes said.

Kevin watched the vehicles creep forward up the rutted, mist-shrouded road in the gathering darkness. Some of the zombies sprinted toward the outpost, outpacing the slow-moving convoy, while the others tried to claw their way into the armored vehicles.

"Okay, zombies coming in fast now," Scott said. "Carpe diem."

The deafening roar of Stokes's light machine gun echoed through the canyon like fireworks as several zombies were cut down.

"Okay, let's get these people inside. We made quite a ruckus, and I bet there will be more on the way," Pete said as the three vehicles entered the outpost perimeter.

The sun tucked itself away behind the mountain, and darkness enveloped the outpost like a living creature eating its prey. People climbed out of the vehicles and moved into the power plant building.

The vehicles were shut off, but Kevin heard a low humming noise. He knew exactly what it meant. "Pete, fire off the next flare."

"Sure thing." Pete ran back over to the mortar and dropped a shell into the tube. The flare showed hundreds of zombies running toward the outpost.

"Bastion, this is Hanzo, over."

"Go for Bastion."

"We are about to be overrun. Not sure we are going to win this fight."

"Overrun?" Pete asked in a panicked tone.

"Pete, you might want to think about joining your people in the building," Kevin said. With that, he lined up a shot and fired.

"No way. I go where you go," Pete said.

"Okay," Kevin said. "Well, it's time to go."

"Aren't we safe up here?" Pete asked.

"With no food and no ammo, up here is not a great plan," Kevin said. "Scott, head down."

"On my way."

"You're out of ammo?" Pete asked.

"Yup," Kevin said as he started down the ladder. The sounds of the light machine gun roared hot as they reached the ground.

"Scott, redeploy up to that walkway," Kevin ordered.

"No problemo."

"Where are you going?" Pete asked.

"Inside," Kevin said. "Where we'll all most likely die."

"What?"

Kevin entered the building and found everyone from the

convoy anxiously waiting. The large room had a crudely welded steel cage in the back, where maybe ten people would fit.

"Pete, have everyone prep for a fight," Kevin said. "If they bust in the door, we'll retreat into that cage. That's where we'll make our last stand."

"Change of plans," Pete said. "My people and I will be in the building for the last stand. Any of your people who come back through that door will get shot."

"That's how you want to play this?" Kevin asked, though he expected this was how it would go.

"Yup." Pete pointed his pistol at him.

"Okay," Kevin said as he headed out the door.

Outside, with the last flare out, only the flashes of gunfire served as illumination. Dozens of zombies climbed over the fence.

"Hanzo, how are we doing, over?" Stokes asked.

"We are clear," Kevin replied.

"Roger that," Stokes said. "All positions, ceasefire, over."

All gunfire stopped. The only sounds were the zombies moaning as they climbed the fence and shuffled across the courtyard en masse. Ahead of them, Kevin ran to the main door to the power plant building and opened it, then slunk away in the shadows. Responding to the only light in the area, the zombies rushed toward it like moths to a flame. Shooting erupted inside, with a mixture of shouts and curses from the newcomers.

Kevin waited until the gunfire stopped before he returned and closed the door. The zombies outside paid no attention to him. He pressed his hand against the wall and walked around the building into the pitch black. He reached the ladder to the roof and climbed. At the mortar, he opened one of the crates and removed a fragmentation shell.

"Fire in the hole," Kevin said into his radio. Then he dropped the shell into the mortar.

A moment later came the fireball, billowing outward, from the explosive impact fifty yards outside the fence. The noise reverberated over the outpost like a thunderclap. The predictable sound of zombies running toward the impact site followed.

"Scott, let me know when they reach the crater, over," Kevin said as he picked up another shell.

Kevin patiently waited for the signal as the zombie sounds faded away as they left the power plant compound.

"They're in the zone," Scott reported.

Kevin dropped the shell, and before it even hit the ground, he climbed down the ladder.

"Bingo!" Stokes shouted as the brilliant flame and dancing white phosphorus of the second mortar illuminated the outpost. "Mission accomplished."

"How long should we leave them in there?" Scott asked over the radio.

"A couple of days," Stokes said.

"Roger that," Kevin replied.

"Yes, ma'am," Scott said.

"Until then, head back out to the ridge," Stokes ordered.

Kevin entered the armory shed and opened a weapons locker. He pulled out another sniper rifle. And the last magazine of ammo.

"Come on, Scott. Let's go," Kevin said.

"On my way," Scott said.

Two days later, Kevin opened the doors to the power plant. The light in the doorway drew out the remaining zombies. Scott, Brady, Stokes, and Kevin took them out with baseball bats as they exited. No need to waste any more ammo.

"You're alive?" Pete asked wearily as he lay on the floor inside the cage with the other starving and dehydrated survivors.

"Are you really surprised to see me?" Kevin asked. A pile of dead zombies littered the room. Reeking of death and decay, the upper torso of a single zombie scoured the floor, slurping up the remains of the fallen humans.

"Let us out," Pete said. "We need water and food."

Kevin noticed the cellar door was open. "Did you go exploring?"

Pete's face twisted into disgust. "We found your food supplies."

The gnawed human and animal parts they kept in the cellar were barely edible.

"Some of it has been there for years," Kevin said. He shivered at the thought of eating another bite of the old frozen meat.

"I get it," Pete said. "This is a trap. Use some of your bullets. Trick us to come in. It's pretty genius, but listen, we're cannibals too. We know where more people are. Just let some of us go, and we can bring them here. We'll join up and have a big feast."

"I don't think so," Kevin said. He glanced at the cage and the ten people who managed to pack inside.

Pete gathered the strength to raise his pistol. "You are going to let us out of here, or I am going to kill you right now."

Kevin shook his head. "That is the least intelligent thing you've said. You're bluffing."

"I saved a few rounds," Pete said, raising the gun higher.

"We made sure you used up every last round by letting those zombies in here."

"Come on, we can make a deal here," Pete said. "I mean, you are cannibals, right?"

"Something like that," Kevin said with a wry smile. He could feel his stomach grumble in anticipation of fresh, unfrozen meat.

"Wait, what?" Pete asked. His eyes darted around the room, frantically searching for some answer. The light from a high window illuminated the zombie lying on the floor—eyes the same strange blue as Kevin's.

"That's not possible," Pete said. His face contorted.

"Anything is possible," Kevin said.

"Right." Pete fired his pistol into Kevin's chest.

Unfazed by the bullet wound, Kevin stepped closer to the cage. "Very noble of you to waste your last bullet on me." Kevin pointed to the lifeless, dark blue-eyed husks on the ground. "We're not all stupid."

Pete's face twisted in horror. "What are you?"

"Hungry. So very hungry," Kevin said.

Growing up in Utah, P.A. Sterling always wanted to be a super hero but somehow ended up writing software for computer games. A fun career, sure, but nowhere near as exciting as being a caped crusader. To fill the void, she got involved in full contact martial arts, skydiving, and finally found herself in the rugged mountains outside of Salt Lake City, volunteering on the county Search and Rescue team. She now works full time in public safety. Aside from writing, she enjoys studying foreign languages, imagining fantastic worlds, competing in triathlons, and hanging out with her retired running buddy, Bella, an eleven-year-old Lab mix.

About this story, P.A. says: "The idea for this story came at a point in my life when it felt like things were falling apart and everything I tried to fix it, just made it worse. I had a dead-end, unfulfilling job, and way too many bills! Almost two decades (and a new career) later, I found the story tucked away in a dusty folder on my old computer. With some encouragement from friends, I worked up the courage to bring it to a LUW meeting for critique and ultimately submit it to the LUW contest and this anthology."

What P.A. doesn't tell you is that "The Cube" won honorable mention in the 2017 League of Utah Writers flash fiction contest. We're very proud to present it here.

THE CUBE
P.A. Sterling

The living room walls had most definitely not been blue five minutes ago. He cocked his head to one side and squinted at the flat, undecorated surface. Of course, squinting did nothing at all to change the color. He distinctly remembered asking for, "Just plain white!" a year ago when he'd had the room redecorated. Now the misbehaving walls were a pale blue.

He looked down at the cube in his hand. It was multicolored and just under three inches on a side. A Rubik's cube. The puzzle had been "solved" when he unwrapped it a few minutes prior, a birthday present his aide had brought in with the morning's mail. Oddly, it had no return address and no to-from card. The note with it had been cryptic, too.

Happy birthday. Remember these? All the fun we had in high school? This one's got a twist, though. You'll love it.

Cryptic or not, the unknown sender was right. He did love a puzzle. In his youth, he had spent uncountable time solving the puzzle and got to the point where he could solve one in under a minute. That had been a long time ago, twenty-five-odd years, but he thought he still remembered the solution.

When he first saw the cube, he had chuckled at the memories, then oriented it so the red face was up. He twisted the top a full ninety degrees to the right, resulting in the blue walls he was looking at now.

He shifted the top face back and watched the walls fade to their normal white. A huge smile spread across his face. "Incredible!" He repeated the previous two manipulations and got the same results; the walls shifted blue then back to white. "I don't believe it."

"Bobby, who sent this?" he yelled. There was no answer. "Never around when you need him," he grumbled to himself. When he located him, Bobby was going to get an earful! Then he remembered he'd sent his aide to pick up his suit at the cleaners. Well, Bobby would get a pass... this time. He returned his attention to the cube.

He turned the green face. Nothing seemed to change. Confused, he got up and wandered around his house for the next fifteen minutes, looking for something out of place or different. It was a large house. He was a successful divorce lawyer, much to the detriment of the opposing parties in his cases.

He glanced out the plate-glass windows that overlooked the valley and noticed things were darker. After disabling the security alarms, he stepped out onto the large wooden deck. The air in the valley was clear for a change, and he could see all the way across the shiny glass skyscrapers of downtown to the mountains.

The sun set behind the snowcapped ridgeline, leaving a deep red gash on the horizon. It should have been late morning, but the sun was setting. He was still in his plush blue bathrobe, for heaven's sake. He twisted the green face to its start position and watched the sun trace a reverse path to its zenith.

He rotated the yellow face to the top and twisted it to the left. As it turned, he watched the sky turn a hazy green and he smelled cinnamon. Instead of turning it back, he rotated the whole cube and twisted another side. His lawn turned from blades of green grass to purple, velvety moss. The effect was just too strange, so he reversed his prior changes. The grass shifted to green blades, but the sky didn't change back to blue.

He looked down at the puzzle, expecting all the faces to be colored uniformly. They weren't. He was also not wearing his comfortable blue robe anymore but instead was dressed in a rough-spun tunic of some design he was unable to identify. The material made his skin itch.

He frowned at his mistake and twisted the colored cube a few times to solve it. But now the colored squares were truly jumbled. He looked out across the now-forested valley. The city was gone, as was his house. His stomach turned to lead. "Oh, shit."

He stared back at the cube, working the puzzle in his mind until he was sure he had it figured out. Positive it would work, he started his manipulations. Turn. Twist. Turn. His fingers became increasingly numb with each manipulation that brought the puzzle closer to the solution.

Now he stood in a desert, flat and featureless. Blast-furnace air burned his lungs when he breathed, and the rays from the red giant sun overhead baked his bare shoulders. "Damn it!" You would think a birthday present would give him better circumstances, not worse, maybe a room full of gold or something actually useful.

A few more turns, and it would be solved. Twist. He gasped for breath in the parched air as his gills collapsed. Horrified, he watched his hands morph into fins, and the cube tumbled to the sand. He fell beside it and flopped around weakly, lidless eyes unable to blink.

Only one row still shifted out of place.

One move away from the solution.

Craig Kingsman writes about murders because committing them would be a real bummer for the victim. He discovered his joy of murder mysteries as a teen and always thought it would be fun to write them. A long career in computer programming got in his way of writing fiction, but he did learn about murder by executing programs and killing bugs. He authored or coauthored two technical books and dozens of magazine articles on programming topics. He has also worked as a radio disc jockey and once worked for the circus. Craig is an active member of both Sisters in Crime (where Misters are also welcome) and the League of Utah Writers, and has presented at several writer conferences and events. You can find him at www.craigkingsman.com.

About this story, Craig says: "The idea, name, and opening scene for this story came to me while sitting in a presentation at the League of Utah Writers Fall Conference in 2016, but it was a year later before I sat down and wrote the story at the Monkey Genre Writers Infinite Weekend retreat. I had fun writing this, especially coming up with the names. And if you're wondering, yes, butler schools really do exist, even today."

A common bit of writing advice is to "avoid clichés like the plague." We're so glad that Craig chose to ignore that piece of wisdom to give us this fun little mystery.

THE BUTLER DID IT
Craig Kingsman

Nigel Remington-Smythe lay on the plush blue carpet of the library. One might think he was staring at the ceiling because his eyes were wide open. The blood pooling under his head, along with the letter opener sticking out of his neck, told a different story. That was the incident we were called to investigate. My name: John Shakespeare, Detective Sergeant, Scotland Yard. My Gov'nor, Detective Chief Inspector Duncan Abrams, led this inquiry.

It was half past ten, and I was reading the lead story in the *Times* about the PM supporting the American president, Kennedy, on the Cuban missiles when we were called to the Bannister Butlering School. The headmaster, Carlysle Eades, had rung the Yard to report the murder. I hadn't even known there was such a thing as a butlering school, but Remington-Smythe must have. He'd been one of the students.

"Can you think of anyone Nigel had crossed?" Chief Inspector Abrams said as he lit a cigarette.

"He had a bit of a row two nights ago with another student," Eades said. "One Frederick Underly."

Eades was the type of person I hated interviewing. As the headmaster of what he called "England's most prestigious butlering school for over a hundred years," he was a pompous blowhard. As if his "acquaintance of the finest royalty and upper class in all of Europe, including the queen herself" gave him license to think he was one of them and treat us as servants.

"What was this row about?" Abrams said.

"A young lady. Seems they both fancied her. It very nearly came to fisticuffs. Professor Blackbourne pulled the two lads apart."

"Who is this young lady?" Abrams said.

"I daresay I don't know. It's quite common for our students to fancy young ladies that live and work nearby, but it rarely comes to a brawl."

"Where is Underly now?" I said.

"All the students were sent to their dormitories when we found young Remington-Smythe lying there dead."

"And what about this letter opener here?" Abrams said. He pulled a handkerchief from his pocket, carefully wrapped it around the end of the handle, and pulled it from the victim's neck.

I cringed at this, knowing it could destroy evidence. "Chief Inspector, should you have done that?"

"Oh! Right you are. Well, it's done now." Abrams turned to the headmaster. "The letter opener?"

Eades said, "Could belong to anyone. The students are all given identical letter openers. Part of the curriculum is the proper method of opening post."

"How many students do you have here?"

"With Nigel dead, it's now seventeen."

"What about staff and faculty?" I said.

"Five distinguished professors at present. It was six, but Professor Pitchfork retired last month after being with us nearly forty years. We have yet to replace him. All are gentlemen, I assure you. As for staff—three secretaries, Mrs. Lancaster the cook, her assistant, Pippa, and the gardener, Mr. Primrose. And of course there's me."

"No maids?"

"The young lads all take part in the cleaning so they know how it's properly done."

Movement in the hallway caught my attention. "Sir, the boys from the crime laboratory have arrived."

"Thank you, Shakespeare." Abrams handed the letter opener to a laboratory technician. I was curious about what he would do with it, so I kept an eye on him and an ear on the chief inspector.

"So this Remington-Smythe, how were his marks?" Abrams asked.

"He was middle of the class, but he got an offer from one of the wealthiest families in Yorkshire," Eades said.

The technician examining the letter opener waved me over and pointed to finger marks in the drying blood.

"Can you get fingerprints from it?" I asked.

"Looks like the killer wore gloves," he said.

Abrams wandered over. "We need to track down those gloves and find out who is missing a letter opener, Shakespeare. Then we'll have our killer."

We began a search of the school, starting with the student dormitories.

Underly's room was first. I could see why a young lady would be smitten with him. He was six feet tall, with blond hair, blue eyes, and a square chin—a devilishly handsome bloke. He waited outside in the hall under the careful watch of a constable during the search. Each student had been given seven pairs of white gloves. Underly's room contained exactly seven pairs and one letter opener. The chief inspector took great care to examine his diary, notebooks, clothing, and shoes.

The next three rooms were searched in the same manner. The fifth room belonged to Nigel's brother, Reginald. I was shocked when I saw him. We hadn't been told he was Nigel's identical twin. He looked every part the butler, dressed in a black tuxedo, white shirt with a starched collar, bow tie, shoes polished to a shine, and hair neatly combed.

The clothes in Reginald's cupboard were precisely laid out. Suits, shirts, shoes. Even his socks and undershorts were perfectly folded. As with the previous room, Abrams examined the clothing, taking a bit longer with the shoes than before. He placed them sole to sole, squinted, and placed them back where they belonged. He riffled through the diary and notebooks, pausing every few pages.

Finally, we came to Nigel's room. It yielded five pairs of gloves. With the ones he was wearing when he was killed, that left one missing pair. And his letter opener was also gone.

We set up a temporary incident room in the headmaster's office. It was huge. One wall contained floor-to-ceiling book-cases, filled with old volumes layered in dust. Apparently, the students didn't clean in here. Another wall was covered with diplomas and framed photographs of the headmaster, including one of him with Winston Churchill.

An enormous desk sat at one end. It was old, solid, and make of oak. It was covered with books and papers and on one corner sat a copy of today's *Times*. Behind the desk were windows that faced out to the garden. Eades sat in a finely upholstered chair facing the large desk and smoked a cigar.

Abrams paced and exhaled cigarette smoke. "Killed with his own letter opener."

"Seems that way, sir," I said. "Or perhaps the killer used his, then took Nigel's to cover his tracks."

"What? Oh, yes, Shakespeare. A possibility. So young Remington-Smythe had a chat with his killer in the library. Frederick Underly had a row with him earlier. I need to talk to this Underly fellow. Fetch him here."

A constable returned a few minutes later and reported that Underly was not in his room.

Abrams blew out more smoke. "Bugger. Find him. No sign of the gloves or the missing letter opener and now no Underly. We're going nowhere. How the devil did he get out? We had constables at every door."

"You know, Chief Inspector," Eades said, "there is one possible exit for the lad. There's an old tunnel that goes from the main building to the carriage house. It hasn't been used in years."

"Well, don't just stand there, Shakespeare. Get on it," Abrams said.

The headmaster led me to the kitchen. From inside a cupboard, he took a torch for himself and handed another to me. At the back of the broom cupboard was a false wall. Pushing on it caused it to open into a passageway. We turned on the torches and walked through the doorway.

We hadn't gone far when a stone staircase took us down several feet. The air smelled of mold and dust that had been there for decades. Spiderwebs covered the walls, and we had to brush them out of our way. It seemed unlikely that Underly had gone through here, but we continued on nonetheless.

After some distance, we went up another stone staircase that ended at a wooden door.

"Look there," I said, directing the light of the torch to the floor. "See where the door made a mark in the dust? It's been opened recently."

"That's it for him," Eades said. "We have explicit rules about leaving the school during the week. He's obviously not Bannister material. Young Mr. Underly will be expelled as soon as he shows up, and I will let it be known to any future employer."

"Stand back. I'll go first. He could be on the other side." I pulled the door open.

We found ourselves in an old stone carriage house with beams so large they seemed to be made from tree trunks. The floor was dirt but over the years had become hard as rock. There was no carriage here now; it was filled with old furniture, boxes, and paintings, some covered by tarps.

I tried the door to the outside. It opened easily. "I do believe young Underly left by this route. I'm going to continue my search. It could be dangerous, Mr. Eades. I'd like you to return to the main building through the same passageway, please."

The headmaster retreated through the underground passage while I headed out into the school grounds. A small pond in the back corner attracted my attention, so I went there first.

A wooden bench sat where the path ended. It looked like a relaxing place to rest and watch the ducks and swans swim. High grass and flowers abutted the back side for a few feet and ended at a stone wall. The smell of blooms and fresh rain filled the air.

As I circled toward it, I noticed a path had been trampled in the grass. Following it, I came across the body of a young man, face down in the bushes. The back of his head had been bashed in. I turned him over to see the face of Frederick Underly.

The next thing I remembered was waking up with a splitting headache. Whoever did in Mr. Underly must have hit me too. But lucky for me, he failed to send me to see Saint Peter. I got to my feet and, despite being wobbly, made it back to the main house.

"Sit down, Shakespeare," the chief inspector exclaimed when he saw me. He called to a constable. "Bring this man some tea."

I told Abrams what I found and what happened to me. I insisted I was fine to continue, but he demanded I rest there and drink my tea. He then set off to inspect the new crime scene himself.

A short time later, he returned, followed by the headmaster.

"Well, sir?" I said.

"It's Underly, all right. Professor Barnaby identified him. I need to talk to Nigel's brother next."

Abrams sent for the lad, and there was soon a knock on the door. "You wanted to see me, Headmaster?" Reginald said.

"Mr. Remington-Smythe, the police have some questions for you," the headmaster said. "Chief Inspector, unless you need me, I have some business to attend to with the staff."

"Very good, Headmaster. We can take it from here."

"One more thing, Mr. Remington-Smythe." Eades paused in the open doorway. "I expect you to truthfully answer every question they ask." With that, he left, closing the door behind him.

"Reginald, I'm Detective Chief Inspector Duncan Abrams. I'm sure you know why I asked to see you. My condolences on your loss. How are you holding up?"

"I am quite well, sir." Reginald's response was dry and flat, his training kicking in. It was as if he'd been a butler for years. He didn't exhibit a single emotion.

"How was your relationship with your brother?" Abrams said.

"It was good, sir. A bit competitive, I'd say, but what brothers aren't?"

"Did he have issues with any of the other students?"

"Just Mr. Underly, sir."

What a butler Reginald would make. His brother had just been killed, and here he was, stoic and at attention. I could not be this way if it were my brother.

I said, "What about this row Underly had with your brother?

Reginald turned to face me. "Both fancied a young lady, sir. Miss Felicity Lancaster."

"We may want to talk to her. Do you know where she lives?"

"No, sir, but I believe she's employed at the Hog and Boar Pub just two streets down."

"Your brother was not at the top of the class," Abrams said, "yet he received a rather impressive job offer, did he not?"

Reginald looked at Abrams. "Yes, sir. He was offered a position with Lord and Lady Blakesley at their country estate in Upper Yorkshire."

"Where did you rank in the class?"

"I was sixth."

"So students who received lower marks than you received offers and you did not. How do you feel about that?"

"I was happy for my brother, sir. As for others, they are going to serve families who are, how should I put this... not up to standards. I have submitted my curriculum vitae to several important families and expect to hear from one of them soon. I am not concerned about placement. Perhaps I may even be lucky enough to replace my brother at Blakesley Manor."

"Very well, Reginald. That's all for now. You may return to your room," Abrams said.

"Thank you, sir." Reginald turned and left.

Once the door closed, Abrams said, "That was certainly odd. In all my years, I have never seen a man so stoic after losing a family member. Quite the program they have here. What do you think, Shakespeare?"

"We should talk to the professors and staff," I said.

"Jolly good idea, Shakespeare. Start with... who was the professor who broke up that row between Underly and Remington-Smythe?"

I looked back through my notes. "Professor Blackbourne."

"Yes, Blackbourne. But let's not overlook the students," Abrams said. "After all, Underly somehow slipped past the constables."

Despite my lingering headache, I went looking for Blackbourne and found him in his office with Professor Barnaby. Both men told me that after Nigel's body was found, they gathered the students and instructed them to remain in their rooms. They both then came here to Blackbourne's office. Other than the row between Nigel and Underly, they knew of no one who had motive to kill either student. Both had been excellent students and liked by everyone.

I moved on to the rest of the faculty and then to the staff. All gave the same story as the two professors. Then I went back to question the students. Some were jealous of Nigel getting a prestigious placement, but no one had a bad word about him.

Underly was a different story. Three students said he cheated on several exams. They reported it but had no evidence, so nothing came of it. That was interesting, but hardly a reason to kill the young man.

I returned to the headmaster's office to give Chief Inspector Abrams my report.

He set down the paper he was reading. "Bugger," he said and ran his hand through his hair. "This investigation is going nowhere, Shakespeare. It's all bollocks. Everyone seems to be in the clear. The question now is who would benefit most by killing both students? We should talk to the young lady the two boys fa— Good lord, how could we miss it? What was the name of the young lady?"

"Felicity Lancaster. The cook! Her name is Lancaster too."

We raced to the kitchen to find the cook getting supper ready. Mrs. Lancaster was a stout lady with graying hair. I guessed her to be about fifty years old.

"Mrs. Lancaster," Abrams said. "Are you related to Felicity Lancaster, the young woman both Nigel and Underly fancied?"

"Yes, sir. She's my niece," she said in a strong Scottish brogue.

"How did you feel about Nigel's and Underly's interest in her?"

"I wasn't happy about it. The wife of a butler is not easy. Butlers earn a pittance, and she would never have a home of her own, let alone have children."

"So you had motive to kill the two of them," I said.

"Kill them? Oh no, Sergeant. I couldn't do that. I couldn't kill someone."

"Where were you when they were killed?"

"Here, in the kitchen."

"Alone or was someone with you?"

"My assistant, Pippa, was with me. A couple of the professors came in and out, and the gardener, too, when he came for his lunch."

"No one else? The headmaster?" Abrams said.

"The headmaster?" Her eyes widened. "He... he wasn't here today. Now if you'll excuse me, the boys haven't had a bite since breakfast—not even tea. I need to finish with supper."

"Very well, Mrs. Lancaster, but you are not to leave the school."

The students and faculty were to have supper in the dining hall. The headmaster arranged for supper to be brought to us in his office so we could continue working. I sat in a corner, balancing my plate on my lap. A small table to my right gave me a place for my teacup. The lamb and potatoes were very good—best I'd ever had, in fact.

I was just finishing when I leaned over too far and my plate slid from my lap and crashed to the floor. I knelt to clean it up and spotted a rubbish bin in the corner. I didn't remember seeing it before. I finished wiping up the floor, then examined the bin. It was full of papers, but underneath, I found a pair of bloody gloves. "Sir, you should look at this."

Abrams stopped dead in his tracks when I held up the gloves. "Bugger. How did we miss those? Were they there before? Get Eades back in here."

The headmaster looked shocked when he saw the gloves. "Good show, Chief Inspector. Where did you find them? Have you figured out whom they belong to?"

"Explain your whereabouts today, Mr. Eades," I said. "Where you were when the murders occurred?"

"I... Now you just hold on there. Are you accusing me of killing my students?"

"The gloves were found in the rubbish bin here in your office. Can you tell us how they got there?"

"What?" Eades said. "In my office? Impossible. I had nothing to do with the lads' deaths. And as for the gloves, obviously someone put them there."

"Mr. Eades," Abrams said. "Right now, based on the evidence, you are the prime suspect. What reason would you have for killing your students?"

"This is outrageous. I have no reason to kill my students. I am entrusted with their education and safety and wouldn't stoop so low as to kill one of them, let alone two."

"But you were missing when Mr. Underly was killed."

"I was discussing a mite infestation in the rose bushes with the gardener."

"I'll talk to him, Chief Inspector," I said and set out at once.

The gardener failed to confirm Eades claims. They had talked about rose bushes, but it was early in the morning, before the first boy was found dead.

"He's lying, sir," I reported back.

Abrams lit a cigarette and paced. "Well, Eades?"

"I— I…" Eades sank into his chair. "I have nothing more to say."

"I suggest you speak now, Eades, or it's off to the nick with you," I said.

"I won't be insulted by this inquiry. I'll say no more," he said.

"Very well," Abrams said. "Shakespeare, bring Professors Blackbourne and Barnaby here. I also want Mrs. Lancaster and Reginald Remington-Smythe to join us. It's time to get everyone together."

Once we were all gathered in the headmaster's office, Abrams began, "You're all here because each of you had reason to kill. Before we're done, the person who murdered Nigel and Underly will be revealed." Abrams walked to the desk and retrieved the sheet of paper he was looking at earlier. "Professors Blackbourne and Barnaby, you were being paid by Lord Wayne, Nigel's soon-to-be employer, to change his marks and give him the answers to the tests. Nigel wrote the answers in his notebooks."

"What? My professors taking bribes?" Eades said. "You two are sacked, effective immediately."

"Precisely, Mr. Eades. But you should sack yourself too because you knew about it. This paper I found on your desk lists the payouts and dates the professors received them. But they are not the killers. You, however, Headmaster, went missing several times today. It gave you opportunity to kill both boys, and you were quick to offer up the passageway as a way of escape for Underly."

Eades stood up. "Chief Inspector, I will not sit here in my own office and be accused of something I did not do."

"Mr. Eades, you will please sit down and listen. And you will do it now," Abrams said.

Eades sat, grumbling, and puffed on his cigar.

"You had a secret of your own. You have been having a romantic relationship with Mrs. Lancaster."

"Mrs. Lancaster?" I said. "The cook? And you the headmaster."

Eades looked deflated. "I couldn't tell you the truth. Victoria and I have been secretly seeing each other for years. We love each other. She's a widow. Lost her husband nearly twenty years ago while fighting the Nazis."

"Then why keep it secret?" Abrams said, pacing.

"She's in my employ. That doesn't look cricket."

"Perhaps the two of you were in this together," I said. "She admitted she wasn't happy with the two dead boys fancying her niece. It would have been easy for one or both of you to slip through the secret passageway in the kitchen to kill Mr. Underly."

"Victoria wouldn't hurt a fly. She's the gentlest, kindest woman I've ever known," Eades said.

Mrs. Lancaster said, "I already told you. I didn't like them chasing after Felicity, but I didn't kill them."

"Right you are, Shakespeare, but neither of them killed the boys," Abrams said. "That leaves Reginald here. Or should I call you Nigel?"

Everyone gasped.

"That's right," Abrams said. "It was Reginald on the floor of the library, and Nigel here who killed him and took his place."

"I hated my brother," Nigel said. "He was always Father's favorite. Always the favorite with the girls. Always the most popular. When he got that job, even though I was the better student, I saw my chance. It was easy to take his place. But how did you know?"

"The gloves were one clue. They weren't here earlier, then they appeared after we summoned you for questioning. But the key to it all was the shoes," Abrams said. "There was one pair too many in Reginald's cupboard and that pair was a size bigger than the others, but the same size as the ones in your room. You aren't completely identical, are you? At first, I thought it was a mistake, but the more I thought about it, the more sense it made that you killed him."

"But what about Underly? Who killed him?" Eades asked.

"That was also Nigel," Abrams said. "You want to tell us, Nigel?"

"I love Felicity. Reginald also secretly loved her. Once he was dead, I just needed to get rid of that toad Underly and she'd be mine."

"You can't have my niece," Mrs. Lancaster said.

"No, he can't," I said. "He's not going to have anyone because he'll hang. Constable, take this man into custody."

"Jolly good deduction, sir," I said when we were back at the Yard. "But how did you figure it out so quickly?"

"It was easy, Shakespeare. Once I considered all the evidence, it was clear which butler did it. The butler always does it."

Jennie Stevens is a wife, mother, copyeditor, and connoisseur of all things nerdy. She lives in Salt Lake City with her husband and their two adorable children, where she drinks too much Dr. Pepper and has a not-very-secret love affair with her Chicago Manual of Style. She can often be found reorganizing her bookshelves, singing along with the radio, or napping. During college, she discovered a deep love of grammar and, since becoming an editor, has achieved her lifelong dream of being paid to read books. Her first short story, "The Albatross," was published in the LUW anthology, Intersections. Follow her on Instagram and Twitter (@jennietheeditor) to find out what she's reading now.

About this story, Jennie says: "I love a good villain. And by that, I mean a villain who believes, in their heart of hearts, that they are in the right. The main character of this story, Myrna, is a murderer and proud of it. She rid the world of disgusting people, and the world is better for it. Of course, her executioners feel the same about her demise. Myrna believes she deserves a beautiful, peaceful death. Her executioners have other plans..."

They say that you should be careful what you wish for, because you may get exactly what you deserve—we think you'll enjoy Jennie's interpretation.

DEATH BY UNICORN
Jennie Stevens

"Prisoner 57806, Myrna Bywater."

The voice drifted into Myrna's consciousness, but she batted it away. She grasped at the fading remnants of her dreams—the only escape from the monotonous dark. King Balthazar had been there, along with his slimy excuse for a nephew. The images slipped away faster. She'd had her knife, her beautiful silver knife.

There had been blood—the nephew's blood.

Red blood on silver.

"Myrna!" The voice echoed off the cell walls and ripped her from her waking thoughts. She cracked open an eye, unwilling to let go of sleep entirely. She slept more often than not these days, despite her rock slab and straw mattress of a bed. Getting old was exhausting.

"Good morning to you, too," she grumbled. "What do you want?"

"It's evening, Myrna."

Myrna deigned to open both eyes.

Beyond her cell bars stood a handsome guard and his obsequious assistant, illuminated in the light of an arc lamp. He was one of the few guards she liked—sweet to the older prisoners.

She liked that he forgot how many of them were cold-blooded murderers. What was his name again?

She rubbed the last vestiges of sleep from her eyes and went about the laborious process of sitting up, her old muscles protesting the movement. "I haven't been able to tell night from day since I was transferred here. That was, oh, ten years back. I used to be right near the surface, could practically feel the sun on my face…"

"That's nice," he said, smiling, not listening. "What have we got for you today?"

He snapped his fingers at his assistant, who handed him a few papers. "Let's see. You've been convicted of fifteen counts of murder and sentenced to death… I'm guessing you know all that…" He shuffled through the papers again, drawing one that wasn't as worn and dirty as the others. "Right, here we are. New orders." Pause. "Oh."

"Lay it on me, handsome," Myrna said. "Another transfer? Deeper into the pit? Near the core where the heat dries you out? Or maybe back near the surface so I can hear the whisper of freedom? Of course not that… I guess the steam couldn't make me look like any more of a prune than I already am."

The guard—Simmons, that was his name—cleared his throat uncomfortably. "Uh, no, Myrna. No transfer. I'm afraid it's the final order."

"Oh," Myrna breathed. "Been waiting on that one. It is about time, I guess."

She rose from her thin mattress with a grunt, bones cracking, and stepped into the light where the guards could see her face. She had once been strong and athletic, but now her spine bent her in half, and she stood only by clutching ancient hands on the bars of her cell. None of that mattered here at the end. Death took young and old alike, and she'd been lucky enough to grow old—even if it was in this hole of a prison.

"Let's get this over with," Simmons said, his voice softening. "Myrna Bywater, you've been sentenced to death by the High Inquisitor of Cicely—"

"That dirty snake," Myrna muttered.

"What?"

"Oh, nothing."

"Where was I? Right. According to the statutes laid down by King Balthazar, the Swift Arrow—"

"Well, you'd have to ask his concubines about that."

"No more interruptions," Simmons said, his sharp tone echoing on the rough-hewn stone.

Myrna swallowed her next insult. No one who mattered was here to listen to them.

"Sorry, Myrna," Simmons said softly. "I've got to get through this. Orders. You know."

"Of course, dear."

He glanced back at his papers. "You have the right to choose the method of your execution, per Royal Decree 648. Here is a list of available methods." He held a sheet of old parchment through the bars.

Myrna shook her hand at it. "You know my old eyes can't read a thing like that."

He read quickly. "Thrown into the lava pits, savaged by wild boars, drawn and quartered, burned at the stake, death by stoning, death by unicorn—"

"You can stop right there. I've had my heart set on that unicorn for years."

Simmons chuckled. "Should have known you'd be a unicorner, Myrna, you bleeding heart."

Myrna smiled slyly back. Once, a smile like that would send

men to their knees—and the point of her knife—but now, Simmons just walked away, shaking his head, his assistant scurrying behind without a backward glance.

That night, Myrna dreamed of the unicorn.

Sunlight fell softly on her face, warming her closed eyes. She was young again, trailing spry fingers through the soft grass beneath her. Her long dark hair tickled her neck and shoulders as the wind gusted through, bringing with it the scent of fresh roses and honeysuckle. Her mind pulled her back, whispering that this was a mirage, she was in a cell, she was about to die, but she resisted. This was a time before the knife, before the red rocks and the steel bars and the endless darkness.

She opened her eyes, her mind quieting as she stood, pushing against the firm ground. A stream rolled by, shafts of light bouncing off its curves and ripples. Golden grass grew high here, swaying in the breeze. The grass moved differently in one area, and Myrna moved forward, knowing what she would find before she saw it.

There it was, hidden by the grass, taking long gulps from the stream. A unicorn. Easily seventeen hands high and white as snow.

Myrna crept now, careful to make as little noise as possible. Still, the beast's ears perked and its head lifted as she approached. Its golden horn, nearly the length of Myrna's arm, glinted in the speckled sunlight.

The two watched each other for a moment, and then stepped toward each other at the same time—drawn together for a purpose. Myrna rested her hand on the unicorn's neck, rubbing its silky mane between her fingers. She looked into its glossy blue eyes and knew what had brought her here. She wasn't afraid. She patted the beast once more and stepped back the length of the unicorn's horn. It lowered its head, and gently—its touch as light as a lover's—pressed its horn against her chest.

Myrna sighed. "I'm ready."

The unicorn pushed its horn through Myrna's heart. There was no blood, no pain, only a beautiful white light that carried her out of her body. As she drifted away, she watched the unicorn curl up beside her fallen body and rest its majestic head against her chest.

A guard came for her the next evening. It wasn't Simmons this time; instead, a bulky man Myrna had never met blocked what little light came through the bars. He flipped a lever on a small contraption in his hand, triggering the lock mechanism in her cell door. Its rusted hinges groaned and protested but finally opened.

"Don't know why they'd need to send a great hulk like you, dear," Myrna said, exiting her cell for the last time. "It's not like I'm running anywhere."

The guard stared, expressionless.

"All muscles and no sense of humor, I see."

"This way," the stiff-faced guard said, pointing down a narrow hallway of sorts.

Myrna followed silently, plastering a smile on her ashen face. Her hands trembled, but she clenched them and thrust her head higher. Any prisoners they passed would see that she wasn't afraid. Good old Myrna, off to meet the unicorn.

They walked a long way, until they passed fewer cells and the walls pressed in on them. Muscles the guard stooped and turned sideways to avoid outcroppings of rock. Myrna placed her hands along the wall for support and walked slowly to avoid tripping on loose stones.

The red stone passage ended in a large, open cavern.

As the copper scent of old blood assaulted her. Myrna pushed down the bile that rose in her throat and imagined instead the soft, warm smell of honeysuckle on the breeze. It was a worn memory she had used many times over her years in the pit, and it served her well here at the end, reminding her of the peaceful dream she'd woken from that morning.

Myrna strained her neck, spotting a small circle of sunlight at the very top. She basked in her last moment of seeing the outside world. If she had the body of a climber and a good three days, she could probably crawl her way out. Instead, Muscles jabbed her in the back, forcing her forward into the center of the cavern, where a group of ten or so people waited. They were more appropriately dressed for an audience with the king than an execution in a dusty cave.

No one said a word; they didn't give an order to restrain her. There was nowhere to go.

She scanned the faces, hoping to see someone familiar, perhaps someone who might remember her fondly—Simmons, maybe. But apparently he didn't warrant an invitation to the show. These grim advisors, lawyers, and witnesses were the last people who would ever see her alive.

"What a depressing lot," she said. "Anyone for a drink? I've got a nice aged brandy in my cell—"

"Myrna Bywater," a tall woman interrupted, emerging from the small crowd. She wore the robe of a king's advisor and small glasses, her face pinched to keep them on. "You are here to be executed for fifteen counts of murder, including the king's nephew."

"Well, he deserved it," Myrna murmured.

"Excuse me?" the woman said, leaning closer.

Myrna spoke up. "The king's nephew. He ran his hand up my skirt. He had that knife coming."

"Enough," the advisor said. "This isn't an inquiry. You've had your trial. Begin the execution."

A lanky man next to the advisor jumped into motion, punching buttons on a small machine in his hand. It looked like the one Muscles had used to open her cell, only larger with more buttons, knobs, and levers. From the floor rose a wall with lengths of brown leather attached to each corner, a drain beneath it. The dam Myrna had built around her fear cracked at the sight of that little drain, imagining what was about to flow down it.

Muscles grabbed Myrna from behind and pushed her toward the wall.

"Let me go, damn you," she said, struggling vainly in his grip.

Muscles kept pushing. Her executioners looked on in imperious silence as he turned Myrna's back to the wall and fastened her arms and legs with the leather straps. She kicked and threw punches, her weak attempts barely registering on Muscles's face. She had once been so much stronger. Her energy and atrophied muscles gave out, and she heaved in breaths as she hung from the wall like a crooked X.

Her eyes flicked frantically to each person in the crowd. On a few faces, she saw something resembling pity. The lanky man moved his weight from foot to foot, glancing at the king's advisor, who remained as stoic as ever.

But she was Myrna Bywater. She had watched the moment of death fifteen times, had reveled as the eyes of the men she had seduced went still, their faces limp. *Death is just a moment,* she coached herself. *Just a moment before something better comes along.*

"I'm ready," she said, willing her voice not to crack. It held firm.

"Bring out the unicorn," the advisor said, and the lanky man pressed a large red button.

A loud screeching ripped through the cavern, echoing off the walls, roaring its way up toward the sky above. Myrna yelled in shock, her voice lost in the reverberations. The noise came from across the chamber. A section of wall rose like the opening of a door, leaving a gaping black hole in the stone.

A moment the length of a long breath passed. The unicorn emerged, shaking the ground with each stomp of its feet.

"God in Heaven, what is that?" Myrna cried as her dam broke entirely.

This wasn't the majestic creature Myrna had dreamed about.

Instead of a pure white body with slender limbs, the beast was ten feet tall and made of silver metal. Visible mechanisms moved its legs in a stuttered walk. Its eyes glinted, not a pearlescent blue, but a dead black, reflecting Myrna's shocked image as it came closer. Atop its head, instead of a delicate gold lance, a thick steel cone twisted into a deadly corkscrew.

As the creature stopped before her, whirring and jerking, the horn began to rotate—faster and faster until it achieved the high-pitched whine of a drill that reverberated off the cavern walls. Steam hissed out of its mouth, blowing hot air into Myrna's face.

Myrna sobbed in terror, all thoughts of dignity vanished. Where was the beautiful, majestic creature she had heard whispered rumors of?

But how could the whispers be true? Anyone who had seen the creature had come here to die.

She turned toward the executioners. They looked bored—an insane juxtaposition next to the terrifying beast exuding smoke and pawing at the ground. They must have spread rumors. They were crueler than she. At least Myrna loved her victims, made them happy before she killed them.

"You bastards," she screamed, but her cry was drowned out as the king's advisor flicked her finger and the unicorn lurched forward, crossing the distance in a mere second and driving its twisting horn straight through Myrna's heart.

It pulled away just as sharply, viscera flying.

Myrna gasped, throat thick with blood. In her final dying moments, she stared into the black eyes of the unicorn. Red liquid seeped down the slowing drill of its horn, running between its eyes and down its cheeks.

Blood. Her blood.

Red blood on silver.

So beautiful, was Myrna's last thought.

Johnny Worthen is an award-winning, best-selling, multiple-genre writing, tie-dye wearing author. Trained in stand-up comedy, modern literary criticism, and cultural studies, his genre-bending comedy-noir, "The Finger Trap," won the League of Utah Writers Diamond Quill award for best book of the year. His newest work, "What Immortal Hand," takes a dark, desert journey into madness and faith. When not haunting writing conferences, Johnny is an instructor at the University of Utah. For more information, visit johnnyworthen.com.

About this story, Johnny says: "I struggle with short work. I often say it takes me a page to write my name so the challenge of a one hundred word flash fiction story was daunting. I took the prompt from the key phrase of Aquarius, "I know," and wrapped it around my constant life companion of death. That phrase used to end the piece, but never worked. Where we start is not where we end, and so from "I know" I came to "infinite peace" at the end of the journey."

In very few words, Johnny has painted a picture of a life well-lived. May we all count ourselves as fortunate.

COUNTING
Johnny Worthen

Seventy-three years, six operations, two cancers, and now not a single painless moment.

Three children and eight grandchildren—Susan pregnant with another. Tomas on scholarship, Betty dating that cute boy from the medical school. Ron through rehab, clean for four years and teaching school in Africa to a class of fifty-five smiling faces staring out of a photo on the dresser.

All well and accounted for. Alice would be proud.

The darkness warmed a bit.

For numbered years he'd sensed the moment, distant but approaching. Halting for Alice, now moving for him. Unstoppable. Undeniable. Now in the house. In the hall. Outside the door.

At the side of his bed.

"I come for thee."

One last breath and infinite peace.

Dr. Masha Shukovich is a writer, poet, chef, performer, visual artist, professor of Gender Studies, mother, and an immigrant from a country that no longer exists. She speaks five languages and has a super power called Synesthesia: her brain interprets words as moving images, numbers as colors, and tastes as shapes, colors, and sounds. She can taste a recipe simply by reading it. Masha is the winner of multiple awards, including the 2017 San Francisco Writing Contest and 2017 League of Utah Writers Creative Writing Contest, and a finalist for both the 2017 Writers' League of Texas Manuscript Contest and 2017 International Literary Awards in Fiction. Her work has appeared in I Come From The World Literary Journal and Permafrost Magazine.

About this story, Masha says: "I was talking to a woman very dear to me about her marriage to a man who, after several decades together, still doesn't really know her. She spoke to me of her desire to find herself after years of taking care of others and neglecting her own needs. 'I just don't know how I could ever leave him,' she told me. 'Maybe you could begin by leaving him a little bit at a time,' I said. I hope this story will help those who need the strength and courage to be their true selves reclaim their lives and begin anew."

Full of quiet hope, "What We Leave Behind" was a finalist in the 2018 San Francisco Writing Contest, and we're very proud to share it with you here.

WHAT WE LEAVE BEHIND
Masha Shukovich

There is no way I could ever leave my husband. He would never let me. And if I did somehow stumble into leaving, he would find me. Or his police buddies would.

And once he found me, he would grab me by the chin and hold my face close to his, my mouth staring at his mouth, like through a foggy window. People may think he is poised for a kiss, and smile.

"How in love those two are!" they'll say.

But they won't see the tightening of his fingers, like pliers, around my jaw. He is feeling for weak spots—little crevices where he can push and prod and poke until the wall crumbles. In his free time, he is a craftsman who unmakes things.

What would he do with my jaw, if he pried it apart? Put it under his pillow? Place it on his nightstand before he goes to bed? Tie a string around it and hang it on his rearview mirror like a charm? Use it to decorate the Christmas tree? Put it in a cardboard box at work and write EVIDENCE across it with a black Sharpie?

And what would I do without my jaw? It's funny how I always forget about that part.

I could never leave him. That much I know. So I start leaving parts of him instead.

I take his slippers to the park. I put them under the bench, lined up neatly, right next to my sneaker-clad feet. They sit there, obedient, like puppies. It seems like I'm sharing the bench with an invisible man who likes his feet to be warm. We sit there for a while, silent, the invisible man and I.

"I have to go," I say finally. "It's starting to rain, and I have a meeting I can't be late to."

I never have any meetings. The word tastes strange in my mouth, like a bite of too-sweet fruit from a land far away where the sun always shines.

"Okay, I'm leaving now," I say to the slippers, firmly.

It's like training for a marathon. One step at the time. Not that I think I could ever run a marathon. But running is a little bit like leaving. You just need to practice it every day. First, half a mile. Then a mile. Then two. Before long, you're half the world away. I used to think someone like me could never be a runner, but now I can imagine myself doing it.

There's no law against imagining, even if you don't have the legs for it.

I wave to the slippers. "Bye."

They seem to understand. Maybe this is what they've been waiting for all these years too. An empty park bench and a little time to gather their thoughts.

"Where in the hell are my slippers?" he roars later that night.

"What slippers?" I ask.

"The fucking brown ones I wear every fucking day!" he screams.

But I can tell by the color of his voice that he is uncertain, wobbly. There's a hint of Egyptian blue in it, like a hairline fracture in the sky. Something is getting dislodged there.

I shrug. He blinks, like a thing that crawled out of a cave into the sunlight by mistake. I've never shrugged like that before. He hardly ever blinks. This is new.

It's his brown socks next, then his pants. How compliant and obliging they are. The pants briefly wrap themselves around my arm, like a cat with its claws out or a child reluctant to follow along, pulling painfully at your outstretched hand. But I'm right there, ready to help.

"It's okay," I say as I pry them away. "You'll like the park."

The white undershirt is the next on the list. It escapes my grip for a moment as I carry it down the street and surrenders itself to the wind. How far would it fly, if I let it? Would it reach the ocean shore? Would a seabird take it to its nest to keep its eggs warm? Do seabirds have nests or do they sleep on top of black rocks amidst the sea spray? Do they ever feel lonely, those seabirds, or are they just glad to be free?

After the first few times, he stops asking about his things.

"I must have left my sweater at the station," he mutters absentmindedly. It feels like there is less of him in the house now, like he is wearing thin. I shrug. I do a lot of shrugging these days. It feels like I'm exercising my shoulders—first left, then right, then both at the same time.

There is a rhythm to it, like running.

Shrug, shrug, shrug, and away I go.

———————

His police hat is the last piece of him I take to the park. It refuses to budge, holding on to the hatstand like a drowning man, but I won't take no for an answer.

"Come on, move it," I say to the hat.

I am emboldened by my newfound strength, my shoulders more flexible and resilient from all the shrugging, my legs sturdier from all the walking to the park and back. If the hat had an elbow, I would grab it, gently but firmly. That's how it's done. Steering them by the elbow is the way to go.

When I get to the park with the hat, it looks like there's a man sleeping under the bench. There isn't, though. It's just all the clothes I've been placing there, gently, day after day. It's strange that no one wanted them. They are good clothes. Anyone can see that. Even I can.

The invisible sleeping man's empty knees are bent at an impossible angle. I cover his imaginary face with the unwilling police hat. Would you look at that: it fits perfectly.

———————

Over the next few days, I go through my own clothes. There's nothing else for me to do, really. This is the next step; there's no question about it.

I find the red sequined dress he bought for me years ago. I never wore it once. How little must he know me to buy me that dress. And even if I wanted to wear it, I wouldn't be able to now. My new shoulders would never fit in it. But it would look lovely on a smaller woman with narrower shoulders. It really would.

"Honey," he says that night after work. "It's the Police Officer Ball tomorrow night, remember?"

At first, I think he's talking to someone else, but there's no one else here, so he must mean me.

"Could you wear your red dress, please, honey? The one with the sequins? It looks so good on you."

Who is this woman he's talking to? I've never worn a red sequined dress in my life. And he's never called me honey before.

The moment he leaves the next morning, I get to work. There's so much to do; it needs to be perfect. That's the least I can do for him.

I place the red dress neatly across the bedspread. It's exquisite, truly. It's just not me. I add a pair of silk stockings, and a Chantilly lace and satin slip with matching panties. A pearl necklace and earrings. A pair of high-heeled shoes he bought after he took a work trip to Sacramento. I never asked what the trip was for, or the shoes. I just said thank you, as one does to be polite. And to keep the peace.

There. She looks lovely. The sequins catch the light like fish scales in bright sunshine. I wonder if she's a good swimmer. I'm becoming a runner, myself. It's like growing into a brand new skin. I'm not very fast—not yet—but my pace is steady, and I don't stop. The two of them will look good together, I'm sure.

Much better than he and I ever did.

This is my parting gift to him, the woman in a red sequined dress, in satin and silk, and high-heeled shoes. The woman who could have been me, only just. It doesn't matter if she's invisible either. She will go well with the invisible man, the one sleeping under the park bench. They can look at the stars together. Maybe they'll even hold hands and kiss in the summer rain, who knows. Keep each other warm at night, in winter. And in this world, who could hope for more?

I put on my sneakers and pick up my purse. That's really all that I need. I leave my keys on the kitchen table and carefully close the door, making sure it locks behind me. I walk down the stairs, each familiar crack and stain a bygone song. The pavement meets my feet with a welcoming thud. I start off walking, but as I come closer to the park, I break into a run. It's as if my legs have a mind of their own, and their mind is set on flying.

I pass by the invisible man and his bench.

One of the sleeves of his sweater flaps in the wind. It looks like he's waving me to stop, but I keep on going. I'll see where it takes me.

Halfway around the world isn't that far when you've learned how to run.

Jonathan Humphries earned a delightfully ambiguous degree in Entertainment Arts and Engineering. He now teaches an equally ambiguous high school media arts class. He often regrets bestowing the great power and responsibility of Photoshop to teenagers, and escapes by writing about the fantasy worlds, convinced it's hip to have imaginary friends. At a young age, he caught a bad case of what people called "the Gay," and no amount of, "Have you tried not being gay?" seemed to cure it. But before boys, Comic Books were his first love. Distract him on Twitter @jonnohumphries

About this story, Jonathan says: "Somewhere in the midst of college stress, this quirky little idea danced its way into my heart. For years, I told myself I wanted it to become an animated short film (my topic of study) á la Disney's Paperman. It nested a hollow idea in my brain, hibernating while I'd tell myself, "someday." When this anthology was announced, the idea poked at me again, adding a few less-than-subtle waves for my attention. While an animation featuring these characters may still be a "someday," the pesky little buggers didn't want their story stuck in the clouds forever."

As a group, all of the editors working on this project agreed that this poignant story of love, loss, and finding a way back from grief deserved a special place in this anthology. We hope that, like us, it leaves you with a smile that is every bit as real as the one the char-acter wears.

PAINTED SMILE
Jonathan Humphries

She's too scared to tell me to just get over it.

My phone's vibrating, dancing, gliding over my faux-wood desk, like it has to pee. It's Mom. She knows it doesn't matter if I answer or let it go to voicemail, the result is the same; she'll talk, and I'll listen.

I plod back to the bathroom mirror, clean-shaven face a ghastly shade of gloom. This is the real me. Lips don't curl upward on their own. I'm lucky, really. Even my heaviest face, dead in expression, still doesn't look as vile or unfriendly as some do. I could be burdened with what Jacob used to call "resting bitch face." That always got a laugh out of me. Grief doesn't show in my lips—it's in my eyes. Iris as black as pupil, they used to glint a little; now they're black holes, devouring the happiness of all who dare look inside. I can't make it ten minutes without living a memory, without thinking of Jacob.

After two years, his face is still tattooed on my mind. Those damn dimples, deep as soup spoons, so much life in his smile. I can still hear his voice, silvery smooth and breathy, like he was ashamed to speak at full volume and had to keep hushed tones. It was like he was always telling me secrets, trusting me with them.

No. I don't let myself stay this way: stern, emotionless.

I paint on a smile.

I've allowed myself time to wade in the lazy river of memories this morning. Now it's time to escape the flood of emotions. It's time to apply my mask, my excuse for not talking.

I start with globs of thick, white paint that clumps between the gaps of my fingers as I spread it over the contours of my face. The paint is cool and soothing. It's particularly hot and humid today—Korean summers can be brutal—and the realization stirs a grimace. I'll have to be extra careful to avoid smearing. The paint clogs in the crevices around my nose, but I even it out as I go, being careful around my eyes. How many times have I stabbed my eye with a slippery finger? It's a miracle I'm not blind.

I use a sponge to even out the white and glide it carefully around edges to form a crisp line under my widow's peak and before the point where chin curls to neck. I'm proud of today's arc around my forehead—a flawless curve.

A ding sounds from my phone. That was a particularly long message. Mom must have had a lot to say about Jin Soo's new job. He finally landed a jeong-gyu-jig position, a stable job manufacturing steel at Posco, so his future is secure. I'm afraid I don't know what he's doing exactly—and I don't ask questions for clarification. A hint of guilt slithers up my esophagus, tightening my throat. They've been so patient with me. I couldn't have asked for a better family. I'll text them and remind them how much I love them. I just don't have the will to *say* it.

I know it's stupid. I recognize I'm probably clinically insane. I mean, most people who come down with a case of selective mutism are kids. And not just kids—kids under five years old. That's why any parent in their right mind would tell me to get over it. It's been two years since Jacob's death. Move on.

But since he passed away, since that day I wore all white to honor him in traditional fashion, alone, in my apartment, I just haven't had the desire to speak. Gay marriage isn't legal. Our union wasn't recognized. No one told me he'd been struck by a bus. They just took his body, contacted his parents, and *shipped* him back home like a Gmarket package. And I got nothing. No closure, no visitation, no viewing. I didn't find out he was dead until two weeks later, from one of his friends in Arizona.

His parents didn't approve of his "lifestyle." He had moved to an entirely new country just to get away and find happiness. And he did. He found me. But he ended with them.

Twirling blades of a cheap fan dry the first layer of paint. White tightens against me, gripping my cheeks like a kitten clinging to a tree. I imagine Botox must feel like this. Seems like everyone uses it now, but the needle would give me pause. Luckily, guys aren't expected to maintain the tautness of teenage skin forever. My hair and eyebrows are as naturally black as the color spectrum allows, but I still have to go back over the brows, which are now frosty white. The fine tip brush leaks an ink-black line over the hairs, matting them against each other.

This next part is always uncomfortable. I have to focus to needle-point precision. It tenses my neck, causing occasional spasms. I draw a stretched triangle under one eye and a diamond under the other, the bristles tickling my skin as they drag. Asymmetry seems to give a mime more life. Quick stabs from the back of the brush, dipped in black, create a series of three dots under the diamond.

My mask is complete. My escape from reality.

I'm already donning black and white—stripes, suspenders,

and black paints, hems folded up to my calf, revealing the should-normally-be-concealed-for-the-sake-of-fashion-and-humanity knee-length white and black-ringed socks.

I pocket my phone. I'll listen to the message when I need a break.

———

I live close to Hongdae and don't mind the bike ride. I get weird looks, that's for sure. It's not every day you see a Korean mime biking down the road, hugging a rainbow briefcase with one arm and a lemon-colored umbrella strapped to his back. But I don't mind.

Wind streams through my hair, the heat daring to coax perspiration from my temples. Thankfully, it runs back into my hairline and not down my face.

I make it to Hongik University, the main student center gapping the street, acting as a building-shaped arch to pass underneath. It's busy out. A few onlookers snicker and bury their faces in books as if they're the embarrassed ones. Some simply smile; I'm a pleasant surprise to an ordinary day of study. But it doesn't matter either way. I won't set up here. It's down the road, near the bustle of café-goers that suits me best.

There are several nooks, corners, or makeshift stages I frequent. I have to distance myself from other performers. Most buskers blast music, to sing, dance, or show off on an instrument. One sits on a high stool with a venomous-looking black and red electric guitar, but I can't hear him over the din of customers. A street dance group always stakes out the prime real estate next to Noona Holdak. I can't fight for that. Especially if I refuse to talk. Plus, the acrid, salty odor of cuttlefish is hardly worth the location. Luckily, many performers only hit the street's night life, leaving daytime open to someone passive like me.

I find a nice spot near one of my favorite *quiet* performers. I'd certainly be his friend if I broke character and chatted with him. That's why being a mime is so perfect. I can blame my silence on my character. We aren't supposed to talk. A mime talking is the equivalent of the motionless Queen's Guard of Britain suddenly breaking down into a boogie-woogie. Out here I'm not allowed to talk—perfect for someone who just doesn't want to.

The unobtrusive performer—whom I lovingly call Panja—gives me a wink and tiny dip of his head as a greeting. "Annyung, chingu yah!"

I give a wave, swooping my hand in a comically large arc and flash him a smile. He called me "friend." Maybe I should come up with a better nickname for him than *Cardboard*. But he always has boxes and cardboard signs to make intriguing points. His performance art has meaning, purpose. He's incredibly brave. I find myself wracked with guilt, that I should be doing more, like him. He can make a difference in this melancholy world.

Wearing his usual rainbow spiraled hat, Panja sits in a cardboard box with three other boxes next to him. Nestled as cute as can be in the other boxes are three stuffed animals. The kitten pokes it head out of a box, its paws like floppy leaves draped over the edge. Written in startlingly vibrant pink in hangul, the box says, "Because I missed the litter box." A plush bear sits in the next box. "Because I ate the good honey" is written on his new home. A one-eared bunny is the final resident, occupying its own tiny space. "Because no one wants a one-eared bunny." Finally, to drill in his glorious point, Panja's own box says, "Because I'm gay."

His message draws a pang of gloom up from my stomach, filling the back of my throat with the taste of bile. My mind is forced to recollect all the horrific things Jacob went through when his own parents discarded him. To throw your own kids out on the street—is there anything more despicable?

I want to thank Panja. Maybe I'll write him a note. But I can't dwell on the pain now. I'll give myself that option at home, where I've created time and space for it. Out here, I'm a mime. A quirky, spirited, silly little mime. And I need the money. Busking isn't the most lucrative position in Korea. I'm fortunate my father is wealthy and owns the apartment I live in. If he forced me to pay rent, I'd be in a box next to Panja. Though even he, I have to hope, has a place to return to after he delivers his poignant message through his art.

A group of golden-haired tourists stop before me, fresh smiles wiped across their freckled faces. American and European tourists love me. They come to South Korea for a new cultural experience, but the moment they see something that relates to home, their faces burn bright as the sun, and their eyes turn to giant orbs of wonder. You should see them during Christmas. They snap pictures of every glinting Christmas tree and fat Santa they come across, as if they hadn't seen enough of those in their lifetime. They also tip better. It's not like tipping buskers is new for Koreans. Street performances used to exist in the form of Madangnori—the theater-based performances of history and mythology. But still, if I weren't in Hongdae, tips would be worse.

I set down my Bluetooth speaker then tilt my bowler hat at the white family, waddle over to them, and set it upside down at their feet. I glance to them, then the hat, then them, the hat, and once more to them. I give a superbly exaggerated wink and nudge the hat slightly closer with my foot. The youngest girl, with hair the hue of a fresh apricot and cheeks redder than hot pepper paste, jumps against her father, wrapping her arms around his legs, letting a tiny giggle slip between her lips.

My cheeks rise into a toothy grin. *I* can't smile. But this mime painted mask can.

I whip my head to the side, like a soldier. Raising my leg past my midsection, I let it fall down to march back to the center of my stage. But when I bring my leg back down, I don't let the other rise. It catches me, like it's been cemented to the floor. I look at it, wide-eyed, offended. *How dare you hold me in place, shoe?* The girl squeals in joy and hugs her leg support hard. A smirk sneaks onto the face of the pudgy middle son.

I pull and pull on my leg, trying to set it free from the invisible force holding it in place. Then I give up and slump my shoulders. My brows furrow and I raise a finger and thumb to my chin. *How could this be?*

I point accusingly at the eldest daughter, the perfect rebellious age to roll her eyes at this and call it "lame." She's chewing gum. I point to my own mouth and start wriggling my jaw around like I'm chewing just as obnoxiously. I blow a fake bubble, then pretend to spit out my gum. I point back to her and pretend to chew and spit another piece.

The mother is delighted and lets out a singsong laugh, controlled and smooth. I'm drawing a larger crowd. A few Koreans might be more amused watching this foreign family than me. I pull my foot again, this time letting it come a slight distance from the pavement. With a *snap*, it locks back into its original position. This time, I pull so hard, pretending the stretch of gum is gluing me so firmly to the ground that my leg is almost in full split. I hurl my body backward, breaking free, and flip around, landing flush on my back.

A few spectators let out a gasp, worried I'd hurt myself.

I stand quickly, looking all around, brushing myself off, and flick my shoulders to a more natural slouch, like my character had meant to do that all along. A few claps resound around me.

I slowly raise two fingers and point them to my eyes, then point toward the gum-chewing fiend. I have my eye on her. She rolls her eyes, as predicted, but she can't hide the flicker across her lips, subtle as a ripple in a calm pond. She's entertained.

"Papa, is he a clown?" a little girl asks from the opposite side of the circle, her Korean slow and annunciated in sharp staccato. She's not terribly far off. Mimes share a fair amount more with traditional Korean clowns than they do with western clowns, those terrifying fake-smiling monsters.

"Watch. It's funny," the dad responds.

Now I have to make sure this girl finds mimes hilarious. No pressure. My semicircle of onlookers has turned into a full crowd. I love it. I adore entertaining people. I avoided high-risk behavior in high school by spending far too much time in a hip-hop dance group. Popping and locking have become my normal way of moving. I've completely forgotten how a human is supposed to move organically. People might think my bones and muscles have been replaced by high-tech robotic parts. Outside of mime, my external emotions might appear just as hollow.

The rigid feel of my mp3 player in my pocket is all too familiar. In my unique case, buttons trump touch screen any day. I flick it on, sending sound to my speaker, and freeze in place, turning to a pretend door as the source of music. The volume is low, intentionally.

I peer through cupped hands, looking through an invisible window. When I grip an imaginary doorknob and pull open the door with one hand, I turn up the volume with the other. It helps sell what I'm doing. I close the door and lower the volume.

Now they know the music is coming from whatever is behind that door.

With a fling, I throw open the door and walk into a night club. Simple bobbing with a dumb grin is sufficient at first, but I ease it into something more, bouncing deeper and deeper with bent knees. Now my whole head is jouncing, the grin deepened to pure excitement.

"He's dancing, he's dancing!" The little Korean girl with a pink bow sewn into her shadow-black hair starts to bob with me. She pops her hips from side to side and throws her arms up —they're so short they don't reach far above her head.

I moonwalk and jolt, pretending I've collided with someone. I gesture to have this "person" dance with me, and show them some of my best moves to win them over—which will, of course, be my worst possible moves—for the sake of humor. I throw in some Carlton moves from the *Fresh Prince of Bel-Air*, and the Americans in the audience die at my flawless Elaine Benes dance from *Seinfeld*. Koreans find the moves hilarious even if they don't know the source material Jacob had shown me, but I'm certain to scrounge up better tips from tourists.

While I'm making a fool of myself, I see a familiar face, lips curled upward, bangs hanging slightly over her eyes. She's seen a number of my performances. I have no idea why I'd have repeat customers. I mean, I'd like to think I'm a joy to watch, but it tends to be new onlookers daily. But she... she keeps coming back. I wonder how many times she has attended and how long it took me to notice. Does she know me? She must be my age. Had we met before?

My gig ends with my umbrella bit. Fake wind pulls it, and me, all around. I time it well. It consistently gets positive reactions. The crowd disperses, some without dropping a single copper coin into my hat. Others are more generous. The blond family slips in a particularly decent-looking wad. I pull a flower from my suitcase and politely hand it to their youngest, back hunched over to her minuscule stature. She departs with the deepest blush I've ever seen, flushed to match the rose I'd given.

The girl with the bangs and the familiar air about her has gone, drifted away, wind in the crowd. Possibly a connection from youth I cannot place.

———————

I perform several times that day.

Later that night, I scrape off the white mask and black-rimmed smile in my apartment. I've assigned time for sadness, time for remembrance, time for tears. I can't let myself dwell on Jacob all day. It would destroy me. So I get an hour before dinner and bedtime. I can look through our pictures, laugh and cry at the goofball faces he always made. It's tough finding a picture where he doesn't have a forced double chin or puffed cheeks.

I never imagined my future with someone like Jacob. I pictured a traditional family, my own biological children, a woman. And in truth, I'm attracted to women. But I always knew I *also* found men attractive. I just ignored it as much as I could. But when you meet someone like Jacob... When you hear his intermediate Korean spoken with his goofy confidence, when someone has such zest for life despite being rejected and abandoned by family, how do you *not* fall in love? I loved the way his eyes rolled back every time he bit into fluffy, sweet bungeo-ppang. He loved those fish-shaped pastries.

Once, he bought one for each of us, stared into my eyes, and said, "You know, there are plenty of fish in the sea, but none as lucky as me." So cheesy—how do you dodge that heart-tipped arrow?

We lived together in our tiny apartment for eight years. I never thought I'd be enveloped in happiness to that degree. We wanted to adopt someday, maybe in our thirties. I was twenty when we met. Jumping into raising kids gave me anxiety, even though my parents seemed to be okay with the idea. Koreans in general? Not so much. They're still learning to love and accept people like me. But it is getting better.

I cling to my favorite photo, framed for safe-keeping. To anyone else, it wouldn't seem that special. Just the two of us lying on Sokcho beach, my head pressed against his. He's smiling, showing off those insane dimples and brilliant blue eyes. I look good, too, which is rare, but that isn't why I like the photo. He'd just told me he loved me. Words I never thought would change my world as radically as they did. It lit a light inside me that couldn't be squelched. At least, I thought so at the time. It was a warm blanket, heavy around my shoulders, comforting in a cold world. I choked the words back at him, voice cutting through pressure clogging my throat, spurring on tears.

He hugged me tightly as I cried. Somehow he found it cute. My entire body shook, only to be calmed by his tight embrace. When I finally snapped out of the emotions, we waited to take the picture so my eyes wouldn't be puffy. It's a moment in time I can't escape. I don't want to escape it. But it's impossible to not hate the universe for what happened. It gave me something I never knew could exist, a love so strong it brought me to a plane of existence I hadn't imagined possible. Then the universe snatched it away.

Here comes the waterfall. Tears race down my cheeks, a competition for which side can fall the fastest. I lie there, hugging the framed photo, bawling. This has been my daily routine for nearly two years. But I need it. I need this hour every night. I can't let myself forget Jacob. He was my everything. I won't let him go. Not all the way.

The sadness has permission to consume me for the hour. But when my alarm rings, my time is up. I focus on chopping cucumbers, mincing garlic, and wokking up beef and an egg for bibimbap, pumping my small apartment with enough sweet chili aroma to mask anything like broken hearts and shattered dreams that still hung in the air.

The moment I need another distraction, I listen to Mom's message. "Hyeok shi yah, I have to tell you about Jin Soo's new job. You'll be so proud of your brother." She goes on to tell me how awesome it is. It does make me proud. Jin Soo has been less okay with my silence. We used to share a lot with each other. He probably feels I've abandoned him, left him alone with the parents. I don't want to dwell on that either. I'm awful for it. But I do text them. They get messages.

I've kept up communication in some form.

The next day, I paint my face and dress in a slightly different outfit, a polka-dot button-up shirt and a navy suit too small for me. Today Panja gives me an excited wave, mimicking the way I'd waved to him. We're becoming familiar to each other. He has a certain quality to his smile I like, his eyes nearly shutting entirely when he's truly happy. He's cute. No one could deny that. But looking at him with eyes beyond acquaintance or friend, I start getting caught up in the past. Thinking of flirting only makes my memories of flirting with Jacob light a forest fire in my mind.

Not right now. I need to focus on my act. This one starts

with an unusually heavy briefcase weighing me down at the office. I keep flashing it open to show a small, neat stack of papers inside, but somehow, the moment the briefcase closes, it becomes a boulder in my hands.

Then I see her. Again. The girl with the shy eyes. Her black hair drapes over her, curling at the tips, a veil concealing her identity. Prominent cheekbones still catch sunlight, preventing her face from being completely hidden. Why is she always here? I swear I can't possibly be *that* entertaining. So much of my repertoire is rehashed and reused. I don't come up with completely original content for each new performance. That would be insane.

I continue with the act, but I can't stop my eyes from flicking her way. Not sure if it's to make sure she's still there, or to try to get a better understanding of why she keeps coming back. Occasionally we make eye contact and she dips down with a sheepish smile. She'll lick her watermelon-pink lips or start chewing them to conceal it further. She's short, making it easy for her to disappear in a crowd.

At my final bow, I keep my gaze locked on her. She's not escaping this time. I have to know who she is. I have to know why she's here. And how, exactly, do I think I'm going to get that information? If I'm too stubborn to open my mouth and speak—how could I possibly learn anything? At the very least, I should give her a flower, thank her for supporting me. I never imagined having a fan.

She's sly. Slipping through the crowd unnoticed to drop in a few coins into my hat. Then she takes off.

I panic. My heart rate quickens. I have to get her a flower, or something. Anything. I scoop up my briefcase and bowler cap prematurely, cutting myself off from a few tips. I can live with that.

The crowd is thick, bodies tightly pinned against each other moving in giant globs. Elbows are barely enough to cut through while ducking and jumping to see under or over the crowd enough to keep her in my sights. My brain doesn't know what my body is doing. *What do you plan to do when you catch her, Hyeok?* Surely I won't break mime code. As if that's my real excuse.

Yet I continue my hustle toward her. Her sunflower-laden summer dress trails in the air, whipping around in wind and movement. When she's finally before me, I reach out—my arm listening to some consciousness outside my own—and tap her shoulder.

She turns, smiles adorably, and gives a tiny head-rock curtsy. I do the same, then pop open the briefcase to reveal a pink rose. I hand it to her, arm outstretched in a comically deep bow.

She lifts it from my hands and touches the petals to her nose, inhaling with closed eyes. The scent of her perfume drifts toward me, and I breathe in with her. It's a pleasant smell, vanilla with a drizzle of coconut. We're sharing an awkward moment now. I hadn't planned anything past this. I don't know what to do. I almost decide to about face and stomp away in military fashion, as my lips part slightly, only barely holding back a few words.

She holds a finger to my lips, then swings her finger from side to side. *Nuh uh uh*, she's saying in pantomime. *No talking.*

She holds the rose to her face and uses it to partially obstruct her shy smile. She points to her eyes with two fingers, then to mine. She's got her eye on me. She waves her hand up and down, gesturing toward my body, then arches back into fake laughter, mouth open, not making a sound. She thinks I'm funny. She's playing into this mime bit to perfection.

I put my hand to my chest as if to say I'm obliged.

She points to my briefcase and holds out her hand.

Confused, I hand it to her.

It drops to the floor in her grip like a ship anchor. She heaves at it, pretending she can't lift it back up, then she stands straight and gives a thumbs-up. Adorable. She must have liked that particular bit. I practiced that one a lot. I'm very proud of it.

I don't have my umbrella today, but imitate the act of popping it open and letting the wind pull me upward and from side to side. With a lift of my shoulders and lips pressed in a line, I gesture-ask her if she liked my umbrella act.

Her hand says more than enough. Outstretched, palm facing the ground, she wobbles it back and forth, thumb and pinkie wiggling. *So-so.* I smile and let out the faintest hint of a chuckle. Her eyes widen in instant shock, and she raises an accusatory finger at me.

I shake my head. *Nope. Nuh uh. That wasn't talking! I didn't cave!*

Dipping her head downward, she keeps her eyes on me, now glaring at me through her bangs. *Sure. Technicality.*

With a quick bite of her bottom lip and a wink, she swipes her hand through the air. *Just teasing.*

And then I see it. Tucked neatly in her ear is a tan hearing aid. My smile deepens. I don't know much, but I know Korean Sign Language for "*Tomorrow?*"

Her face lights up when I make the sign, and she nods rapidly, cheeks flushing pink.

And in that moment I realize something. I'm smiling. Not my mask. Not my character.

Me.

ABOUT THE EDITOR

Lyn Worthen began her career as a professional writer and free-lance editor sometime in the previous century. She currently divides her time between technical writing, fiction editing, and writing fiction in multiple genres under various pen names.

Contact her at *www.camdenparkediting.com*

ABOUT THE INFINITE MONKEYS

www.luwgenremonkeys.wordpress.com

The Infinite Monkeys are the genre fiction chapter of the League of Utah Writers (LUW). They support writers from novice to professional with the goal of publication. The chapter has a heavy emphasis on speculative fiction, but writers of all genres are welcome.

The infinite monkey theorem states that:

"...a monkey hitting keys at random on a typewriter keyboard for an infinite amount of time will almost surely type a given text, such as the complete works of William Shakespeare..."

As a League chapter, the Infinite Monkeys believe such things shouldn't be left to chance and strive to provide education for those individuals desiring to acquire or develop their literary skills in the genre fiction field. Meetings are designed to improve craft and support writers at every stage of their path toward publication. Geared toward the needs of genre writers, the Infinite Monkeys lift one another through inclusion.

Visit the Monkeys at *www.luwgenremonkeys.wordpress.com* to discover more.

www.ingramcontent.com/pod-product-compliance
Lightning Source LLC
Chambersburg PA
CBHW070928100726
47908CB00001B/139